The valley was devastated. *How could anyone possibly be alive here?* Before anyone could dissuade her, Bimily dismounted and took off at a fast walk toward the huge monoliths that waited eerily in the center of the ruins. When she finally reached the circle of towering stones she stepped into their midst. Her body wavered for several seconds before a thunderous cracking sound rent the air. They all gasped as Bimily was transformed into a column of stone.

Shunlar was the first to realize she couldn't move. Loff, Avek, and Ranth came into her field of vision, shouting at her and gesturing but she couldn't hear them or respond in any way. Then her vision faded to black, taking her awareness with it.

Other Avon Eos Books in
THE SHUNLAR CHRONICLES *by*
Carol Heller

THE GATES OF VENSUNOR
THE SANDS OF KALAVEN

THE STONES OF STIGA

A NOVEL OF *SHUNLAR*

CAROL HELLER

AVON • EOS

This is a work of fiction. Names, characters, places, and incidents either are the product of the author's imagination or are used fictitiously. Any resemblance to actual events, locales, organizations, or persons, living or dead, is entirely coincidental and beyond the intent of either the author of the publisher.

AVON BOOKS, INC.
1350 Avenue of the Americas
New York, New York 10019

Published by arrangement with the author
Library of Congress Catalog Card Number: 98-94800
ISBN: 0-380-79081-5
www.avonbooks.com/eos

First Avon Eos Printing: June 1999

Printed in the U.S.A.

WCD 10 9 8 7 6 5 4 3 2 1

Thank You To...

Marilyn for sending the manuscript to Charlie who sent it to Jane who sent it to Jennifer. I thank you. Shunlar thanks you. Also big hugs for the love and support of my family and friends.

And as always, to my darling Stuart, for the late-night consultations and the perfect martinis.

Prologue

It was early morning and Ranth's backside was numb from sitting still for so long atop his rocky perch. At first he thought the dim light was playing tricks on his vision, but when he clicked a signal to his companion nearby, she, too, saw the motion.

It looked to be one horse with a rider carefully maneuvering its way across the rocky ground toward the entrance to Kalaven. As Ranth, from his observation point, studied the person who advanced, a shudder passed through him. He again signaled his companion, who in turn sent a message to hers. Soon Ranth and several others were making their way down to the sandy floor of the portal, something that the rider and horse did not miss.

Seeing the figures moving in the distance, the horse snorted and stamped, but its rider kept a taut grip on the reins to prevent it from bolting. Having to control the animal helped her control her own desire to turn and flee in the opposite direction. Because the wind was steadily blowing, her heat trace sight was useless. The wind wiped away any traces left upon the air that her special sight normally could see. But the tiny hairs at the nape of her neck had risen and begun to tingle nearly thirty minutes ago. Forewarned that sentries would be posted, and where, she could do nothing to stop the automatic response of her trap warning neck hairs. She could, however, calm her mount. With its flanks quivering, the tired animal, now wide-eyed and alert, kept its steady uphill pace.

As the rider neared the entrance, her sharp eyes counted the sentries climbing down from their lookout points to form a living barrier with their bodies. She surmised that because of the war there were twice as many as she had anticipated. This made her neck hairs dance.

The clothing they wore blended so well with the encompassing rocks that, eerily, when they stopped moving it was as though they vanished, and she had to blink several times to be sure they hadn't. Their faces, like hers, were masked to protect them against the constantly blowing sand. None had weapons drawn. As she guided her horse into their midst, she felt their eyes assessing her. Eyes that didn't miss the fact that one slender hand gripped the pommel of a sword while the other controlled the horse.

"I come for Ranth sul Zeraya," she called loudly.

Recognizing something familiar in the accented voice that echoed off the surrounding cliffs, Ranth demanded back, "Who asks for him?"

"When he sees me, he will know. I refuse to give my name to any but him," the woman answered defiantly. "He gave me this for safe passage within your city." From beneath her tunic she pulled a thick chain with a gold medallion on it, holding it up for everyone to see.

"Shunlar?" whispered Ranth in disbelief as he unfastened his mask.

For several minutes they stared at one another. Only when her neck hairs relaxed did Shunlar push back her hood, unfasten her mask, and open her cloak, enabling everyone to see the small face that peered out from the bundle she carried against her chest. The wind became curiously still as a small child with a head of curly black hair squirmed out of the sling he was wrapped in. One small chubby hand came up and pointed at Ranth. The child smiled, then hid his face within his mother's bosom, shyly.

"I have brought you your son," Shunlar announced quietly.

One

An awkward silence of several minutes passed as Ranth tried to make sense of the words he had just heard and the sight of the woman and child before him. Here sat Shunlar upon a horse, encrusted with sand from an obviously long journey. In the crook of her arm was an active, bouncing boy, and she had just said this was his son. His face felt hot as he tried to remember to breathe.

Clearing her throat, the sentry closest to Ranth decided to step forward and take control of the situation. "We bid you welcome. If you please, lady, we will give you refreshment and see to it that you are rested after your journey." Once the welcome greeting was spoken, the remaining sentries bowed to Shunlar; all, that is, except Ranth. He remained standing, blinking in disbelief, trying desperately to regain some self-control.

Shunlar, too, seemed overwhelmed. Avek had been teaching her the Feralmon language all winter, but her understanding of the tongue remained rudimentary at best.

"It seems that you know one another, Ranth sul Zeraya." The woman beside Ranth observed wryly.

"Yes, Captain," Ranth answered.

"Then I would suggest you offer her welcome in a tongue she understands, for she looks confused," the captain urged.

Dumbstruck but regaining a sense of propriety, Ranth

bowed to her and slipped easily into Old Tongue. "Um, please my whims, Lady Shunlar, be welcomed. If you will come with me, I will take you to meet my parents, and then to lodgings and refreshment. I know Benyar will be pleased and most surprised to see you . . . both of you." He took the reins from her hands and led the horse through the entrance to the city, confusion, joy, and sadness tumbling through him all at once.

The sentries neither spoke nor moved until Ranth and Shunlar were gone from sight. Then one by one they took up their posts, maintaining their strange silence. It would be impolite to speak of Ranth behind his back, and these people knew how to keep their tongues and thoughts to themselves. Only a raised eyebrow or two or nods were exchanged as they climbed the rocks to find once again a perch and resume watch.

As Ranth led Shunlar through the city streets, people recognized the son of Zeraya sul Karnavt, Ruler of Kalaven, and Benyar sul Jemapree, First Guardian, and they bowed to him, bows he returned automatically. Though they recognized that he brought a stranger into their midst, none stared or regarded her with curiosity. Discreet looks were exchanged by some when they saw that the woman Ranth led through the streets held a child.

The people they passed emanated a natural inquisitiveness, yet only once did Shunlar hear a stray thought, and that came from a very young child whose mother quickly covered it with a velvety-soft mind protection. Taking a cue from that mother, Shunlar did the same to her son.

The excitement of being in Kalaven at last heightened Shunlar's senses. After the long journey through endless desert, colors seemed to jump out at her. The designs and shapes of the houses were like nothing she had seen before, and Shunlar relaxed as her eyes absorbed the soft roundness of the buildings. Built to blend into the surrounding rocks, Kalaven's structures were fashioned from the stone and sand that was available. Each dwelling was decorated in delightfully imaginative ways with the color of the inhabitant's clans. Doors and window frames were brightly painted in several colors, and most windows had tinted glass panes. There were murals on large, round tents, and each one sported multiple banners of a single color.

There were so many new sights to take in that before she knew it, they had reached the palace, or at least the courtyard. A stable hand quickly appeared to take the horse. Shunlar dismounted easily enough, but once on her feet her weariness nearly got the better of her. Her knees turned soft, threatening to buckle. She had only to glance Ranth's way, and he immediately took the boy from her.

Surprised to be in the arms of a stranger and walking down an unfamiliar corridor, the child's tiny bottom lip began to tremble, and within minutes he was wailing loudly. This brought several servants from the household staff, who seemed to be accustomed to responding to a child's cry. They were astonished to see Ranth carrying a boy in his arms who looked to be around nine or ten months old and resembled him greatly.

Following close behind Ranth was a lovely woman who stood nearly as tall as he. Her auburn hair, liberally streaked with gray, had two white streaks at the temples and was pulled back in a warrior braid. That she was familiar with fighting showed in her bearing and the weapon at her side. Though she was not of the people, someone had outfitted her in leathers that were cut in traditional desert style. As Ranth and Shunlar passed them, the servants merely bowed, only their eyes betraying their curiosity.

Exhaustion and excitement made Shunlar's breath come faster than she liked. It was difficult for her to be here, but she had too much pride to let mere tiredness overcome her now. She smiled wearily as she quieted her son.

''If you wish, you can rest first before greeting my mother and father,'' Ranth offered. ''Surely they will understand that you are tired after your journey.''

''No, I would see them now. Later will be time for

rest. But a drink of water would be appreciated."

Ranth gestured to a servant, who bowed and hurried away for the water. He invited Shunlar to sit on a low bench against the wall while they waited for the servant to return. Sitting with her and the child, Ranth could not help but feel anxious. He wanted answers to all of his questions at once, but with so many questions swimming in his head Ranth could not seem to put words into any kind of order. Instead he focused his attention on the baby, who sat calmly on his lap, regarding him with eyes the color of dark amber, a look much older than was possible in their depths.

Sitting beside Ranth as he held their son for the first time, Shunlar realized she was dangerously close to tears, something she refused to allow herself to do. To distract herself from even the thought of crying, she squeezed her left hand so tightly that her nails broke the skin. Though it took a surprising amount of effort, she forced herself to study Ranth's face. What she saw startled her.

He looked gaunt, a bit worn, and slightly thinner than when she had last seen him. His skin tone had a somewhat unhealthy cast, and there were dark circles under his eyes. Even his hair seemed to have lost its dark luster. The curls she had expected were formed into many braids, which were twisted intricately to form one long braid down his back. In the middle of his chest, beneath his shirt, bulged something that hung from a leather cord around his neck. When she raised her gaze back to his face, their eyes met, and he looked away quickly, clearing his throat.

Finding his tongue, Ranth began to speak, but in the language he had grown accustomed to. Catching his mistake in mid-word, he immediately stopped and began again in Old Tongue. "Please my whims, lady, one request I make of you. It is the custom of my people to keep their thoughts very closed from one another. In fact, they see it as an insult to do otherwise." He paused, waiting for an answer, watching emotions play across her face.

"No one will hear my thoughts," Shunlar answered, more coldly than she intended. "What about my son? Do I cover his mind as well?"

"No. A child his age will have little to say that would distract adults."

Shunlar regarded Ranth for a moment with one raised eyebrow. Just then the servant returned, carrying a tray with a pitcher of water and cups. Shunlar filled a cup for her son, who noisily gulped it down as she drained another.

"Inform my mother and father that I request an immediate audience and I bring two guests, please," Ranth quietly ordered. One of the women bowed and hurried on ahead to do his bidding as he waited for Shunlar to quench her thirst.

Placing her empty cup on the tray, Shunlar nodded a polite gesture of thanks, and they continued on their way down the corridor.

Two

At this time of day, Zeraya and Benyar would customarily hold audience with the townspeople, settling disputes, meeting with officials, planning committees, and the like. But today the meeting was with the officers and scouts, and what they planned was war.

In anticipation of their arrival, the double doors to the audience hall gaped wide. Before each door were positioned six guards at rigid attention. Ranth carried the child and Shunlar walked beside him as they entered into the midst of the guards. As each pair of guards was passed, they bowed, then turned and followed Ranth and Shunlar into the hall, the last two closing the doors quietly behind them. Only after Shunlar had passed through the doors did she realize they were panels of opaque, multicolored glass in swirls of impossibly brilliant colors.

The great hall was long and wide, with a high ceiling from which hung three large, woven fans. Servants were stationed at intervals, pulling the ropes that kept the fans moving and the air circulating. The room was light because two opposing walls contained clear glass windows across their length; the walls and floor were painted off-white. Fragrant rushes were stacked in the corners, the smell of incense further freshening the room. Men and women, able fighters all from the looks of them, stood conversing in hushed tones in groups of three or more around the room.

When Ranth and Shunlar passed beyond the threshold, the conversation stopped and the warriors bowed low to them. Ranth returned the courtesy, though not as low, as befitted his rank. Following his example, Shunlar returned the greeting, after which they began to walk the length of the room, closely followed by the six guards. As they passed by, the warriors took their places in an order Shunlar guessed was according to their rank.

Only when she saw the woman and man waiting upon thrones at the far end of the room did Shunlar remember that Ranth's mother, Zeraya, was the Queen, and Benyar, his father, was her consort. Until this moment it had all been mere words. The power Zeraya wielded was obvious. Shunlar began to doubt whether she had made the right decision in coming here. She had imagined the first meeting with Ranth's parents would take place privately, between them and her. But here she stood in a great hall with a full contingent of warriors surrounding her.

Quickly assessing the room, Shunlar noted that off to the side there were four long tables, covering an entire half of the audience hall. Placed end to end, they were strewn with maps, charts, and a model of the city. Though from the look of things they had been hard at work, the men and women assembled—numbering around twenty-five people—who were the generals, captains, and scouts, presently stood at attention in two orderly lines on both sides of the dais where Benyar and a lovely, raven-haired woman sat waiting upon thrones. The woman's throne was more ornate and set slightly forward of the one Benyar sat upon.

Shunlar was amazed at how silent and void of thoughts everyone in the room seemed to be, then she remembered what Ranth had told her about the custom of his people. Her own thoughts were tightly concealed behind an exterior of tired determination. She raised an eyebrow when she saw Benyar, and recognition passed between them. He looked much the same to her, handsome and dark, as the Feralmon were. Benyar's black eyes looked wary, and she noticed that when he smiled, only his lips turned up; his smile did not reach his eyes. His black, curly hair was pulled back in an elaborate warrior braid, and a small jewel glinted in his left earlobe. Benyar stood and bowed politely to her, then introduced Zeraya sul Karnavt, Ruler of Kalaven, bowing low to her as he did so.

Zeraya seemed impossibly young, too young to be Ranth's mother. Then Shunlar remembered that Benyar had been on a quest for over twenty years, looking not only for his son, but for his wife's Lifestone as well. When the infant Ranth had been abducted during a raid, Zeraya had been seriously wounded and her Lifestone stolen. Benyar had told Shunlar how the High Priestess, Honia sul Urla, was keeping his wife alive in a state of suspended life while he searched year after year. Only by reuniting Zeraya with her Lifestone could her life be fully restored. She apparently had not aged at all while she remained in her healing sleep.

Zeraya's raven black hair was braided in several plaits that were so long they coiled upon the floor. Her pale face made her dark, almond-shaped eyes seem even more brilliant. She was dressed in a sheer peach-colored gown with matching robe, the sleeves of which were embroidered with gold threads. Upon her feet she wore golden leather sandals encrusted with jewels. On her brow sat a circlet of beaten gold and around her wrists were matching bracelets. Rings set with dark jewels were on most of her fingers.

With a start Shunlar realized she had been staring, and she quickly bowed before Zeraya. Another raising of eyebrows, but this time they were Zeraya's. Aware that she was being scrutinized inch by inch, Shunlar bowed her head and allowed Zeraya to continue her scrutiny. When she had finished, Zeraya did the same to the child, and then to Ranth. Her eyes flashed, a telltale sign that her temper was rising, and the entire room became uneasy.

Benyar gestured to a servant, who brought a tray with

the traditional visitor's cup. He poured three goblets and picked one up and presented it to Shunlar with his own hands. As Shunlar bowed and accepted the cup, she and Zeraya exchanged quiet glances. Benyar handed the second to Zeraya, then he picked up the third. After the three toasted one another's good health, the room began to relax. Ranth continued to stand, holding the boy, watching, his face an unusual mixture of emotions.

"Tell me, Shunlar, what brings you and this child to Kalaven?" asked Zeraya without hesitation. Ranth's eyes darted from Zeraya to Shunlar. The look on Shunlar's face told him she was having trouble forming an answer in the language.

"Mother, if I may suggest, Shunlar might best answer you in Old Tongue," Ranth offered. Zeraya nodded her approval with a curt dip of her chin.

"Please my whims, I have brought my son to meet his father. The boy has yet to be named, and I wished his father present at the naming. I never doubted Ranth would grant that wish." Shunlar glanced hopefully at Ranth before changing her expression back to an unreadable mask.

Zeraya's eyes narrowed as she carefully scrutinized the baby who squirmed in Ranth's arms. She rose from her throne, descended the steps, and slowly held her arms out to the boy. He reached his arms toward her and went to her easily. A smile spread itself slowly across Zeraya's face, and the furrow between her brows melted as she cradled the babe in her arms. She felt transported back in time as she stared into his remarkable eyes.

"Yes, he is your child. Can you not feel it, my son?" Zeraya quietly asked Ranth.

"Mother, I can," he quietly replied.

But what Zeraya heard from the child surprised her even more. The baby spoke to her in a language she had never expected, strongly demanding in Old Tongue to be returned to his mother. Astonished beyond words, Zeraya held him at arm's length and laughed out loud as she handed him over to Shunlar.

"Well, little one, it seems you are a unique boy." To herself she added, *And who can this Shunlar be that she speaks the old sacred language? I will find out, if we can persuade her to stay.*

Holding her child, Shunlar could speak directly to his mind. She comforted him saying, *Hush, my little one. Soon we will both rest. Be patient.* Safe on his mother's hip, he laid his head on her shoulder and began rubbing his eyes sleepily.

As they returned to their thrones, Zeraya and Benyar touched hands and they exchanged a meaningful glance. Suddenly everyone was more at ease, and Benyar's face softened. Shunlar couldn't be sure, but she thought she saw tears in his eyes. Turning his attention once more to the men and women in the audience hall, he beckoned for them to come forward to be introduced to Shunlar and Ranth's son.

Bowing low, each person welcomed her and the boy graciously. So much acceptance nearly melted Shunlar's cool exterior. After the pleasantries were exchanged, the room emptied, leaving Shunlar, Ranth, and his parents alone together, with the child in their midst.

With yet another gracious bow, Benyar offered, "Let us make you comfortable after so long a journey. Rooms are being prepared for you where you may bathe and rest. We ask you to join us and other members of our family at our evening meal. All of them will want to meet you and your son." His eyes rested on Ranth with an unusual look before he bowed to Shunlar and summoned a servant.

No sooner had Shunlar and her child left the great hall than Zeraya began to question Benyar about her.

With the help of his Lifestone, Ranth wrapped a subtle, protective cover over himself. He stood by and watched as his mother questioned his father, knowing his turn would come next. He would be prepared, as Benyar had taught him.

Zeraya was greatly recovered, having by this time spent more than a year with her Lifestone restored to her. The more her health improved, the more she showed her true mettle, and Ranth learned each day just what kind of woman his mother was.

After Ranth had been called by his Lifestone, he had taken over caring for his mother, stepping in when Septia announced that because of her advanced pregnancy she could no longer perform that duty. Zeraya thrived under his careful healing, her mind, too, growing sharper by the day.

Benyar was clearly not the same person he had been when he and Ranth had first returned to Kalaven. He deeply loved his wife, and, remaining true to the laws of his people, he acquiesced to Zeraya in all matters. Perhaps it was that it had been so deeply ingrained in him from birth, for in their society women were the rulers. Ranth believed otherwise. Ranth knew Zeraya had demanded to know the full story of why and how she had been injured. What exactly had passed between them no one was certain, yet everyone could see that Benyar was a changed man.

Explaining what he could of the situation, Benyar told her it had been his enemies who, having gained access to their city, had nearly killed her and had abducted their son. Zeraya's wrath after all this time seemed to Ranth to be merciless and petty. Benyar began to sink into a depression, becoming more morose and brooding as the days passed.

At the time of the raid, the attackers had been heard to cry: "For Ticides," as they fought. One in particular had even declared himself to be a direct descendant of Ticides, the man who had had blood feud with a long-dead ancestor of Benyar's, Ferala. After the raid was over and the bodies of the enemy examined, it was discovered that they were, in fact, from Tonnerling.

Centuries ago, when the feud began, all parties had lived in Stiga. When Stiga fell, the descendants of Ticides fled to the mountainous seacoast to found Tonnerling. Ferala's descendants became the nomads known as Feralmon, named for their stealth and their fierce fighting methods.

But while Zeraya blamed Benyar, he blamed himself

even more. She had spent nearly twenty-two years frozen in time, kept in a state of stasis by Honia sul Urla, the High Priestess. Once her Lifestone had been restored to her, she came alive again, but the years that had been lost were difficult for Zeraya to accept. When she had been placed in the protective sleep she had been a nursing mother. Now her son was fully grown; in fact, Zeraya was two years younger than Ranth.

Her actions were those of an immature young woman, and she focused her irrational anger on the person closest to her, her husband Benyar. Zeraya declared to Benyar that she would set him aside as First Guardian and take another man as her consort if the person responsible for the raid was not found and killed.

That task, Benyar knew, was impossible to perform because when Zeraya's Lifestone had been found, mere fragments of human bone and cloth had been left behind in the snow, the work of predators. He would have to piece together a twenty-year-old mystery, or travel to Tonnerling to discover if the man yet lived. Since they were at war with Tonnerling, that was out of the question.

Ever since the day Benyar had confessed the truth to Zeraya, Ranth had not been permitted to speak to his mother alone. At Benyar's order, his son was kept at a distance. Benyar not only believed that Zeraya's judgment was not to be trusted, but also that she was capable of doing physical harm to Ranth. He was correct; however, Zeraya was not entirely to blame. The young priestess, Septia, who later became Ranth's wife, had been placed at Zeraya's side to nurse her shortly after she had awakened. Under the guise of healing, Septia administered drugs to Zeraya that prevented her from fully recovering, and clouded her mind as well. Only after Septia had been arrested did everyone discover the truth.

However, another even more startling discovery was made. Septia and Korab, Ranth's cousin, had been secret lovers. And worse, the child everyone thought was Ranth's was really Korab's.

No longer under Septia's spell, Ranth discovered what she had done to him only after she was gone. By secretly slipping the juice of the poppy into his wine or food, Septia had given him a physical addiction that made it easy to bend Ranth to her will without his knowledge. It had taken a toll on his normally robust physique, but, he, too, was nearly recovered, thanks to his Lifestone. Once he had answered the call, the Lifestone had strengthened him.

Overnight Ranth's life had seemed to turn to dust before his eyes. He knew that he, too, must seem like his father. Though he had tried to speak to Benyar about the situation, it did no good. Little by little he had realized that his parents were strangers to one another, and he felt very much in the way. Now that Shunlar had shown up on the scene, would things change? Ranth stood by watching and waiting for his mother to begin questioning him about Shunlar and his son.

Three

SHUNLAR REMEMBERED BOWING POLITELY, then saying nothing. Servants had been summoned forward to lead her to rooms, these same women that she followed now. Swooning from exhaustion and overwhelmed at seeing Ranth again, she was very nearly numb. Once they had entered the sumptuous suite, a woman carefully took the sleepy boy from her, placed him in the crook of her arm, and began to nurse him as Shunlar looked on. Another woman got her attention by gesturing to a curtain on the other side of the room.

Shunlar followed her slowly, allowing a smile at last as the curtain was pulled back to reveal a private alcove with a sunken tub in the floor so large that five or six people could fit comfortably. Three women gathered around her, bowed, then cautiously began to remove her clothing and weapons. She stood and let them unbraid and brush her hair and help her step down into the tub of steaming water. One on either side of her, they slowly washed her body and her hair. When she was clean to their satisfaction, they brought the boy to her and they washed him, too, with much giggling and splashing.

After the bath she was dried with soft towels then laid upon a table where expert hands massaged away the aches and knots from her muscles. Her body was pampered and oiled. In a dream-like state Shunlar felt the hesitation of the masseuse when she touched the places on her back where tiny scales grew, but the woman only applied more oil.

Her hair was plaited, desert fashion, with tiny beads woven into the many strands and these braided into one solid warrior braid down her back. She smiled to herself when she noticed the servant who plaited her hair stop, then check herself and continue, when she encountered the patch of green-tinted skin at the nape of her neck.

After what seemed like hours of luxury, Shunlar fell into a deep, restful sleep. Awakening from her nap, she had the boy brought to her and nursed him while servants passed before her a seeming endless procession of clothing. But she refused to dress in any of the clothing, choosing instead her best set of leathers from her saddlebags.

Shunlar arrived at the evening meal greatly refreshed. Dressed in a soft leather vest dyed a dark russet color with matching breeches, she carried her diaper-clad son on her hip. Her hair glinted with faceted beads, small gold loops pierced her ears, and the gold medallion Ranth had given her as his parting gift hung about her neck. Also around her neck was a leather thong, worn under her vest so that what hung from it could not be seen. This sparked Ranth's interest, but he soon forgot it once he looked at her face. Shunlar's skin seemed to glow, and Ranth could not take his eyes from her as she was seated between Zeraya and Benyar.

Separated from Shunlar by his mother, Ranth's mood was readable not only on his face, but in his posture. His appetite gone, he sampled only a small portion of the roasted fowl and a few bites of fruit, tasting neither. He sipped small mouthfuls of wine and listened and watched as Fanon sul Eliya and Ketherey sul Jemapree, his aunt and uncle, were introduced to Shunlar and the boy. They had been the appointed Regent and First Guardian during Zeraya's long sleep, while Benyar searched. Now as Zeraya's strength increased, their duties diminished daily.

Next came their daughters, Tilenna and Cachou, more cousins, and something called oath-brothers, so that soon

Shunlar's head was swimming with names and faces. The person who sparked the most interest in Shunlar, however, was Zara sul Karnavt. She knew this woman was Avek's foster-mother and took a good, long look at her face to commit it to memory. Her resemblance to Zeraya was apparent, the same black, almond-shaped eyes and full mouth. Zara's skin was a dark coppery brown color, her gleaming black hair braided similar to Shunlar's. Strong, muscled arms showed she was familiar with weapons and hard work. The proper time would come when Shunlar could tell her that her son was well, for now she merely inclined her head to the woman, which left Zara with a bemused look on her face. Shunlar had not greeted the others so.

Once everyone had been introduced, Shunlar handed her tired child over to the care of a wet nurse. The boy was content to be carried from the dining hall, sucking noisily, practically asleep before he left his mother's sight.

The table conversation began with Zeraya's polite query about several of the cities Shunlar had stopped in on her way to Kalaven. Someone asked how the war effort went along the border that she had so recently passed through, and she answered as best she could, with her limited vocabulary, thankful that she seemed to be able to provide useful information. When translation became necessary, Benyar obliged. Never once did anyone ask questions of a personal nature, something Shunlar was vastly relieved about. Thus the first evening passed with Shunlar and Ranth attending dinner under the scrutiny of Benyar, Zeraya, and other members of Ranth's family.

Ranth had little to say; nor did he ask any questions. In fact, he never once spoke directly to Shunlar in the course of the evening, which she noticed with growing unease. Remembering then the Feralmon law that forbade singles to speak to one another without the accompaniment of a family member, she reconciled herself to that as an explanation.

Truthfully, Ranth could speak to her, he was merely

afraid to, afraid he would blurt out something inappropriate. After all the time that had passed since they had parted, he found that he wanted to know everything. Why had she never written and told him of the child? Why hadn't she ever replied to his many letters? Did she know he had been married and that his wife, Septia, along with his cousin, Korab, had betrayed him and their people, and had been banished? He tried his best to hide the emotional turmoil he was going through as he watched Shunlar sitting calmly, precisely answering questions.

Ranth was miserable. Nearly overcome with sadness and grief, he became aware of his state only after his father cast him an uneasy look. Before he betrayed himself further he composed himself by reciting a calming meditation as he sat rigidly in his chair, watching Shunlar and remembering. He longed to touch her, to hold her close, knowing at the same time that he would be just as content to see her smile or hear her laughter. *Later tonight, we can be alone, and I will ask my questions,* Ranth promised himself.

Shunlar was first to excuse herself from the dining hall, saying that she was tired from her journey and wanted to check on *my* son, using the word "my" deliberately. Her choice of words wounded Ranth at first, then he found himself strangely rankled and did not pursue any thoughts of a conversation with her that night. He and she were both heavily shielded against one another.

Ranth rose when Shunlar did and bowed to her as he would to a woman he did not know. Shortly after she left the dining hall, he took his leave of his parents and retired to his chambers, but not before checking on Septia and Korab's daughter, Iola sul Fanon. Korab's mother, Fanon, had given the child her name and would raise her as her own. Septia's mother, Esca sul Patia, would not; it was too shameful for her because of the crimes her daughter had committed. She preferred to think of Septia as dead and wouldn't take another in her place.

Because Ranth wasn't able to part from Iola yet, Fanon had taken up temporary residence in the quarters next to Ranth's that had been Septia's until he could bear to let the child go. Coming to the realization that his wife had never truly been his in any way except in his mind, that the child he loved wasn't his, and coping with the difficulties of addiction and weaning himself off the drug were too many things to handle at once. So, the child lived close by until he felt she had accepted Fanon as her mother and Ketherey as her father, though everyone knew Ranth also needed to be weaned and not torn apart from her. In an effort to make that possible, he saw less and less of the child each day.

The child was sleeping peacefully. Not quite four months old, her small heart-shaped face was so like Septia's that it brought tears to his eyes, and for a long time Ranth knelt beside the cradle, staring at her. When Iola stirred, Ranth backed away and motioned for the wet nurse to attend her. After Iola had settled back into sleep, he returned to his suite.

But he couldn't sleep. Several times he paced the length of the room, then called for a servant and asked for wine. He drank some and paced more, but still his mind would not quiet. He finished the wine and was about to call for more when there came a knock at his door.

"Come," he called.

It was Benyar and he was very troubled by Ranth's reaction to seeing Shunlar again. He more than anyone felt responsible for his son's pain and, indeed, to an extent he was. Had he not been so focused on Zeraya, he would have noticed that there was something very wrong between Ranth and Septia.

"My son, I found I could not sleep either. Will you walk in the courtyard with me and speak about what's troubling you?"

Reluctantly, Ranth joined his father. Thoroughly drunk, he refused to let his guard down and speak, remaining stubbornly mute, listening sullenly as his father tried to engage him in conversation. Finding no way to reach his son, Benyar left Ranth to his pacing.

Four

RANTH HAD BEEN UP ALL NIGHT AND LOOKED terrible when he showed up at Shunlar's door early the next morning. Dismissing the servants, he waited patiently as the women filed quietly from the room, leaving Shunlar sitting on the bed nursing the boy. When the child saw Ranth, he gave up the nipple and pointed at him. He said, "Da," smiled, and went back to his breakfast.

Suddenly weak in the knees, Ranth crossed the room and sat down in a chair beside the bed. Confused, bewildered, he put his face in his hands and sighed heavily, near to tears, the awkward silence between them building.

"I suppose I must be the one to begin the questions," Ranth stated finally. "So, I will. Why did you not answer any of my letters?"

The color drained from Shunlar's face. "You're telling me you wrote to me? I received nothing, and I sent more than ten in all to you. I even wrote to tell you about a plot against your father's life by someone named Korab. Do you recognize that name?" she demanded, some of her color returning.

"What are you talking about? Of course I know the name—I'll never forget it. Where did you hear such a thing?" Ranth demanded back.

"In Tonnerling. Last winter Gwernz had me accompany him there as an escort so that he could marry Klarissa of Tonnerling. Because it was so late in the year, we were forced to winter there after an avalanche closed the passes. One evening as I sat in a tavern, three men came in who I discovered were Feralmon and they spoke of offering a large amount of gold for the head of Benyar sul Jemapree. As soon as we returned to the Valley of Great Trees we tried to contact you by asking Delcia and Morgentur to send secret couriers from Vensunor, since none of my letters had gotten a reply. Did any ever reach you?"

"None."

"Gwernz also had Delcia and Morgentur attempt to reach Benyar by calling to him in his dreams. Curiously, though, they were intercepted by a woman who claimed to be a priestess who guarded the family. Who is she that guards you so well that no one can reach you at all?" Shunlar was agitated. She rose to put the sleeping child down in his cradle before her temper woke him.

"Septia," Ranth muttered under his breath.

"That name even I know," she answered him back. "She is your wife. Tell me, has she given you children?"

"No," he answered stiffly. "There is much you don't understand." He stood and began to pace, his head pounding.

She watched for several minutes before asking softly, "What would you have me understand?"

"Only this, I did write to you, and I had every intention of returning within one year to meet you in Vensunor. The fact that I had no word from you in so long and my obligation to my people helped me to agree with my parents when they persuaded me that I should marry."

"So it's true. You forgot our pledge and married another," she accused.

"My wife," his voice cracked with emotion, "is dead. Also dead is Korab, my cousin, who betrayed us all. This is the last time I can speak of them, for it is forbidden even to utter their names. And I caution you against asking my father or mother about them. They will not take kindly to someone who is an outsider asking questions about those whose names have been stricken from the record of the Temple.''

Ranth conveyed an unusual mixture of sadness and anger. The man who stood before her looked broken apart by anguish; his eyes seemed unwilling or unable to focus. Shunlar wondered what could have changed him so. When she had last seen Ranth, he had been so determined, so sure of himself; now that was gone. She found herself looking anywhere but at him.

Clearing his throat he continued with a partial lie, ''I carry a message for you that was the purpose of my visit this morning. Bimily is here, and she wishes to see you.'' Ranth paused as his words settled in.

In disbelief she said, ''Bimily? Here?''

Nodding, Ranth continued, ''Her mate, the eagle, was killed, and she was gravely wounded shortly after she left Vensunor. Bimily tried to fly to safety but was captured while in the shape of a small bird. As fate would have it, a caravan brought her here and she was purchased as a bird in a cage for entertainment. I discovered who she really was, but she was so weak she needed Benyar's and my help to return to her human form. She has been recovering ever since but must return to her people if she is to live. I will have someone take you to see her now.'' Finished with his explanation, Ranth bowed to Shunlar and turned to leave.

She scooped up the boy and followed Ranth through the doorway, where a servant was instructed to take her to Bimily. Questions ran through her mind as she watched Ranth walk away stiffly without a backward glance. *Why did Ranth refuse to tell me anything about Septia? He says she is dead, and Korab, too, and their names stricken from the record. What in the name of the three moons does that mean? Perhaps Bimily will answer my questions, for it appears Ranth can't and Benyar won't.*

Though she had been under the constant care of the healers of the Temple, Bimily the Shapechanger remained extremely weak. To shapechange while wounded or ill put one at risk of forgetting the true self, which is exactly what had happened to her. Furthermore, being in the shape of a small bird for nearly a year had drained Bimily of much of her vital energies, weakening her powers. In fact, she had lost such a significant amount of her inner essence that only her people could restore it to her. If not, she would surely die from the wasting illness that had settled upon her.

Preparations to travel were under way when Shunlar appeared at the gateway to Kalaven. Hearing that her dearest friend had come, Bimily was anxious to meet with Shunlar again—after all, more than a year had passed since they had seen each other. As the lovely, green-eyed, copper-tressed woman waited for her friend to arrive she speculated that Shunlar would be angry. She remembered all too well the way the young mercenary's mind worked. Bimily would have to apologize first to cool her temper. Then, and only then would she be able to explain how she had disappeared from the face of the earth for so long and reappeared here in Kalaven.

The knock at the door came at last. "Come," Bimily called out, rising from her chair to greet her old friend. In mid-step she froze and her jaw fell open. Shunlar carried a small child in her arms and he resembled Ranth so strongly that there was no question who his father was.

"It has been a long time, Bimily," Shunlar said in a soft voice as she embraced Bimily. "Ranth explained what happened to you, and I am truly sorry for the loss of your mate as well as for your illness."

"You're not angry? I prepared an elaborate apology and now you don't want it? And who is this sweet boy?" Bimily had only to look at the boy to know the answer. "He is Ranth's, yes?"

"Yes, and he is also the reason I'm here. Marleah agreed to raise him while I was in Vensunor with Loff, protecting the surrounding countryside from the army of Tonnerling. But over the winter, while Avek helped me recover from an attempt on my life, I realized I must bring my child here to meet his father and to be named.'' Suddenly Shunlar scowled deeply. ''Even though Ranth had no idea he had a son. But tell me of yourself,'' she said abruptly.

''Wait. Just back up a few paces. Avek? Who is Avek, and who threatened your life?''

''Ah, a long story for another time. Perhaps I will tell it to you on our journey. You do need a traveling companion, someone skilled at finding her way in unfamiliar territory who is good with a sword?'' Shunlar flashed a huge grin.

''But you just arrived. I couldn't possibly take you away just yet, and I must be on my way very soon.'' Bimily's face had become pale in the last minutes. The effort of standing and engaging in conversation exacting such an immediate toll told Shunlar her friend had little time.

''Besides, all the preparations have been made by Ketherey, Benyar's brother. I am to be provided with four warriors who will take me to my people. We leave when I am well enough to travel.'' Weary, Bimily plunked herself down in a chair, then held her arms out to the boy, who happily came to sit on her lap.

''Now, my little man, since your mother is being so close-mouthed, perhaps you can tell me just who this Avek is, huh?''

The boy stared intently into her eyes for several seconds, then pointed a small finger at her. *Bird*, Bimily heard in her head. Astonished, she jumped and looked at Shunlar, who stood watching, grinning.

''He speaks in Old Tongue! And he called me bird!'' said Bimily, her eyes growing rounder.

''Don't look at me. He spent the last six months with my mother, though I suspect my father, Alglooth, had more to do with his language than Marleah. And while I am speaking of them, Cloonth has given birth. She and Alglooth have six children and they are living in the Valley of Great Trees so that they might have help raising their brood.''

"I know your foster-mother is an extraordinary woman, but please explain how one of her stature could bear six."

"Bimily, there is so much you don't know." Taking a deep breath Shunlar began, "At Creedath's palace when the Lifestone of Banant exploded, Cloonth and I were standing next to each other." Shunlar told her tale, and her old friend listened intently, making few interruptions. "One piece of the Lifestone embedded itself in my right forearm, one pierced Cloonth's left arm. Somehow the combination of her pregnancy and the tainted Lifestone of the evil wizard under her skin changed her into a dragon. I witnessed it with my own eyes!"

Bimily's breath became shallow for several heartbeats, then she asked Shunlar to continue.

"My pregnancy also changed me." Shunlar looked around the room, and asked, "Are we alone?" A nod from Bimily and Shunlar began to change before her. She grew taller and thinner, and her hair turned completely white. Small scales covered most of her arms, chest, and thighs, and iridescent wings unfolded from beneath her tunic. It brought tears of joy to Bimily's eyes.

"Beneath the skin of my arm I will always carry the sliver, for it has become a part of my bone. Cloonth had the piece removed because it was foretold it would make her ill, perhaps even cause her death." Sparks and smoke came from Shunlar's mouth, making Bimily cough.

"I'd better return to my natural state before someone comes," Shunlar said, quickly altering her shape.

"Nearly as good as me, or how I used to be," said Bimily wistfully.

Rather than let Bimily begin to feel sorry for herself, Shunlar said, "Last night Ranth told me that Septia and Korab are both dead but he refused to explain how they died or when because of this strange taboo they have that forbids speaking of the dead. What can you tell me?" Shunlar asked, exasperated.

Bimily explained, "Do not be too harsh with him, my friend. Ranth has suffered much since returning to his people. As it turns out, he was married to Septia in name only. She was a priestess and would have one day ruled these people with Ranth at her side as First Guardian. In Kalaven, women are the rulers, an arrangement I agree with, wholeheartedly." Bimily winked.

"It seems Septia and Korab had secretly expected to marry one day. All that was changed when Benyar found his son, Ranth, and brought him home to take his rightful place as consort to the next ruler. As the only child of Zeraya and Benyar, he was persuaded to marry Septia. Since she had access to secret Temple texts, no one is quite sure yet just what she did, but we do know that she had been slipping the juice of the poppy to Ranth without his knowledge. That made him extremely easy to manipulate, as you might expect, and you can see how much he's changed. What really damaged him, however, was finding out that the child Septia gave birth to almost four months ago was Korab's, not his."

Shunlar's mouth dropped open. "No wonder he got so upset when I asked him if she had given him children . . ."

Bimily rolled her eyes, and said, "And I thought I was the only one who put her foot into it." Shaking her head, she continued, "While I was trapped in the body of a songbird, the Tonnerlingans who brought me here by caravan spoke the word 'korab' many times, but I had no idea what it meant. When I allowed Ranth and Benyar to touch my mind and listen to my memories, they understood and realized that Korab had somehow instigated the war. Later, when they questioned him, they discovered why he had done it.

"Septia and Korab were banished together for their crimes, their names stricken from the permanent Temple records and their child taken by Fanon to raise. As is their custom, they were taken into the deep desert and abandoned without food, water, weapons, or horses, just two weeks ago. Only by a miracle could they be alive." Thinking about that for a moment, Bimily added, "Or some devious planning. Knowing their reputation, I would not put anything past them."

Shunlar was stunned.

"He has a Lifestone, you know," Bimily added.

"No, I didn't, but I felt a difference about him," Shunlar answered. "And I have not yet looked at him with heat trace sight. Perhaps I should do that soon," she mused.

"Now will you please tell me about Avek?" Bimily pleaded.

"Oh yes. He waits in a small town nearby with Loff, my half-brother."

"Loff traveled with you? Whatever could have torn him away from the woman from Vensunor he was so infatuated with, though I never understood why," Bimily taunted, tilting her chin at a haughty angle.

"Now it's my turn to caution you, my friend. Ranla died, and Loff is not yet over it. She carried Creedath's child, forced upon her, of course, and his seed turned out to be as much of a demon as the father. It killed her before it died. If you want to keep Loff a cheerful companion, don't mention Ranla to him." Bimily nodded agreement.

"And . . . Come on, Avek is who I asked about," prompted Bimily. "You also mentioned that someone made an attempt on your life. Do you know why or who was behind it?"

Reluctant to dredge up those memories, Shunlar was quiet for a long time before she began telling the story. "In a very weak moment, one that I am ashamed to recall, I was hit over the head and thrown into a foul prison where I was drugged, beaten, and interrogated for three days. The woman who interrogated me knew about my son and demanded to know where he was. At the time I was positive the woman was Deeka, who was from Kalaven. She and her partner Orem had been Avek's trail companions for several weeks as they traveled to Vensunor. The first night at our fire, however, Deeka tried to touch my thoughts, and I sent her away.

Afterward, whenever I encountered her it made my skin crawl.

"When I was rescued, two corpses lay facedown in the dirt near the door, and I was told they were the bodies of those who held me captive. If I had been in better condition, I would have tried to read a heat trace, but I was still under the influence of whiteflower root and could barely keep my head up.

"Now that I recall the events of those three days something else occurs to me. Over the course of the year I wrote to Ranth many times. He never received any of my letters nor I the ones he wrote to me. In one of my letters I told Ranth we would have a son." Shunlar began to glower. "I'm beginning to suspect it was Deeka who intercepted our letters, else how could she have known about my son?"

Bimily agreed. "All indications say yes. We must speak to Ranth about this and ask him if he recognizes the names. Perhaps there are others who could be questioned as well." But to herself Bimily added, *What I worry about now is Avek's involvement.* Listening to her friend going on about Avek made Bimily grimace.

"Avek has turned out to be the most wonderful man to have beside me. In combat, his arms seem tireless. He and Loff and I became campmates in the mercenary camp we were attached to outside the gates of Vensunor. Avek is from Kalaven, in fact, his foster-mother is Zara sul Karnavt, Zeraya's sister. It was from him that I learned that Ranth had married Septia. She was the reason Avek was banished for two years. Do you know of the law his people have that forbids unmarried men and women to speak to each other unless a family member is present?" Bimily shook her head.

"When Avek learned Ranth and Septia were to marry, Avek spoke to her while they were alone, telling Septia of his love for her," Shunlar finished.

"Doesn't it seem a little convenient that you and he should meet, when he also confessed that he loved Septia?" Bimily asked.

Shunlar considered her question for a moment, then

dismissed it with a shake of her head. "No. I trust Avek completely. And I do love him. It's very difficult for me to be here in his city when he is banned from entering the gates." Shunlar sighed, then looked at her son. Bimily grimaced again. Acting like a lovesick girl was so unlike her friend, but she watched and said nothing.

The child had fallen asleep on the bed next to Bimily. "What could have happened between Ranth and me will never be known. We have a child between us that will keep us in contact over the years, but that is all now. Too much time and too many hard feelings have made us strangers to one another." Shunlar's voice conveyed sorrow.

"Have you spoken to Ranth about Avek or any of these feelings? Perhaps it isn't too late," Bimily urged.

"I've made up my mind. Avek is the man I want to be with. Besides, Ranth seems to be so settled into life with his family. I had no idea he would become so docile and agree to a marriage, us barely six months apart." Now her voice had a sarcastic edge.

"But Shunlar, think on this," Bimily brightened suddenly. "If Zeraya should become pregnant and have a female child, that girl will become the heir, replacing Ranth. As it is, he is merely destined to be First Guardian. If he should marry again, his consort, whoever she might be now that Septia is dead, will rule, not him."

"I wasn't aware of that. Are you sure they would so easily discard him after all he has been through?"

"Probably. Ranth has no oath-brothers, nor does he have any close friends. Since he returned with his father, all of his time has been spent learning the proper way to conduct himself among these people. When he married he became a slavishly devoted husband, though Septia had much to do with that. He has yet to recover his full strength."

"How do you know these things? Did Ranth tell you?" Shunlar asked.

"Not exactly. He told me some things, and I managed to piece together the rest of the tale from listening to servants' gossip. You see, they don't suspect that I can understand much of what they say, and I don't let on that I do. When they tend me, I listen, sometimes pretending to sleep so that they feel free to speak. It's a bit dishonest, but I learn many things,'' Bimily confided.

Shunlar shook her head, looking puzzled, and asked, ''Why doesn't he leave then?''

''He can't. That much Ranth has confided in me; he feels like a prisoner. No person in this city may leave without first asking the High Priestess, Honia sul Urla, for permission. Everything—hunting, festivals, planting, betrothals, marriages, every aspect of their life—is governed by the scrying she does. If he were to try and sneak away, Benyar would only send someone after him to bring him back, willing or not, and it would cause the clan great shame.''

''I had no idea his life was so structured and proscribed. To look at this palace, the servants, the guards . . . Oh, I see now, guards are everywhere. They are not merely there for his protection, are they?'' Shunlar asked.

''No, you can be sure of that,'' Bimily answered quietly.

''What can he do? Surely once he has recovered from the effects of the drugs Septia gave him he will want to leave or escape somehow. I'm surprised he is not off fighting the war.''

''Ranth will probably never actually fight—he is the only heir. If I were him, I'd pray mightily for a sister,'' Bimily concluded.

Five

PICKING UP HER FEET TO TAKE ANOTHER STEP was more than she could bear, but Septia willed herself to do it. She and Korab had been walking for days, and there was still no sign of the men who had assured Korab they would come to their aid. They had found the first bundle of waterskins and food that had been buried near the rock formations as promised, but that was mostly gone now. It might last until tomorrow, but she doubted it.

Their lips were cracked, blistered, and bleeding. Their sparse clothing offered no protection from the sun. The part of the desert where they had been left was far from any source of water, plant, animal life, or shelter. It was the intent of those who punished them that they should suffer greatly before they died for their crimes.

Septia's throat was raw from the effort of breathing. Her skin burned and her legs felt heavier with each step. Korab was not in much better condition. The supplies that had been left were noticeably insufficient for sustaining life under the full desert sun. Properly clothed, they would not have been burned or used all the water by this time as they had. The Tonnerlingans had not left the agreed-upon supplies, and Korab vowed someone would pay for his suffering.

They had only been given water for two days before they had been loosed into the desert to die. The small group that had brought them to be banished and witness their shame consisted of Korab's parents, Ketherey sul Jemapree and Fanon sul Eliya. Ranth sul Zeraya and his father, Benyar sul Jemapree, and Septia's parents, Esca sul Patia and Morot sul Tarok.

Their crime had been betraying their people and beginning a war with the people of Tonnerling that had resulted in the loss of countless lives. Though Septia and Korab were guilty, no one yet suspected the depth of their betrayal. Among other things, they had promised a faction of the enemy access to the last-known source of Lifestones in the Temple in the heart of Kalaven. When it became known in Tonnerling that it might be possible for anyone to again possess a legendary Lifestone, every young man enlisted to fight the Feralmon.

Unknown to the High Priestess, Honia sul Urla, Septia had been studying the secret texts of the Temple, and she had discovered the long-guarded secret that anyone, no matter what their station in life, could be prepared for a calling by a Lifestone. But it was a secret no more.

The clandestine meetings between Korab, his oath-brothers, and the men from Tonnerling had all been going as planned until Benyar returned with his son, Ranth, to resume his post as First Guardian and Consort to Zeraya, the Queen of the Feralmon. Korab remembered the day well; it marked the time that all of his careful weaving of plots began to unravel. As he took another faltering step, pure hatred coursed through his veins. He cursed Ranth silently and trudged toward the horizon and the appointed meeting place with grim determination.

When Septia fell, Korab slowed his pace only a little, not looking back until her faint cry for help tugged at his heart. His breathing labored, Korab turned slowly and sent a chilling look at the woman who reached for him with an upturned hand. Again he cursed, but he turned around and stumbled toward her, roughly grabbing her hand, all signs of patience or gentleness gone. Pulling her to her feet in one abrupt motion, he draped her arm around his neck, then encircled her waist with his arm. He dragged Septia along beside him until she could manage to step on her own.

"Hate, Septia. Let yourself be filled with hate, and it will sustain you," he whispered to her through clenched teeth. A shudder passed through him, and he felt stronger, his head becoming clearer.

Suddenly Septia went limp beside him. He realized in that moment that it was not hatred that fortified him with the will to live, but Septia, and the cost might be her own life, for she had transferred some of her vital energy to him when they touched. Cursing her under his breath, but more gently this time, he picked her up and began carrying her slender, limp body across the sand, his lips set in a thin, determined line.

Six

DECIDING THAT SHE MUST SPEAK TO RANTH with Bimily present—he would be more relaxed with her there—Shunlar summoned a servant and handed the woman a note for Ranth. Besides, she told herself, should they reach an impasse, Bimily could be counted on to relieve the tension of the moment with an off-color comment or a verbal jibe. Thirty minutes later the servant returned with Ranth's written agreement to come to Bimily's apartment at the appointed hour. Shunlar smiled.

When Ranth entered Bimily's room, Shunlar activated her sense of heat trace sight. A small spark of green jumped into her vision, her forehead became pale, then a greenish tint washed across it and vanished just as quickly. Deep within her vision a light that only she could see marked Ranth's path across the room. She watched, fascinated; the heat trace she remembered for Ranth was very different in color and width from what she currently saw before her.

Each person left a unique trail and only if one were adept at changing her shape or altering her appearance by illusion would the pattern change. Bimily knew of Shunlar's ability to see the heat trace as did Cloonth and Alglooth, but Ranth did not. Shunlar knew she would have to tell him if he were ever to understand what she was talking about.

"Good morning, my friend," Bimily said cheerfully.

Yet when she took a closer look at Ranth's face she felt compelled to ask, "Are you feeling well?" He looked absolutely haunted, and the circles beneath his eyes were darker than ever.

"I would be lying if I said yes, though truthfully my problem comes from lack of sleep." The pain his voice conveyed nearly brought tears to Bimily's eyes.

"Ranth, is there any reason that you would cast an illusion over yourself?" Shunlar asked.

"No, lady, I would have no reason to. Why do you ask?" The three of them had fallen easily into speaking the tongue of Vensunor, and it made Ranth realize how much he had missed hearing it.

"Something has changed your heat trace. Before you ask me what I mean, I offer to show you." Shunlar held her hand out to Ranth. After a several-second pause, he reluctantly grasped it. As their hands touched, their minds opened to each other, a flood of emotions rushing through both of them. They gasped, she at what it felt like to touch his thoughts again, he at what he saw floating on the air before him.

There appeared to be a band of color clearly marking his movements, following him like a thick ribbon through the room and clinging to him as if it were alive. "What is this?" he demanded to know.

"I have the ability to see this path left on the air by people and animals. I remember yours clearly, but it was not like this. It is now, somehow, strangely different."

Ranth thought for a moment, continuing to study the unusual phenomenon. "I see only mine. What about Bimily's or yours, or the servants' for that matter?"

"Watch and I will open my vision up to that." Still gripping Ranth's hand, Shunlar concentrated until he was able to see the tangle of colors that wove across and through the room. Disoriented, he shook his head at the jumble and she narrowed what she saw back to just his heat trace and Bimily's.

"I am told it is the heritage of my dragon grandmother; Cloonth and Alglooth also have this sense. Until now only Bimily knew, but I tell you this secret because

I wish to understand why your heat trace has changed so since last I saw you. Bimily told me you are now a keeper of a Lifestone. Perhaps that is the reason,'' she concluded, letting go of his hand.

Released from the vision, Ranth's hand went to the bulge under his shirt. He curled his fingers gently around it and closed his eyes. When he opened them several minutes later, both women were sitting quietly, waiting for a word or an answer.

''I asked my Lifestone and it informed me that I must show you my scars. Then it whispered, *azkrey gaht.* What does that mean?''

''Those are very old words in a very ancient tongue. It means, 'helpless captive,' '' answered Shunlar with a worried look. ''What scars do you mean? Have you been wounded?''

Shaking his head, he explained, ''These are clan markings that only the men of the Feralmon inflict upon each other, beginning at a very early age. At certain times of the year my people revert to an ancient custom of men and women living separately. The men perform a sparring ritual wherein they cut each other with the mark of the clans. These small cuts are then rubbed with a dye that colors them. My clan's color is dark green; there is also red, blue, yellow, black, and orange.'' His voice had taken on a slight singsong quality.

Shunlar had learned about the scarification practices from Avek, but she decided this was not a good time for her to admit that knowledge, or its source. While Shunlar and Bimily watched, Ranth undid the lacings and pulled his shirt over his head.

To Bimily's great surprise his body was scarred with markings on his chest and upper arms that blended into a beautiful pattern on his torso. The patterns on his arms looked familiar to Shunlar, and she realized they were shaped like the scales of a dragon, not unlike the ones on her arms when she took on the form of half-human, half-dragon.

Although the pattern of his breathing had increased, Ranth let himself be examined by the two women. He turned around slowly, raising his arms so they could get a better look. Behind him Shunlar made a hissing sound. ''Ranth, who made these marks?'' she asked, tracing a particular pattern.

''I have no way of knowing who could have made a specific cut. Because I am Zeraya and Benyar's son, members from all the clans participated in my initiation.'' Though he tried to conceal it, his voice rumbled a deep frustration.

''Korab was the instigator of my initiation. It occurred on the first night I spent in the clan's pavilion, coincidentally my first night in the city. Normally the scarring would have begun when I was a young boy, had I been raised here. Benyar was attending to my mother, Zeraya, and when he found me, he explained that though I had been treated unfairly, if I chose to have the scars healed and removed, the initiation would only be repeated. I didn't want to endure the pain again, so I relented and he rubbed pigment into the cuts. It was that or I would be an outcast.''

Tracing one of the scars with her finger, Ranth's memory of that night flooded Shunlar with such intense pain, fear, humiliation, and frustration that she began to cry in shock at the barbaric initiation, unable to remove her hand or block the memories. Very carefully he reached around and pried her fingers away. As he released her hand, he sent a message directly to her mind saying that he was no longer aware of those feelings as strongly. In order to survive he had buried them.

Calming herself, Shunlar wiped her tears away with the back of her hand. ''Ranth, take hold of your Lifestone and place it on the small of your back.''

Removing it from the pouch, Ranth touched it to his skin. The Lifestone flared up with a bright yellow light, then it winked out.

''Curious. What did you feel?'' she asked as she examined the spot he had touched with the Lifestone. It looked almost sunburned.

''A warmth spread across my back. Now it feels numb.''

"Bimily, look at this!" Shunlar pointed. Two identical sets of markings, one on each side of his spine were growing brighter. Surrounded as they were by the other scars, they had remained invisible. But because they had been touched by the Lifestone, they stood out and could be clearly seen.

"I need paper to copy this." As Shunlar drew the pattern, she explained, "In Stiga when I was young, Algooth taught me the meaning of the secret, sacred texts. If I am correct, these symbols on your back mark you for a slow, painful death. Some symbols can take months, even years to develop fully. How long have you had them?"

"How long? Nearly a year and a half."

"More importantly, who could have hidden them so skillfully?"

As realization sank in Ranth began to glower and pace. "This I cannot tolerate," he whispered in a voice tight with anger. "Who else but Korab could have placed these marks on me? My cousin resented my return and being restored as next in line of succession so much that he systematically undermined my chances to succeed with my own people. The man hated me," he stated with finality, putting on his shirt.

He turned to face Shunlar. Gently placing his hands on her shoulders, he looked deeply into her eyes, and said, "The one woman I truly loved, I betrayed by forswearing my oath to her and marrying another. Now all we have left to remind us of what we once meant to one another is a son. Perhaps I should die, for why would I want to remain alive if it means I must do so alone?" The anger in his eyes had been replaced by a look of despair and confusion. Abruptly he stepped away from her and left the room.

"Someone must be told about this, and soon," she heard Bimily say as though through a fog. Her senses seemed to have been blurred by Ranth's touch. Slowly the fog cleared, and she found herself understanding more of what Ranth's life had been like since they had parted. Soon she found herself sobbing on Bimily's shoulder.

"I must speak to him and ask him to tell his parents. Surely they will want to know his life is in grave danger. And, I never got the chance to ask him if he recognized the names Deeka or Orem." Bimily nodded agreement. Shunlar splashed water on her face and left to speak to Ranth.

When she reached his door the guards knocked to announce her and she was admitted immediately. Ranth looked tired and resigned, but he bowed graciously and escorted her to his private outdoor courtyard. Once she was seated she noticed on the table the piles of scrolls and books that he had obviously been studying.

"I hope I am not interrupting anything serious," she began.

"No, lady. There is nothing serious here for me to do or that I am allowed to do. The interruption is very welcome." His voice softened.

"You know I'm deeply worried about our discovery. If nothing is done, you will die. Surely you can't just resign yourself to that?" she asked, bewildered.

"Resignation is an emotion I have become familiar with since returning to the bosom of my family. Were you sitting here, you would see that it is best not to question or desire too much." His voice sounded tight.

"I *am* sitting here, and I don't like what I see. Are you telling me you're willing to die—to let another man win—rather than try to find a way to stop this sentence of death that's been placed on you?"

He laughed, a sound that made her feel uneasy. "This past year has been one of the most remarkable of my life, so I am told. There is not much I remember, you see, and I have to rely on others to fill in the details. I'm left alone much of the time, to recuperate, so I have been told. Even my tutors are not as interested in coming around much. They whisper behind my back that my mind is unstable and my health is in decline while to my face they say that time will heal all this. Most nights I cannot sleep, for my dreams are so vivid that they awaken me. My Lifestone is the one thing that has kept me from going mad.''

Listening to him made Shunlar shiver. She was not too sure that he wasn't mad, and after all he had been through, she wondered that he had a shred of sanity left.

''Then let me go to Benyar and speak to him about it,'' she pleaded.

''NO! I will do it in my own time.'' Gesturing angrily with his hand, his eyes made Shunlar turn away.

''Then do it within the next seven days, for that is how long I will keep quiet about this awful discovery. Wallow in self-pity if you must, but do not speak to me in that tone of voice again.'' She was angry and let him know it.

''Take your frustrations out on someone who deserves it, like Benyar. I never trusted him—he sold me to Creedath for gold. What was his price for you?'' Color reddened her cheeks as she angrily spat out her words of accusation.

Ranth said nothing. He sat with his eyes growing colder and more detached by the minute. She shivered when she saw them.

Finally, he promised, ''I will speak to Zeraya and Benyar within the week.'' With those words they parted, the tension between them unresolved.

Seven

Two days later Shunlar received a visit from three young novices sent by Honia sul Urla, the High Priestess. Their politely distant manner made Shunlar wary of them. They were dressed in identical ankle-length, pale yellow shifts, with veils of a similar color draping past their knees. The first novice, a young woman of about fifteen, bowed deeply, lifted her veil, and introduced herself.

"My name is Calenda sul Honia. Please my whims, I have been asked to deliver a message from my mistress. She requests that you bring your son to the Temple tonight at the tenth hour for the ceremony of his naming. Since you are his mother, you are the first person to be summoned, and I am to ask who else you wish to accompany you on this occasion."

The young woman's soft-spoken invitation in Old Tongue changed Shunlar's mind about her, and she returned the bow. "If it pleases, my son's father should be there, Ranth sul Zeraya. Also my friend Bimily. And, since I understand none of your customs, I would ask that you deliver a message for me to Zeraya sul Karnavt and Benyar sul Jemapree. Can you do that?"

"Yes, lady," answered Calenda.

"Invite them and ask them to invite whoever should be present at the boy's naming, at my request."

"Of course, lady. I will leave you now to do your

bidding." Calenda bowed and withdrew, the two novices accompanying her.

The appointed hour found Shunlar and a small group of Ranth's family members gathered before the doorway to the Temple's sanctuary. Since she had never been inside before, it was explained that the only way one could enter was in bare feet and weaponless. She complied at once, removing her wrist dagger and three small throwing daggers that were hidden in secret vest compartments, placing them in the alcove provided.

The inside of the Temple was a wonder to behold. They walked to the left, careful not to tread on the design of the centermost floor, a mosaic of cut glass that represented the night sky. There were gauzy draperies hanging at intervals from the ceiling high above that swayed gracefully as they were passed.

At the far end of the room waited Honia sul Urla, High Priestess of the Feralmon, dressed in a robe of brilliantly dyed deep blue silk that shimmered in the light of hundreds of candles blazing near and around the altar. Some candles were set upon the floor, others were in elaborate holders, while others were placed by the dozens in large sand-filled hanging glass cradles that were suspended from the ceiling by silver chains.

The altar itself was covered with a tapestry intricately embroidered in runic patterns of gold and silver threads. In the middle of the altar sat a bowl of dark, cobalt blue glass that was three feet around and about six inches deep.

With her son on her right hip and Ranth at her side, Shunlar led the procession into the Temple. Bimily followed close behind on Shunlar's left. Next came Zeraya and Benyar, then Fanon and Ketherey with their two daughters, Tilenna and Cachou. Following them were Zara and Jerob and their three children, Menity, Falare, and Jessop. Young Jessop looked to be around six years old and held his head high, proud to be present at so important a ceremony.

As the procession approached, Honia bowed to them three times from her place at the back of the altar. Then she picked up a water-filled pitcher of the same blue glass and slowly poured its contents into the bowl.

The child saw this and clapped his hands with glee, his small voice filling the chamber with laughter. This brought a smile to everyone's lips.

Yes, my son. Today is the day you shall choose a name, Shunlar spoke directly to his mind. In rapport with her and out loud he called in his small voice, "Name!"

"Welcome, little son," Honia's voice rang out in Old Tongue.

"Welcome," he echoed back to her in the same language, again clapping. Honia's eyebrow arched, and it was apparent she was fighting to remain solemn for the occasion. Finally, however, she smiled at the little boy before her, who was so obviously engaged and aware of what was happening.

"If you are ready, I will say the words that will begin the ceremony."

Without hesitation his voice called back to her, "Moon!" Then he pointed to the bowl.

Honia's eyes grew wide. She bowed her head to him, and began, "Great Mother of our People, this child comes before you to ask for a name today. Hereafter he will be called by what he draws forth from the scrying bowl. May the three moons, Malenti, Daleth, and Andeela guide his hand as he chooses."

Shunlar carried him close to the altar and held him up to the bowl. Seeing his reflection in the water he laughed, covering his mouth with his hands, squealing with excitement. Something caught his eye on the other side and he reached for it so that Shunlar had to hold his little body completely over the scrying bowl. Then a bit of vapor rose from the water gradually forming into the shape of a hand. Enclosed in the fingertips was a tablet, which it offered to the boy. He took it and squealed again.

None of the adults present seemed to be breathing. Honia was pale; her lips parted open from surprise, and she trembled. As soon as the vaporous hand disappeared beneath the surface of the water everyone bowed their heads, except for Shunlar and Bimily.

Since no one seemed to be moving, Bimily stepped forward to ask, "May I see what you were given, young man?"

Without hesitation the boy held his small hand open, his tiny palm nearly covered by a tablet with the rune known as "tavis." It meant "one who escapes." Shunlar and Bimily nodded to each other, satisfied that he had chosen well.

"Ranth, I present to you your son, Tavis," Shunlar said into the quiet. He smiled warmly at her and his son.

"Tavis sul Shunlar, welcome to the heart of the people," was his answer in a voice tight with emotion. Then he came forward and embraced Tavis, kissing him on each cheek. One by one the rest of his family did the same. As each person spoke the greeting, Tavis proudly held up the rune for them to see. His eyes seemed to grow older and contained more depth than Shunlar remembered ever seeing in them. He was evidently very proud of his name.

When the last and youngest member of the family, Jessop sul Zara approached, Tavis looked him deeply in the eyes and spoke his name. When Jessop gave him the welcome embrace of a kinsman, Tavis reached out and returned it. A bond had been struck between the two young boys, and Tavis went to Jessop's arms from Shunlar's, his small arms wrapped tightly around his older cousin's neck.

Tavis grinned and held up his tablet proudly for everyone to see. Then he loudly shouted his name again and giggled, the sound of his delight bouncing off the walls of the Temple. Jessop laughed, too.

Now that the ceremony was complete Honia spoke her words of welcome. "Tavis sul Shunlar, you are truly a son of the people now. To celebrate your naming, as custom demands for a child befitting your rank, we shall meet with the clans tomorrow night. You will accompany your father and his father and observe your first ritual. Do you understand?"

Honia waited for Tavis to acknowledge her question. If he did not, it meant he was yet too young and would stay with his mother in the women's pavilion for their ritual. Tavis became suddenly very quiet. He looked from Honia to the tablet in his hand. Then he pointed at Ranth and Benyar. After several seconds of tense silence, he turned to Honia and crossed his tiny arms over his chest. Then he answered her.

"Yes."

The adults were astonished but none more than Shunlar. Tears coursed down her cheeks, and he raised his arms to her to take him back from Jessop. Secure in his mother's arms once more, Tavis laid his head on her shoulder as one tiny hand patted her back to comfort her.

Seeing this, Honia sent them on their way.

Eight

THE NEXT MORNING SHUNLAR APPEARED REquesting an audience with Zeraya and Benyar. Her intention was to ask them to rescind the sentence of exile that had been placed upon Avek. Standing before the dais where Zeraya and Benyar sat in judgment of all who sought their counsel, Shunlar felt herself losing some of her courage as a drop of sweat trickled down her side beneath her tunic. There were perhaps fifty others in the chamber watching her, the outsider. Though none spoke the word aloud nor did any stray thoughts reach her, she could read the body language of those who waited their turn. Because of who she was, she had been singled out to be the first supplicant of the morning.

She bowed low but remained standing, refusing or forgetting to kneel. Benyar returned her courtesy first, then Zeraya inclined her head just barely enough to be polite. Inhaling deeply, Shunlar spoke in Old Tongue into the uncomfortable stillness.

"Highness Zeraya sul Karnavt, First Guardian Benyar sul Jemapree," she began with the proper protocol as the chamberlain, Hadida sul Yelenna, had instructed.

"Please my whims, I come before you to beg a favor. There is a man who saved my life who is from your city. He is responsible for bringing me and my son, Tavis, safely here from my mother's people in the Valley of Great Trees. He did not join me when I rode to the gates of Kalaven because to do so might endanger his life. He was exiled and has one more year to complete his exile. The favor I beg is this." Shunlar went to one knee. "Lift the exile from him so he may enter Kalaven."

Zeraya's gaze softened when she saw Shunlar finally bend her knee to her. *Perhaps there is some hope yet for this arrogant young woman,* she thought to herself, forgetting that Shunlar was older than she.

"Rise and come closer, daughter." Though Zeraya might choose that word to address all younger women, Shunlar grew suspicious as she slowly stepped closer.

"What you ask is beyond my power alone to grant. Honorable Honia sul Urla must be the one to lift the ban on the man you have not yet named. Tell me, who is he?"

"Avek sul Zara, foster-son of . . ." she was cut off.

"We know his parentage," Zeraya shot back to her coldly. "He broke one of our oldest laws. Why should we grant him special privilege and change our sentence?"

Knowing she had to think fast, Shunlar blurted out, "Because of the circumstances and who he was involved with when he broke your laws. Is it not possible she might have held sway over Avek in some way? Couldn't you at least consider it?"

Several people in the back began to whisper. "Silence. No one was given leave to speak," Zeraya ordered, her eyes flashing with anger. Benyar reached his hand over and placed it on top of hers. It relaxed her instantly, and Zeraya clamped her lips tightly together. It was Benyar who turned to address Shunlar.

"As you can see, Shunlar, this subject is troublesome to us. Let us consider your request while you speak to Honia. She will have the ultimate word on it, after all." With that Benyar nodded and Shunlar knew she was dismissed because the chamberlain, Hadida, was at her elbow. Without touching her, he conveyed the message to follow him, and she turned on her heel and stomped out of the audience chamber.

Beyond the doors and anyone else's hearing Hadida turned to face Shunlar. "Lady, if I may speak bluntly." He waited for a nod from Shunlar. "I urge you to practice caution and humility when you present this matter to Honia sul Urla; for, after all, it will be in your best interest."

When Shunlar looked puzzled at his words, Hadida remembered her rudimentary knowledge of the language. He considered a moment, then slowly said, "Bend your knee to Honia," demonstrating the meaning of the words.

She bowed in thanks to Hadida, nodded several times in understanding, and said in a thick accent, "Thank you," not altogether convinced that she would actually do it. Satisfied that he had done what he could, Hadida summoned a young female servant, instructing her to take Shunlar to the Temple. He bowed to Shunlar and was gone.

Perhaps it was the way Shunlar immediately bent her knee that helped her words persuade the High Priestess to reconsider Avek's sentence. She was impressed to see the efficient way Honia's orders were carried out by her assistants. As she sat waiting, several men and women entered the Temple for an audience with Honia. Within the hour two riders were chosen and given instructions.

Knowing the heat of the desert would take its toll on rider and horse, they were cautioned against taking unnecessary risks, but because they had been dispatched by Honia, no one questioned the order for haste. It was early afternoon when they departed for Obboda, the small oasis city where Avek and Loff awaited a message from Shunlar. When they rode into Obboda, and finally found the inn, it was full dark, and they were told that Avek and Loff were sleeping. Sure of themselves, they were asked to be shown to the room.

Learning that Shunlar had gotten Honia to consider ending his exile, Avek persuaded Loff to leave for Kalaven immediately. Anxious to return home, he chose to ride through the night rather than wait until the messengers had rested. Besides, he argued, riding in the desert at night meant it would take half the time. Thanking the men profusely, he first saw to it that they and their horses would be well cared for. Then he and Loff threw their few belongings into saddlebags, saddled up, and rode into the night. He was right, as with the first blush of dawn they approached the entrance to Kalaven.

Not much missed the keen eyes of those who guarded the gateway to Kalaven. Avek had been spotted by one who knew him well from the way he sat astride his horse. Immediately one of the sentries was sent to the palace to inform Ranth that Avek and another rider had been seen. The fact that he was accompanied by an outsider was obvious to the sentries, even though Avek had taken great pains to clothe Loff properly. Both of them wore hooded robes over their riding leathers, for warmth as well as protection, and masks to keep the sand out of nose and mouth.

Their tired horses puffed and grunted as they cantered up the final slope, giving their last bit of strength as if they knew their journey was over. Avek and Loff dismounted and immediately Avek knelt, then touched his forehead to the ground, which Loff mimicked. When Avek took a pinch of sand in his fingers and touched it to his tongue beneath his mask, Loff did the same. But only Avek removed his dagger from the sheath at his belt and made a small cut on the back of his hand, letting droplets of blood fall onto the sand in front of him.

That part of the ritual over, Avek stood and Loff came to his feet beside him. Now they must wait. As Avek had informed Loff, not only was he not yet welcome, he was not permitted to show his face to any of them. To support his friend, Loff decided he would not remove his face mask either. The minutes stretched by as Avek and Loff stood in the center of a circle of motionless sentries waiting for an escort to arrive who would offer them official welcome and bring them into the city.

When the escort finally came through the gate, Avek felt his heart jump when he recognized Shunlar among them, but he was forbidden to speak to anyone. Holding his tongue, he and Loff bowed to Shunlar, Ranth, and the others who approached as the sentries stepped back, opening the circle.

Normally the sentries or family members who welcomed a returning traveler would now approach and exchange greetings; however, this was not a usual homecoming. Avek was still considered an exile. A group of eight stern warriors moved in to escort Avek to the Temple. Two of them came forward and took the reins of the horses. From among those warriors Avek's oathbrother, Emun sul Setta, stepped forward to take his weapons.

His eyes conveying the emotion he dared not speak, Avek placed his dagger firmly on Emun's open palm. Secretly their hands touched, physical contact allowing a message to pass between their minds. The words *welcome, brother* echoed in Avek's head, and he squeezed his eyes shut to keep them from tearing up, bowing his head to Emun in thanks.

Ranth had remained exceptionally distant from Shunlar that morning as they hurried in the half-light of dawn to meet her brother and Avek at the city gates. Benyar had informed Ranth that he was the family member who had been chosen to meet Avek at the gates. When Ranth learned the reason why Avek was being called back, his jaw set in a tight clamp and he dismissed himself from Benyar's presence.

The only words he had exchanged with Shunlar, besides a polite good morning, was to explain that she must not speak to Avek, embrace him, nor show any signs of familiarity with him in public. Knowing that Shunlar and Avek were lovers chafed him even more as he watched them greet one another wordlessly. His face closed and tight with emotion, Ranth gave Avek a kinsman's embrace with just enough contact to show civility. Yet he was genuinely happy to see Loff, who though made nervous by everyone's somber behavior, was excited at the prospect of finally entering Kalaven, the city of the Feralmon.

Breaking the silence, Ranth embraced Loff, and said, "Be welcome to our city, Loff sul Marleah. As Shunlar's brother you will walk beside her. Avek must now walk between the escort of guards." Loff removed his mask and greeted his sister with a huge grin.

Ranth had been sent as a representative of his and Avek's clan to remind Avek of how he must comport himself on their way to the Temple. Ranth, as the son of Zeraya and Benyar, and Avek, his foster-cousin and clan member, must, of all people, set an example.

Adhering to custom, Avek's face remained covered as he entered the city surrounded by guards. It was a sign to all that he was returning to ask permission to live among them once again. Having been banished, he couldn't let anyone look upon his face until he was declared "back into the heart of the people."

Tired, sore, and grimy from riding all night, they must first bathe before being presented to Honia sul Urla. Since speaking directly to Avek was also forbidden, Ranth decided it was best that he join them so that Loff would have an interpreter. Leaving Shunlar and their escort of guards in a waiting area, the three men entered the baths in silence. At this hour few others were enjoying a soak before beginning their day. Seeing one enter who was masked, everyone moved aside quietly, bowing to Ranth when they recognized him.

An attendant appeared and quickly escorted them to a small alcove with a private tub that the three of them would easily fit into, filled with hot, steaming, herbal-scented water. Two more attendants appeared and began to remove their clothing. It was then that Loff saw the unusual, green-tinted scars on Avek's and Ranth's bodies for the first time. Though he tried not to stare, he couldn't help himself. Having never seen anything like this before, he was naturally full of questions but stopped as the attendant who was helping him disrobe made a small sound and backed away from him.

A quick exchange of words from Ranth and the attendants left them alone, pulling the curtain across the doorway for privacy. Once they were gone Ranth apologized and explained, "The scars are traditional clan symbols and every man has them. In fact, it is considered shameful for a man of our people not to carry these scars."

He turned to Avek, saying, "You may remove your mask while we are alone." Having said that, he turned and stepped into the tub.

Something about the tone of his voice prompted Loff not to ask any more questions. That and the way Avek held his finger to his lips and shook his head. Instead Loff joined Ranth in the water, thanked him for his explanation, and began to wash. It felt thoroughly wonderful to submerge himself and soak his tired muscles.

"Loff, I hope you understand that I am in a difficult position here. I realize you have many questions about our customs. Tonight the clans will meet and if you will join me, I would be honored to have you sit beside me. If Avek were permitted to invite you, he would also." Ranth looked at his cousin for confirmation of his words. Avek had a longing-filled look in his eyes as he nodded silent agreement, then bowed his head to Ranth. Loff sat between the two men feeling more than a little uncomfortable.

Once they were clean, they dried off and took turns braiding each other's hair into elaborate, more formal warrior braids. Satisfied that they were more than presentable, Ranth stuck his head through the curtain and quietly ordered attendants to bring their clothing. Avek's and Loff's saddlebags were set inside the room, and another bundle was given to Ranth. Dressed in more formal attire, Avek once more donned a mask and the three of them joined their waiting escort.

It was an emotional moment for Avek when he entered the Temple and saw his family present. Zara sul Karnavt, his foster-mother, along with his father, Jerob sul Ansilla, and their three children were gathered in the atrium, near the doorway, eager to welcome him with open arms. But until Honia had declared him welcome, he could neither show them his face nor speak to them.

Avek entered the Temple in his bare feet, walking alone ahead of the others. His family followed close behind and behind them came Shunlar, Ranth, and Loff.

The guards that had escorted Avek waited outside.

Honia called his name in a booming voice that startled him. "Avek sul Zara, come forward."

Before her he went to his knees, bowing his head. Honia stood before the altar, Zeraya and Benyar flanking her.

"You have been summoned before us to plead for return into the heart of the people. Since it has been brought to my attention that you may have been under the influence of a person who used her knowledge to do great harm to others, I will consider it possible that you have been unjustly banished for two years. You have spent more than one year in exile, and your family and friends have influenced my decision. What have you to say for yourself and your conduct? Remove your mask and show me your face." Honia's voice was strong, but not without compassion.

Avek slowly pulled the mask away. With eyes lifted to Honia's he answered, "Because I broke the law my punishment was just. If an influence was placed upon me, I ask that you touch my thoughts to find it. Truthfully, I do not know." Finished, he lowered his eyes.

"You appear to be a man without guile, Avek sul Zara. Your willingness to accept your fate tells me much about your character. There will be no need to touch your mind. Your sentence has been fulfilled. As of today, you are welcome back to the heart of the people. Stand and let all see your face."

Avek was near to tears. He sprang to his feet, grinning happily, turning toward his family. His smile was mirrored by everyone present as his family and friends rushed forward to embrace him. When at last his oath-brother, Emun sul Setta, had thumped him firmly on the back, Avek turned his attention back to Honia. He went to his knees once again and bowed, placing his forehead on the floor before her as a sign of his profound gratitude.

"If I may be permitted," he began.

"Speak, returning son," Honia answered.

"I must speak of matters of the heart before anything

else. Some six months ago I met and came to love a woman not of the people. She is present here today and because of her I have been allowed to walk within Kalaven once again. I gifted her with a carved pendant, which she accepted, understanding that it meant a pledge. It must be said now, not later, that I intend to have Shunlar as my mate, unless she has accepted another.'' Honia eyed him suspiciously for several seconds, then called Shunlar forward.

''Have you accepted this man, or any other as your mate?'' she asked in a voice gone cold as ice.

Suddenly unsure of how to answer in the language of the Feralmon, something compelled her to ask in Old Tongue. ''Please my whims, but ask me again in this tongue for I cannot be sure I understand you otherwise.''

Before Honia could speak, Zeraya whispered something to her. Honia nodded, and asked in Old Tongue, ''Have you accepted this man as your mate?''

All attention was focused on Shunlar. On his knees before Honia, color rose to Avek's cheeks as he waited for her answer, his gaze on the floor.

''Please my whims, Avek is my sword brother and traveling companion. We have not formalized our partnership with a pledge to one another yet. Since I am within your city and must adhere to your rules, I will comply,'' she answered.

''Do not take this lightly. I did not ask you to comply. Avek is one of our precious sons and not a man whose affections are to be trifled with.'' Honia fixed a stern look on Shunlar, then over those assembled before her. ''If there is any among you who can speak against this union, do so now.'' When she set her eyes upon Ranth she could see the turmoil in him.

''Child of Zeraya, please my whims. Does this union trouble you?''

''Honorable Honia,'' he answered with his eyes downcast, ''I would be lying if I said no, but I will not speak against it.''

Avek knew what was passing without being able to understand. He raised his head to speak, and Honia recognized his anguish. "If I may be permitted," he began, "Shunlar and Ranth have a child between them, this I know. Shunlar and I have love between us, this I also know. If time is needed for her to respond to my proposal, then time must be given." He spoke very softly and when he was finished he lowered his head again.

Things suddenly had gone wrong, Shunlar could tell. "Avek, what are you saying? What am I supposed to do?"

"Child, he cannot answer you now, unless one of your family is present," answered Honia, switching language.

"My brother Loff is here," she fairly shouted. Loff hurried forward and went to his knees before Honia. Shunlar quickly explained that because she and Avek were unmarried, a member of her family must be present in order for them to be permitted to speak to one another.

"Are you this woman's brother?" asked Honia through narrowed eyes. The resemblance was faint, and Honia suspected it was not true.

"I will answer for him," interrupted Ranth. "In Vensunor my father and I met Loff. He is her brother as she says." Benyar confirmed Ranth's answer.

Honia raised her hand for silence. Before anyone could speak another word, she said, "This is my decree. Shunlar and Avek are to remain apart until the time comes when she knows the true voice of her heart. Until then, Avek will return to his family and Shunlar to her residence in the palace. Go now, for tonight the clans will meet to celebrate the naming of Tavis sul Shunlar."

The entire group bowed to Honia as Shunlar and Loff looked on. Before anyone could explain to Shunlar what had been said, Honia turned and left the Temple, leaving Shunlar full of questions. She began to suspect that things had gone badly.

"Avek, speak to me, please," she pleaded. "Loff is here by my side. Tell me what just happened."

With great sadness he spoke in a very controlled voice. "We must live apart for now, that is what was said."

"No, we will come with you—Loff, the boy, and I. We will be together as we have been for the last six months."

"It is not permitted." With a final gesture Avek turned to leave, but Shunlar grabbed his arm. "Please, let go," he said, putting his hand over hers. "If you continue, it will only make things harder on me, not you. Honia has just allowed me to walk among my people again and to question her judgment would put me in a very bad position. Later I will speak with you. Now I must return to my home and attend to my family." He gently removed her hand from his arm and, not looking back, joined his family, who waited for him.

But Shunlar had heard Avek's thoughts when they touched. He said in mind-to-mind rapport, *Make your peace with Ranth. Then, and only then, when you are sure, come to me.*

His tone had been firm, and she knew he meant every word of it. Avek was near heartbroken, from the sound of his voice, but he remained true to his word. He loved her, was devoted to her, and was willing to risk losing her to another man to prove the strength of his feelings. He had brought her here to Kalaven, after all, where Ranth waited.

Frustrated, Shunlar watched Avek leave before she turned her attention back to the small party that waited for her. Loff stood patiently beside her, but with a bewildered look on his face. Benyar and Zeraya stood off to the side, talking to Ranth in hushed tones. Suspicious, Shunlar sent a careful tendril of her awareness toward Ranth.

She heard Zeraya saying in a firm voice, "Do what you can to convince her and the child to stay with you. You now have a son who is truly yours."

Suddenly Ranth turned toward Shunlar. The look of self-loathing in his eyes made her cringe. "She has heard you, Mother," was all he said before turning and walking away. Zeraya watched her son leave, then, with an exasperated shake of her head, she approached Shunlar as if nothing had happened.

"Return with us to the palace. All that can be done here has been done."

"Are you quite sure, Highness?" Shunlar asked defiantly as she turned to catch up to Ranth. Thoroughly confused, Loff followed her.

But catching up to Ranth was no easy task. He practically ran from the place, from the people, angry beyond words. *Why do I let that woman get under my skin so?* He had no idea where he was going, he just walked as fast as he could. Several minutes later he remembered that Shunlar and Loff would eventually find him, because of her ability to follow his heat trace, so he stopped where he was and waited for them, leaning against a pillar with his arms crossed against his chest.

"Why are you following me? Can't you see that I have no desire to speak to anyone?" Perhaps he could drive them away with words.

"Ranth, you haven't told them about the symbols on your back yet, have you?" She carefully asked him in the tongue of Vensunor so that only Loff would understand their conversation.

"No one knows, and I must choose to tell them or not. It is my business, and this must be my decision." He was very angry and gestured with his fist.

"Excuse me, but what are you talking about?" interjected Loff.

"Quiet!" Shunlar shouted at him. He backed off a few steps with his hands raised before him.

"Not if it means your death. Ranth, there are things happening to both of us that demand explanation. I promised you I would tell no one about the markings for seven days, but I doubt I can keep my word after this. Why didn't you warn me of the possibility that Honia might choose to make Avek and me live apart? What is your motive?" she demanded.

Ranth's eyes were narrow as he carefully chose his words to answer her. "There is no way I can learn the mysteries of Honia's mind. As for a motive, must you hear it to know? I still love you. I have tried to put those feelings aside because of my kinsman, Avek, but it hasn't worked. Now there may be a chance for me, and I find I want that chance. I want to be taken seriously for a change and not treated like a child. I want a chance to prove to you I am the man who should be by your side.'' His voice had risen, and his cheeks were flushed. People who passed by in the street were surprised but hurried past with their faces averted. Already Ranth knew he would be reprimanded for his behavior in public. He didn't care.

He continued, his voice louder, ''I want, more than anything, to live somewhere where I can be free to make my own decisions, where no one will scrutinize every minute decision and say it is for the betterment of the clan.'' His anger loosed, Ranth found that the more he ranted, the better he felt.

Shunlar stood before him, her hands on her hips, her smile growing wider each time Ranth made another statement. ''That's more like it. I was beginning to wonder if someone had castrated you by the way you were behaving. Good. Now we can proceed. Meet us after the noon hour in Bimily's quarters. We have much to discuss.''

She turned to Loff and said, ''Come, brother, you look like you could use some sleep.'' He yawned, and Ranth heard him ask, ''Did you say Bimily? What's she doing here?'' as they walked away.

Ranth was left standing alone in the street, breathing heavily but feeling somehow cleansed by his outburst. It seemed anger was good for something.

Nine

JUST AFTER THE NOON HOUR RANTH FOUND himself reluctantly on his way to Bimily's quarters. He had successfully avoided seeing his parents since this morning, when Avek had been told he could not be considered Shunlar's mate. Ranth found himself distrusting them and their motives more and more.

His knock on the door was answered by Bimily calling, "Enter." Stepping into the room, Ranth saw that Bimily and Shunlar had assembled a great pile of provisions. Only then did he remember that Bimily would soon begin her journey home. Loff greeted him with a genuine smile as well as a hearty thump on the back, gestures that improved Ranth's mood.

"Lady Bimily, I have been so involved in my own life that I forgot you will be leaving us. If I were permitted, I would join you, but you know that asking permission to accompany you would be a futile gesture."

Bimily smiled a secret smile, then cast a look at Shunlar. "Perhaps not as futile as you believe. Hear what my friend has to tell you, then see if you are willing to cast your lot with ours."

Shunlar flashed Ranth a genuine smile, saying, "We want you to come with us, and I am willing to abduct you from under everyone's noses if that's what it takes. How will I manage that? I needed to have you here in private to show you something. You see, since becoming pregnant with our child I have acquired the ability to change my appearance.'' She watched Ranth before continuing.

''Remember the awful nightmares I had that began after Creedath died?''

''How could I forget? They nearly cost me an eye!'' Ranth smiled a lopsided grin.

''The reason for the nightmares is no longer a mystery, though no one can say why they occurred. When Banant's corrupted Lifestone exploded, a sliver embedded itself under the skin of my arm. The Great Trees explained that the heritage of my dragon bloodline mixed with the sliver of Lifestone and being pregnant caused what I am about to show you.'' Smiling wryly, Shunlar closed her eyes. Ranth stared at the impossible taking place before his eyes.

Her height increased first, and gradually her hair turned white. Next small scales became visible on her arms, throat, and legs. Finally, from beneath her sleeveless tunic wings unfurled and grew until they were nearly ten feet from tip to tip, the scales upon them glittering in a rainbow of colors.

''If you like, I can also breathe a stream of fire across the room,'' she offered, a curl of smoke rising from her delicate nostrils.

''No, what you have shown me is sufficient,'' Ranth answered, looking at Loff for support. Her brother nodded. Though he had seen Shunlar in this form before, he had never watched the change take place.

Shunlar bowed her head to him and soon she returned to looking like her usual self. ''Good. Now you know how I will abduct you if the need arises. Please tell no one of my ability to change my shape.''

''I swear no one will learn of this from me,'' Ranth agreed.

''Good. Now you and I will pay our respects to your parents. I have a proposition to make to them that should make them very happy and will also serve us. I want to leave Tavis in their safekeeping while you and I search for a way to remove the markings from your back. Because the journey will be dangerous, I will not risk the life of our child."

"Why would you do this for me?" Ranth asked quietly.

"Our son needs his father alive," was her whispered reply as she bestowed a very gentle smile on Ranth. He inclined his head to her in appreciation.

"Bimily's people should have the knowledge we seek. If they don't, we will return to the Valley of Great Trees and enlist help from Gwernz and the Great Trees or Alglooth and Cloonth. Surely one of them can give us an answer to this mystery."

"Lady, I want more than anything to accompany you, but I doubt if you will sway Zeraya, Benyar, or Honia to agree to my leaving," Ranth answered, his voice thick with emotion.

"Then you will simply disappear. Several days after we are gone I will return for you while everyone else sleeps. But first, let us see if words can do their work and persuade them to answer in our favor." She winked at him then, suddenly sure of herself.

Ranth sent a guard ahead to inform his parents that he and Shunlar wished a special audience with them and Honia within the hour. Then he and Shunlar went over the details of just how they were going to ask his parents and Honia for permission for him to leave Kalaven. Though he was nervous and unsure, Ranth finally relaxed enough to believe they might agree to the proposal. Encouraged by Bimily and Loff, Ranth and Shunlar left for their audience.

As they wound their way along the corridors of the palace to the wing where Zeraya and Benyar resided, Ranth found himself hopeful for the first time in a year. He let his feelings grow and before Shunlar could stop him he took hold of her hand and they slipped into a small alcove. He reached out to touch her face with trembling fingers. Shunlar allowed his touch and opened her thoughts to him for the first time since they had seen each other.

Ranth saw her memories and felt the longing and loss

for him that she had buried so effectively. Tears welled up in his eyes as he sent his painful memories to her. Without a word passing between them they forgave each other for the past hurts and, with deep sighs, embraced. Ranth's kiss was tender upon her mouth, and she returned it with remembered passion.

Reluctantly Shunlar began to close her thoughts off from Ranth but not before he was able to see Avek in her mind. He felt her love for Avek, but it was not enough to stop him from trying and he told her so very gently. It seemed to have the desired effect, for Shunlar looked confused as she stepped away from him.

"I will do all I can to make you trust me again," was what Ranth whispered before turning to lead the way to the royal apartments.

The guards at the doors bowed to Ranth. They knocked three quick taps to announce their arrival, and he and Shunlar were admitted immediately.

Honia was already present, having been summoned by Zeraya. Both women inclined their heads to Ranth and Shunlar but did not speak to them. They were not in good temper, unaccustomed as they were to being summoned. Zeraya cast a quick glance at Benyar, who bowed in greeting to Shunlar and his son, then asked them to be seated. Once they were settled into chairs, Ranth began talking.

At first Ranth remained calm, but as he described the lethal symbols on his back and how they were discovered with the help of his Lifestone, his temper rose. Finished with his explanation, he removed his shirt so that Zeraya, Honia, and Benyar could examine him. The familiar numbing sensation spread across the small of his back when he touched his Lifestone to his skin. Ranth heard his mother suck in a fast breath.

But the meeting did not go as well as Shunlar anticipated. Zeraya steadfastly would not hear of Ranth leaving Kalaven to accompany Bimily on her journey home. Even hearing that Tavis would be left in her keeping while Shunlar and Ranth sought an answer from Bimily's people could not sway her.

Certain that Honia would be as unreasonable as Zeraya, Shunlar held her tongue, deciding not to push; after all, she had an alternate plan. Though she was angry, Shunlar knew a show of temper would do no one any good, especially Ranth. She waited impatiently for him to speak up for himself. When he didn't, she encouraged him with a severe look. But nothing would change Zeraya's mind, and Benyar conceded. Ranth would not be given permission to leave.

Honia insisted she would find the way to remove or change the deadly words on Ranth from the ancient texts of the Temple. After all, she reminded them, someone had uncovered the mystery from the very same books that were in her possession. And everyone, even Shunlar, knew just who that someone was. Only Septia could have violated the law of the Temple and sought knowledge that was forbidden to her until she had come of age. Honia vowed to Ranth and his parents that she would not rest until she had found the text and learned how to reverse the process.

Hearing reference to Septia made Ranth uneasy. His level of distress increased to a point Shunlar had not seen before. Seeing this made her more determined to take him away from this strange life of his. For what kind of life would Ranth have if he could never pass beyond the confines of the city? Upon leaving the royal suite she cast a baleful glare at Zeraya.

Ten

THE APPROACHING EVENING FOUND RANTH RE-clining in his courtyard, indulging in self-pity. He had known he would never be granted permission to leave Kalaven. Gods, what must he have been thinking to even ask? Shunlar had been so persuasive, and Bimily and Loff had added to her already over-inflated sense of confidence. But at least they had given him some sense of hope. He tried not to even think about the plan Shunlar had mentioned about abducting him. The very idea that he would be taken away by a flying woman was so absurd, anyone would believe it sheer fantasy on his part. He laughed at that, something which lightened his mood, finally. Ranth rose and began to dress for the night's special occasion.

Soon Benyar would come to collect him, his son Tavis, and Loff. Together they would take Tavis to the clan's pavilion, where the celebration of his naming would take place. He turned his thoughts to the importance of the evening's festivities. On one hand, Tavis and Loff would be experiencing their first ritual battle. Though Tavis was too young to be initiated—he must be at least five years old to take part in his first blood-letting—Loff would be given the option to stand and join in. Ranth had a lot of explaining to do. Suddenly he was happy that Avek would be there. He decided to ask Avek to sit on the other side of Loff and instruct him in the finer points of the "dance."

Shunlar and Bimily had been invited to accompany Zeraya to her clan for the evening's festivities, but both women had declined. Bimily because she was too weak; Shunlar because she was too angry. Since even the servants would be attending their separate clan gatherings, Shunlar would look after Bimily that evening while the servants were gone.

A knock at his door and Benyar entered. "Good evening, my son. Are you ready?" Ranth nodded. "Good," Benyar said, grinning from ear to ear. "Then let us proceed to Shunlar's quarters and collect your son." Benyar opened the door for Ranth and the two men who were so similar in looks and stature proudly strode down the hall.

"Father, Loff has asked to be initiated into our clan tonight. After giving it much thought, I wish to ask Avek to sit beside him and explain our customs to him." Having said that, Ranth felt suddenly relieved.

"I don't see how that could be a problem. After all, Loff and Avek have traveled together for months. Having been campmates and fighting together as long as they have will give Avek the knowledge neither of us has about Loff's sparring abilities. I say you've made a wise choice. It might also do much to help settle any problems that come between you and Avek." Benyar paused and gave Ranth a knowing look.

"I imagine it must be hard for you to sit by and watch Shunlar being courted by another. Think of how it must be from Avek's point of view. This is not the first time clan brothers have wanted the same woman. If it were long in the past, you would both stand a chance or solve it by duel."

"What do you mean?" asked Ranth, very curious.

"Long ago it was customary to take several mates, not simply one. Many of the Feralmon took two, and sometimes, though not often, three mates. But in those days, our people traveled constantly, eking out our very existence from the desert. Rarely would all the mates be in camp at the same time. If the person chosen for Second One was not someone that the First One agreed with, a duel would be the only way to settle it. Though most times it was the women who dueled. It seemed they were the ones who vied for the position of First One.

"Once we settled in Kalaven, that way of living did not work very well because most times all the mates were under the same roof at the same time. Too many women and men began to die in needless duels. It was then that your mother stepped in, making it unlawful to take more than one mate at a time. Certain factions who disagreed decided to leave and continue living in the old ways. We could not stop them and have not seen or heard from any of them since."

"But don't you ever run across any tracks or sign of them when you hunt? How could they just vanish?" Ranth asked intrigued.

"We Feralmon can be very secretive when we choose to. How much did you know of our people before you returned home with me?"

"Practically nothing. Everyone assumes we are still a nomadic people. Not even Delcia or Morgentur suspect what a grand city exists here. I begin to understand more each day, but just when I think I have learned all there is to know, something like this crops up." Ranth got very quiet for a moment, then asked, "Tell me, does Avek know about the old custom of taking more than one mate?"

"Indeed he does. Else he would not have needed Zara for a foster-mother," answered Benyar quietly. "The women of your mother's clan have long been skillful fighters," he added just as they reached Shunlar's quarters.

Ranth gave Benyar a questioning look before knocking on the door. A servant opened it, and as Ranth entered the room he heard Tavis squeal, "Da," in his high-pitched voice.

Tavis was dressed in robes that matched Ranth's in color and design. Ranth and Benyar could only grin with delight when they saw him. Shunlar alone seemed to be in grim spirits.

"We thank you for allowing us to present your son

to our clan. Rest assured that he will be treated with love and respect.'' Benyar bowed to Shunlar.

''I'm relieved to hear it. Tell me he won't be cut or treated like his father was on his first visit to your clan,'' Shunlar demanded.

''What you may have heard about Ranth's own initiation happened because of my fault alone. No other is to blame but me. My absence is what allowed another to act. Never will I leave the clan's tent this evening while this child is present. I vow this to you solemnly.'' Benyar bowed low to Shunlar, who regarded him for several minutes before accepting his words.

''Good. I accept your promise. And yours . . .'' she waited for Ranth to add his vow to his father's.

Ranth was holding Tavis in his arms, their foreheads pressed together, their eyes closed in deep rapport. When Ranth opened his eyes, Tavis did, too. Together they faced Shunlar, their combined gazes conveying such intensity that she held her breath. Their faces were shaped similarly, and it was apparent that Tavis would grow to look much like his father.

''Tavis will be in my safekeeping. Never will he leave my side. He asks his mother not to worry,'' Ranth told her.

Satisfied that her son would be safe, Shunlar put his cloak over his small shoulders, pulling up the hood. Dressed like his father, Tavis looked around with twinkling eyes. He laughed, pointed at his mother, then waved, saying, ''Bye-bye. Go.''

They were out the door and down the hall, stopping only briefly for Loff. To say he was excited would be an understatement. As they walked, he asked so many questions of Ranth and Benyar so rapidly that they could barely answer him before he fired off another one.

Into the large tent that was the clan's meeting place Ranth carried Tavis. He followed his father, Benyar, who led them to their places, with Loff close behind. As their guest, Loff would be given much leeway, but he had been instructed to remain silent for now.

The Feralmon were a dark-skinned, black-haired people, so Loff's lighter coloring made him stand out. Since he was in the company of Benyar, the highest-ranking man among them, Loff was regarded with the utmost courtesy. Knowing that he was Tavis's uncle also gave Loff special status. But it had been rumored that Loff had requested initiation into their clan. As he passed by, each man took his measure.

To Loff the large oval tent was a marvelous construction of tanned, waterproofed leather. Painted across the sides and ceiling were the symbols of the clan: the footprints, claw marks, and form of the giant poison-clawed sand cat. There were hanging lamps burning a smokeless oil that gave a soft, golden glow to everyone and everything. The center of the tent appeared to be perfectly smooth sand that no one walked upon, and in the middle was a fire pit, where the wood was stacked, waiting to be lit. Covering the perimeter of the tent were beautifully woven carpets, and it appeared each man had his place.

Just as they began to settle into their places, Avek entered the tent with his father, Jerob, and their oath-brothers, five men in all. They bowed to Benyar, Ranth, and Loff, who returned the greeting. Tavis immediately recognized Avek.

" 'Vek. 'Vek," he loudly called out to him, reaching for Avek. Ranth watched as his son readily went to the arms of the man who was his rival for Shunlar, and now, it seemed, his son also. He had a hard time hiding his feelings. He watched, swallowing hard several times as Tavis hugged Avek. At last Avek whispered something to Tavis and the child turned and reached for Ranth.

"My lord Benyar. Cousin," Avek greeted them, bowing again, lower than he needed to.

Ranth's face softened once Tavis was back in his arms. Beside him stood his father and Loff. Ketherey, his uncle, had joined them, with his two oath-brothers. In his arms Ranth held his son, the child they were gathered to honor this evening. Never had Ranth felt such a sense of family or belonging. Though he envied Avek his alliances, he realized he had not put himself into any situation that might have allowed friendships to build. Tonight he decided to change that.

"Cousin, I would ask a favor," Ranth began.

"If it is within my power to grant, it shall be done gladly," Avek answered solemnly, his face suddenly looking wary. The men surrounding them recognized how tense the moment had become, and they all grew even more silent. Ranth's next words must be carefully chosen else a feud start within the clan.

"Please sit at my left, as a brother tonight." Ranth's eyes glistened. There, he had done it. He was asking Avek to become his sworn oath-brother. If Avek refused, as was his right, Ranth would be shamed. To ask another for this type of commitment was usually done when the two were in private, not publicly.

But Avek had watched Ranth closely from the first. After he had arrived and endured his highly controversial initiation, Ranth had withdrawn into himself and his studies. Avek doubted he could have withstood the pain or that he would have handled himself so well. Having been a reluctant participant in Ranth's initiation, Avek knew Ranth had been put through torture at Korab's insistence. Secretly he had always admired Ranth and might have asked him to become his sworn brother if it had been allowed. Placement within the ranks of the clan was of the utmost importance. Because Ranth was above Avek in rank, it was up to Ranth to do the asking. Though this made already complicated matters worse, Avek knew he could not refuse.

"I would be honored to do so," Avek answered, with a genuine smile. Someone let out a sigh of relief.

Ranth smiled and nodded. He, too, realized how much more he had just entangled things, but he didn't care. It was done, and for the first time since he had arrived in Kalaven he felt as though he had truly made a friend.

"Loff," Ranth called. He stepped forward, and Ranth explained what had just happened in the language Loff could understand. Then Ranth asked Avek, "Brother, if you would explain things to Loff throughout the evening, I will be most grateful, for doubtless Loff will have questions.'' Avek guffawed out loud. Though Loff was usually quiet, once he got started, his natural curiosity could be overwhelming.

With that settled, Benyar put his hand on Ranth's shoulder. ''It is time to begin, my son.''

As each man took his place on the carpet's edge, the lamps were snuffed out until the only source of light came from a small boy who stood on the edge of the sand. He carried a torch to the fire and Ranth realized it was Jessop, Avek's half-brother. He smiled proudly as he expertly got the blaze to catch. Then he bowed to Tavis and took his place next to his father, Jerob.

Ketherey unstopped a wineskin and handed it to Benyar, who in turn passed it to Ranth. Everyone in the circle took a drink, even the young boys. Tavis was no exception though he made a face and rubbed his mouth, much to everyone's amusement.

Loff swallowed a larger gulp than he had intended because just as he was tilting his head back, Avek clapped him hard on the back. It immediately made him feel giddy, and the heat of it warmed him like nothing he could remember. Avek had a most amused grin on his face as he took the wineskin from Loff. When Loff looked around the tent the men seemed to be speaking slower, and his attention was drawn fully to the fire.

Ranth stood and put Tavis upon his shoulder so that everyone could see him. The entire pavilion of men began clapping a rhythm. When they reached a crescendo they stopped. Into the silence Tavis clapped and laughed aloud. He was welcomed by all as in one voice they shouted his name, ''Tavis sul Shunlar! Be welcomed, little brother!''

Then Benyar and Ketherey rose and shed their robes. Dressed in loincloths the two brothers began to circle one another slowly on the sand. Crouching low, they made sweeps with their legs. They turned upside down to balance on their hands and flip expertly to their feet again. They executed each move perfectly, and the rest of the clan encouraged them with their clapping rhythm and occasional shouts or whistles. As their bodies warmed up they began to glisten with sweat by the light of the fire. Soon their one-handed cartwheels and flips had them moving so fast they were a blur of motion.

At a word from Benyar they stopped suddenly on one knee in front of Tavis, who was staring wide-eyed, his arms wrapped tightly around his father's neck. The boy grinned and reached out to Benyar, who picked him up with a whoop and tossed him up into the air. Then he returned him to his father, bowed to Ranth, and took his place next to him, panting.

Four more men paired off, riding the wave of excitement, and began to spar. Loff was entranced. Occasionally he would ask a question of Avek, who in turn explained particular kicks or thrusts to him with hand gestures and much good humor. When the time came for Ranth to spar, he handed Tavis to Benyar, who by now had caught his breath. Ranth slowly removed his clothing as the pair of men finished their dance in the sand before him. Dripping with sweat, they bowed to one another, then to Tavis, who squealed with delight. Then they took their places. Ranth stood and turned to face Avek, who sat next to him in the place of honor.

Avek slowly removed his robes. He was a head taller than Ranth and more muscled, his chest and arms proof of the fact that he was an exceptional swordsman. Neither of them wore foot blades, as oath-brothers did not inflict marks on one another. Yet Ranth was confident that he and Avek would dance well together. And they did.

In the year that Avek had been gone, Ranth had learned to fight as well with his feet as he did with his hands. Avek's reach was longer, but Ranth's shorter stature made him seem quicker. They stopped each blow just short of inflicting a bruise, calling out with a loud whoop when contact was made. Ranth kicked out in a fast sideways sweep that landed Avek on his back. Surprised, Avek grinned as Ranth pulled him to his feet. They began the rhythm again and as Ranth ducked a kick from Avek's left foot, his right foot swept out and landed Ranth in the sand.

When they finished, their fathers, Jerob, and Benyar, who still carried Tavis, rose and approached them. Standing beside their sons, they handed them their oath-daggers. Ranth and Avek each made a cut across the back of his left forearm. They raised their arms, pressing the cuts together as Jerob, looking very serious, took a leather thong and wound it around their arms.

Jerob and Benyar spoke together, "As your blood mingles in the sand, so your lives will forever be entwined; pledged until one or both of you dies. More binding than the taking of a mate, you are bound before us all."

Ranth and Avek watched the droplets of blood make small black spatters in the sand between their feet. Their eyes locked and they smiled a deliberate half smile to each other. The serious business over, the leather was unwound. They embraced, clapping one another on the back, and took their places.

Now it was time for the younger boys to spar. One tall, lanky, youth sauntered over to stand before Loff, much to his dismay. "What should I do?" he asked Avek.

"Stand and take your first step into real manhood," was Avek's answer. With a grin he helped Loff off with his robes and sent him onto the sand with a slap on the backside.

I asked for this, didn't I? Loff said to himself as the adolescent nearly sent him sprawling on his face with a sweep of his leg. Suddenly aware that all eyes were on him, Loff went into a low crouch, determined not to let this lad who was ten years his junior best him. The next sweep was easily jumped but as Loff landed on his feet the youth spun around and kicked out at Loff, his foot leaving a stinging sensation on his chest that took him totally off guard. Looking down at his chest to see why it stung so much, he took his eyes off his opponent. The lad's heel landed on the side of Loff's chin, spinning him around and knocking him to the sand. Loff spit sand and got to his feet. Brushing himself off as he slowly rose, he bestowed a grin that was partially a sneer on his younger opponent. Checking his hand, he noticed it was dark with blood.

The clapping rhythm picked up its pace. Quickly glancing down at his chest, Loff saw a curved scratch from which a thin trickle of blood ran down his stomach. The youth came at him again with a high kick to his head this time. Loff ducked the kick easily and went down on one knee. When the lad spun around again, Loff held his stance, holding his chest out for the cut he was ready to accept.

The second sting left the other side of his chest burning. Loff now spun into action. Being a seasoned warrior, he was a better fighter than his young opponent. As the grinning youth raised his foot for yet another kick, Loff went into a deep crouch and swept out with his leg, quickly toppling the boy onto his back with a jarring thud that left a very surprised look on his face. Before he could move, Loff flew through the air in a one-armed cartwheel, landing in a deep crouch, straddling the boy's chest, one fist inches from his nose. Several of the older men nodded their appreciation of Loff's maneuver, and he was declared the winner with loud applause.

Proudly he helped the youth to his feet. They bowed to one another, after which Loff took his place next to Avek. Their match was the last of the evening and several men made a point of coming over to Loff with congratulations, one of them introducing himself as his young opponent's father. Afterward Loff tried not to wince as Avek rubbed green pigment into the cuts on his chest, but it stung.

The hour was late. Tavis had fallen asleep and lay wrapped up in a blanket between Benyar and Ranth. The men were tired from the evening's sparring and slowly began to drift off to their blankets. But Loff was wide-awake. Avek knew the feeling well. He brought out a jug of *taloz* and passed it to Loff. Taking a healthy pull, Loff passed it to Ranth, who gladly accepted it. The three of them sat for another hour whispering about the sparring, enjoying each other's company.

Just as Ranth turned in, Tavis started fussing. He

needed changing and said, "wet" several times. Ranth put a dry cloth on his son, and the boy fell back to sleep. As he looked around the pavilion at the shapes of the sleeping men around him, Ranth felt content for the first time. "I have you to thank for this, my son," he whispered to Tavis as he stretched out on the pallet next to the boy and closed his eyes.

Eleven

While Septia, Ranth's former wife, had been nursing her back to health, Zeraya's dreams had been exceptionally vivid. She thought they were simply the result of the herbs her daughter-in-law had been administering to her, herbs that later were found out to be slowly killing her instead of building her strength.

In one recurring dream, a large black eagle would circle close and swoop in to scream at her, as if to warn her of something. In another, a tall, slender woman with white hair and brilliant green eyes appeared from the sky, swooping in as the eagle had, her wings glinting in a rainbow of colors as she passed overhead. She looked as if she were searching for someone or something. And in yet another, Zeraya saw a man and woman; they, too, had white hair, but their eyes were a golden color. She told the women of her clan about the dreams but had never discussed them with Benyar. Had she done so, Zeraya would have known that she was not merely dreaming.

Zeraya had invited Shunlar to join her and the women of her clan in celebrating Tavis's naming. Even though Shunlar was a foreigner and not of the clan, Zeraya had the secret hope that she and Ranth would rekindle their love and marry. This child was Zeraya's blood, and even though Tavis would never become the ruler, he was of the people. Females ruled in Kalaven. The highest rank a male could hope to attain was First Guardian, as consort to the Queen. Because of the child, Shunlar was already her daughter-in-law in the eyes of the people, something Zeraya forbade Ranth to tell her.

But Shunlar had declined Zeraya's invitation to join her and the women of her clan, not fully realizing it was an order, not merely a request. It infuriated Zeraya. She was not a woman who was accustomed to being ignored or turned down. Her temper molten, Zeraya had her sister Zara accompany her as she hurried through the halls of the palace to Shunlar's quarters, intent on giving her one last chance to comply with her wishes.

Having just placed Tavis in Ranth and Benyar's care for the night, Shunlar planned to spend the evening with Bimily in her quarters. Opening the door to her suite just as Zara had raised her fist to pound on it, the two women startled one another. But when Shunlar recognized who was at her door, she bowed and asked them to enter.

"We have come one last time to ask you and your friend to join us in celebrating your son's naming day. It is a special occasion, and I would have you there," announced Zeraya matter-of-factly.

"Am I ordered, Highness Zeraya?" Shunlar asked, her eyes meeting Zeraya's squarely.

"Yes, you are ordered. By my command, you and Bimily will join us. If, as you say, Bimily is too ill to join in, she may watch from a bed. All means of comfort will be provided for her, be assured."

"Then we must do as you command," Shunlar answered, bowing.

Zeraya turned in a whirl of cloak and was gone. Zara had watched the battle of wills taking place before her with real amusement. She knew too well how determined her sister could be when she wanted her way. And Zeraya always got her way.

With a sigh Zara turned to Shunlar, saying, "If I may offer some advice. Leave your anger behind with your sword." After Shunlar unbuckled her belt and laid her sword aside, Zara gestured for Shunlar to proceed her through the door. They stopped for Bimily, whom Zeraya persuaded in the same fashion to join them.

Zeraya led them through the palace and out into the streets. There were yet many people on their way to their respective clan gatherings. Zeraya was given room to pass by, all people bowing low to her.

Their clan's tent was a beautiful oval of tanned animal skins painted on the outside with the design of the giant poisonous lizard, its footprints and claw marks. Identical in size and construction to the other clans, it housed about thirty women, children, and young girls comfortably. Oil lamps hung at close intervals cast a golden light on everything inside. Thickly woven carpets of the softest wool covered the outer ring of the interior, leaving the white sand in the center of the tent mostly bare. At four distinct points the elaborate designs of the carpets appeared to pour the colors and patterns onto the sand. In fact, sand had been dyed in the same rich colors of the carpets and the pattern painstakingly duplicated by hand.

Most of the older women were dressed in robes of dark colors, while the younger ones wore lighter shades. Everyone spoke in hushed tones that were occasionally punctuated with the sound of laughter. Zeraya found the joyful mood of the women contagious, and she was soon smiling proudly as she led Zara, Shunlar, and Bimily to their places. Since Shunlar was being honored as the mother of the newest member of the Feralmon, she was to sit at Zeraya's left. Already a little pale just from walking to the pavilion, Bimily was settled onto a pallet directly behind Shunlar and Zeraya, covered with a blanket, and propped up with pillows.

As each woman took her place in the circle at the edge of the sand, Shunlar noticed that those who were nearest the sand paintings took great pains not to disturb them. She followed the example of the women around her by removing her sandals and sitting cross-legged at the edge of the carpet. When Zeraya had at last settled into her place, the lamps winked out one by one and all conversation ceased.

A young girl held a torch high. At a nod from Zeraya

she approached the fire pit in the center of the circle and set the wood to blazing. Bowing to her, the girl returned to her place beside her mother, careful to return in her own set of footprints.

"We meet in the old way tonight to do honor to the mother of a child who is special to my heart. Her son was conceived by the seed of my son, Ranth. My hope is that Tavis sul Shunlar will be a great warrior, like his mother and his father before him."

The air was rent with a ululating call from the women, which made Shunlar jump and automatically place her hand on her hip, where her sword would normally be.

Seeing the motion, Zeraya laughed. "There is no need for a weapon. If our cries frighten you, what will you do when you face one of us?"

Shunlar frowned. "I didn't realize I would be fighting with anyone tonight. Why did you insist I leave my sword behind?"

"Because there is no need for it. No one will approach you tonight. Be at ease. We are here to celebrate and nothing more." Zeraya gave Shunlar a reassuring smile that seemed to convey goodwill, but Shunlar wasn't quite sure.

Honia sul Urla was seated several places to Zeraya's right. Careful to avoid stepping off the carpet, she approached Zeraya and handed her a round, squat, deep cobalt blue glass bottle with a short neck. Zeraya took hold of it by the neck with one hand and placed her other hand on the bottom. Putting it to her lips, she tilted her head back and took a long swallow.

"Drink and be one of us, Shunlar sul Marleah," Zeraya said as she passed her the blue jug.

Warily Shunlar sniffed it and thought she heard a snicker from Bimily as she tilted her head back to drink. The taste reminded her of damp earth mixed with another flavor she could not place. When the liquid touched her tongue, a tingle filled her mouth and passed through her torso. Never had she experienced such immediate, intense pleasure. In her mind's eyes she watched as a brilliant flower opened, the color and fragrance a heady mixture that brought a wave of dizziness. She sucked in her breath with a gasp and shuddered. She was aware of someone gently removing the bottle from her hands before she accidentally dropped it.

As though she had swallowed something alive, wave-like spasms began in her middle and spread to her limbs. For several seconds Shunlar panicked, but that feeling left nearly as soon as it began. There was nothing she could do to control or stop what was happening, and she realized her desire to stop it was also gone. Ripples coursed through her once more and a smile turned up the corners of her mouth. Acceptance replaced all other feelings, an acceptance so deep that it brought tears to her eyes. There was kinship here. There was a sense of belonging, of fulfillment that included a comforting sense of safety.

Aware of the quiet surrounding her, a familiar sound drew her attention. The sound grew louder, and she recognized it as voices. Only then did she realize her eyes were closed. Opening them, she slowly cast her glance around the circle. Each woman acknowledged her with a quick nod of recognition before continuing with her conversation.

As Shunlar watched, they all began to change before her. The older women appeared younger and stronger, the blush of youth on their cheeks. One woman who had never borne children (somehow Shunlar knew this) had several around her and looked to be pregnant. Another who was shorter in stature than her sisters had grown taller. Shunlar became the greatest surprise of all. She began to transform before them into her half-human, half-dragon self, with white hair, glinting scales, and wings. None appeared frightened or surprised. Zeraya had told them of her dreams, after all. Shunlar felt respect emanating from everyone, most especially Zeraya.

Zeraya looked much the same except that she no longer wore the robes of her office. Dressed in a leather hunting tunic and breeches, Zeraya carried a spear and had belted at her waist a weapon that was a cross between a long dagger and a short sword. Her long black tresses were no longer loose, but braided into a style of warrior braid that Shunlar was not familiar with. The muscles on her arms and shoulders were chiseled, and Shunlar found herself facing a warrior she would consider to be an admirable opponent.

It was this Zeraya who matter-of-factly began to question Shunlar about her intentions toward Ranth. Being under the influence of the potion she had drunk, Shunlar could only answer the truth. Yes, she still cared for Ranth, but Avek had taken a solid place in her affections. When Zeraya heard Avek's name she was not surprised, but she was not pleased either.

But another change had appeared in Zeraya. Her belly was swollen and gave her the appearance of being several months pregnant. When Shunlar mentioned this to her, Zeraya nodded, and answered, "I have been told that I will have other children. Since that is my desire, it shows in this way." Shunlar nodded acceptance of her explanation.

Someone began to beat a slow rhythm on a drum. She was soon joined by another, then another, and as the circle took up the rhythm, two women rose and began to spar. Shunlar watched in fascination as their bodies crouched, spun, tumbled, and leaped through the air. She had seen Avek fight in several skirmishes with the mercenaries while they defended the gates of Vensunor, but he had never shown her anything like this. Secretly she prayed no one was going to ask her to spar in this beautiful yet deadly dance.

As if her thoughts had been spoken aloud, Zara, who sat beside her, laughed aloud, then reassured her, saying, "Never fear, you are the guest of honor tonight. We are merely putting on a show for you. But, my clan sisters are a sight, are they not?" Pride swelled Zara's chest. Shunlar nodded her agreement.

When the last two partners ended their match they bowed to one another. The tent became silent once again. From somewhere a breeze stirred. The sand directly in front of Shunlar began to roll and shift as patterns appeared. The patterns became black letters that became words. Not sure if her eyes were deceiving her, Shunlar turned to Zara and then to Zeraya. They also saw the words for their gazes were transfixed on the sand before them.

Honia's voice broke the silence. "Prophecy is at hand. Speak the words that show themselves, Zeraya sul Karnavt, so that we may all learn."

"Wrought in pain, severed by death, bound by oath. Step above the world to live once more." Zeraya's voice had an eerie tone to it.

Shunlar took her attention away from the sand to stare at Zeraya, who remained transfixed by the letters before her. When she looked back, the black letters were gone. Behind her Bimily had turned pale, but she shrugged and shook her head when Shunlar gave her a look of inquiry.

"Who are the words a message for?" Zeraya asked Honia.

Honia looked uneasy, answering, "I must contemplate the meaning before giving a definitive answer." She was as puzzled as everyone else. "Now I believe it is time for us to retire." Speaking in this way, Honia closed off any further discussion on the subject.

Zeraya had a look about her that said she definitely wanted to pursue the subject, but Honia gave a minute shake of her head and cast an uneasy glance at Shunlar just as Zeraya opened her mouth. Pressing her lips together, Zeraya dipped her chin quickly in a gesture that showed her reluctant acceptance of Honia's wishes. Immediately after, Honia closed the evening with a prayer of thanks.

Though the evening had ended in this unusual way, everyone agreed that they were all tired. Lamps were lit, the beds rolled open as the women quietly prepared for sleep. The hidden meaning of the words in the sand was on everyone's mind but no one dared to mention it. After the last lamp winked out, the fire in the center cast the only light in the tent.

Soon Shunlar was the only person who lay awake, troubled, listening to the sounds of the women sleeping around her. She remembered another night long ago when she had stumbled upon a message that had been left by Benyar beside the river. It, too, had kept her awake. His words had been in another language, encrypted in a code that the correct question unlocked.

This time the words that had appeared in the sand before her had been translated, but no question that she asked seemed to be the code. Each time Shunlar saw and heard the words, she wondered, *Who is this a message for and what can the words mean?* Though she rephrased her question for hours, she heard no answer.

TWELVE

KORAB FOUND THE LAST CACHE OF FOOD AND water in the rocks just as he was about to collapse. Carrying Septia, who was too weak to walk, he had started at sundown, to avoid the heat and wind of the day. Traveling in the dark, he had nearly passed the tiny oasis that consisted of half-buried rock formations and several dead trees, the water long ago dried up.

Blankets, clothing, and medicines were in the pouch this time as well. Korab silently hoped it wasn't too late for Septia as he gently eased her to the ground. Once he made her comfortable, he began applying salve to her burned lips and the skin of her face and arms. She mumbled something to him, and he gave her water to drink, after which she fell asleep.

He sat next to her with his back to the rising sun, pulling the hood of the cloak over his head, his face covered with a mask. The wind was beginning to blow again, and he knew he had better cover Septia's face or her burned skin would be scoured away by the blowing sand. She struggled with him, pushing his hands away when he tried to fit her mask in place. After several attempts he finally gave up, content that he could at least pull the hood of her cloak over her face. He didn't bother to communicate directly with a mind-touch because he knew their pain would also transfer to one another because of their weakened conditions. He hurt enough already.

Korab was too spent to be as furious as he wanted to be. Someone had reversed the order of the supplies. The robes and masks that would have protected them from the elements should have been left in the first drop-off location. As he sat glowering, he wondered if the mix-up had occurred because of a genuine mistake or had been purposely done. All he could do now was see that Septia was comfortable and try to conserve his energy. Someone would answer for the pain they had caused him.

Exhausted, sitting beside Septia who lay huddled beneath a blanket, his body giving her partial shelter from the wind, Korab fell asleep. A noise startled him awake, making him jerk upright. It was dark, and though he couldn't see them, Korab could sense the presence of many men surrounding him and Septia. Something sharp jabbed into his ribs as a hand searched his body for weapons. Relieved of his dagger, his hands were roughly tied behind his back and he was hauled to his feet by his arms.

Facing his captors, Korab knew they were from Tonnerling by their stature and dress. He greeted them in their language and was rewarded with a vicious backhand across his face that caused a trickle of blood to run from the corner of his mouth. Once more he spoke up, and this time two men attacked him, laughing as the first punch sent him sprawling onto his back. They continued to kick him until a third man commanded them to stop. Korab was lifted to his feet but only managed to stay standing for a few seconds before he fell to his knees, gasping for his breath, the result of another blow to his stomach. After that Korab decided to remain silent.

Septia was uncovered and one of the soldiers prodded her with his foot. Seeing it was a woman, horrible grins lit up their faces, and she was scooped up into a pair of strong arms. Through all the lifting and prodding, Septia remained limp, hardly breathing. Korab watched in silent horror as the man shook her repeatedly. After several tries to waken her, the man gave up and roughly dumped her back onto her blankets and covered her face as though she were dead. Korab couldn't see well enough in the dark to tell if that were not so.

It took them three days to reach the encampment. Septia remained alive, but just barely. Since his capture, the ropes on Korab's arms were only removed morning and evening. He was given time to eat a small meal, try to feed Septia, and relieve himself, and then he would be bound again. During the day he walked beside the horse that pulled Septia's litter, attached to the saddle by a long rope around his neck. At night, once he finished seeing to Septia, he was bound and his cloak thrown over him. Though in great pain, Korab kept up the pace. He knew if he did not, they would kill him and take Septia, and he refused to let that happen.

It was fully dark when they reached the river. Korab couldn't tell if Septia was alive or dead. They hadn't stopped since morning to rest or to eat as usual, and Korab was on the verge of collapse. He smelled the water before he heard it and it frightened him to think he might be forced to cross it. Without the use of his arms, in his weakened state, he now began to believe he would die.

Stumbling along with his head down, Korab raised his head and tried to focus his eyes. Countless fires burned within a camp, and large numbers of men crowded around the blazes for warmth. Korab was aware that all eyes were on him and the small group of soldiers as he weaved unsteadily on his feet through the encampment.

In addition to being sunburned and dehydrated, Korab was nearly blind and numb from trying to keep up the pace for the past three days. He wasn't even aware when the horses had come to a complete stop in front of a small tent. Before he could stop his feet, he stumbled into a soldier who blocked his path. The man knocked him down with a curse.

Korab blinked hard. He was dizzy, panting, and only realized that the rope attaching him to the horse had been removed when he saw the animal being led away. What did register was that someone was carrying Septia, and Korab refused to let that man out of his sight. The soldier and Septia entered a small tent, with Korab practically crawling behind him. When the man placed her on a pallet on the ground and stood up, Korab was hovering too close for his liking, and he knocked Korab down with a hard punch. Before he left the tent he threatened Korab again with his fist. Korab remained on the ground until the soldier was gone.

Alone in the tent with Septia, Korab struggled to his knees and made it to her side. Her breathing was shallow and he was helpless even to give her water. The tent flap opened and two soldiers entered, followed by a third man who carried a lantern and had a leather bag slung over his shoulder. The man examined Septia with much shaking of his head. He was a healer, but Korab didn't place much faith in his abilities.

Knowing he had nothing much to lose, Korab decided to speak to him. "Sir, are you a healer?" he asked.

Startled either by the question or by the fact that Korab could speak his language, he just stared at Korab for some time. Finally, he answered, "Yes. How long were you in the desert?"

"I've lost track of time. Perhaps five days, perhaps seven. Tell me, is there nothing you can do to save her?" The desperation in Korab's voice made it crack.

"No. She won't last the night." Then he gathered up his bag of supplies and left.

Korab remained kneeling near Septia, bent over her as closely as he could, whispering to her now and then. The very real prospect of losing her brought tears to his eyes but he blinked them away when he sensed that the soldier who remained guarding him at the tent flap was watching him with a sneer. Korab had no doubt that the soldier enjoyed watching him groveling on his knees near his woman.

Resigning himself to the fact that Septia was going to die, he straightened his back and turned to the man who guarded him. Remembering the proper words, Korab bowed his head and in the most humble voice asked, "Please, I request an audience with Quintas of Tonnerling."

"Why?" demanded the leering soldier.

"Because he will know my name and know that I am not to be treated in this fashion," Korab answered through clenched teeth.

"You'll be seeing Quintas soon." The soldier laughed, the sound sending a shudder down Korab's back. But he was no match for Korab. Fear produced a sense of urgency in Korab that effectively gave him some of his strength back. He sent a mind-touch toward the guard and easily planted the suggestion that he would do his bidding. As a haze settled over the man's features, he blinked hard several times, turned, and left the tent. Moments later he returned with another man, who looked to be an officer.

The officer bent closely over Septia, watching how shallowly she was breathing. "A shame she won't be with us much longer. We've had only three women in the camp all winter and grow tired of them."

Korab grew more frightened with each passing second. This wasn't how his escape was supposed to happen. He and his oath-brothers had planned for him and Septia to be rescued by a company of soldiers from Tonnerling, but obviously not this company.

Turning to Korab, the officer warily asked, "How do you know to ask for Quintas?"

"Months ago it was planned that we were to meet with Quintas of Tonnerling. My name is Korab sul Fanon and my oath-brother Tadim sul Kleea arranged this." He spoke quietly, watching Septia breathe.

"Ah, too bad, Feralmon, Quintas is dead. One of his own soldiers killed him in his sleep. The rest of his men are now part of my company. Harpe is my name. But, before you join the woman on the other side of life, I will try to confirm your story. Perhaps there is someone among Quintas's men who was present at that meeting." Turning to leave, Harpe spoke to the soldier guarding

Korab. Both men glared warily at Korab before Harpe left the tent.

What seemed like hours later the flap of the tent was thrown open. Harpe entered followed by two soldiers and the healer. "Korab sul Fanon, these two men were present at the conversation between your man and Quintas. Prove to them that you are who you say you are, and you will be treated properly."

Korab was near the limit of his strength. Since they had believed Septia would die anyway, no one had thought to give her or Korab food or water. Korab might as well have been a condemned prisoner. His stomach growled loudly, and he watched as a cruel sneer crossed one of the soldier's faces when he heard it.

Fighting to keep his rage from overpowering him, Korab trembled as he described in great detail the meeting that had taken place between Tadim, Quintas, and the two soldiers present. As he spoke, he continually kept his attention on the healer who hovered over Septia. His throat tightened and tears might have begun to well in his eyes had he not been so dehydrated when he saw Septia take a few sips of water, but he cleared his throat and continued speaking. The only sign of emotion he allowed to show was anger.

As Harpe and his men listened, they became convinced that Korab was who he claimed to be, for they believed that only one who had been present at the meeting with Quintas could possess the kind of information he did. While it was true that Tadim had been at the meeting, he had never related these particular details to Korab. What Korab had done, and done easily, was read the memories of the men who stood before him, something that was effortless because of the way they did not close off their thoughts.

Begrudgingly Korab's ropes were cut and his hands were freed. Trembling from pain and rage, he did his best to control his first impulse, of picking up a sword and thrusting it through these men who had mistreated him. Harpe bowed to Korab when he recognized the look in his eyes, hoping it would placate him. The others quickly followed his example.

"Lord Korab, I regret the treatment you have suffered at our hands. But you must understand, my soldiers mistook you for enemy scouts. It in no way should reflect on our loyalty or the agreements we have made. After all, we were never told you would be traveling alone, with a woman." He gestured awkwardly before continuing. "I will personally see to it that you are housed in more suitable quarters and all your needs fulfilled." Harpe bowed again and waited for acknowledgment from Korab.

"Yes, you will," Korab snarled. "I will need servants for myself and my woman. Since none of my men have yet arrived, I must pick from yours, Harpe." His sneer was terrible to see. As he rubbed his arms to get the blood moving through them, Korab winced from the pain. Not only had his arms been bound for days, his skin was sunburned as well.

One of the soldiers who had beaten him when they had first captured him was standing near the tent flap, inching his way out. In a blur of motion Korab was beside the man and backhanded him to the ground. "This one I will take as a guard, and when I am finished with him he will know what it means to follow orders to the death."

The man lay on his side, looking from Korab to Harpe. When he saw that there would be no rescue from his captain, he quickly wiped the blood from the corner of his mouth with the back of his hand and scrambled to his knees before Korab.

"Hand me your sword. You will be my personal servant until another more suitable one can be found." Korab was in a foul mood, and he kicked the kneeling man as he took his sword from him.

"My lord, this man is a soldier, not a body servant. I extend to you the services of my personal servants who are impeccably trained and will please you in every way," Harpe said, trying to intervene on the soldier's behalf.

"Perhaps when my anger has cooled I will take you up on your offer. For now, this man will suffice." Turning to the kneeling soldier, Korab ordered, "Bring us food, water, and wine, in that order. Then we will need water for bathing and clean clothes. Is that clear?"

"Yes sir," the soldier answered.

Korab's hand flew in another backhanded blow that nearly knocked the man over. "Address me as Lord Korab, not sir. Now hurry."

"Yes, Lord Korab," he answered. He shakily got to his feet and backed from the tent to do Korab's bidding, wiping the blood from his chin with the back of his hand.

Harpe and the rest of his men withdrew as hastily as they could. Only the healer remained, and Korab stood behind him watching his every move. When he had finished, Korab dismissed him. Septia's eyes opened once they were alone. Korab watched her grow stronger with each breath. She smiled at him.

"Tell me this was deliberate, Septia. You are well and merely playing being at death's door," Korab entreated.

"Yes, my lord Korab," she laughed. She had heard everything. Knowing that she would be raped when they were captured, she pretended to be hanging on to a thread of life. "I did not tell you so that it would seem more real to our captors. We make a fine team, do we not?" Septia held her arms open to Korab.

"Septia, I will not lose you. You have come to mean more to me than I would ever want to admit. You gave your life's essence to me while we were lost in the desert. Why did you risk yourself?"

"You are the stronger of the two of us, and I needed so little to survive. I knew you would carry me to safety and beyond. It meant that we would both live, but I cannot do it again for I have only enough strength left for myself now. It will be several weeks before I am able to travel."

Korab knelt beside Septia and embraced her tenderly. For the first time she felt he was being truly loving to her. Of course, when Septia had fortified Korab with her essence, it naturally produced a desire in him to want to treat her more kindly—something she counted on—something he would never detect. They were alone together, at last, on their way to fulfilling their destiny.

"Tell me, do you intend to kill that soldier who angered you so, or are you just going to punish him for a while?" Septia whispered in his ear.

He grinned wolfishly. "That man caused me physical pain. He will never forget the lessons I teach him, if he survives, and he will, I'll see to that. No one treats me like an animal and does not suffer for it."

The tent flap suddenly opened and the soldier was there. Bowing from the waist, he spoke, "Lord Korab, please follow me and I will take you and your lady to proper quarters. Food, water, and wine await your pleasure. There is hot water being poured as I speak and clean clothes waiting. We have also provided a litter for the lady." Head bowed, eyes on the ground, the man backed away, holding the flap open.

Korab cautiously peered outside, blinking at the daylight. To his amazement it was morning and two lines of soldiers marked the path he and Septia would walk. His eyes followed the lines of men as they snaked around to the left and then right to a small hilltop where a very large tent the blue of a brilliant summer sky squatted. As he stared, Septia joined him, a shudder running through her when her eyes rested on the tent.

"This is either an elaborate joke or the truth. What do you say we take a walk?" Septia nodded as he picked her up in his arms. She clung tightly to his neck as they stepped from the tent. Very gently he laid Septia upon the litter.

The soldier who had arranged everything remained bent in a low bow. Korab stood before him, and asked, "What are you called?"

"Gustov Maren, my lord Korab," he answered proudly.

"Then lead on, Gustov Maren, lead on," Korab declared loudly.

Gustov Maren straightened and led the way. As they

passed each soldier, the men saluted smartly. The first two made Septia jump, but Korab took hold of her hand and walked beside the litter as they continued on their way. At last, at the top of the hill could be seen Captain Harpe and two young men who were dressed in tunics, not soldiers' mail. They were introduced to Septia and Korab as Linq and Dennik, the body servants Captain Harpe had promised. They followed Septia and Korab into the tent, closing the flap behind them.

"Gustov Maren," Korab called loudly. The man entered the tent and went down on one knee.

"You called, Lord Korab?"

"Arm yourself and a companion. Guard the door, day and night. No one comes or goes without my permission, understood?"

"Yes, Lord Korab." Gustov Maren saluted and was gone.

It would take Septia the better part of four weeks to recover from her ordeal in the desert. Korab seemed to spring back to his usual vigorous strength but because she had transferred her vital energies to him so that they would both live, she was much weaker than she even allowed Korab to see. Though the healer, whose name they learned was Ferrik, supplied her with herbs, she tired easily, and early each afternoon would nap. After the evening meal she could not manage to stay awake for more than an hour, much to Korab's displeasure.

Being rescued and treated like royalty did much to excite Korab's already overblown feelings about himself. He was soon introduced to General Bergoin and began to meet with the general and his officers each night, preparing them for the taking of Kalaven. Afterward he expected Septia to warm his bed. The first few times when she could not—Korab suspected she refused him deliberately—he became surly.

This evening the hour was late and as Korab returned to the tent his mood began to plummet. When Gustov Maren, who had become his bodyguard and somewhat of a shadow, pulled open the tent flap, Korab fully expected to be greeted by darkness and the sound of Septia sleeping. To his surprise, she was awake, and several lamps blazed brightly near her pallet.

She looked up and gifted him with a sultry smile. "Ah, you have returned at last. Come here, and I will show you what secrets I have uncovered tonight."

Korab was wary. "What is this?" he asked, remaining at the entrance.

"Surely you remember the book that was in our hidden supplies? I had it delivered to Tadim sul Elera by one of the young priestesses. She didn't realize what she was doing because I had taken control of her mind," Septia reassured him. "This book may well be the key to finally taking Kalaven and the Lifestones."

Though Korab seemed very interested, she knew it had nothing to do with her words. Septia watched him approach and was able to read the passion in his eyes. *First things first* she said to herself. As Korab sat beside her on the pallet he pressed his lips against her throat. Much to his surprise, she returned his embrace with fervor. *This will be over soon,* she quietly ordered, reaching toward Korab with a manipulative mind-touch.

Sooner than he would have liked, Korab was spent, lying beside Septia, who sat up quickly to rearrange the folds of her clothing. Then she began to matter-of-factly inform him of the contents of the ancient text.

"Because of its age and where it was kept, I knew this volume had special information. Yet I was prevented from reading it by Honia. She continually promised that one day I would be privy to the book's knowledge." Septia laughed a scoffing sound. "Pity I won't be present to see her face when it is discovered that the book is missing."

Korab scowled. "Is this all such a game to you?"

His words had the effect of a blow. "Have a care, dearest Korab. I have always taken my part in the taking of Kalaven's Lifestones very seriously." She looked at him long and hard before continuing. "I have risked and lost everything I held dear to me, save for you. Our child has been taken from me along with our position in society that gave us a real chance to rule Kalaven. This is not and has never been a game to me.''

Her words had the desired impact. Korab found himself apologizing to her. ''You remind me of a painful time that I would not have wished upon an enemy. I meant no harm by my words, but see that I have caused harm. Forgive me.'' He reached for her hand and kissed it. Finally, Septia took a deep breath and nodded, accepting his apology.

''You have something to tell me. I am listening now,'' he said with a lazy smile.

''This map pinpoints another location where Lifestones can be found, but it does me no good because I cannot find the name of the city. Here, see what you can make of it.'' And Septia thrust the open book at Korab.

''What makes you think I can understand the words?'' he asked as he pored over the strange script.

''Perhaps your eyes will see something mine have missed. Just look, please,'' she urged.

Reluctantly he began studying the page. ''What do these words mean?'' he asked, pointing to faint letters nearly hidden in the inner margin.

''Let me see,'' Septia said excitedly, her eyes leaping across the page. When she saw what she had overlooked, she sat back. ''You've done it. How could I have missed that?'' she murmured, checking the page again to be sure her eyes weren't deceiving her. ''Korab, this names the location as Stiga.''

Stiga was a place forbidden to the Feralmon, thought to be legend. The chance that it really existed unnerved them. From the time they were children, the Feralmon were cautioned against returning to Stiga. They were told that to do so would be punished by death. Many young people believed Stiga was something their parents and elders conjured up to frighten them.

Her eyes shining with elation, Septia told him, ''I have made a very interesting discovery today. According to this text, there is a type of Lifestone which is considered to be dangerous, although I have yet to understand why.

"Listen to this," she began reading breathlessly. "Only one who can control the lightnings that pass through the dark Lifestones will be able to hold one. Many have tried, at the expense of life and limb. Many have died. The dark ones do not blend with a person like the others, but the person who possesses the strength of will to control it will be able to use it for strong magic."

"You tell me you wish to possess a Dark Lifestone. Are you also saying that you have a text that instructs you how to take one? Tell me that is so, Septia." Now Korab's eyes sparkled with excitement and something more like greed.

"I hold the key in my hands before you, dear Korab," she grinned. "All that remains now is for us to learn how to be prepared for one, safely. Together we will be unstoppable, you and I. We will regain our child as well as our dignity. People like Honia, Zeraya, Benyar, and pitiful Ranth will be made to suffer as we were by watching all they hold dear to them destroyed."

A shudder passed over Korab as he lay on his pallet beside her, watching her read the ancient text. He had never known her to seem so completely taken over. Soon he drifted to sleep and dreamed of Septia clutching the book in her lap, studying the words, as jagged white lines of lightning jumped up from the pages beneath her nose. Sometime later, when he opened his eyes to total darkness, the smell in the tent reminded him of winter nights in the desert after a lightning storm.

THIRTEEN

TWO DAYS LATER AT DAWN BIMILY, SHUNLAR, and Loff rode to Kalaven's gates with Ranth, Benyar, and Ketherey escorting them. Although her stay had been short, Shunlar was anxious to leave Kalaven. The escort of four Feralmon that had been picked to travel with Bimily had been replaced by Shunlar and Loff, something the warriors were relieved about, though they would never openly admit it. None of them wanted to escort this strange woman who had appeared one day in their midst. Bimily made them all uneasy.

Saying good-bye was difficult for Shunlar, but not for the obvious reasons. She had to pretend, after all, that she was leaving Ranth behind to care for their son, and she played her part well. With tears in her eyes she recalled saying good-bye to Tavis just an hour ago. She had carefully planted her feelings of love securely within the recesses of his young mind. Feelings of loss were erased, and she made sure that he was filled with the understanding that she would return. It was curious for one so young to have a grasp of such things, but Tavis did.

Squeezing Ranth's hand tightly, Shunlar said, ''See that Tavis is not left alone too much of the time. I know you have your duties, but he has much of my father in his nature and will only get himself into trouble if he is bored.'' Ranth looked puzzled for a moment, thinking, *Tavis is not yet one year old, what trouble can she mean?* But the words were more for Benyar's benefit than Ranth's.

Continuing to hold Ranth's hand, Shunlar relayed a message directly to his mind. *Say your good-byes to Tavis only on the night you will be leaving. He does not understand the concept of a secret yet. Trust that he will be fine.*

Ranth answered, *I understand,* as they parted.

That evening when they made their first camp, Shunlar took stock of their provisions as she unloaded the pack animals. There were bags of travel cakes, dried fruit, cheese, and smoked meats. She had left Bimily in charge of quantity because she was the one with the largest appetite. Though early spring was a pleasant enough time for travel in the desert, they were not a hunting party. Even if game were plentiful, it required cooking and a fire was out of the question until they knew for certain that no scouts from Tonnerling were nearby.

Grain for the horses must also be provided which meant they needed to have an additional pack horse. Shunlar had chosen a tall, sturdy, gelding for that, something Loff noticed but did not comment on. It seemed a wise choice to him, for the animal was large and muscular.

When Bimily explained to the servants that, because of her illness, she needed extra food to sustain her on their journey, additional bundles had been prepared for them with no question. They were securely lashed onto another pack horse. Bimily had planned that this horse would become Ranth's mount. Somehow she had also managed to procure a saddle, and it was carefully concealed beneath the extra provisions. Though she could no longer change her shape at will, it seemed her powers of persuasion had remained intact.

When Shunlar asked her friend how she had done it, Bimily answered, "A flutter of eyes can do many things to a man, make him forget or make him more generous.

All was done for Ranth's comfort, of course,'' she said, giving her head a dramatic toss.

''Sly fox that you are, what other 'provisions' have you gathered for the journey? A case of *taloz,* perhaps?'' Though she joked, Shunlar's voice sounded hopeful.

''Half a case will have to do,'' the shapechanger answered, knowing that the cactus alcohol of the Feralmon was Shunlar's favorite drink. Bimily laughed out loud when she saw the look on Shunlar's face.

Loff chuckled conspiratorially as he rummaged through one of the baskets, pulled out a clay jug, and tossed it to his sister. Laughing out loud, she unstopped it, took a long swallow, and smacked her lips appreciatively as the liquid warmed her.

Luck seemed to be with them as far as the weather went. Spring was usually the time for rain and cold nights in the desert. The first two nights had, thankfully, been dry but very cold. Shunlar had spotted fragments of the heat trace of several men on horseback. When she examined their tracks, she determined there were three of them and suspected they were scouts. When she reported her findings to Bimily and Loff, it was decided that even though the riders appeared to be traveling in the opposite direction, they would not risk a fire. The possibility always existed that the night wind might shift and send the smell of their fire to the enemy.

Their third night out, once full dark had settled, Shunlar transformed into her half-human, half-dragon self and took to the skies to search the area for the enemy scouts. It took some time to find them, for they were a good three hours' ride north; but the aroma of smoke eventually led her to them.

Circling high over their camp, Shunlar observed the three soldiers sitting and eating around their smoldering fire. Normally she would have gone by now, but something prompted her to linger. To her complete surprise, three other men stepped out of the shadows into the light. The wind had erased their heat trace so well that she had not seen them until they walked into the firelight. Even though she shivered with cold, Shunlar was happy that she had trusted her instincts and waited longer before returning to her camp. Otherwise, she would not have seen these other men.

A smile crossed her lips. Knowing they'd never be able to distinguish between the scent of smoke from a distant fire and their own, she began to imagine heat seeping into her bones. Satisfied that there was no danger, she turned her wings toward camp, the scent of smoke heavy in the air. The thought occurred to her that the amount of smoke couldn't possibly be coming from that one small fire below.

She turned to fly farther north until she found what she suspected. Soldiers in a large encampment were living at the edge of the Thrale River. Apparently these men of the north couldn't keep away from the water for too long. Now she knew her assumption that these men were scouts was correct. She couldn't wait to warm herself beside her own campfire.

The blaze made their camp much more cheerful, putting everyone in a better mood once hot mugs of tea began to warm their insides. The small oasis where they camped provided a source of water and dried palm branches for burning. A tumble of stones that had once been a dwelling provided much needed shelter from the wind and sand. The air had the smell of rain to it. They drowsed before the fire, listening to the sizzle and crackle of the wood, listening to the horses crunching the grain in their feedbags.

Into the quiet Shunlar announced, "I am leaving within the hour to return to Kalaven for Avek. We will be back before sunrise, assuming all goes as planned."

Bimily and Loff were speechless. They had known Shunlar would be bringing Ranth to their camp, but she had not mentioned Avek to either of them. Now Loff cast a meaningful look at the familiar, sturdy pack horse.

"You arranged this with him and not us, your traveling companions?" accused Bimily, thoroughly exasperated.

"No. For the sake of secrecy I didn't even mention this to Avek. What you don't know is easier for you not to hide within your thoughts. I believe I can convince Avek when I find him; besides, we may need him. Tonight as I scouted the area, I not only discovered the fires of a large encampment of Tonnerling soldiers far to the north, but three others surprised me when they appeared from the shadows, joining the three who had set up a camp. Although we travel away from them, they seem to have a network of scouts who range across this territory with regularity.

"Avek's strength will also be a great help to us, for soon I fear you will succumb to the toll all this travel is taking on you, Bimily. You are fooling no one, my friend. Another pair of strong arms will be most welcome." For once Bimily had nothing to say.

Stretching in preparation for flight, Shunlar said her good-byes and began to transform. Once she had her wings unfurled, she lifted off gracefully and flew into the night air, leaving Loff and Bimily to fend for themselves.

Loff reassured Bimily they were fine, encouraging her to get some sleep as he took up watch. He kept watch while Bimily slept, knowing that his sister would soon return with his friend Avek. He agreed with Shunlar that Avek would be a welcome addition to their party. They had been comfortable traveling companions, and he missed the tall, quiet man and his easy smile. If anything, his turn at watch would be shorter with another person to relieve them. The thought of sleep reminded Loff how tired he was as he yawned again, then got up to shake his arms and legs and stretch.

Some hours later a rush of wind from above scattered the embers of the fire. Loff was on his feet and alert, straining for the first sight of Shunlar's arrival. Then his eyes picked out a glint as the scales of her wings reflected the glowing coals. With another whoosh of air, Shunlar landed and as her feet touched the ground, so did Avek's. He settled wearily onto his knees, dropping the saddle he carried against his chest with a noisy thud, his personal belongings securely lashed to it. Loff and he exchanged a kinsman's embrace, and Bimily woke to greet him. Soon they were passing a jug of taloz all around, Shunlar and Avek sitting shoulder to shoulder.

Bimily offered to sit watch but Shunlar reassured her that it wasn't necessary. "There is little need. Avek and I scouted as we approached, and there was no evidence of man or beast close by. We can all get some much needed sleep. I for one am ready." Shunlar cast a secret glance at Avek; he nodded, and they took their bedrolls to the other side of the ruins for privacy.

Hours later Avek awoke with the uneasy feeling that they were being watched. He left his bedroll silently, not bothering to slip on any clothing. His dagger in hand, he slipped into the night. He had just completed circuiting the camp when he heard a sound far in the distance. Noiselessly Avek dropped to the ground pressing his belly to the cold, rocky sand. Raising his head, he was able to see two people trotting away on foot. From the way they moved, they were Feralmon, though what they were doing so far from Kalaven puzzled him. As he watched them fade into the distance, the skin on his arms prickled.

The next day when they broke camp Avek rode over to the spot where he had seen the two people. The ground held no signs for him. Yet, as he was about to turn back and rejoin his companions, another feeling overcame him. He rode a bit farther and smelled death before he came upon the man. Riding around a pile of rocks and brush, Avek's horse started.

Sitting slumped over against the rocks was a tall, blond man dressed in the tabard of a soldier of Tonnerling, his throat neatly cut. Whoever had killed him had purposely left him where he could be discovered. Checking the ground around the body, Avek finally found one footprint. The print appeared to be made by a soft leather boot, and the style was Feralmon. Another prickle ran up his back. He stood for a time sweeping the area with his eyes before mounting and returning to his friends. For reasons of his own, Avek did not mention the dead man or the footprint to anyone.

* * *

It was the appointed night. Ranth waited under the stars in his courtyard with his sword and dagger belted securely. Saddlebags that included a change of clothing and his personal kit were slung over his shoulder. Soon he felt the rush of wind on his cheeks and a tall, winged form landed lightly in the moonlight several yards from where he stood. He called out with a tentative whisper and Shunlar answered him.

She was taller than he by nearly two heads, and he found himself looking up into a face that was familiar yet strangely alien. *Am I making a great mistake?* he asked himself.

Surprised by her strength when she scooped him up in her arms, Ranth was aloft before he realized his feet had left the ground. It was then that he noticed a growing desire for her but as soon as he felt it, he heard the echo of her voice order very firmly: *Don't.*

They flew into the night, keeping their thoughts closed off from one another. Several hours later he smelled the smoke of a fire and knew they must be close. Then he noticed a pinpoint of light far ahead of them that gradually grew until he could see a small campfire with two people rolled into their blankets sleeping nearby.

Shunlar touched down and set Ranth on his feet. From the shadows a third person, who had been keeping watch, came forward to greet them, and it startled Ranth to recognize Avek.

"Cousin," Avek bowed. Ranth stiffly returned the greeting. He felt he was owed an explanation and he turned his attention to Shunlar, waiting for one.

"What?" she asked, annoyed at the silent way he and Avek regarded her.

By now Bimily was awake and she began to laugh. "It would seem that you have two husbands now, my friend. You should sleep well tonight, or at least warm." Bimily chuckled.

Not amused, Shunlar asked no one in particular, "I suppose you're going to tell me that's another one of your quaint customs?"

"As a matter of fact," Avek offered hesitantly, "it

is, especially when the intended is stolen.'' She eyed him suspiciously, but just rolled herself into a blanket close to Bimily muttering curses under her breath. Bimily was about to make another comment, but seeing Shunlar's agitated state thought better of it and held her tongue. Tomorrow would offer her ample opportunities to remark on the situation.

Ranth recognized that if he wanted to know why Avek had joined them he would have to wait for Shunlar to offer an explanation or ask Avek himself. He was sure Avek had arrived at the camp in the same manner he had, but Ranth was baffled by the fact that Shunlar had not mentioned Avek's presence at all. Tired, confused, yet elated at being free, Ranth found a bedroll. Assuming it was his, he crawled into it and went to sleep.

Later that night Shunlar had a vivid dream in which both Ranth and Avek joined her in her blankets. She tossed and moaned until an urgent hand woke her. It was Bimily, and she had a rude smile on her lips.

''Now that is what I call a very exquisite dream,'' she whispered wickedly. Shunlar guffawed at her friend and pushed her hand away. *Ach*—rubbing her face—*by the moons, this will not do at all,* she told herself. She sat up and quickly checked to see if Ranth and Avek were sleeping. They were, and thankfully they also seemed to be unaware of her dream. Parts of the dream still tugged at her mind and she firmly pushed those thoughts away, thinking instead of her son and how much she missed Tavis.

With a deep sigh she got up and went to relieve herself in the pit that had been dug near to where the horses were tied. On the way back someone waited for her in the dark, and from the size of him and his unique heat trace, she knew it was Avek. He wrapped his arms tenderly around her and kissed her long and hard. She missed him, but she kept her thoughts quiet and closed off from him. Abruptly he stopped and walked away. When she returned to the embers of the fire, Ranth was awake. He cast an accusatory look at her, then at Avek's empty bedroll before lowering his eyes and turning onto his other side.

They broke camp just before dawn and were on their way in under an hour. Bimily led the way with Shunlar beside her. Loff rode between Ranth and Avek, trying his best to engage them in conversation. Somehow he got Avek to tell hunting stories and even Ranth managed a tale or two. By midday, when they stopped to eat and rest the horses, everyone seemed in a tolerable mood though Ranth remained very quiet.

True to his nature, Avek had graciously accepted the fact that Ranth would be joining their party. When he learned the reason for taking Ranth to Bimily's people, he understood it was a life-or-death situation for Ranth and seemed determined to be a pleasant traveling companion to him. He had a small, pink scar on the back of his left forearm to remind him of the pledge he and Ranth had made to one another in front of their clan, and he was determined to live up to that pledge.

The first day they managed to stay out of each other's way, and Avek treated Ranth with respect when they did speak, deferring to him as one who outranked him in the clan. His behavior seemed to have a positive, even calming effect on Ranth. By the second day, Ranth, too, remembered the blood oath that he and Avek had made to one another. What better man could there be to have with him on his quest to save his life?

After that, as they traveled, everyone fell into a natural rhythm. It was as if they had always been campmates. Avek's careful eye sought fresh meat for their dinner, and he managed to kill several small lizards. When they made camp later in a small oasis, Ranth helped a very exhausted Bimily to her bedroll, then he unfurled the other bedrolls, placing them around the fire pit Avek had dug. Shunlar and Loff gathered scrub wood and palm branches. Striking a flint, Avek started a fire, skinned the lizards, and spitted them while Loff fed the horses and Shunlar dug the latrine.

Returning to the fire just as Avek was portioning out pieces of hot, sizzling lizard, Shunlar's cheeks reddened when she realized her bedroll had been placed between Avek's and Ranth's. Both men merely smiled politely; she responded with a scowl. Bimily laughed. Loff raised his eyebrows, then put his head down and began intently eating his piece of leather-tough lizard.

Dinner was eaten in silence after which Ranth offered to sit first watch. As soon as full dark set in Shunlar left on a flight to scout the surrounding area. As on the previous nights, she saw no evidence of soldiers nearby, something she thought a bit odd, but she was thankful. The only other evidence of life around them was the heat trace of what looked like two large animals, but as the wind kicked up they were soon erased. Satisfied they would sleep safely again, Shunlar returned to camp.

In her blankets, Shunlar was lulled to sleep by the comforting sound of Avek breathing beside her. She woke once aware that Avek was gone and she recognized the sound of Ranth sleeping on the opposite side of her. Everything seemed perfectly calm, and she fell back into a dreamless deep sleep.

But Bimily progressively grew more ashen every day. Their pace was exhausting her and even though she was anxious to be on the way, everyone knew she must not push herself if she was to survive the journey. This was the seventh morning of travel for the original group; Avek had joined them four days ago, and Ranth three. In three more days they would come to the Thrale River. Once crossed, it should take them another five days to reach Bimily's people, that is, if she was able to keep up the pace.

However, the next morning it was painful to watch Bimily mount her horse. Careful not to let her see, worried glances passed between the others as they rode out. By midafternoon they had to stop and help Bimily down from her mount because she didn't have the strength to dismount by herself. Avek's keen eyes had discovered a small cave, and they decided to stop for the day though Bimily protested. It was the third time they had rested since morning, and her face was even more pale than it had been at dawn.

"I am afraid we will be overtaken by a party from Kalaven. Please, we must continue while we can," she begged. But it did her no good to try and persuade her companions. After drinking the hot herbal mixture Avek had prepared for her, she slept. The four of them were quiet as they made camp, careful not to awaken her. Avek left with Loff to scout the surrounding area and hunt for dinner, leaving Shunlar and Ranth to look after Bimily. So far they had seen only evidence of camps that were weeks old, but they knew Tonnerling scouts could be nearby.

From their vantage point on the hillside, Shunlar and Ranth watched as Avek and Loff carefully picked their way across the floor of the arid, rocky valley. Yesterday they had entered a different ecosystem, finally leaving the ever-pervasive sand behind. Small brush grew in sparse, scattered clumps, becoming increasingly greener and thicker at the far end of the valley. Off in the distance the snowcapped mountains were covered with green forests, something that comforted Shunlar greatly. Ranth seemed a bit more at ease than he had the first days of their travel. The air smelled clean, and there appeared to be rain clouds approaching slowly from the east.

"Now that we are alone would you mind telling me why you failed to mention Avek would be accompanying us?" Ranth's carefully controlled voice asked, startling Shunlar.

"If you had known, would you have stayed behind in Kalaven?" she countered, an edge to her voice.

"I don't know. What I do know is I don't want to argue with you. Can't you see that my feelings are overpowering my judgment? I expected you were taking me on this journey as your mate. That last night, when we made our peace in the palace alcove. What did that mean to you?"

"Just that, we made peace. I have real, deep feelings for Avek."

"Can't you bring yourself to say the word 'love'?"

"All right, I have real, deep love for Avek. Does that satisfy you?" Now Shunlar was angry.

"No. Surely you remember how we once pledged ourselves to one another. It may seem fine to you to wait, but I am unwilling to. I may not have that much time, and we are together now." Ranth closed his arms around her and backed her against the rocks. He tried to kiss her, and she pushed him away with such force that she knocked him over. He lay on his back, surprised.

"Stop it. We're here to escort Bimily to her people to see that she lives. There we will seek a cure for you or a way to remove those words of death marking your back. That is why you are here. Avek is here because I have made my choice. He is the man I want for a mate. Believe it and leave me alone." She stomped off to check on the horses.

The horses were fine, just as she knew they would be. What did it matter whom she loved? This was all so confusing. Maybe it was a crazy idea to have both of them along. What could she have been thinking? She knew she loved Avek. But if forced to tell the truth, she would admit she also still loved Ranth. When she thought of their child it seemed the most natural thing to want to be with Ranth. Just now, feeling his arms around her, his desire, made her irrational with longing. She was supposed to be thinking about Bimily's welfare and caring for her, not obsessing about a man or, worse, two.

The sound of a pebble clicking behind her made her whirl around. Ranth had stopped several feet away, and he slowly raised his open arms to her. Looking into his eyes, her heart pounded. Hesitating for a second, she made a decision, not caring what the consequences might be.

Fourteen

THE OLD MAN'S BROW WAS, IMPOSSIBLY, MORE furrowed. He scowled as he woke from his dream, trying hard to remember. He couldn't recall exactly what, except for a feeling of unease and distrust. It was as if something evil hovered nearby.

For months from his hermit's retreat far above the city proper Da Winfreyd had been aware of certain activity in Tonnerling. He refused to believe any of the insane ramblings of the rabble, but last night he had dreamed that a war had been declared and men were being recruited daily to fight. Who were they fighting, and for what? It took some several minutes before the answer came to him. The people of Kalaven Desert. Didn't it seem a little absurd that they would fight a war so far from their beloved mountains by the sea? What could be the impetus for such a ridiculous action? He must find out.

Calling for his assistant, Brother Boringar, Da Winfreyd asked him to mix a strengthening elixir for him so that he would be able to rise from his bed, something that had become increasingly difficult as of late. How many more years were left to him, he did not know, but he prayed daily for release from his present body. He was, after all, older than any of his brothers of the monastery. Few were left who recalled how long he had even been there. But release seemed to be far away for now.

After drinking the draught he sat on the edge of the

bed, slowly contemplating his next move. He bathed, with the help of the younger brother, and slowly dressed himself in soft cotton undergarments, warm woolen breeches, and tunic, covered over with the soft, dark brown cowled robes of his office. The lightweight fabric clothed and blanketed all the brothers in the monastery, keeping them warm even on the coldest winter nights. He caressed the fibers with his gnarled, old fingers, sighing, remembering how as a young man he had learned to shear the goats, card their silken hair, and spin the wool for the weavers. His occupation kept him busy still, something he was grateful for. No matter that he couldn't be up and about from his bed most of the time, he could still card and spin. Though his fingers were bent with arthritis, constantly moving them kept the pain at bay.

His appetite full upon him, he was ready to break his fast. Already he could feel his body responding to the herbs, and he smiled. Today would be the day he would find out the answers to his many questions. Perhaps he would even venture to the main city to see how Dolan and Klarissa fared.

What was it he was supposed to remember? Ah yes, he snickered to himself, Klarissa had been gone for many months now, married to that outlander from the Valley of Great Trees, what was his name? Gwernz! Such a serious fellow, he recalled, but Klarissa seemed more than content. It seemed that she had made a love match.

Brother Boringar watched his mentor closely to see that the herbs took effect. He was never sure that he trusted them completely, but the old man did, and they certainly made quite a difference. Color flushed Da Winfreyd's cheeks, and his appetite reappeared in full force. Boringar smiled with love upon the old man, who patted his hand affectionately when he served him more cheese and bread.

"Today, Boringar, I fancy even a taste of red wine. But, just a taste, mind you. More than a sip or two will

set my head reeling and the herbs' effect will be gone."
He winked conspiratorially.

Boringar poured a small spoonful into the simple wooden mug. He shook his head as his old master smacked his lips in appreciation and winked again. Something was afoot, and Boringar knew if he were patient, Da Winfreyd would soon let him in on the secret.

Sure enough, within minutes Da Winfreyd announced, "Today I wish to leave my lodgings and visit my young friend Dolan. Surely your duties can be set aside for several days while you accompany me, eh Boringar?"

"Da Winfreyd, you know the only duties that I have now are to make sure your days are as comfortable as possible. But, are you sure you're up to so long a journey, sir?"

"Young man, the sun warms me as have the herbs and that sip of fine wine. I feel life running through my veins again, and so I must act. There will come a day when not even the strongest draught you mix for me will enable me to rise from my bed. But let us not dwell on the future when the present beckons!" He smiled broadly and Boringar immediately set to packing their meager belongings, laying in a good supply of herbs for his mentor and changes of clothing for both of them.

Within the hour they were off, Da Winfreyd nimbly astride his gentle gelding, Boringar on his mare. As they rode slowly past the brothers working in the terraced gardens, all of them went to their knees for a blessing. Da Winfreyd raised his hand and called for the spirit of the guardians in the stone to protect and comfort them. Back on their feet, many waved while others cheered as he rode on down the mountain path. It was rare for the venerable old man to be out riding, and surely their plantings would increase twofold now that he had bestowed his benediction.

Continuing on their way, Da Winfreyd explained to Boringar, as he often did, his recent disturbing dreams and thus why he wanted to visit Tonnerling.

"I believe that something is greatly amiss in the city

of our people. Have any visited in the past six months to tell the news?"

"No, sir, not to my knowledge," was his honest reply.

"Have you spoken to any of our brothers about their dreams or have you had any that could tell us what might be happening below?" Da Winfreyd gestured to the city that slowly appeared before them as they traveled down the mountain path.

"Only this can I report, now that you ask. For the last month I have had dreams of war and horrible, bloody killing. Many of the other brothers have also reported they have woken at night with the same terrible dreams. Could it possibly be true, sir?" Boringar asked, sick at heart.

"That we are not merely dreaming? Yes, I believe it is happening. War has come to Tonnerling, and I must find out why men are killing one another when so long ago their fathers vowed it would never happen again." The old man's stern look made Boringar shudder. It had been years since Da Winfreyd had seemed so full of life, so determined. It didn't seem possible that mere herbs could stir him so deeply and produce so much activity—just yesterday Boringar had reported to the head of the monastery, Da Florin, that he doubted if his charge would see another winter.

"We are nearing the women's monastery, and I wish to stop and ask some questions. Stay with me and keep an open ear. Notice everything and let all feelings move freely through your body for you are yet a young man and I would not have you report that you were disturbed by the sight of so many women."

"Sir, I have been with you for over thirty years and I have never given you reason to admonish me as if I were yet a schoolboy with the blush of youth on his cheek. My vows are permanent . . ." And he stopped in mid-sentence, his mouth open.

"Ah, Boringar, how easy it is to trick you still!" Da Winfreyd laughed as he caught the younger man's look of astonishment. Soon Boringar, too, was chuckling and shaking his head good-naturedly at how effortlessly the joke had been played. How he loved this old man.

After Boringar pulled on the bell rope several times, the doors were opened and two novices led the horses into a courtyard. Inside the walls were terraced gardens that, like their counterparts, were being tended by the diligent sisters. From the chapel drifted the sounds of melodious voices lifted in songful prayer. Tranquillity seeped into the two men as they dismounted, the elder being assisted by his companion.

Soon footsteps announced the arrival of the Reverend Mother closely followed by her assistant, Sister Nomia, a tall, thin woman whose remarkable blue eyes pierced Boringar to the core. He remembered well their first meeting, many years ago, and he bowed his head to her as a smile warmed her eyes. She returned the bow and ushered them to a quiet alcove with two benches and a small table, offering them a cup of cool water from the well.

Boringar assisted Da Winfreyd to his seat, and took his place behind Da Winfreyd as the younger woman took hers behind the Reverend Mother. Allowing himself one more look at her face, Boringar lowered his eyes and remembered his place as well as his vow. Had she been willing, Nomia and he would have been married, their betrothal arranged by their respective families before they both could walk. But one night she escaped from her father's house and fled to the women's monastery on the hill. From her smile, Boringar knew they had both made the correct choices, for he, too, had answered his calling high on the mountain. Nonetheless, it was always a bit unnerving to see her.

"Mother Enissa, it is good to set my old eyes upon you again, though I doubt you feel the same about seeing me," began Da Winfreyd.

"Brother Winfreyd, your visits are most often preceded by the most peculiar happenings. Just yesternight several of the sisters were telling me of their disturbing dreams, which I took as a sign that you would soon be upon our doorstep. Again, I was correct. What is the news, or do you have any to tell me yet?"

"Sorry to say, dear lady, but we are only just on our way down the mountain. It has been six months I daresay since we have had any news from Tonnerling, and I assume the same for you?"

Mother Enissa answered with a nod.

"Then, we will stop on our return to report what we have learned on our foray. I trust we have not taken you from anything important this morning and I will keep you no longer. Remember us in your prayers."

The two elders rose and bowed to one another. As they turned to leave, Mother Enissa remembered something. "Do any of your brothers report dreams of Lifestones?" she asked.

That stopped Da Winfreyd in his tracks. That was the important missing piece that he had seen only too briefly in last night's dream—a young man clinging desperately to an amber crystal, crying out, his words unintelligible in the howling desert wind. Slowly Da Winfreyd turned around.

"I thank you, Mother Enissa. You have helped me to recall an important detail. I begin to understand the severity of the situation, and I will be sure to send word the minute I learn something. In the meantime, pray that my worst fears do not come true."

They bowed to one another, and the two men mounted their horses, once again on their way. Clearly worried, Mother Enissa leaned toward her assistant, Sister Nomia. "See that the Dreamers Council is assembled as soon as possible."

"But Mother, they have just retired these two hours past. If they are wakened too soon, they will suffer."

"Oh, if only there were more time. Yes, I remember now, child. Don't worry. Let them sleep. When they are refreshed, let me know, and we will reconvene." She patted the younger woman's shoulder affectionately.

"Yes, Mother," Nomia answered as she watched Boringar and Da Winfreyd ride through the gate.

"Regrets?" Mother asked.

"Always and never, Mother. I would be lying if I said

no to either. But I see clearly where the threads of our lives touch and no longer wonder at the reason for our betrothal. He and I together will yet play a part in the lives of our people. I am convinced of that."

Mother Enissa looked squarely at Nomia, many questions apparent in her gaze, but she merely knotted her brow. "We must speak of this later, child."

"Yes, Mother," she answered quietly.

About an hour later Da Winfreyd and Boringar came to the first vantage point on the mountain road. They were both stunned and speechless; there appeared to be a military encampment in the distance where none had been before. There were men drilling, sparring and being trained in the application of the tactics of war. Worried now, they rode on.

Arriving in the late afternoon at Dolan's home, they were greeted warmly and informed that Master Dolan would be home for the evening meal. Until then they were shown to quarters and made comfortable. Relieved to be out of the saddle, Da Winfreyd fell asleep as soon as his head touched the pillow.

Later that evening the three men supped together, retiring afterward to the overstuffed chairs in front of the fire.

"What can you tell me of the war that is being waged on Kalaven?" Da Winfreyd asked.

Startled to hear the question from the old monk, Dolan asked, "Since when do you involve yourself in the business of war? Surely I thought you had come to speak of my bethrothal and ask questions of the bride-to-be."

"But I know nothing of your wedding. Why didn't you tell me as soon as you returned home this evening? Is the young woman from a good house? Do you love her?" Da Winfreyd asked with a wink.

"I suppose I will come to love her. Her father owns several ships, and if the match is a good one, we will go into business together. So, I will do whatever I can to make the marriage work. It is, after all, best for business," concluded Dolan with a weary sigh.

"This is the perfect opportunity for me to meet your intended. Invite the family here for a betrothal dinner, which I will preside over and bless your union."

"Excellent idea, Da Winfreyd," Dolan replied, but he looked worried. "How I wish Klarissa were here. She would know what to do to impress her mother. I fear the woman might take a dislike to me and refuse my offer to her daughter."

"Let us talk to Cook and see what she comes up with." Da Winfreyd winked. "I'll bet she has a few secrets in her apron pockets that will impress the most dour prospective in-laws."

"How I have missed your company, Da Winfreyd," said Dolan with a smile of relief. "The house is so empty without Klarissa. My hope is that within a year I can be married, and I won't be alone in this drafty old place."

"I would hardly call it drafty," the old monk answered, as with Boringar's help he propped his feet up before the fire. "Now let us return to my former question. What can you tell me about the war?"

For the next hour Dolan told Da Winfreyd and Brother Boringar everything he could of the reason that Tonnerling had declared a war upon Kalaven.

As Da Winfreyd had predicted, the betrothal dinner went along splendidly. Cook outdid herself in the preparation of each course, from the soup to the dessert. Most impressed was the mother, whose severe features began to ease as she sampled each dish. She was even smiling by the time the roast fowl was sliced and delicately placed on her plate. Cook supervised each and every detail, and Dolan could tell she was doing her best to make this dinner an evening to remember for her young master.

Dolan's bride gift was a choker of four strands of pink pearls that closed with a gold clasp encrusted with white sapphires, with earrings to match. In Tonnerling the custom was for the men to bestow pearls on their women, and the wealthier the man, the more strands of pearls.

Four strands was a very auspicious beginning.

When she opened the box, Ariaste, the bride-to-be, gasped, and her mother smiled approvingly. Her father, who was busy gulping down yet another goblet of wine, raised his head long enough to squint his bloodshot eyes, counting the strands of pearls. He picked up an eyebrow as either a sign of approval or greed, Dolan could not be sure which; but he made a mental note to himself to find out, since soon they would become business partners.

So far the evening had gone well, and his gift fairly made Ariaste swoon as Dolan fastened the clasp at the back of her neck. Her skin was warm and soft to his touch. His fingers trembled as he fumbled with the clasp.

His intended bride was four years his junior, making her fifteen, yet she seemed so much younger. Perhaps when they were alone he would find out if that were so or if she were just acting childishly with her mother so close. Many of his married friends had predicted that would happen, and it was proving to be the case tonight.

With the presentation of his gift Dolan knew the evening would soon be over, something that he looked forward to wholeheartedly. He had never been so nervous in his entire life. Da Winfreyd rose and bestowed a blessing on the upcoming union of the young couple, and soon the guests were rising to leave. The parents were ushered from the room by Da Winfreyd, as if he knew what was on Dolan's mind. Without skipping a beat, Dolan took the opportunity to speak to his betrothed alone.

If he was reading the look in Ariaste's large blue eyes correctly, it bespoke wariness and beneath it intelligence. She curtsied and offered her hand for him to kiss before he even reached for it. A bold move, he thought. Her gaze met his eyes steadily. Dolan liked that. Her breath came fast, and he was aware of her lips parting when he took hold of her hand.

"Thank you for the pearls. They are the loveliest I have ever seen. I will be the envy of all my friends."

Her voice was low and sweet, and the sound of it made Dolan very warm.

Momentarily speechless, he kissed the back of her hand, and her perfume of lilacs filled his nostrils. She was quite lovely, though her eyes seemed a little wide set. Her nose was strong, not too large for her face, and her lips full, not at all like her mother's. He wanted to kiss more than the back of her hand. Suddenly his arms went around her and he planted a warm, soft kiss on her lips. She had just begun returning the kiss when the sound of someone clearing his throat behind them brought them back to reality.

Ariaste jumped back, curtsied, and ran from the room, passing Boringar, who they had forgotten was present. Dolan straightened his jacket, thankful that it was cut long and full in the front. He nodded to Boringar, who bowed as the young man passed him. Boringar smiled to himself and just shook his head.

After seeing their guests into their carriage and safely on their way home, Dolan breathed a sigh of relief.

"There, there," Da Winfreyd consoled him. "You will see Ariaste soon enough I think. No need for such sounds of longing."

"Sorry to disappoint, sir, but it is merely a sigh of relief you hear. If I'm not mistaken, Ariaste's mother was smiling when she left, and I don't know if I felt more uncomfortable with that smile or her usual sour expression."

Taking Dolan's arm, Da Winfreyd laughed. "I know very well what you mean. Come, let's partake in a bit of brandy after that fine repast and we will discuss your future in-laws. I may be able to shed some light on the lady in question." Dolan cast an unusual look at his old friend. What secrets would he learn tonight, he wondered? Da Winfreyd was a fountain of knowledge and never ceased to amaze Dolan with his information.

Boringar met them at the double doors to the main hall. "Ah, just the man I want to see," gushed Da Winfreyd. "Be a good lad, Boringar, and sit with us. You don't mind, do you, Dolan? Boringar and I are old friends, and perhaps someday he will be your advisor, after I'm gone.'' Dolan and Boringar exchanged a meaningful look, and Boringar bowed.

''Gladly will I join you, but are you not ready to retire? It has been a long evening, and you have pushed yourself these past five days.'' Boringar tried to persuade his mentor to consider going to bed.

''Pah, with the two of you for company and a glass or two of brandy, I will keep you both awake.'' Da Winfreyd grinned his challenge.

Once they were settled into their chairs, Da Winfreyd asked, ''Which of you can tell me why there are no wizards in Tonnerling?'' Dolan and Boringar again exchanged glances.

''Perhaps you should tell us,'' Dolan ventured.

Taking a sip of his brandy, Da Winfreyd smacked his lips in appreciation, then began. ''When our ancestors abandoned Stiga, generations ago, it was because wizards had been waging war upon one another and their allied houses with their horrible weapons. Once they had settled here and established a council of elders to be lawmakers, Tonnerling's law forbade public study of wizardry.'' Da Winfreyd stared at Dolan several seconds before continuing. ''But we know that in secret many sons learned from their fathers, don't we, Dolan?''

Dolan thought before answering in the affirmative with a nod of his head. A look of shock crossed Boringar's face for a second; then he composed himself, making his expression unreadable.

''Daughters were seldom taught because of a prejudice against women. You see, the wizard from Stiga who had destroyed most of our ancestors was a woman. Female wizards proved to be the most ruthless when it came to revenge,'' Da Winfreyd added.

''Vinnyius, your father, young Dolan, studied the ancient art but it was not widely known, nor would it have been accepted if it had been. Tell me, young master, how much did your father teach you?''

''Sir, I am uncomfortable speaking of this to you, especially in front of Brother Boringar. While I mean no disrespect, how could I possibly explain what I know in terms that you would understand?''

''And just where do you think your father learned the art in the first place?'' Da Winfreyd asked, taking a sip of the brandy with relish.

Dolan's mouth fell open. Boringar's followed.

''Come now, you look a bit like a fish. Close your lips upon your glass and have a quick swallow, there's a good lad. You, too, Boringar.''

''Well now, I can see you have both been startled by my revelation, but that's not why I asked you to join me tonight. This evening I may have stumbled upon a bigger secret, and it concerns Ariaste's mother.'' He let his words sink in until the two men began to fidget in their chairs.

''You may have already guessed, but she, too, has been instructed in the ancient arts. At this evening's dinner I noticed something peculiar about the lady, and I did what I could to touch her mind without her knowledge. She is quite powerful, and you must do whatever you can to make her an ally, Dolan. Otherwise, I shudder to think what an adversary she will make.''

Dolan seemed suddenly to lose some of his color, and sweat beaded up on his brow. ''I recognized something in her, too, but I refused to believe it could be possible,'' he said quickly. ''What about Ariaste?''

''It appears the daughter is not skilled, but she may know some fundamental tricks. Did you have occasion to touch her for any length of time this evening?''

''Well.'' Dolan hesitated, then looked at Boringar. ''As Brother Boringar will probably tell you, I did kiss her. But briefly!'' he protested at Da Winfreyd's upraised brows.

''Let me see if there is any residue that might give me information. Stand and face me fully and don't be afraid. Boringar, bar the door.''

Rising from his chair, Da Winfreyd slowly made his way to stand before Dolan. He pulled a pouch from beneath his tunic and opened it. Taking a large, many-faceted amber crystal from the pouch, he held it near

Dolan's head. Dolan became immobilized as a beam of light moved across his features. It felt warm and left a slight tingle on his skin. When it came to his lips, they became icy cold. Dolan could hear whispers in the back of his skull as the beam roved across his body. As it crossed his chest and arms and finally his fingers, all parts of his body that had come in contact with Ariaste seemed to turn suddenly cold.

"Well, you are no worse for the wear I see, but I caution you against touching the young woman again. For now," he added, seeing the look of dismay on Dolan's face. "I'll be able to teach you a counterspell to the one set upon Ariaste by her mother, one that Lady Tumnia will not suspect, nor Lord Raspin, though I doubt if you have much to fear from him." He put the Lifestone back into its pouch and slipped it under his tunic.

"What did she do?" demanded Dolan, his face red.

"She merely put a spell in place that would allow her to see if her daughter and you touched. Her motive is unclear, but if she can do that, she can certainly read your thoughts through Ariaste's. Did you have any thoughts—besides the obvious—as you embraced her?"

"I, I, don't remember," Dolan stuttered. He was panicked. No one in so long had known his secret, only Shunlar, and she had never learned more than the fact that he had certain abilities. He trembled.

"My young friend, calm yourself. Remember what your father taught you about protective spells. I will be here to help you, in fact I promise not to leave until you are safely secure in your knowledge." Da Winfreyd smiled and placed his hands on Dolan's shoulders, calming the young man down. "See how easy it is?" Dolan smiled and nodded, then he embraced the old man.

Da Winfreyd stayed with Dolan for months, teaching him and Boringar many spells and protections. The art of wizardry was strong and alive in him, and he passed on most if not all of his knowledge. In that time Brother Boringar and Dolan became quite good friends.

Da Winfreyd gathered all the information he could

and sent it to the men and women of the monasteries on the mountain, as he had promised. They, in turn, prepared for war as best they knew how; growing and preserving extra food, and healing herbs, weaving extra blankets and cloth for bandages, even training men and women in the healing arts. When called upon, they would be prepared to nurse the sick and the wounded.

Fifteen

Having slept for an entire day, Bimily was awakened by the aroma of meat roasting over the fire. Her stomach rumbled, and when she turned her head and opened her eyes, she saw the concerned look on Shunlar's face. Shunlar sat cross-legged on the ground beside her, a cup of hot herbal tea in one hand and a jug of taloz in the other. One look told Bimily something was wrong. She propped herself up on her elbow and reached toward her friend. Placing her hand upon Shunlar's knee, Bimily was made immediately aware of what troubled her.

She removed her hand and shook her head, then smiled. "Cheer up. Your secret is safe with me. Tell me, will you be able to choose one over the other if it comes down to it?"

Shunlar shook her head. "I don't know. I don't even want to think about it. Avek suspects nothing, or if he does, he won't show it. What came over me? One minute I know my mind and have a firm decision made, the next, I'm swooning like a girl and let my passions trample me like a runaway horse." She raised the jug to her mouth and took a hefty swallow.

Footsteps announced someone entering the cave. Shunlar straightened up and handed the cup of tea to Bimily as if no conversation had occurred. Avek was behind her and he bent down on one knee to offer them each a plump, steaming bird upon a plate. The aroma made Shunlar's mouth water, and she smiled at him. His dazzling grin set her heart pounding, bringing color to her cheeks, and as she took the food, he kissed her full on the lips, handed Bimily her food, and left.

"A man of few words, they say, is a man of action," Bimily taunted. That made Shunlar laugh at last. "Good, I was beginning to wonder where your sense of humor had gone. It occurs to me that you're the only one worried about what you've done. Ever since Ranth arrived, Avek has acted as though he expects you to be a threesome. Remember, it's not foreign to their culture to do so."

"But it's not *my* culture. One man at a time should be enough for one woman," Shunlar said with some finality.

"Well, mark my words. Tomorrow Loff and Ranth will go hunting and you and Avek will be left alone, together, to watch over me." Exasperated by the thought, Shunlar concentrated on her food.

True to Bimily's prediction, it did happen that way. The day Bimily had spent sleeping helped her regain some strength and brought her color up to merely pale. Another day would do her wonders, everyone agreed. Soon after breakfast Ranth and Loff saddled up and rode out to scout the area and hunt for food. As they rode away, Ranth raised his arm in a salute to Avek, who returned it, bowing his head as he did. Shunlar was puzzled but said nothing.

After checking on Bimily and finding that she was sleeping soundly, Shunlar returned to sit beside Avek. He was busy replacing a worn-out piece of leather on a bridle and smiled warmly when she joined him. Together they watched from the same spot where she and Ranth had sat on the previous day.

"What did that salute mean?" Shunlar asked finally, unable to stop thinking about it.

"Salute?" he asked coyly.

"Between you and Ranth. What did it mean?"

"That I will take his place until he returns."

"Take his place as what?" she asked warily.

"As First One. I am second to him being first. That's all."

"That's all? You're second. First One what?" she asked unsure about whether she truly wanted to hear the answer.

"First husband. It has been settled between us, and I am content. Clearly you wanted both of us or you would not have stolen both of us."

Shunlar's eyes widened in disbelief. "Am . . . am I to understand that you and he have decided without me that you are both going to . . . to . . . share me?" she stammered. "What kind of a woman do you think I am? This is pure horse dung. I won't be handed a decision that I had no part in making and surely one that I have no intention of keeping."

"But we both assumed from your actions that this is what you wanted. Is it not what you want?" Avek wasn't joking. He looked anxious.

"By my actions? What action besides abducting you from the city do you mean?" she asked suspiciously.

"That is precisely the action I speak of. Also, Ranth told me of your pledge to one another. That promise is as binding as a marriage. In the eyes of our people, because you have a child, you are married."

"You mean the entire time I spent in Kalaven, everyone assumed I was married to Ranth? And he didn't tell me?"

"Ranth was under orders from Zeraya to say nothing. I suspect it was because she had seen him so badly hurt by Septia, but also you are not one of our people. Zeraya sul Karnavt is not an unfeeling woman, after all. The day you sought special audience with her and Benyar, she was waiting for you to come forward and declare you claimed Ranth for a mate. When you asked for my exile to be ended instead, she forbade Ranth to tell you."

"But, not to tell me that it was already assumed we were married? And then this archaic custom of not speaking to me unless Loff was present."

"Oh, that was never imposed on you and Ranth. Just me," Avek answered with a sigh.

"But I assumed Ranth was bound by it because he wasn't speaking to me. Perhaps I assumed too much. Tell me, if it is true that your people have more than one mate at a time, then why don't Benyar and Zeraya have other spouses, or Ketherey or Fanon? What about Zara and Jerob, your parents? And, now that I think about it, why didn't Septia marry Korab as well as Ranth?"

"It was common practice with us to have more than one wife or husband. That was in the days before Zeraya and Benyar were declared Queen and First Guardian. You see, when Zeraya founded the city, she declared that we would no longer live as nomads. Soon afterward she began to change some of our laws.

"The first thing she did was to ban the custom of multiple marriages, decreeing that everyone was permitted only one spouse at a time. Needless to say, it was an unpopular law at first. Perhaps it would have been changed—Zeraya was very young when she made it law. But then she was injured and put into stasis. Until her death actually occurred, the law could not be changed."

"But what could have been behind her reasoning if this was an ancient custom?" asked Shunlar, very interested.

"When questioned by the High Priestess, Zeraya answered that it would put a stop to unnecessary death. You see, it was also common practice for a duel to be arranged if the first spouse did not agree with the choice for second. And since the majority of the duels were between women, many were dying. My own mother died in such a way, when I was very young. By Zara's hand," he added quietly. "Zara herself was severely wounded in the fight and after nearly losing her sister, Zeraya declared her new law.

"There was a large faction of the Feralmon who refused to live the way Zeraya demanded. They rebelled and left Kalaven to continue living as nomads as they had for centuries. I'm not sure how many remain today, but I am told they are few in number. When they first left, many abductions occurred, and those who were taken were never seen again. We hope they have been treated well.''

Speaking of the Lost Feralmon made Avek remember the dead soldier and the one footprint he had found the first morning after his abduction. He knew the print was either a deliberate message or a warning, and until he determined which, he chose not to mention it. Instead he simply watched Shunlar's expression change as she listened.

The information stunned Shunlar into silence. For several minutes she could think of nothing to say, words jumbling in her head. When at last she spoke she began to explain how it had been for her growing up, ''I was raised by Cloonth and Alglooth in near seclusion until the age of ten. I assumed many things about other people and their customs. When I was taken to Vensunor for my first glimpse of how other people lived, Vensunor became my model. It was my first look at the world, after all, because Stiga was deserted except for us.''

''You're telling me Stiga really exists?'' Avek gasped.

''Now surely *you're* joking?'' She laughed.

''No. My people tell a fable of leaving a great city of magics behind, but it was long ago and we are all forbidden to return on pain of death. Not that anyone of us would want to travel there. There are stories of great demons that fly who spit fire . . .'' His mouth fell open as he remembered Shunlar's transformative abilities.

''So. I was waiting for you to make the connection.'' Bimily stood at the mouth of the cave, looking rested but very thin. They hadn't heard her rising and subsequent eavesdropping, but she had heard everything.

''Stiga is very real and it exists to this day, though now it is a great ruin and uninhabited. All of us including the Feralmon, those from Tonnerling, from the Valley of Great Trees and Vensunor originated there. Even my kind originated in Stiga,'' Bimily said quietly.

Now it was Shunlar's turn to look puzzled. ''How can that be? None of the texts spoke of shapechangers. From studying the ancient texts one could learn how to cast an illusion over one's self, but nothing was mentioned about changing one's shape."

"You won't find any information about my kind in the texts, no matter how ancient. But I am not permitted to speak of this to anyone. Even if I were to try, my tongue would fail me and the words become garbled. And no images can be transferred directly to your mind from mine. The secret is locked firmly within my memory.

"When the wizard wars had decimated the population of Stiga, those who remained fled to found the four distinctly different cultures I mentioned, though parts of Stiga's traditions were taken by all. It has always been interesting to me to see the way societies form," mused Bimily.

"Do you tell us that you witnessed the destruction of Stiga?" asked Avek in astonishment.

"You could say I was there at the beginning of the end," she answered with a faraway look.

"Bimily," said Shunlar quietly, "I never asked you how old you were. I always assumed you to be somewhat older than me, but not centuries. Had you known Cloonth and Alglooth long before you and I met?"

"I was present at their birth." Looking tired, Bimily turned and went back to her bedroll, leaving Shunlar and Avek to contemplate her words.

Sixteen

FINALLY, THEY STOOD AT THE BANKS OF THE Thrale River. Along this part of the river the trees remained sparse—a few saplings at best—making it impossible to build a raft for crossing. Though Bimily insisted she could easily ford the river, no one was willing to risk her being washed from her horse by the current. Getting wet would be bad enough. None of them wanted to face the prospect of swimming after Bimily in the icy water. Though shallow near the banks, the Thrale was quick and deep in the middle, and at this time of year, spring, it ran faster than usual.

So, the only reasonable alternative was decided. Shunlar would transform into her larger half-human, half-dragon self and carry Bimily across. But to do it in daylight posed too great a risk.

"We can camp by the river this evening, and before dawn I will carry you across and most of the supplies as well. That way nothing will get wet or lost to the river," suggested Shunlar. They agreed to her plan though Bimily felt they were coddling her unnecessarily.

"What if I want to get wet?" Bimily asked stubbornly. "I haven't bathed in over a week now, and I'm beginning to think my horse smells better than I do."

"Ah, it's a bath you want. Why didn't you say so? I'll race you," challenged Shunlar, laughing as she pulled off her boots, flinging clothing. That was all the challenge Bimily needed. In seconds she was doing the same. Each woman grabbed soap and a towel from her saddlebags and ran for the river's edge, giddy as girls, leaving the three men with their horses and bemused looks on their faces.

Loff shook his head saying, "I'd wager we'd best gather extra wood and build a large fire that we can dry ourselves by, for as sure as I'm sitting on this horse, we will be the next bathers, if those two have anything to say about it. And I'm sure that my sister will."

"Aye," echoed Avek and Ranth.

Later they were all seated around a blaze drying their hair, happy to be clean again. As they ate a dinner of fire-roasted fish, Bimily explained that the Lesser Thrale also waited for them to cross, in at most three more days. She assured them it was smaller, quite shallow, and would be easy to cross. After that, another two days would finally bring them to her homeland.

Their crossing of both rivers went without incident, and on the afternoon of the fifth day they arrived at the entrance to a barren, rocky valley that Bimily claimed was her home. Though they had just ridden through some of the most lush, green, countryside any of the others could remember, this valley looked to have been recently destroyed by a fire. Far in the distance, near the center of the valley, loomed a circle of standing stones of enormous proportion that appeared to have also been blackened by fire.

"This is where I must leave you for now," Bimily told them as she slipped from her horse. "Before I can take you with me to meet my people, I must be received and granted entry. Don't look so worried, all will be well."

None of them believed her. The valley was devastated. How could anyone possibly be alive here, they all wondered? At first glance there appeared to be only dozens upon dozens of burned-out buildings scattered about the remains of lace-like charred orchards. Before anyone could dissuade her, Bimily dismounted and took off at a fast walk toward the huge monoliths that waited eerily in the center of the ruins.

They watched Bimily recede into the distance for what seemed like hours. When she finally reached the circle of towering stones she stepped into their midst. Her body began to waver for several seconds before a thunderous cracking sound rent the air. They gasped together, helpless, as Bimily was transformed into a column of stone.

Shunlar was the first to realize she couldn't move. Loff, Avek, and Ranth came into her field of vision, shouting at her and gesturing but she couldn't hear them or respond in any way. Then her vision faded to black, taking her awareness with it.

Bimily felt an ecstatic sense of release when she stepped softly into the circle of standing stones. A sudden rippling of the air passed before her eyes and suddenly she was no longer flesh and bone but had turned to stone. In this state she recognized several family members around her, but the most significant feeling was that of being in another shape, something that her weakened state had prevented her from doing.

At first no one recognized her. What remained of her soul had taken on the characteristics of the black songbird she had been for more than a year. Knowing full well that she must seem like a stranger to them after all the years that had passed, Bimily reached out to her family by whispering her name.

"Bimily. It is Bimily," someone whispered back, followed by another voice. One by one they began to recognize and acknowledge who she was.

The condition of the valley began to change as well. It regained its pastoral look. Houses returned to their solid shapes as the trees, lush grasses, and flowers sprang to life. The standing stones encircling Bimily transformed into the family and friends she knew and loved. They surrounded her and caught her up in their arms, transforming her as they did so from a column of stone back to her human form. By touching her they were able to ascertain that Bimily was near death. For several moments the feelings of joy that brightened the mood of everyone faded, to be instantly replaced by a sense of determination. They would now begin the process that would bring her back to life as she knew it, restoring her abilities and her soul.

A sound touched Bimily's ears, reverberating through her body like a liquid balm entering her pores. Several particular notes struck memories stored deep within her cells and brought them to the forefront of her vision. In the midst of the memories, as if watching a performance, she saw herself being carried by a group of people through a portal in the hillside that led to steps that descended deep into the ground.

She next became aware of being in a long, damp corridor that brought the smell of musty, comforting earth to her nostrils. Then another familiar note of sound touched her ears, and she reached toward it with her senses, wanting to taste it and feel it as well as hear it. It became a tune played on a flute, and the melody soothed her to her bones.

Those carrying Bimily took her through the damp tunnel until they came to a short doorway. Bending low, they entered an ovoid chamber. Beside the fire sat a person dressed in black, her face covered by a transparent black veil that sparkled at the edges with a blue light when she stood. "Leave us," her resonant female voice echoed within Bimily's skull. Then came the sensation of being gently placed upon a narrow, high bed in the center of the room by careful, loving hands.

As the last person backed through the doorway, Bimily was aware of the wall closing over, the doorway disappearing with a faint crackling sound. Though she could not move and her eyes were closed, she was able to see, hear, and feel everything that happened in the room around her. A part of her had somehow stepped into the skin of the other woman, enabling Bimily to see through her eyes. When a question about the woman began to form in Bimily's mind, another sound washed over her like a sigh, and the question dissolved.

She was safe in this womb-like cavern. Somehow she knew there were several more doors that led to other chambers similar to the one she was in, but they, too, had become part of the wall. There were no questions or curiosity about this place, no fear, merely acceptance and remembrance.

With the next sound, Bimily's eyes opened, and this time she looked down into the room, as if she were perched on the hanging lamp suspended above her body. On the walls opposite from her head, her feet, to the left and right of her, four columns of light appeared and began to glow, pulsating and growing brighter by the second. Gradually each column resolved itself into the shape of a woman, which then separated from the wall and slowly moved into the room to stand around her.

They began to stroke her, with long, gentle caresses, and each part of her body that felt their hands grew stronger, as if it were re-forming under their fingers. She blinked; when her eyes opened again she was on the narrow bed, and the four women gazed lovingly back at her with her face. Beginning on her left side, the apparition rose in the air to hover over her body. Like an opaque blanket the form drifted down over her, and, as it touched, a surge of power rippled through Bimily. The one on her right side did the same, dropping down and delivering another surge. Then the one at her head came next, the one at her feet going last.

Bimily's breath was fast and a sheen of sweat covered her face and body. She felt stronger and more clear-headed than she had in more than a year. Tears welled in her eyes, and she reached to wipe them away. She opened them again just as the woman draped in black began to descend upon her. Now there was fear and confusion. Bimily screamed. The black shroud fell away, revealing her own face, as the apparition dropped onto her and dissolved beneath her flesh. She sat bolt upright in one quick motion, noticing for the first time that she was naked. In the next several seconds her skin began to itch terribly.

Examining herself Bimily could see tiny bumps that seemed to dance along under the skin of her arms and legs. Then she began to change. One moment Bimily was covered in fur with a long, bushy tail, her fingers and toes turned to claws. Those melted away before her eyes as her arms turned to wings and she sprouted multicolored feathers. Next came fish scales, and her arms and legs disappeared to take on the shape of fins. Again her body changed, and, as the fins fell away, the skin of a snake covered her, and she was twisted, turned, stretched, and curled in all parts of her body. Gradually the shapeshifting slowed down and finally stopped. By this time Bimily was panting, shaking, and dripping with sweat.

The sound of water caught her attention and when she raised her head, a large tub that hadn't been there seconds ago squatted in front of the fire. It was being filled with steaming water from a pipe that extended from the wall. Once the tub had filled, the flow of water stopped and the pipe retracted and disappeared into the wall. The hot water was most inviting. Bimily slid from the bed and slowly padded across the hard-packed dirt floor to the bath. The lovely scent of lavender insinuated itself into her nose as she raised a leg, testing the water with her toes. Satisfied it was at a comfortable temperature, she slipped gracefully into the water, sighing deeply as she submerged her head below the surface.

When she came up for air Bimily felt a presence in the room. She turned to see her mother, Filomena, and her sister, Bresia, smiling down on her. They came near the tub and began to wash her. By then Bimily was spent. Though she had been given back much of her lost essence, she remained weak from the ordeal. When she was clean they helped her from the tub, and after drying her with soft towels they helped her into the large bed that now took up most of the room. Soon Bimily was sleeping soundly, and the two women left her to rest.

Awakening later to the gentle sound of her mother's voice, Bimily opened her eyes. Bresia was also there, her smile radiant.

''Daughter, we have come to take you to your audience. Sleep has completed the work that was begun. Are you able to rise?'' Filomena asked.

"Of course, Mother," Bimily answered. Putting her feet on the floor, her sister came to one side of her and her mother offered her arm, helping her to stand. She walked slowly to a marble topped table that held a basin of steaming, herb-scented water, and towels for washing. Picking up one of the soft cloths, Bimily washed the sleep from her face, the herbs doing much to revitalize her.

Together her mother and sister helped Bimily dress. A sleeveless shift of blue gossamer silk was slipped over her head. On top of that came a dress with long sleeves of a heavier weave in the same material. A silver-link belt with a silver eagle claw clasp was put around her waist. Bimily was adorned with a matching silver necklace, bracelets, and earrings. Her mother and her sister braided her hair in three long braids, one hanging over each shoulder and one down her back, narrow silver ribbons tied around the ends.

Similarly dressed, though in gowns of different colors, Filomena and Bresia smiled at Bimily, and the three women happily embraced. Filomena's dark, coppery hair had retained its sheen though it now had gray liberally streaked throughout. Her flawless skin remained smooth. Only her great green eyes crinkled at the edges when she smiled. Bresia looked the same, still tall and thin with long curls of reddish blonde hair, a trait inherited from her father. Her eyes were hazel specked with gold.

Crying tears of joy, Bimily opened her mind to her mother and her sister, showing them the events of her life, particularly explaining how she had come so close to death.

"How is Father?" Bimily asked when they stepped apart.

"He is fine and waits to greet you in the great hall. We have come to take you there now, for you must speak to the Elders." Filomena's voice sounded tight as she brushed the tears from her cheeks.

"Is there something wrong?" Bimily asked when she heard the constriction in Filomena's voice.

"It is time we should leave for your audience," was her only answer.

With her mother on her right and her sister on her left, Bimily left for the great hall, to be received by the Elders. At the doorway waited the unmistakable tall form of her father, Sloan. His smile nearly made her cry and when he encircled her in his arms, she felt reassured and safe. Holding her at arm's length, Sloan looked her over. His hair, too, was highlighted with gray, but was still mostly blond curls. His ice-blue eyes looked deeply into hers and she heard him say, *I have missed you, daughter. You have been away too long.*

Bimily merely nodded her agreement, unable to speak. Reassured by the presence of her family around her, Bimily turned her attention to the audience with the waiting Elders. The distance from the entrance to the end of the hall seemed interminably longer than she remembered. As she walked the hall's length, she searched the room for Shunlar, Ranth, Avek, and Loff. When she did not see them standing together in one of the clusters of people, she grew a little concerned but not overly; after all, she was home, and she expected her people to treat her friends well.

As Bimily neared the dais and the Three Elders seated there, she thought to ask Filomena just where her friends were. Her mother's answer was a grim expression. When Bimily gave her sister, Bresia, a questioning glance, she colored and lowered her eyes. Now Bimily began to worry. Despite the fact that her people had never encouraged or invited outsiders, she had expected them to receive her friends openly.

Standing close to the steps, Bimily bowed low. The Three Elders, Leatha, Menadees, and Thricia, inclined their heads to her when she looked up. The lines on their faces were deeper and their hair whiter than the last time she had seen them, but they, too, appeared about the same.

"We greet you after your long absence, Bimily," said Leatha, who was the eldest and spokesperson for them.

"And I am most grateful to be welcomed and restored

of my health. For that I thank all who were responsible.'' Bimily's voice could be heard clearly throughout the great hall.

''I am troubled to see that the four people who accompanied me are not present in the hall. If not for them, I never would have been able to return. I would most probably be dead by now.'' She let her words sink in and waited for the murmurs in the hall to subside.

''One of the men, my friend Ranth sul Zeraya, has come seeking your help in removing ancient symbols that were carved onto his back by an enemy. I am sure you must be aware by this time that he is also a holder of a Lifestone,'' Bimily concluded.

''We are aware that one of the men has a Lifestone upon him, but have not examined him further. Your request is something that we must consider carefully. But, you must be aware that you have brought abomination into our midst. The woman who accompanied you must die. We have not made our decision about the others yet.''

Bimily could scarcely believe her ears. She felt her knees go weak. ''Surely you cannot mean to kill Shunlar.''

The Elders looked on impassively for several long minutes. Finally, Thricia spoke up. ''Explain to us who this woman is, and we will consider whether or not we will allow her and the others to live.''

''But I alone cannot speak for them. Awaken them and you will find out for yourselves that they are worthy human beings and should be granted life,'' Bimily pleaded.

''If we leave them in their current state of sleep, they will die peacefully and it will be painless. If we bring them back now and are not convinced by your words or theirs, knowing that they are to die will cause them great anguish.'' This time it was Menadees who spoke.

Realizing that she must speak more convincingly than ever before in her life, Bimily began. ''Shunlar is the child of Alglooth, and Cloonth is her foster-mother. How can you say she is abomination when her blood and ours is mingled?'' At the mention of their names the Elders suddenly became interested. Several people could be heard murmuring off to the side.

''She is Alglooth's child? How is it that Alglooth fathered a child? That was never supposed to have happened,'' grumbled Leatha.

''Pardon me for saying it, but if you had not chosen to leave the outside world and sequester yourselves in this valley, you would know that Alglooth had mated with a woman from the Valley of Great Trees.'' Bimily bowed her head, hoping her tone of voice was humble enough. When she ventured a glance at her mother, Filomena's face was pale.

Leatha spoke again, her voice impassive. ''Nevertheless, she cannot be allowed to live. It is unnatural for her to be alive. You know all of our kind were appalled when the mating between Grazelea and the wizard occurred; she who had been the last dragon alive among men, the one we could not convince to leave behind her dragon form and become a shapechanger because she was so old. She thought she would live out her days in seclusion.

''Even we were surprised with the strength of Banant's heinous spell. When it was discovered that Grazelea had given birth to two children, some of us were determined to prevent them from having children of their own. Some of us did not believe they would try,'' concluded Leatha.

''Do you mean that you were responsible for their first child's death?'' asked Bimily, horrified.

''No. The poison in the stones, the result of the hideous weapons the human wizards had invented, did our work for us. However, once it was known that a child had come from their union, to assure that there were no further children we placed a spell on Alglooth and Cloonth. It didn't occur to us that Alglooth would seek another mate outside the confines of Stiga. He wasn't supposed to leave,'' Leatha said with finality.

''There appears to have been a flaw in the spell,'' Bimily blurted out before she could stop herself. Praying they would take her comment at face value, she further hoped they would think she was criticizing their shortsightedness. She had suddenly become afraid of what they might do if they found out that since Alglooth fathered Shunlar, he and Cloonth had had six children of their own. Even worse, what might they do if they were to find out about Shunlar's child? Bimily felt as if her blood were turning to ice in her veins as she waited.

The Three Elders conferred for several minutes before Menadees softly replied, "It seems we have disclosed more information than you needed to know. The abomination we speak of has to do with Banant of Stiga. Because we recognized his taint about the woman it was assumed by us that she was Banant's offspring, not Alglooth's. This is a different matter altogether, which we must contemplate."

"Continue, Bimily," ordered Leatha. "What news do you bring from the outside world? Do men still fight and kill one another as well as beings they don't understand?"

"I am sad to report *that* part of human nature has not changed. The Feralmon of the southern Kalaven Desert are currently being threatened by people from the north who settled near the sea in a place they call Tonnerling."

"You also mentioned the Valley of Great Trees. I take it men have settled there as well. How fares Stiga? Is it under the control of Banant's evil offspring?" asked Leatha.

"Stiga has been abandoned for centuries. Banant's last-known descendant was killed by the explosion of his Lifestone as it rejected him, but that happened in Vensunor. It was a death I myself witnessed, as did Shunlar, Alglooth, and Cloonth. When it exploded two slivers from it pierced Shunlar and Cloonth's arms, which they discovered much later. That must be the taint you recognized in Shunlar, the piece of Lifestone in her right forearm!" At the mention of this, a louder murmur traveled around the room. Menadees raised his hand for quiet and urged Bimily to continue once everyone settled down.

"The cities I mentioned are where those who fled Stiga settled. There is another, a great walled city called Vensunor near the banks of the Thrale River. Alglooth and Cloonth knew Shunlar would someday seek out humans, so they began to introduce her to living among full humans when she was still a child. It was in Vensunor that we met and struck up a friendship. She is loyal and brave, and I will spend my last breath to convince you that she must live." Bimily had become pale in the last few minutes.

The Three Elders stared at Bimily impassively, waiting for her to continue. The great hall remained silent behind her as if it had emptied.

"These four people brought me here so that I could be restored to health, knowing it was the only way to save my life. Can you not do the same for them? Give them their lives," Bimily begged.

Leatha fixed Bimily with a cold stare before speaking. "When we chose to live here in Vash Darlon, sequestered from the world as you put it, we did so to preserve our remaining lives. Our kind could no longer coexist in the world of men. They looked upon us as demons, hunting us down and killing us. We decided, with the exception of Grazelea, to become shapechangers and never again to take on the body of the dragon. All other animals were permitted, but not our true form. We vowed that if one of us did take on the form of a dragon, the punishment would be total loss of powers.

"We have all felt the existence of a dragon in the world and thought it to be you, since you are the only one of us who remains alive of those few who left Vash Darlon. Now that we have heard your story we are inclined to believe that it was not you. Because you returned to us of your own accord, we were willing to listen to your story before pronouncing sentence upon you, but understand this, you were brought before us today to be stripped of your shapechanging abilities." Leatha's words echoed in Bimily's head, and she suddenly felt very cold.

"What you have told us about Alglooth fathering a

child is most unexpected. If this woman, Shunlar, is truly his offspring, it must be she whom we have felt taking on the dragon's body. It cannot be permitted to continue,'' Leatha announced with finality.

Upon hearing Leatha's smug tone, anger replaced Bimily's fear. Unable to contain it, she shouted, ''Who are you that you pronounce life or death on another as easily as swatting a fly? How can you justify killing her? Is it for her human nature or her dragon nature that she must die? Or is it jealousy?''

Leatha was out of her seat at those words. She stood over Bimily and peered down at her from the dais with hatred as she raised her fist to strike her. Before she could, Menadees grabbed her arm from behind. Leatha jumped at his touch and turned on him.

Menadees released her arm and stepped back several paces. ''She has posed excellent questions, dear Leatha. We three must confer before we can answer. Shall we retire now and contemplate?'' His calm voice had an immediate effect. Leatha straightened and turned her attention back to Bimily.

''Forgive me. I seem to have lost my temper. We will need time to think over all you have told us. Several days, I believe. We will send word when we are ready. In that time your friends will suffer no harm, but they must remain in their sleep. Go now and wait for our summons.'' With a curt nod Leatha walked sedately from the great hall, followed by Menadees and Thricia.

As soon as they were gone, people rushed forward to gather around Bimily. She was welcomed back and given hope for her friends' future, but their many kind words offered little comfort. Bimily could not help but feel frightened.

Though much of her strength had been restored, Bimily had been shaken by the audience more than she imagined possible. She leaned heavily on her father as they walked from the great hall to their home. Once she had rested she asked to be taken to see her friends. Reluctantly, Bresia took her to the underground chambers where Shunlar, Loff, Ranth, and Avek lay in a deep sleep. In separate rooms, similar to the one Bimily had been in, they appeared to be comfortable and resting peacefully.

At Shunlar's bedside Bimily tried to communicate directly to her with a mind-touch but was unable to because of the strength of the spell. Not knowing what else to do, Bimily remained beside her friend for hours, worrying, occasionally crying from sheer, helpless frustration. Finally, long after dark her mother appeared at the doorway.

"Daughter, it is late in the night. You have been here all day without food or water. If you don't come away to eat and rest, all of our good healing work will be for naught. No harm will come to your friends, I promise. What good can come of making yourself ill again?" Filomena held out her hand to her. Accepting her mother's words, Bimily reluctantly followed her from the chamber.

Seventeen

Shortly after Bimily left, a procession of eight people bearing torches entered the underground chambers. It was the Three Elders accompanied by an ancient man named Erroless. He had been the First Elder until his advanced age had led him to step down from the post. Though mentally alert, Erroless became easily fatigued, thus no one had been surprised when he had announced his desire to pass his duties on to a younger person. In addition, each Elder brought along an assistant, someone they trusted, who would not merely observe as the four captives were questioned and examined, but would also be instrumental in helping to reach a fair decision about their futures.

The fact that Shunlar was the daughter of Alglooth interested all of them greatly, having sparked several heated discussions before questioning even began. Leatha had been ready to pronounce a death sentence on Shunlar when she mistakenly thought Shunlar to be Banant's descendant. In fact, that was the reason Erroless had been asked to join them. Menadees was against her death and Thricia was reluctant to oppose Leatha. Needing another mind to make a decision about Shunlar, Erroless was consulted. Ultimately it was Erroless who saved her life.

The piece of corruption from the past, which Shunlar carried in her arm and which also placed her in danger of forfeiting her life, would be the focus of their investigation. Entering the chamber the Elders and their assistants formed a circle around the narrow bed where Shunlar slept, her chest rising and falling in what appeared to be a peaceful slumber. One by one they closed their eyes and matched their breathing patterns with hers. Soon they were able to see the young woman's body floating gracefully before them in an upright position.

She appeared to be wearing a hooded cloak that completely enveloped her, covering even her hands and feet. A quick flick of Erroless's hand and the cloak dropped to reveal a stunning half-human, half-dragon female. Dressed in a sleeveless tunic and leather breeches, she extended her multicolored wings slowly as she hovered in the air. Her wings and arms, from shoulders to elbows, were covered with tiny scales that glistened in the light of the torches. Her eyes were the color of dark emeralds with gold and amber flecks. Her white hair was swept back in a warrior's braid. Though her eyes were open, she was not aware of any of the people who scrutinized her. Shunlar continued to float upon the air, slowly rotating before them.

Erroless knew that he looked upon Shunlar as she appeared when she changed her shape. Though she was much taller than he had expected, there was no indication that she had changed herself into a dragon.

Several of the people in the circle simply stared as tears trickled down their faces, struck by the beauty and blending of Shunlar's two natures, the pain of their loss visible. Leatha had no tears. Fury and vengeance were the emotions playing across her face.

Another quick motion from Erroless, and Shunlar's skin became transparent, making her bones visible to them. Someone sucked in a breath upon seeing her right forearm. There between the two bones was a luminous glow, the piece of Lifestone that had become part of her bone. Though the very core of light it cast was a sickly, greenish color, it was outlined by a golden aura that effectively encapsulated the evil-tainted piece. Everyone seemed instantly relieved.

To this point no one had tried communicating directly

with Shunlar. Leatha, ever the impatient one, told Erroless she wanted to initiate a mind-touch so that she could begin questioning her. Erroless was so involved with investigating the physical features of Shunlar's body that he nearly let Leatha proceed. But something at the back of his memory stopped her just as she reached toward Shunlar's mind.

"Do you recall, Leatha, the cloak this young woman was wearing when we first encountered her on this plane?" Erroless interrupted.

"I do. What of it?" Leatha returned, not bothering to hide her annoyance with him.

"Think, impatient one," he chided, not caring that his words would inflame her. "She is protected. The cloak should have told you that or are you so blinded by your own agenda that you refuse to see the obvious?"

Leatha's eyes blazed. Her temper flared so hot that she could no longer control herself. Suddenly the air around her shimmered red and standing in Leatha's place was an enormous black panther. Her howl rent the air with a savage sound. Not to be outdone, Erroless also changed his shape. His cat was even larger. With ears laid back the two animals hissed and spat, circling, striking out at one another, claws fully extended. Erroless pounced, knocking Leatha to the ground. His maw wrapped around her throat, his huge back claws poised to rake open her belly. Leatha moaned a low growl admitting her defeat.

Are you ready to listen to reason and put aside your hatred? Erroless asked with a mind-touch.

Yes, she answered.

The air around them shimmered with color. As they returned to human form, Leatha's anger cooled, for the moment. Because Leatha chose to spend much of her time in the shape of a black panther, its temperamental nature took precedence. Quick to anger, quick to jump to conclusions, she was also quick to change when she recognized she was wrong. Leatha apologized to Erroless as the others watched. Menadees smiled at her with relief when their eyes met.

Returning to his place in the circle around Shunlar, Erroless explained, "The protective spell this young woman is cloaked with would most probably have seriously injured Leatha as soon as she had initiated a mind-touch. The only way we can safely question her is to bring her mind out of the dreamless sleep spell." The entire circle bowed their heads in acquiescence.

Erroless approached Shunlar carefully and softly ordered, "You who are bound by the Spell of Reposing, hear my words. Waken only your mind. My voice alone will you hear. Your answers will be truthful or none."

As the words began to seep into her, pulling her awareness up from the deep spell of sleep, Shunlar blinked and opened her eyes. She could see an elderly man step out of the thick fog that surrounded her. Looking closer she knew that he was covering himself with a strong protective spell by the way his image rippled, as if she observed him through the heat of a flame. Seven others who were similarly cloaked stepped from the fog to encircle her. A different color sparked around each person's edges, similar to the blue light she remembered seeing around Bimily when she changed her shape. It was then that Shunlar remembered the journey, her friends, and the last thing that had happened to her. She became frightened.

Recognizing her fear, the old man bowed and introduced himself. "I am called Erroless. And you are?"

"Shunlar." Reassured by his voice, she bowed to him.

"Who are your parents, child?"

"Marleah is my mother. Alglooth is my father," she answered instantly.

He asked, "How is it that you are able to change your shape?"

Before she could stop herself, Shunlar answered, "It was nothing I learned. When I became pregnant with my son I began to change physically." *Should I have told him of my son?* she asked herself as soon as the words were spoken.

His brows went up. "You have a son?"

"Yes," she answered immediately.

"Can you tell me who it is that became a dragon then?"

Again, before she could think, Shunlar blurted out, "Cloonth, when she became pregnant." *What is wrong with my tongue?*

"Cloonth has had a child?" The way he blurted out the question told Shunlar that Erroless knew who Cloonth was. It soon became obvious from the expression on his face that he had not wanted to disclose this bit of information either. The murmur coming from the people in the room had distracted Erroless. Exasperated, he quickly silenced them so that he could hear Shunlar's answer.

"Because of her size she managed to have six at once," Shunlar answered. "But once the children were born she regained her usual appearance."

"Six you say?" Erroless chuckled. It was becoming clearer to him that the spell they had placed on Cloonth and Alglooth so long ago had grown too old to be effective. He knew Leatha must be hopping mad hearing that the half-dragon couple had had six more offspring.

Unsure of why she was blurting out this information to Erroless, she asked, "Why is it that when you ask me questions I must answer?"

"My dear, your mind is awake but your body is not. You answer all the questions I put to you truthfully because I have placed a Spell of Compulsion over you. I am sorry to have to do that, but if I were to awaken you fully, you might be able to counteract the spell. And, as I have determined that your mind is protected in some way, I had no wish to come to harm, nor risk the well-being of my companions either. They can hear you, but you can hear only my voice for now."

Remembering her trap-warning, Shunlar reached to touch her neck. The hairs were flat, as she expected them to be. Erroless was telling the truth, she could not help but answer truthfully, nor could she retaliate in any way while under his spell. What he did not know, however, was that she wasn't as helpless as he believed. Now that her mind was awake and she realized she was a captive, Shunlar acted. Undetected, and with little effort, she split her awareness, sending a part of herself into a gray, featureless, plane that she was familiar with, to seek help from her father.

The Spell of Compulsion did only that—compel her to speak the truth when asked a question. It didn't prevent her from asking questions of her own or from acting on her own behalf. Neither Erroless nor any of the others who were present suspected Shunlar might possess the knowledge that enabled her to send a message for help while being questioned. It had been such a very long time since they had encountered anyone from the outside world that they were lax, something Shunlar took advantage of.

"But why put a spell on me at all?" the part of her that remained in the room asked innocently. Then she remembered the others, and asked, "Where are my friends? Have they been kept like me in this dreamless state?"

"Let me reassure you that the three men who were with you are held by the spell of sleep, as you have been. No harm has come to them."

"We have all come to seek your help, after all, and it would do me no good to tell half-truths or lie to you. What purpose would that serve?" Shunlar had his attention.

Erroless laughed again at her honesty, shaking his head. "You say to me while under the Spell of Compulsion that you would not lie, and that is the truth. However, I cannot be sure it would happen that way if you were not held by the spell."

"We traveled here to save the lives of Bimily and Ranth. Please tell me that you are able to help them both." Again the truth.

"You can rest easy. Bimily has been well cared for and grows stronger with each passing hour. As for the one called Ranth, we have not learned the nature of his affliction because we have not yet examined him. What can you tell me of it?" he asked.

"Ranth was scarred by his cousin in an initiation ritual with ancient words that were cut into the flesh of his back. I am certain he will die if they are not removed or altered in some way. Surely you will be able to decipher the markings."

A look of extreme consternation knit Erroless's brows. "Do you tell me that you are able to read the words on his back?"

"Yes. They are the symbols *azkrey gaht.*" Speaking the words, Shunlar saw the effect they had on the people around her. The Three Elders and their assistants became nearly frantic. Only after much pleading from Erroless did they quiet down.

"Who taught you these words?" he asked her with some dread to his voice.

"My father, Alglooth, and foster-mother, Cloonth," she answered truthfully again.

The seven others seemed to be rebelling against Erroless. As Shunlar watched, one woman spoke to them, her eyes filled with fury. Her words, were doubtless furious as well. Though Shunlar could not hear her, she knew this woman was not on her side.

Desperate, Shunlar began to plead with Erroless, "Please, we don't have time to waste arguing. Allow me to hear what the others are saying. You are Bimily's people, and you have ancient knowledge. If you are telling me now that you aren't able to help Ranth, set us free so that we can find someone who can, for Ranth may be closer to death than we suspect." Her words were not merely truthful, but they conveyed the deep love she felt for Ranth.

"While Ranth sleeps, the spell is arrested, so time will not affect him. But tell me, why should we save Ranth's life? Who is he to you?" Erroless asked.

"He is the father of my child."

Hoping he was not already too late, Erroless enclosed Shunlar completely in a spell that prevented her from reaching beyond the room where her body slept. She felt the effects and gave him a hard look as her image began to fade.

"Why imprison me like this, for surely you have?" she demanded.

"Do you mean you felt that?" he asked with trepidation.

"Yes," she answered, straining to clamp her mouth tightly shut so that she wouldn't blurt out any more information than she already had. Her control over her words held but her body that lay upon the bed became restless as her shadowy form settled over it.

Erroless released Shunlar from the Spell of Compulsion and sent her back into sleep, not realizing he was only partially successful. The part of her that remained in the room could be returned to the sleep spell, but not the other half of her that had gone in search of Alglooth. She would never let them know that, of course. Just as her form settled back over her sleeping body, her other half returned from its visit with Alglooth in time to watch the group file silently from her side. As soon as she touched her prone body, Shunlar learned all that had transpired while this half of her had been gone.

Anger welled up in her that she kept at bay. *Best not to let on that I am no longer under their control. First I need to know what they are doing to Ranth, Avek, and Loff.* However she tried, Shunlar could not pass the barrier that had been placed around her. Unable to leave the room to check on her friends, she tried to contact them on the dream plane. She soon found out that, too, was impossible since they were all covered by a Spell of Dreamless Sleep. In fact, there was little she could do but wait.

The group of eight that had surrounded Shunlar worked swiftly to enclose Ranth within a shell of secrecy. Once they made contact with his Lifestone, touching him was permitted, but only after they reassured it they would inflict no harm.

Unlike their questioning of Shunlar, Ranth was not awakened. It was decided not to question him because, being fully human, he was not deemed worthy. Instead, his shirt was removed and he was turned onto his stomach. Never had any of them seen the scarification on a Feralmon's body. They were both shocked and mesmerized.

For hours the group worked at the mystery of how to remove the letters that were carved into Ranth's back. At last, they determined, with help from his Lifestone, that he had four choices. He must either have them removed by peeling away layers of his skin. Second, he could have the letters changed, something which could only be done by the person who placed them there. Third, he could become someone else by taking another name. Or, finally, he could die and be restored to life by his Lifestone for the symbols to be made impotent.

Eighteen

Six weeks had passed since Dolan and Ariaste had married. The wedding ceremony and banquet had been presided over by Da Winfreyd. Dolan's three sisters, their spouses, and children attended, as did Ariaste's parents along with her three sisters and two brothers. The most anticipated guest, Dolan's sister Klarissa, sent her regrets by letter, promising to come soon to meet her brother's bride.

Klarissa knew she would not be considered a welcome guest by her family, nor Ariaste's family if they were the class-conscious people she remembered them to be. The fact that she had married Gwernz, a man who had been a captive, made her a pariah. So she decided it was best to wait until after the wedding, something that did not surprise Dolan, but he was disappointed nonetheless.

But these six weeks had put a tremendous strain on Dolan, for Ariaste continued to behave like a very young, frightened girl. Except for their wedding night, which as far as he was concerned had been a total disaster, he had not attempted to approach her bed but once.

As the weeks passed and she saw how Dolan truly attempted to please her, Ariaste became a bit calmer, but she still jumped and cowered when he came into the room. She had known about what was expected of her in the marriage bed, but considering that she learned about it from her mother, she hadn't expected to like it.

Being the eldest girl in her family and the first from

her circle of friends to marry, Ariaste had no other women near to her age to explain things to her. Young girls in Tonnerling led a very sheltered life. But now that she was a married woman and away from her mother's severe scrutiny, Ariaste was determined to do things her way. What that way was, she had no idea.

It was evening, and Ariaste had eaten alone, again. She was sitting patiently before the fire, watching the patterns the flames made, remembering how she had cried herself to sleep last night. Why wasn't Dolan here beside her? Was it something she had done to keep him away? The last time he had "visited" her in her bed-chamber, she had again cried when he had finished, and he abruptly left. But that was what her mother had told her to do. Perhaps that was it. Perhaps she didn't need to cry so loudly, or so much. Perhaps, she dared to think, she didn't even need to cry at all!

She jumped up as the doors opened and cool evening air rushed into the room. Dolan stood in the doorway, excusing himself for interrupting, preparing to leave her alone while he grabbed a quick supper in the kitchen.

"Husband," she began shyly, "would you mind if I joined you?"

He was surprised by her request and secretly delighted. Until this moment she had not shown much interest in him or being around him, and, being busy, he had not made much time for her either.

"Please do. I would much rather eat in your company than alone." His smile was tender as he held his hand out to her.

"I have taken the liberty of asking Cook to set you a place at table in the dining hall." She looked at him for approval. He smiled again as he put her hand in the crook of his arm and slowly led her to the hall.

They sat together by candlelight, Dolan eating and talking, telling her of his day, Ariaste listening intently. The two servants who stood in the shadows exchanged quiet glances, nodding approval. Something was changing here.

Dolan also noticed something was different in Ariaste.

After several long silences, he cleared his throat. "Would you kindly leave us?" he said to the servants. They bowed and quietly exited the room.

"I'm afraid it must be terribly boring for you to listen to me babble on about something you have no interest in," he said once they were alone.

"Not at all. Please tell me more of what you and my father plan, husband."

"Ariaste, you can be honest with me. I don't need to speak of these things, for spirits know, I have been going over the details of this business all day with Lord Raspin." He blew an exasperated breath and propped his head up with his hand, rubbing his eyes.

She blushed upon hearing him call upon the spirits. "I . . . I didn't mean to upset you. If you d . . . don't wish to talk about it, we can change the subject," she stammered, bowing her head, fearful.

What had he done to produce this fear in her, he wondered? Just when they seemed to actually be conversing at last. All of their dinners and subsequent evenings together had been so painfully quiet—she never venturing to speak unless he asked a question. It was becoming very tedious. Had he made the biggest mistake of his life by marrying a woman as young as Ariaste?

Not to mention that their intimate encounters had produced such a prodigious volume of tears afterward that he had no desire to approach her again. Secretly, he was afraid that he had injured her in some way, and he was too embarrassed to ask. Yet she seemed more at ease tonight, and it gave him a glimmer of hope.

"We can discuss anything you want to," he reassured her in his most soothing voice. "Here, have some wine." He poured a glass and offered it to her.

"Oh, I couldn't. Mother says I sho . . ."

Dolan gently cut her off in mid-word. "Ariaste, you are a married woman now and you are fully able to make decisions for yourself. This is our table, in our house. I am your husband, and I offer you this wine. If you want it, by all means accept the cup. If you don't, refusing it will not offend me, I assure you."

Wide-eyed, she took the goblet in a delicate, trembling hand and sipped. That and his words produced the desired effect. She smiled, sitting up a little straighter before setting the cup down on the table. "Please continue, husband. I find what you are saying most interesting." Then she blushed at her own boldness and looked down again.

"Ariaste. Wife, look at me. Is something wrong that you color and turn your eyes away? There are only the two of us in this room, and I would be happy to continue our discussion, especially if you wish it. Do you wish it?"

She raised her head slowly and took a deep breath. "I do wish it."

"Good. Now what was I talking about?" He asked, laughing. A tiny laugh bubbled up from her as well.

"If I may say so, you were speaking of the difficulties you seemed to be encountering with my father. Please remember that I have been listening to my father speak of such things as shipbuilding and cargo for more years than you. Perhaps I can offer some ways to deal more effectively with him in the future. He *can* be persuaded if you know the ways to do it." She smiled, suddenly not quite so shy.

Dolan grinned widely. He enjoyed this side of his young wife immensely. He began explaining that her father had been approached by the city fathers to construct a fleet of ships for the purpose of transporting troops downriver to Kalaven. Dolan wasn't sure if such a thing could be done since none of the men from Tonnerling knew if timber was available so far south. Their only source of information came from traders who traveled overland, and most Tonnerlingans said they couldn't be relied on for accuracy.

"Why not send your own delegation of men whom you trust with the traders to seek information? That way you will be assured of their loyalty," she offered, boldly now that she had Dolan's ear. And from the looks of him, his full attention.

"You know your idea of sending men to scout ahead

for timber and a suitable site is intriguing. Please continue,'' Dolan offered.

''Have you given thought to them carrying messenger doves to relay a message back once information is obtained?'' she asked, matter-of-factly.

He was clearly astonished. It was as if she were reading his mind, and he urged her to say more. Continue they did until, yawning, Dolan rose from the table and began to blow out the candles.

Ariaste's face drained of color when he held his hand out to her. She swallowed hard, took it, and stood up, her jaw tight, her shoulders raised. Dolan was once more puzzled by her fearful pose.

''I will escort you to your bedchamber, wife,'' he announced softly.

All the way down the hall she refused to look at him. Her breath was short, and by the time they reached their suites, she was shaking.

''May I ask you a question?'' he ventured.

''Of course you may come in,'' she answered breathlessly, and curtsied.

''That wasn't my question.''

''Oh, I didn't mean to presume . . . that is . . . I . . .'' Now she was on the verge of tears, and he had to do something.

''Come with me,'' he said without thinking. Grabbing hold of her hand he turned and headed for the stairway at the end of the long hall. At the top he turned the key and threw his shoulder against the thick door. It scraped open onto a balcony that extended the length of the house. Ariaste had never known it existed until this moment, and she looked around curiously at the narrow walkway, marked by a path of bootprints the length of the balcony.

''What is this?'' she asked.

''My father would come and pace here when he had something bothering him. My sister Klarissa found herself here many times while she waited for Gwernz to return and marry her. In the last six weeks, I, too, have come here to think and worry.'' Dolan stood close behind her, the warmth of his body very near hers.

"What cause do you have for worry? Surely the business dealings with my father are not so important that they should keep you awake . . ." Her voice trailed off. He was touching her, caressing her shoulders. She suppressed the urge to stiffen, instead relaxing beneath his hands. But her breath quickened.

"Ariaste, why do you cry so when we bed together? Do I hurt you that much? I must know if we are to continue. I thought you seemed to experience pleasure from my touch, but when you cry afterward . . ."

Had she heard him say, "if we are to continue?" She blinked tears away and tried to answer through her constricted throat. "Is that not what women are supposed to do, afterward?" she finally got out.

"I haven't known other women," he whispered into her hair, breathing in the scent of her. He turned her around and kissed her passionately, a kiss she returned much to his amazement. "Do you want to cry? Does it make you so unhappy to be with me?" he asked, genuine concern in his voice as he pressed her against his chest.

"I have wanted to laugh or cry out with joy, but my mother assured me that a man wants to hear and see tears afterward."

"Not this man. Why ever would she tell you such a thing?"

"Many's the night that I recall hearing the crying from my mother's room. But I also remember other noises first, like shouting and slapping. Horrible noises." Dolan listened as she told him of how things were between her parents, and then the abuse she and her siblings suffered at their mother's hands. From this night on he would forever look upon her parents with different eyes. Da Winfreyd had warned him that the woman was powerful, possibly dangerous, but this?

"This is unbearable. Never did my father raise his hand to me or my sisters, nor my mother." He grew quiet for a moment, gently stroking her hair, before asking, "Why would anyone want to be cruel to her own child?'' She had no answer for him. Ariaste stood with her head against Dolan's chest, listening to his words and the beating of his heart.

''I think I understand what you meant when you said I must make my own decisions about what I want, Dolan,'' she finally said. They were both trembling in the wind, holding tight to one another in the darkness.

''Husband, this is such a cold, sad balcony. I pray I am never again the cause for your pacing here in the night. Come and I will warm you. There will be no crying from tonight on, only tears of happiness, if any at all,'' she promised.

He squeezed her tightly. ''Sweet Ariaste. I promise I will try to produce only tears of joy and laughter from you.'' Kissing her fingertips and taking her hand firmly in his, he led the way down the stairs to their suite.

The next morning they were awakened by Patia, Ariaste's maid, pulling open the heavy curtains. When she saw that her mistress was not alone, but that she and Dolan were wrapped in a tight embrace in the tangle of bedclothes, she gasped, curtsied, and ran from the room, nearly bursting at the seams with the news. This was the first morning that their young master and mistress had woken together in the same bed since their marriage six weeks ago.

Later at breakfast, Cook herself served the morning repast, eager to see from the expression on her young master's face if what Patia had reported was true. But neither Dolan nor Ariaste seemed to notice the smiles, whispers, and glances of the servants around them. They had eyes only for one another.

After kissing Ariaste's hands yet again, Dolan left the courtyard reluctantly, looking over his shoulder twice before he had walked the length of the yard and reached the gates. As happy as he was, Dolan felt guilty this morning. The one thing he had not mentioned to Ariaste last night was that he had volunteered to be part of the party leaving Tonnerling within the week to search for a suitable site on which to build ships.

Last night they had had their first real conversation—

ever! He had been so delighted that she spoke to him as an equal, with none of the reticence that usually accompanied her answers. No, last night she began talking to *him,* at last! She even offered a most practical suggestion of sending messenger doves with the men who looked for suitable trees for shipbuilding. Just last week he had suggested that same strategy to the council. He hadn't wanted to interrupt her and tell her that he would be one of those men. Before last night he had wanted to get away. But that had changed.

Dolan hurried through the day, eager to be home and in Ariaste's company. When at lunch, several of his younger friends chided him for being so cheerful after weeks of sulking, he nearly blurted out the reason for his happiness. But seeing the look of caution on his father-in-law's face, he simply toasted, "To my bride, Ariaste!"

Excusing himself early from the day's meetings, Dolan made his way to the Avenue of Jewelers. He had decided a gift might ease the news of his going away, and he had already chosen it in his mind: a long strand of pink pearls that matched the choker he had given Ariaste as a betrothal necklace, fashioned by the same maker. The package secure in his pocket, Dolan hurried home.

Upon entering the courtyard he recognized Lady Tumnia's carriage, and his mood changed. *Ach, I pray we don't have to endure her presence for too long,* he thought to himself as he hurried up the stairs and let himself in the kitchen entrance. The scene that greeted him was not what he expected. Cook and three of the maids, one of them Ariaste's personal maid, Patia, stood whispering in hushed tones, wringing their hands. They jumped when they realized it was Dolan coming in the door not Janow the doorman. All of them clamped their lips tight and curtsied. He bowed and gave them a puzzled look.

"What is it?" he asked, suddenly concerned. "Is Ariaste ill?"

"No, Master Dolan," Cook answered quietly, closing her lips in a firm line.

"Then tell me, what is wrong? Does Lady Tumnia turn you all mute?" At his question Patia paled and clamped her hand over her mouth. She had been Ariaste's maid since she was a child of twelve and Ariaste five. Patia was devoted to her young mistress and Dolan didn't like seeing Patia's frightened expression.

"Where is my wife?" he demanded loudly.

"In your suite, Master Dolan," answered Cook quickly. "You'd best hurry, sir."

Panicked, he ran from the kitchen and down the hallway to his and Ariaste's suite. Through the partially opened door he heard Lady Tumnia warning viciously, "Your insolence will cost you, girl." Not bothering to knock he quietly slipped into the room. Ariaste was facing the door and when she saw Dolan she opened her mouth to call out to him. But, as Dolan stepped into the room, he watched in disbelief as Tumnia slapped her daughter across the face.

"Lady Tumnia, by what right do you strike my wife?" His voice made the woman jump and emit such a snarl that Dolan thought she might fly across the room and hurl herself on him.

She looked back at her daughter, then at Dolan, and a calm rippled over her. Dolan knew immediately she had just covered herself with a spell of some kind that would have gone undetected if he were an ordinary man. Dolan mumbled a phrase under his breath, covering him and Ariaste with a subtle protective spell, aware that Lady Tumnia could not see it.

"Why I was merely patting her cheek," Tumnia began.

"No, that is not what I saw. If it were so, Ariaste wouldn't have a red handprint across her face."

"But I thought you had done this to her!" She raised her voice in accusation.

"Enough. I'll have no more lies. This is my house, and you have no right to touch her," Dolan warned.

"She is my daughter and that gives me every right," Lady Tumnia snarled at him.

But Dolan refused to show her an ounce of fear. He had been raised by a wizard, after all, and Da Winfreyd had let him know just how powerful a man his father had been. Until two months ago, much of Dolan's knowledge had lain dormant. Da Winfreyd had shown him, among other things, how to set a strong compulsion on another using merely his voice.

"I am her husband and she is under my protection now. You will never strike her again. Leave us." The words of the spell floated upon the air, Dolan alone able to see them.

He watched in fascination as each letter split in front of him then fast as a breath, entered Lady Tumnia's ears. The woman's eyes were wide with shock and as the last word disappeared into her ears, she clapped her hands over them. She was bent over in what looked like pain when suddenly she stood bolt upright and shuddered. Her hands fell to her sides. Without another word she bowed to Dolan, picked up the cloak she had thrown casually across a chair, nodded to Ariaste, and left.

Ariaste was dumbfounded. Holding her hand against her left cheek, she began to hyperventilate, gasping for breath in loud gulps. Dolan rushed to her side as Patia came running into the room, tears streaming down her face.

"Oh, Mistress," Patia cried out.

"Bring your mistress a brandy," ordered Dolan as he carried Ariaste to the bed, propping several pillows behind her. Only after Ariaste had taken several sips was she calm enough to tell them what happened.

"My mother wanted me to submit to her so she could read my thoughts," Ariaste began, waiting for a sign from Dolan to continue. Patia was holding her breath from the tension.

"What do you suppose she wanted to know?" he asked.

"I am not sure, but I refused her, and never before have I been able to refuse any of her demands on me until today.'' Though her voice trembled, Ariaste held her head high.

''From this day on Lady Tumnia will have no hold over you or your mind. I vow to protect you from her, and I shall,'' Dolan solemnly promised.

''But you don't know what she is capable of,'' protested Ariaste.

''Everyone in my household will be safe from her, never fear,'' he reassured both women in a calm voice. ''It has been a long while since magic of the sort I am about to make has been practiced under this roof. Listen carefully and don't be afraid.''

Dolan stood up and whispered under his breath. He touched his fingertips lightly to his chest, to both ears, then his lips. He slowly turned his hands away from his face, opening his arms in an upward motion.

''As long as I breathe, no harmful spell, no substance from Tumnia or anyone she may send against us can touch Ariaste, any of my blood, or my household. This I vow.'' Again Dolan saw the words as they issued forth from his lips to dance upon the air.

Each servant also heard his spoken Spell of Protection; at the sound of Dolan's words, every person paused, and the words became buried deeply in their memories. Ariaste blinked at Dolan, staring at her husband with a look of awe.

''Oh thank you kindly, Master Dolan.'' Patia was blubbering, all smiles and tears.

''If you don't mind, I wish to speak to your mistress alone,'' Dolan said quietly.

Patia curtsied, then left the room.

Dolan returned to sit beside Ariaste. Very slowly he took her hands in his and kissed her fingertips. Then he pulled a velvet pouch from his jacket pocket, placing it in her hands. She opened the bag and pulled out the strand of pink pearls. ''Oh, they are so beautiful,'' she gasped.

''Ariaste, I must tell you something that I hope will not be too upsetting. Last night I couldn't bring myself to tell you that I will be going on that expedition to scout for a place to build ships. My decision to leave was based on how we were not seeming to fit together as a married couple. I thought giving you some months of time to become accustomed to living here would help. Now I find that I do not want to leave you behind, but I'm afraid it can't be changed."

"No," Ariaste gasped dropping the pearls. "You don't know what she will do to me if I am alone." She trembled in fear, her lips gone white. "Take me with you. I beg you, Dolan, don't leave me behind." Her hands tightly squeezed his arm.

"It's much too dangerous for a woman to go on this expedition. No, I couldn't possibly allow it, and I would never forgive myself if anything happened to you."

"Something will happen to me, at her hands, if you leave me behind," she cried tearfully.

"Calm yourself. We'll think of something. I'll send for Da Winfreyd and perhaps he or Brother Boringar will come and stay with you when I am gone," he said.

"No, they are strangers to me. He is an old man who couldn't possibly protect me against her. You must take me with you, please," she begged.

"For now, let me think on it. I will consider it, I promise," he conceded. "Just stop crying. I'm still here, and I'm not going anywhere for at least two weeks." He bent close and kissed her tenderly.

True to his word, Dolan sent for Da Winfreyd. Two days later he arrived. Dolan explained what had happened between himself and Lady Tumnia and the subsequent spell he had placed on Ariaste and his household. Though it was strong and seemed to be foolproof, Da Winfreyd agreed that Ariaste would be in danger without Dolan. It was decided that she must leave with her husband, in disguise, of course.

NINETEEN

THE EARLY MORNING RAINSTORM SEEMED TO drone on and on with its never-ending spatter. Spring in the mountains was a miserable time to travel, Dolan decided. Even their heavily oiled canvas tent was beginning to smell of mildew from seven solid days of rain. Dry firewood had been impossible to find these last three days, and he was beginning to wonder if they would ever be truly warm again.

Having Ariaste with him on this adventure had been sheer joy. Not one word of complaint had passed her lips; he couldn't say the same for himself or the other men. Did she keep silent simply because she was the only woman, he wondered? She seemed to truly enjoy being with him, slogging through the endless mud, dripping wet at the end of the day, shivering with the cold as she threw her clothes off to clamber naked beneath the piles of cold blankets and furs. Not one word of complaint.

Her physical strength was something he hadn't expected either. Ariaste's mother had insisted that Ariaste learn to ride astride and as well as sidesaddle. Begrudgingly, Dolan had to admit he was grateful to the woman for something.

Since all the men were dressed similarly in waterproof clothing that included large hats and heavy woolen cloaks, it was easy to hide his wife's true identity. Dressed as a young groom, aided of course, by an illusion cast over her by Dolan, Ariaste was perfectly disguised.

Dolan had told only one other member of the expedition that Ariaste was coming along, but not how. Haukkon was not happy in the least hearing Dolan's decision to bring along his young wife, but nothing he said seemed likely to change Dolan's mind. Dolan feared for her safety and when he told his friend that Lady Tumnia was a wizard, Haukkon's face paled, and he agreed to keep silent about Ariaste.

The morning of their departure, when Haukkon saw Dolan with only one groom in tow, he brightened. Perhaps his words did have some impact after all. The first night, however, he became suspicious when Dolan and his groom slept together in their small tent. The second night, he was sure he heard laughter, and a woman's laughter at that. The fourth morning, Dolan announced to all the men at breakfast that indeed, he had deceived them. Ariaste stepped from their tent into their midst in the bright-morning sun, unmistakably a woman and not the young groom they had seen.

The leader of the expedition, Captain Looren, was outraged. "What do you mean by this charade?" he demanded loudly. "This is no place for a woman. We are all men, some of us yet single, others of us soldiers. We have serious work to be done, and she will hamper us with complaining and special needs. After traveling this far we cannot take her back. Our army is depending on us to meet them on a specific date. You and she will return at once and you will do so alone," he barked, obviously a man used to being obeyed.

"My regrets, Captain Looren, but we will not. She is my wife and therefore my responsibility, and I say she comes with us. Ariaste is well accustomed to riding, as these last three days attest." He gestured to Ariaste, and she came to his side.

"Wife, how do you fare so far?" Dolan asked her.

"I would be lying if I told you I was not tired, but the pace so far has not been overly difficult. I assure you, Captain, all of you, that I have no desire to slow any of this company down. I will do my part as I have done so far.''

It was true, now that they remembered, Dolan's groom had taken care of both horses and his equipment these past three days on the trail. There had been no complaints. In fact, ''Ari'' had made himself a very useful groom, happy to do more than his share of the work.

One of the men, a seasoned soldier named Balint, laughed and offered, ''If I can be as cheerful as Ari, er . . . excuse me, madam, Ariaste, after riding all day, I say let him, I mean her, stay. I'd much rather look at her face once in a while than stare at your ugly mugs for the rest of this trip. No offense, of course, young lady, young sir.'' He tipped his hat to Ariaste and Dolan.

''Captain, my wife will continue to perform her duties as groom or wood gatherer, or whatever is assigned to her, as equally as the rest of us. I will, of course, accompany her whenever possible. No one will accuse either of us of shirking or not fulfilling our duties.''

''Captain, I wish to be useful to you on this expedition as well,'' Ariaste announced. ''I know that the purpose of our travel is to find and mark suitable sites for shipbuilding. My father's business is shipbuilding and since I was a small child I have heard him discuss his business. All of my knowledge is at your disposal.'' She bowed to the captain, and his face reddened, his scowl deepened, but he returned the courtesy.

She had made an instant hit with most of the men, and Ariaste settled into life on the trail. The younger men were in awe of her; none would ever have suspected a woman could be in the company of men and maintain such a pleasant disposition. Some of the older men, except for Balint, eyed her with suspicion, as if she might suddenly turn on them, waiting for her to make a mistake, or complain in such a way that they could say, ''I told you so.'' But even in the miserable rain, her laughter punctuated the air regularly; her smile was readily given to all.

When at last they did reach the banks of the Thrale, it was in a driving downpour that had effectively drowned out the sound of the fast-flowing river. Ariaste and Dolan sat beside one another upon their tired horses staring in disbelief at the raging water. Swollen from the spring thaw and the recent rains, it looked ready to overrun its banks. As they silently observed their first glimpse of the river they planned to transport troops down, both of them were suddenly afraid. What could the leaders of Tonnerling have been thinking? There was no ship that could navigate these waters! If all parts of the Thrale were this treacherous, then the plan would have to be discarded.

Neither of them heard Captain Looren approach in the rain, but their horses stamped and shifted; the captain's mount was an old stallion who gave way to no other animal, much like his rider. As the downpour continued, the captain gestured at them to follow. The sixteen riders proceeded silently in single file down a game trail, dripping and miserable in the cold rain.

The landscape gradually changed. There were fewer trees this close to the river, and large rock formations became more prevalent. Turning a bend they came upon the cave, which had been formed by a gigantic rock shelf that jutted out from the hillside. Enclosed on three sides, it comfortably housed the riders, their horses, and pack animals. The most welcome aspect of the cave was the enormous pile of firewood that was stacked back against the far wall.

Two fire pits had been dug by previous inhabitants and soon there were two fires blazing. Tripods were assembled and large kettles hung. As the smell of hot stew filled the air, everyone's mood changed considerably. Mugs of hot tea were passed around, warming hands as well as bodies. Someone passed a wineskin.

Ariaste's hands shook as she warmed them on her cup. Sitting near the first fire in nearly a week she took the offered wineskin and expertly aimed a stream into her mouth to the cheers of the men around her. They huddled together shoulder to shoulder near the fire, their clothing steaming as it dried. Her breath, when she laughed, sent a cloud of steam billowing from her mouth.

When Dolan saw it, he was reminded instantly of Shunlar. Where was she now, he wondered? How ironic, he thought, that the first woman he had fallen in love with had also been so at ease in the company of men. Who would have thought Ariaste would seem to be so comfortable under such adverse conditions? Dolan considered himself to be a very lucky man. His smile sparked an inquiring look from Ariaste, but he only reassured her with a quick squeeze of her hand. She smiled back as she flicked a wet strand of hair from her forehead.

The next morning they awoke to the first sun they had seen on the entire journey. Without the sound of the rain, the swollen Thrale River could be heard as it burst and dashed itself against the rocks, careening away downstream. There was a smell of sweetness to the air.

Dressed and breaking their fast, Dolan and Ariaste decided to explore. It took them most of the morning to climb up to a vantage point that gave them a bird's-eye view. Ariaste was thrilled to see the size of the forest that surrounded them. She pointed out cedars, pine, and oak, all excellent woods to consider for the building of ships and they were plentiful. Even Captain Looren would be pleased to hear that news.

Now that the weather had cleared they also saw how close they were to the ruins of a large city that had been built into the mountain. Camped on the plain at the foot of the ruins was a small army. There looked to be hundreds of men. This was part of the force that Captain Looren had told them they would rendezvous with. In the coming weeks more troops would be arriving overland from Tonnerling, after which they would be transported downriver to meet with the remainder of the army, which had wintered farther south, closer to Kalaven.

"Dolan, what are those ruins?" Ariaste asked.

"Have you never heard of Stiga?"

"No. Should I have?" she asked.

"Stiga is the great city where all the civilizations began. Our ancestors came from there. Surely your mother mentioned it to you. Knowing what I do now of her, I am certain she could give us much information about Stiga," Dolan told her.

"You forget, husband, that my mother told me little and used my innocence to gather information about others. Tell me what you know about this place, for I feel an unusual attraction to it." She shuddered, but not in an uncomfortable way.

Dolan put his arm around her shoulder protectively. "Will you open your thoughts to me and permit me to feel what you do? I only want to be sure that you are safe, believe me," he assured her.

With wide eyes she said, "You can do that?" He nodded. "Only if it won't hurt. Promise me it won't hurt," she pleaded.

"Never would I hurt you. Never would I touch your thoughts without your permission." Then he thought to ask, "Did your mother's touch cause pain when she read your thoughts?" With tears in her eyes Ariaste could only nod.

He held her close and they both grew very quiet. For a long time she sobbed against his chest. They stayed that way until finally her tears stopped and Ariaste relaxed. Once she was calm, she whispered, "Tell me what to do."

Dolan opened his mind to her and softly called her name. Her head jerked up. "Did you hear me?"

"Yes. It tickled my ears." Ariaste was grinning.

"That is how it is done when you have the person's permission. Now you try it. Just relax and feel me close beside you. Say my name, but quietly," he instructed. DOLAN boomed in his head. He winced.

That was well done, but try it even quieter, he said patiently. This time he was speaking directly to her mind-to-mind. Ariaste seemed not to notice at first.

Dolan. I heard that, but your lips didn't move, she thought to him.

I know. Neither did yours, he pointed out. Laughing,

they continued in that fashion for some time. Dolan told her the history of Stiga as he instructed her how to temper her communications to him. When they came to the end of the lesson, Dolan asked her to open her mind for the pull she had mentioned to him earlier.

She concentrated and soon there came a feeling like a deep longing. Ariaste's knees went weak; this time she heard the sound of her name being called. Dolan supported her so that she could stand; yet no matter how hard he tried, he could not hear the voice she did.

"What does this mean? I'm frightened," Ariaste said.

"I'll protect you, don't worry. But I'm afraid I can't explain what it is you hear, nor who it could be that calls. I heard nothing."

"You believe me, don't you? I wouldn't make this up. Dolan, help me. It reminds me too much of my mother's power over me, and I can't stand for this feeling to continue, not knowing what it is." She was panicking. Dolan quickly placed a protective spell around her, closing off the sound. Once she no longer heard it, Ariaste breathed a great sigh of relief.

"I believe you, don't worry. My hunch is that the sound has something to do with Stiga. It is, after all, known for the wizardry that was practiced there. Would you be willing to enter the ruins so we can find out for certain if it is the source of what you heard?" Ariaste thought for several moments, then nodded in agreement.

"Good, then let us return to the cave and see who we can recruit to go with us. For now I think it best we tell no one the reason why. Let's just make it on the pretense that we're curious, nothing more. We may have a bit of convincing to do with Captain Looren, but I do believe he'll let us go if we promise to be very careful." Their plan established, Dolan and Ariaste returned to the camp.

But when they approached Captain Looren with a request to investigate the ruins of Stiga, he would not allow them to leave. "No. It is an impossible request. There will be men from the army also exploring, and I will not risk it. In fact, it will be better for everyone if you were to remain close to camp at all times.'' They agreed with his restrictive measures for the time being, but Ariaste didn't like it.

Twenty

THE MORNING OF DOLAN AND ARIASTE'S fourth day along the Thrale River, the reinforcement troops began arriving. Looking tired and ragged, they had obviously pushed themselves to join the main force and get the building under way. Their orders were to settle the matter of the invasion as soon as possible. Accompanying the order to expedite the campaign came a change that made everyone breathe a sigh of relief. They were to build rafts, not ships, for the former were much more easily built and took less time to construct.

Upon their arrival, the soldiers set to work felling trees, hauling logs into camp, and sawing them into lengths that were lashed together for great rafts that would eventually transport troops and supplies downriver. It had become increasingly obvious that there was no ship that would sail down this river; the spring snowmelt had turned the Thrale into a treacherous torrent. The spring rains also made matters worse, adding water where none was welcome. Rafts were the only vessels likely navigable in this surging torrent.

They learned valuable information from the scouts who had spent the last seven months in this vast territory. They told of the southern city the river would pass on their way down the Thrale called Vensunor. Although it was guarded by an army of mercenaries, several men had volunteered and successfully infiltrated the camp by pretending to be mercenaries, gaining valuable information in that way.

Similarly, others had entered the gates of the walled city by pretending to be traders. Because Tonnerling was a city of traders and many dialects were spoken there, those posing as traders could speak some of the language, making it easy to remain inconspicuous when asking certain questions. Traders needed to know, for their safety, which routes were perilous in these times of war. In this way much about the workings of Vensunor became everyday knowledge to the Tonnerling troops.

But most fascinating to Dolan and Ariaste were the stories of the dead city called Stiga. In Vensunor tales of Stiga were told, vividly describing how the wizard wars had poisoned the stone of the mountain, making it uninhabitable to all. Only the birds had returned, and just in the last thirty years or so, it was speculated. Hearing that, Dolan and Ariaste anxiously waited for an opportunity to sneak away and explore Stiga.

They planned carefully, spending nearly two weeks in the cave, monitoring the movements of Captain Looren and his men. Being the disciplined soldier that he was, he followed a daily routine remarkably impressive in its repetition. Knowing where he would be at all hours helped Dolan and Ariaste decide when it would be safest for them to ride from the camp and enter Stiga. Though Captain Looren had specifically cautioned them against going alone, they ignored his warnings.

That Captain Looren and his men would adhere to their tight schedule, Dolan and Ariaste had no doubt. It was easy to rise when everyone else did and leave unobserved as the men dispersed, on their way to their assigned duties. As they did every morning, Ariaste and Dolan saddled their horses and rode out, taking the same route at first. Once they were sure that all were involved in their duties, they easily changed direction and, unobserved, pointed their horses toward Stiga.

They skirted the camp of soldiers, who had spread their tents and fires across the grassy plain. Ariaste was dressed in the only clothes she had with her, those of a young servant. Her blonde hair was pulled back into one long braid and tied with a piece of white leather that signified the wearer was in training as a warrior. Dolan's hair, which was chin-length by this time—having been shorn as a sign of mourning for his father—was worn loose. He dressed in the well-cut riding clothes of a trader of considerable means. Confident that no one would hinder their passing, they rode toward the ruins as the sun began burning off the early morning fog.

As they rode through what remained of the gates to Stiga it was evident by the cleared path that the soldiers had been through here. There were stones and debris piled up on the sides of the streets that evidently had seen riders coming and going. Captain Looren had mentioned that the soldiers regularly entered Stiga's ruins to explore.

Seeing this, Dolan placed a protective spell over himself, Ariaste, and their horses.

''Do you expect we will meet up with anyone while we are here?'' Ariaste asked, her words echoing off the walls.

''No. Well, perhaps. But it is always better to be prepared and not taken off guard,'' he concluded. They rode on without speaking, the clop of their horses' hooves echoing off the buildings.

As they neared the center of the city, Ariaste began to feel the pull she had felt the first time she and Dolan had seen Stiga from atop the mountain. Like the call of a lover, the voice whispered her name, and she sighed out loud.

''What is it, dearest?'' Dolan asked when he heard her sigh.

She nearly didn't answer, but sighed again and this time her face became flushed. ''Oh Dolan. The most wonderful sound and feeling is happening. Tell me that you can hear it, too!'' She was excited, he could tell, but he just shook his head. Dolan heard nothing but it was obvious to him that Ariaste did. And, whatever it was, it had managed to make itself heard despite the protective ward he had cast. He began to worry.

Overcome by a feeling of elation, Ariaste kicked her

horse into a canter so that she passed Dolan, leading the way up the twisting streets, faster and faster, calling out for him to hurry. He could only follow, knowing that to caution her might do more harm than good. The narrow street was coming to an end; as they passed through a stone archway they rode into a massive open courtyard paved in enormous white-marble blocks with streaks of gold and silver running through them. At the opposite end of the courtyard were steps of the same marble, at the top of which was the Temple.

Cantering to the steps, Ariaste jumped from her horse and began to run up them two at a time. At the top she stopped only because Dolan was pleading for her to do so. When he made it to the top step beside her, she wrapped her arms around his neck and kissed him. She was flushed, but not as out of breath as Dolan.

"Isn't it spectacular?" she asked, as they took in the view. From where they stood, the valley was visible and the forest beyond. They could see the Thrale running wild and cold. On the embankment the tiny forms of the soldiers could just be made out, busy at their task of raft making. The plain where once the cattle and sheep herds of Stiga grazed was dotted with the tents of Tonnerling's army.

"We must never leave here, Dolan. This is where I wish to stay and raise our family," she said, looking up at his amazed expression. Before he could answer her, Ariaste bounded off again.

For several moments she stood before the massive doors to the Temple, with her head cocked at an angle, as if listening. Stepping to the left, she walked very slowly, then went to stand before the wall at a place just adjacent to the doors. She bent low and began running her fingers across the tight seam of the wall in a searching way. In one of the grooves she felt a chink of loose marble, which she pried out. Into the small opening she stuck her fingers and touched a metal ring. Slipping two fingers into the ring, she gave it a pull. The block of marble, which was about three feet by three feet, moved aside until she could grab the corner with both hands and pull it open. She went down on her knees and peered inside, then crawled through the opening just as Dolan called out loudly for her to stop. His heart pounding, Dolan was crawling after her as fast as he could move, terrified at the way Ariaste was acting.

Inside the wall a soft glow of light illuminated everything. The narrow tunnel carved into the rock went on for about ten feet, emptying into a wider corridor wherein he could stand. He hurriedly stepped down from the tunnel onto huge, ancient stone steps that could not have been made by humans, from their size and spacing. Panic rising, he called out to Ariaste, not sure which way to continue. She answered him and urged him on, but he couldn't see her. Following the sound of her voice, he ran down the steps, one hand brushing the wall, the air growing damper as he descended.

Finally, with his sides heaving as he wiped the sweat from his brow with his sleeve, Dolan stepped onto a flat surface. He raised his head and saw he had entered a cavern that seemed to be a shrine, for the walls appeared to contain faintly glowing luminaries. He heard Ariaste singing, and turning, saw that she was sitting on the ground, crooning, holding a heart-shaped, amber stone so large that it covered both her palms.

When Dolan looked closer at the walls he realized that set into each of the hundreds of niches was a stone, not a candle, and each was more impossibly brilliant than the next. The stones in this cavern were the source of the light. Daring to believe what he saw, Dolan knew he looked upon a cavern filled with Lifestones.

Gazing down at Ariaste, the sight of his young wife brought tears to his eyes, and he cautiously came to her side, half-afraid that this vision might disappear. Never had he seen her so radiantly beautiful. Da Winfreyd had told Dolan that only specially chosen people were called in the way Ariaste had been. Smiling, she gestured for him to sit beside her, her eyes containing a glimmer of amber in their depths.

Kneeling beside her, he was about to speak when they heard the scrape of leather against stone. Into the lighted cavern from an adjoining corridor strode Lady Tumnia, escorted by several large men bearing torches and weapons.

"No," was all Ariaste was able to gasp. Then her throat closed.

"Lady Tumnia, release your hold on my wife," Dolan screamed as he tried to get Ariaste to breathe.

Ariaste's terror-filled eyes watched as the guard came up from behind and knocked Dolan unconscious. Seeing her husband fall, she fainted. At Tumnia's order, one of the guards scooped Ariaste up and carried her away. Because Ariaste and the Lifestone were yet in the process of bonding, it was powerless to protect her.

When Dolan awoke he was alone in the dark and his head was pounding. Trying to stand left him nauseated, so he rested his head on his knees. Putting his hands to his head, he felt a painful, wet lump on the left side. His hands sticky with blood, he groped along the floor of the chamber until he reached the wall.

The wall offered support and he pulled himself up slowly, continuing to search for the opening and the way out. Once his fingers began to fumble along the wall, his hand fell into one of the niches. Only then did he recall that the wall contained hundreds of such recesses and each held a large, many-faceted stone. But something was wrong. When Ariaste had been here, the stones had all been glowing, casting light into the cavern.

"What happened to the light?" he asked aloud.

Just then the pads of his fingers brushed against a large stone and for a moment there was a burst of purple-blue light. Dolan curled his fingers around the stone and suddenly he didn't feel alone or lost; a sense of purpose flooded him. No longer needing to support himself, he stood away from the wall. The stone began to glow with a soft amber light, and he was able to see the large steps he had followed down into the chamber.

Bounding up the steps with newly found strength, a soothing voice whispered inside his head, *Yes, this is the way to Ariaste. I will heal your head as you climb out of this chamber. It feels so wonderful to be moving at such a fast pace again.* The voice continued talking, and Dolan's head soon stopped throbbing.

With the Lifestone leading him on, Dolan soon found himself turning this way and that until he came to a door. *Caution*, said the voice, as he put his hand on the latch. Without understanding how he knew to do so, Dolan reached up and opened a peephole in the middle of the door. Bright light poured through the hole, and it took several seconds before he could put his eye to it.

Peering through the peephole, he could see into a large room alight with torches held by the same burly guards who had been Tumnia's escort. Ariaste's limp body lay on a table, motionless. His hand on the latch, Dolan jumped when Tumnia walked across his field of vision. Gripping a dagger in one hand, she approached her daughter.

Thinking fast, Dolan put his lips to the peephole and whispered into the room. As the words of his spell touched her ears, Tumnia's body snapped and went rigid, her hand poised over Ariaste's throat.

The guards jumped and some began to stagger, as Tumnia's controlling spell began to crumble. At that moment, Dolan entered the room. Though the guards saw him, several of them had already fallen to the floor unconscious; the rest were leaning against the walls, groaning in pain.

Praying that Ariaste was alive, Dolan continued weaving his spell on Tumnia. He gave Tumnia a wicked vision of slitting her daughter's throat in one cruel, swift motion. Then he gave her the illusion of her fingers wrapping around the Lifestone, while her own child's blood poured over her hands, and pulling it from Ariaste's grip. In reality, Ariaste's fingers did release their hold on the large amber Lifestone, but only because she was unconscious. Light began to pour from the Lifestone in great flashes, and Tumnia cried out. Howling in agony as she burned, Tumnia released her hold on the Lifestone.

Her cry woke Ariaste. When she saw Dolan, she ran to him, forgetting the Lifestone on the table. The moment Ariaste realized what she had done, it was already too late. Holding his wife in his arms, Dolan foolishly dropped his guard, and his spell on Tumnia broke.

Blinking several times, Tumnia snarled when she realized Ariaste was not lying dead before her. Whipping around, she saw her daughter in Dolan's protective embrace, and, laughing cruelly, she snatched the Lifestone. Several seconds went by before she realized her hands were burning. Her flesh was being seared and she could not drop the stone, even as smoke rose from her hands and her arms began to glow. The Lifestone pulsed with a bright orange glow of inner fire that transferred to Tumnia's hands, arms, and into her torso, surging up her neck and face until her body was consumed in the orange glow. Within seconds she burst into flame.

The Lifestone hurtled through the air, spinning end over end, and landed with a great noise in the corner of the room, spraying chips of marble floor into the air. Ariaste ran to it and picked it up, gently cradling it to her chest, cooing soft words as she would to a child.

Ariaste's smile was brilliant as she turned to him. "My husband, we have found our home. My Lifestone informs me that it wants us to remain here and build a great city to rival the former one," she whispered in his ear. "We must keep secret the cavern we found." Happy beyond words, Dolan nodded in agreement. It was then that he remembered that he, too, had been chosen by a Lifestone. He brought it from his pocket and showed it to Ariaste.

The men who had witnessed Tumnia's demise were all coming around, befuddled by the residual effects of the spell. One by one they approached Dolan and Ariaste and went to their knees before them with their heads bowed. Finally, one spoke. "Young Master and Mistress, please believe me when I tell you that we were all under the control of that evil woman. We would never knowingly do harm to either of you, for we don't know who you are. Please have mercy on us when you report this to our captain.'' They had no doubt that he was sincere.

''You will not be held responsible for your actions, we promise,'' answered Dolan. ''But tell me all you recall about what happened here today so that I can be sure you are free of her hold over you.'' What Dolan really wanted was reassurance that none of the men could remember they had been in the cavern of Lifestones.

One by one they reported remembering little, if anything of the events during the time spent under Tumnia's spell. Hours later, they left Stiga, this time under the watchful eyes of the guards who had been Tumnia's escort. Hurrying back to their camp and the cage containing the messenger doves, the couple sent Da Winfreyd a coded message about the Lifestones beneath Stiga. Specifically they told him they needed the help of all the hands who wished to join them in settling there.

Several days later, when Da Winfreyd received the message, he bade Brother Boringar gather supplies and be ready to leave the next morning. He also sent a monk down the mountain to the abbey, requesting that Mother Enissa ready Nomia and several other women to travel with the monks, trusting she would give the women whatever she deemed necessary information in preparation for travel.

Only to Mother Enissa did he explain the reason, and it was this: they, Boringar and Nomia, were to become the spiritual leaders of Stiga. Though he had known this for many months, Da Winfreyd had told no one, he had simply waited for the message to arrive from Dolan. Knowing, too, that Stiga was where he would die, Da Winfreyd prepared for his last journey.

Twenty-One

THE VOICE INTRUDED UPON HER WITH ITS INsistence. *Waken only your mind to me,* she heard whispered. Shunlar floated, dreamless, bobbing like a leaf in the sea. Again, there was that niggling, nagging pull to awaken. *Waken only your mind to me,* she heard again, but this time it sounded like a command more than a suggestion. That annoyed her. *Finally,* she heard some part of her say. She sucked in a great gulp of air feeling as though she had just broken the surface of the water after a long dive. Confusion overwhelmed her. *Where am I and how did I get here? The last thing I remember is watching Bimily walk into the ring of standing stones. Have I died? Am I awake? Bimily! Is anyone there?*

Her words didn't even echo; they were strangely muffled as if she were enclosed in a room of solid stone. At that thought the room she was in became brighter and she was able to see that she was in a small chamber and, it appeared, underground. The hairs on the back of her neck were tingling, yet when she touched them they were not standing on end. Now she knew she was trapped in a spell. Whoever had done this had been powerful enough to keep her from the dream state—until now. Anger flared up for a brief moment which she quickly damped.

Revenge will come later. I have a trick or two that

will surprise whoever has me held in this state. Shunlar smiled a wicked grin.

The place, cold and gray as it was, was one she knew because Alglooth had taught her well. Once she was able to close her deeper mind off to the influence of the voice that summoned her from sleep, Shunlar split her awareness. Having done that, she summoned the path. As soon as she touched upon the thought of it, the path appeared as a ribbon of multicolored light, and she took flight, following the one color that led straight to Alglooth. Looking back over her shoulder for a brief moment, she could see people filing into the small chamber to stand around her body, which remained sleeping upon a narrow bed. Then she turned her attention back to the path and finding her father.

Because of the real physical distance between them, the journey to Alglooth took longer than she anticipated. Just as Shunlar was about to call out to him anxiously, however, he appeared in the distance, flying toward her. As always, Alglooth embraced her with his arms and wrapped his wings around her, happy to see her.

"What troubles you, daughter?" he asked, concerned.

"I am a captive of Bimily's people, as are Loff, Ranth, and Avek. I fear that our lives are in danger." As soon as she had uttered the words, she knew they were true.

"We traveled with Bimily to her people's valley," Shunlar began. Alglooth listened intently as she told her story of their journey and the reason for it.

"Tell me the direction this valley lies in and I will come to your rescue, never fear. If I have not reached your side when you are fully wakened and questioned, say to them: 'I demand The Thousand Things.' Return to yourself now and be assured that I will be there. As a further protection, I will send you on a dream journey. As long as you dream, no further spells can be placed upon you."

They embraced once more and parted, though Shunlar was reluctant to leave him. Her awareness returned almost immediately to the room where her body lay sleeping, the return journey being much shorter with Alglooth's help. Surveying the room before settling into herself, she could see her form floating in the air above her body, encircled by eight people. The oldest man among them was asking her questions. When she saw their interview was at an end, she watched as he compelled her floating form to return to her sleeping body, then they all filed out of the chamber.

So this is the man who has put a spell upon me. If I am to know what he said to me, I must reconnect my mind to itself. First, I need to see about my companions.

She tried to follow the group to the room where Ranth lay sleeping but was prevented from leaving by a strong barrier, the effort of doing so making her unusually tired. Realizing she must rest, she slipped back into her body. As soon as she did she knew all that had taken place since she had gone down the path searching for Alglooth. Secure in the knowledge that Erroless could not trap her again, Shunlar began the dream journey that Alglooth had promised he would send her.

She was in an enemy camp with a man whose identity she wasn't sure of. He accepted a welcome cup, and, as she watched, he took only token sips. A woman approached them and invited him to join her in a strange dance, which he accepted. Shunlar watched as others began to perform the same dance.

While everyone seemed to be occupied with watching the dancers, Shunlar slipped away in search of her horse, only to be ambushed by warriors from the enemy camp who were hiding in the grass. Several of them attacked at once, and no one came to her calls for help when she was captured. Not knowing why, Shunlar heard her voice loudly demand The Thousand Things. Hearing those words, the burly man who had her arms pinned behind her back instantly released her.

Her elbow slammed into his diaphragm, making him double over as her fist flew up in a solid backhand blow to his nose. It cracked with a painful sound, and blood poured down his lip. A quick backward sweep of her foot toppled him onto his back. Stunned as he was, it was easy for her to place one foot against his throat. Several others made an attempt at her but she again demanded The Thousand Things in a loud voice. At first there was no response to her demand so she applied more pressure to the man's windpipe with her foot. He gestured frantically for the others to do as she demanded.

Someone ran to find her possessions. As things were tossed to her, she could see that each piece was damaged in some small way. A stone gouged from a ring, a dent in a bracelet. But none of these things were hers. What she wanted were her weapons, not jewelry. She waited, increasing the pressure on the man's throat with her foot, sneering as he coughed and sputtered.

A stone from a sling came hurtling through the air. Shunlar caught it in her hand and hurled it back the way it had come with an angry curse. Finally a man approached leading her saddled horse. Her weapons were tossed to her, and she mounted, sword in hand, a dark scowl creasing her brow. "Take my advice and don't follow me," *she warned.* "I will not spare the life of any who does. Use your strength to fight your real enemies." *Kicking her mount hard in the flanks, she caused the already terrified animal to grunt and bolt, sending clods of dirt flying into the faces of her tormentors as she galloped off.*

For the time being they heeded her words, and she rode away alone, not bothering to look back, forgetting her companion. No arrows whistled after her, nor stones from slings, but she knew it was just a matter of time and knowingly abused her horse to get all the speed she could from the poor animal. Soon it was lathered, the whites of its eyes showing as it poured all its strength into answering her demand to go faster still.

Something was very wrong. Why should the horse seem so terrified and its breath be so labored so soon? Just as that thought came to her, the horse's gait faltered. He was lame, having been damaged by her captors. Easing up on the reins, she let the animal slow down as she scanned the horizon for a place to hide herself from those she knew would soon be coming after her. Already she imagined the face of the man she had bloodied swimming before her, twisted into a grimace made uglier by his broken nose.

With no way to outrun them she must make a stand. In the distance a dust cloud could be seen as her pursuers drew closer.

As suddenly as it had begun, her dream dissolved, and Shunlar realized she was not alone anymore. She opened her eyes and looked into the face of the ancient man whose name she remembered was Erroless. He did not smile but had a puzzled, accusatory look on his face. ''It seems she has awakened on her own,'' he announced.

Twenty-Two

In all the months that Septia had cared for Zeraya, no one suspected that her daily dosing included a slow-acting poison. Septia had taken great pains to formulate a mixture that gave Zeraya a false sense of recovery and by nightfall produced such exhaustion she could barely walk. And, all the more sinister was the fact that Septia knew how to hide what she did not only from Zeraya and everyone around her, but from Zeraya's Lifestone as well. It should have been able to detect that what Zeraya ingested each day was using her strength, not building it. Septia was far more dangerous than anyone had suspected.

When Benyar had first returned and reunited Zeraya with her Lifestone, he rarely left her side. Many nights he slept in a chair by her bedside, she holding on to his hand as he poured his very life's essence into her. They had been intimate rarely, because Zeraya remained so weak, and even those times had been at her insistence. Benyar had even told her that it felt to him as though he were using her, not making love to her.

Though Honia sul Urla, the High Priestess, had proclaimed that Zeraya would beget another child, possibly more than one, their few encounters over the last year had produced nothing. To make matters worse, in the last three months, Zeraya and Benyar no longer shared a bed. She had decided that because Benyar's ancestor's enemy was the person responsible for the war, and he had not succeeded in killing that enemy, Benyar was to blame. Zeraya, acting every bit the immature young woman that she was, had decided his was guilt by association. She even hinted she might set Benyar aside and take another as Consort.

Benyar did not take that news well. His wife was alive again after twenty years of constant searching. His son had been found as well, and this was how she repaid him: with blame and threats. However, there was nothing he could do about it. Zeraya was the Queen, and her word on the subject ultimate. He was merely her consort and First Guardian, for now.

Truthfully, Benyar was much weaker than he knew. The hours spent healing his wife drained him so that his powers diminished and he was unable to communicate openly with his Lifestone. If he had, he would have thought to ask it if the enemies that Zeraya demanded be hunted down and killed were yet alive.

Honia had not proven Benyar's ally either, and she fully supported Zeraya in her accusations. When Honia scried to ask if Zeraya's information was correct, the oracle answered with a resounding yes. Had she asked another, more important question, the answer would have been a resounding no. The question: Was Benyar's ancestor's enemy the person responsible for instigating the war? Everyone just assumed it must be so.

At the time, no one knew or suspected that Korab was the viper in their midst. Only when he was confronted by Benyar and Ranth and their Lifestones was the awful truth finally revealed. Hearing that her nephew, and not her husband's enemy, was the instigator of the war had done much to soften Zeraya's attitude and feelings toward her husband. Benyar had been welcomed, once again, to her chambers on the occasional evening, but he still slept alone most nights.

Last night had been no exception. Benyar had retired alone, as usual. Waking before dawn the next morning, he was deeply troubled by a dream that had been disturbing enough to waken him. He closed his eyes as he recalled the fading threads of the dream.

He saw himself and the others in the desert, watching, as the banished Septia and Korab walked away from them across the sand. The question burning at the back of Benyar's mind suddenly came into focus. He ran after Septia, grabbed her and took firm hold of her shoulders, demanding to know why Zeraya had not conceived. She merely laughed a hideous-sounding laugh in his face, turned, and ran to Korab's side.

Benyar sat up in his bed, sweat beading on his brow. *Could the reason Zeraya has not conceived be because Septia administered herbs to prevent pregnancy?* he asked himself. Astounded by his own question, Benyar removed the Lifestone from the pouch around his neck. Holding it in his hands, he posed that question to it. It confirmed his suspicions, answering, *Yes. Septia's herbs prevented the quickening of Zeraya's womb.*

The answer filled Benyar with a strange sense of elation, but he didn't know whether to laugh or cry. Septia had been imprisoned for months, once it was established that she was Korab's lover and accomplice. That meant Zeraya had not been given any herbs to prevent conception for at least four months. Though she had not spent many nights in his arms, the possibility existed that Zeraya could be with child. It filled Benyar with hope.

Again taking a firm hold on his Lifestone he asked it: *Does Zeraya carry my child?* The answer he heard was: *Yes.*

Feeling genuinely happy for the first time in many months, Benyar rose from his bed. He decided to visit the public baths, and it occurred to him to ask Ranth to join him so he could tell him what he had just learned from his Lifestone. If Zeraya gave birth to a girl, she would be next in line of succession, something Benyar knew Ranth would be relieved to hear. It was a well-known fact that Ranth had no desire to take his place as First Guardian. Only because Zeraya had not had another child was he the considered choice.

But Ranth was not to be found in his suite, and the guards had not seen him leave. *Curious,* Benyar said to himself. Perhaps he had left the palace grounds by his private courtyard gate as he was sometimes known to do. Looking around the room, Benyar noticed that Ranth's sword was missing. He made his next stop the sparring yard, but Ranth was not among the warriors hard at practice in the cooler, early morning hours.

From the sparring yard he went to check the clan's pavilion, only to discover that Ranth was not there either. Finding his son's disappearance rather odd, Benyar discreetly engaged several of the palace guards on a search for Ranth. Now that he thought about it, he had not seen Ranth for two days. His duties beckoning, no time remained for the baths, so Benyar hurried back to his suite to prepare for the morning of meetings at which he must officiate alongside Zeraya.

Zeraya, too, had woken up that morning with unusual feelings. She was nauseated and immediately remembered how she had appeared in the women's pavilion the night Tavis's naming had been celebrated. Clutching her Lifestone firmly, Zeraya asked the question. It confirmed that she was indeed pregnant.

Benyar would be happy, she knew. She had been considering setting him aside for another, though there was no other man who had caught her attention. In reality she had been holding a grudge and wanted to make Benyar suffer. Why, she couldn't seem to remember clearly.

Hasn't he suffered enough already? The voice of her Lifestone startled Zeraya so, she nearly dropped it.

Why is it that I can hear you so clearly today? she asked.

Several seconds went by until she heard the whispered reply, *You are now completely free of the woman's influence. Until now I was rendered helpless by her.*

What woman? Zeraya asked, frightened for the first time in a long time.

Septia, came the whispered answer.

Panic seized Zeraya, and she loudly called for her servants. Once she was no longer alone, Zeraya calmed down and let the women help her dress and bring her breakfast. Soon, she promised herself, she would tell

Benyar the news. But not yet. Perhaps tonight. For now she wanted to keep this to herself.

When she appeared in the audience hall, it was apparent Benyar was preoccupied. As on most days, he seemed remote and deep in thought as he rose and bowed to her when she approached the throne. She found his mood unappealing and decided to tell him that. But as she was about to berate him publicly, her Lifestone warned her in a most unsubtle way. She felt heat radiating into her chest and as she put her hand around her Lifestone's pouch she heard, *Remember who the man at your side is and the sacrifice he has made of his life for you. He is not to blame for his mood. You are.* Zeraya blinked back tears, desperately not wanting to believe what she heard was true, but knowing that it was.

For the first time in a year she looked tenderly at Benyar, really looked at him. His hair was showing a bit of gray at the temples, but he looked much the same as he did when they had first pledged their love to one another. Certainly he had a few wrinkles at the corners of his eyes, but he loved her and had never left her side until she had sent him away.

"Husband," she called him as he kissed the back of her hand. "There is much we must discuss. Tonight, after we have had dinner, come to my chambers," she said with finality.

Benyar looked at her with something that could have been fear. She felt her heart jump, knowing she caused this feeling in him. She smiled, but it seemed not to change his expression. There appeared to be much more damage done than she had imagined. How could she not have seen what she was doing? Zeraya was near to tears when she heard the chamberlain, Hadida sul Yelenna, loudly call out the name of the morning's first supplicant. She jumped and pulled her fingers from Benyar's hand. Swallowing to relieve her throat of its tightness, Zeraya nodded to Hadida, indicating she was ready to begin. Soon she became absorbed in her work and forgot about Benyar's mood.

He, on the other hand, watched her warily throughout

the morning. What was it they must discuss? Had she finally decided to set him aside for another? Did she know yet that she was going to have a child, his child? There was nothing he could do but wait until night.

The wait, however, was long and drawn out. Everything had taken longer than seemed possible. And, of the people Benyar had engaged to find Ranth, none had reported back to him. But finally it was evening, and Benyar stood before Zeraya's door. So anxious had he been that he had not attended the evening meal; instead, he had paced in his room until a servant delivered the message that Zeraya had returned to her suite and awaited his presence.

Hesitating, Benyar breathed deeply before he asked the guards to announce him. He entered and saw that Zeraya was waiting for him upon a chair in the sitting room. She smiled at him, and he grew wary. Something was happening, and he wasn't sure what. Zeraya dismissed the servants and beckoned him to come to her side. He found himself afraid. He approached her and went down on one knee.

''Husband, rise and come closer. Being formal isn't necessary. We are alone.''

He raised his head and found that he couldn't look at her. Certain that he was being set aside, Benyar found that he was having a difficult time breathing. Seeing the state he was in, Zeraya rose from her chair and hurried to his side. She placed her hand gently on his shoulder so that she could communicate her thoughts directly to him.

Finding himself submitting to her touch, Benyar opened his mind slowly to Zeraya. His thoughts, when she heard them, were jumbled and confused. She tried to explain that she wasn't setting him aside, but it didn't register at first. He began speaking as fast as she was at the same time, apologizing for not finding the man or men responsible for injuring her all those years ago. It took several minutes for her words to begin making sense, but when they did, Benyar slumped on the floor. He covered his face with his hands, relief and fear overwhelming him. This was not like him. Now Zeraya began to worry.

Have I produced this in him? Have I driven him to madness by my careless treatment of him? Zeraya asked her Lifestone. Its answer—yes—sent her to her knees beside him.

"Benyar, look at me. I only wanted to tell you that I am going to have another child, that is all. There will be no setting you aside. I see that I have much to make amends for."

He was unnerved but managed to ask, "How long have you known about the child?"

"Just since this morning," she answered, taking his face in her hands. He began to sob then, and she comforted him as he cried, pulling him close. "I am so sorry for all the hurt I have caused. I never should have sent you away," Zeraya whispered to him as she held him in her arms.

Sitting on the floor, her arms protectively encircling Benyar as he lay in tears with his head upon her lap, Zeraya began to hear the voice of her Lifestone speaking to her. She listened and transferred what she heard directly to her husband.

Because Benyar was so involved with your healing process, he could not notice his powers were being diminished, her Lifestone said in a chastising voice. *His magic became affected by his self-doubt. When you withdrew your love, Benyar became lost. His Lifestone was not able to help him either.*

Benyar's breathing became more even and quiet as he listened to the words.

You have caused great pain to a man who loves you unselfishly. It is time to repay him for all he has done for you.

Now Zeraya was in tears. "I accused you, and you remained faithfully beside me, tireless in your desire to make me whole again," she managed between sobs. "I will never forget that. There is no other who will ever take a place beside me. Can you forgive me for the anguish I have caused?'' asked Zeraya, looking deeply into his eyes.

It was Benyar's turn to comfort her. ''From the moment I first set my eyes on you, I knew we would be together. I never expected it to be easy, knowing your volatile nature, but I could not be content with another. I forgive you, willingly,'' he said quietly, kissing her.

By this time she had stopped sobbing. Benyar rose and offered her his hand. She stood and they embraced. Together they opened their minds to one another and began to travel through Zeraya's body to her womb to observe the new life growing there.

Too small yet for awareness, the cells were busy forming, splitting, growing. In the months ahead they would continue to monitor their child. Soon, they knew, they would be able to determine what sex the child would be. For now, they were content to watch as the cells continued to divide again and again.

When they had untangled their minds and pulled back into their respective bodies, Zeraya took Benyar's hand and led him to bed. ''Never leave my side again,'' she whispered to him as they lay down together.

The next morning Benyar awoke slightly before Zeraya. He propped himself up on one elbow so that he could watch her sleep. She seemed to glow in the morning light, and when at last she opened her eyes, she smiled at him. For the first time since her near-fatal injury, Benyar believed his wife had truly returned to herself and to him. He sat up against the pillows, and she laid her head against his chest. They remained this way, talking quietly, until the servants entered to begin the morning ablutions.

The servants also noticed the difference in their queen and the quiet, efficient manner in which they went about their duties conveyed an air of calm. Knowing beforehand that Benyar occupied the royal suite, his body servants were also prepared. The men entered the suite and helped him bathe and dress alongside Zeraya, a natural rhythm taking place. The Queen and her consort were certainly acting like newlyweds. They couldn't take their eyes off one another.

Dressed for their morning, they sat down to breakfast together, dismissing the servants. Between bites of food they talked about the child. It was then that Benyar remembered sending several people off to investigate Ranth's whereabouts.

"My dear one, yesterday I sent people to find Ranth. I asked them to report to me as soon as possible with any information. Since I am anxious about this, would you mind if we interrupted our breakfast and sent for them?"

"What do you mean? Surely our son is either in the palace or the clan's pavilion. And what about Tavis? He is here, isn't he?" Zeraya's voice sounded a little frantic.

She called loudly for the servants, who assured her Tavis was fine. She insisted he be brought to their suite anyway. As always, when Tavis was carried into the suite by his wet nurse, he was all smiles and happy to see them.

But when the warrior who had been in charge of finding Ranth appeared, his look of concern worried both Benyar and Zeraya instantly.

"Tell us that you have found our son," ordered Zeraya.

"My Queen, I wish that I could," was Takoth sul Tash's quiet reply. "It seems that Ranth is nowhere to be found in Kalaven. I have also discovered that Avek is missing. Since they are oath-brothers, we feel they may be together. If I may ask, has anyone consulted the High Priestess?" Takoth asked.

"We have not," answered Benyar. "Perhaps you would do us the service of reporting this to her. Tell her we are greatly concerned, and we wish to speak with her within the hour." Zeraya agreed with Benyar, as he knew she would. Besides, they had other news to tell Honia.

When they were alone again, Zeraya asked, "Husband, do you think it is possible this could be a mate abduction? Both our son and Avek were, after all, vying for Shunlar's affection.'' Before Benyar could answer, however, Tavis began wailing loudly.

Hearing his mother's name caused Tavis to remember that he missed her and his father and 'Vek, as he called Avek. Taking his grandson in his arms, Benyar held him and comforted him. Then, he began to toss him up in the air and catch him, something that always made Tavis laugh. It worked. Soon the youngster was giggling happily, forgetting that half a minute ago he had been crying for his mother.

Both Benyar and Tavis were laughing and breathing hard when Benyar stopped tossing him and sat down, putting the boy to bounce on his knee. Tavis turned to his grandparents, pointed up with a small finger, and announced proudly, ''Momma fly.'' Zeraya and Benyar exchanged startled looks.

''Husband, let us leave now for our audience with Honia,'' Zeraya calmly announced. ''There are several things I wish to ask of the oracle today.'' He agreed with her and handed the boy back to his nurse. As soon as Tavis left their sight they departed for the Temple.

They arrived with an escort of four guards. A young priestess who waited at the door hurried off to announce them. Upon entering the Temple, Zeraya and Benyar felt a tingle of excitement run through them. Holding hands, they walked the length of the hall, their love for each other nearly making them glow. Taking note of this, Honia smiled, bowed, and gestured for them to approach the altar.

As always, the scrying bowl sat ready, filled with water. Honia extended her hands over the water and whispered the words of a prayer. Her words had impact. As the water rippled, from the middle of the bowl a tendril of vapor rose that gradually darkened and took form.

The vapor became a woman who, when the face could be seen, was undoubtedly Shunlar. The face and shape of the body changed, grew taller, more elongated, and, most surprising of all, sprouted large wings. More vapor rose, forming itself into the shape of a man who was lifted up to be carried in her arms. Clearly it was Avek, by the size of him. In awe they watched the flying form of Shunlar set the form of Avek down and turn to another male form that had risen from the vapors of the bowl. The second man was clearly Ranth.

The mystery of how Avek and Ranth disappeared seemed to have been solved. The logical reason they were taken seemed to point to mate abduction, but Benyar was not entirely convinced of that. He recalled how Shunlar and Ranth had come to them days ago to beg permission for Ranth to be allowed to leave and join her and Bimily on their journey to her people in the hopes that they might have a cure for the markings on his back.

The vapor dissolved slowly, and another form rose from the surface of the water. It was clearly Zeraya, and she was heavy with child. Honia cast a furtive glance at her queen and could see by the way Zeraya gazed into Benyar's eyes that it was true. Overjoyed, a small sound escaped from her throat as she covered her mouth with her hands. When Zeraya and Benyar looked up, they saw the image of Zeraya that floated above the scrying bowl just as it began to dissipate.

"Yes, Honia, it is so, as the oracle foretold. Benyar and I are going to have another child," Zeraya said, more content than she could remember being in a long, long time.

The High Priestess bowed to them, saying, "I will offer prayers for this child. Foremost I will ask that it be born in a world not torn apart by war. Now we must discuss what we have been shown by the oracle. Come, let us retire to my apartment and some refreshments."

Twenty-Three

AT HONIA'S INSISTENCE, ALTHOUGH THEY HAD misgivings about doing so, Zeraya and Benyar agreed to alert the population to the fact that Avek and Ranth had been abducted by Shunlar.

"What if Shunlar returns to the palace for her son? If the servants are not prepared, they will be terrified and unable to protect him," Honia argued. She certainly had a point.

Though it was rarely done, Honia suggested that a telepathic image of Shunlar as a woman with great wings, carrying the men away be mentally transmitted throughout the city by Benyar and Zeraya, assisted by their Lifestones. None would question the sight when they learned the oracle had given them the vision.

Honia called her priestesses to her to begin preparations. The heads of each clan were given the message that an announcement would be made and when. Efficiently, that message was passed along to every clan member.

When noon came, the great gong in the Temple sounded. Benyar and Zeraya opened their thoughts to each other. Linking their minds they duplicated what had appeared to them that morning: the image of Shunlar hovering over Honia's scrying bowl. Holding their Lifestones in their hands, they sent the image of Shunlar in her winged form across the expanse of the city. People were, of course, in awe of what they saw, and an eerie quiet settled over Kalaven. Many secretly admired the finesse of the mate abductions, and it remained the favorite topic of conversation for weeks afterward.

Jerob sul Ansilla, Avek's father, was hidden within the rocks in a sentry post at the entrance to Kalaven when the image of Shunlar was passed on. Jerob had been in a rather foul mood ever since he had learned that Avek was missing. He thought, actually hoped, that Avek had been with his oath-brother, Emun sul Setta, for the last two days, renewing their friendship. Discovering that he was gone and had left without the permission of Honia made him doubt his son's honesty and willingness to live by the rules of their society. No one, not even Benyar, could leave without Honia's consent. Everyone lived by that rule. He worried that Avek might have grown so used to coming and going on his own in his year of exile that he might throw caution to the wind and up and leave.

Seeing the image of the flying woman clutching the man in her arms tightly to her chest gave Jerob some hope. He and everyone else, including Honia, agreed it was a mate abduction. That was also the feeling that Benyar and Zeraya conveyed along with the image. Whether or not it was true remained to be discovered. Benyar was not convinced, but he kept that thought to himself.

Breathing a great sigh, Jerob felt his composure returning. Everyone else had remained motionless at their posts, only their eyes constantly moving, seeking any telltale sign of intruder. The guards at the entrance had been doubled since the first attack by the Tonnerling soldiers. Only the seasoned, older men and women were rotated in shifts nowadays. No young adult would likely be trained or allowed to take up the post until the war was over.

As if the earth just coughed them up, two people appeared from a small outcropping of rocks in the distance. They were walking toward the entrance to Kalaven. Every sentry seemed to see them at the same instant and only their years of training kept them seated and still.

By their movements and stature, the couple appeared to be two young women, masked and dressed in desert leathers cut in an old style. When the couple was nearly upon the first two sentries who sat farthest from the portal, the sentries came slowly to their feet. Their clothing blended into the rocks so perfectly that once they stopped moving, they seemed to disappear. The two strangers were startled by the sudden movement of the sentries, whom they obviously hadn't seen, and they froze in their tracks. Seeing that no one barred their way, they continued, picking their way carefully, noiselessly, to the entrance, until they had passed the two sentries who had startled them.

Impeccably trained, the sentries returned to their sitting positions, once more becoming part of the landscape. With hesitant steps the two women continued walking until they reached the flat, sandy spot that marked the entrance to Kalaven. Stopping at that exact spot, they went to their knees, bent forward and touched their foreheads to the ground. When they sat back on their haunches, they found themselves surrounded by a force of twenty men and women. Seasoned warriors all, they kept their faces covered as a sign that the two people before them were strangers and not yet welcome. Now the women flinched, the first sign of fear they had shown.

Standing in the forefront was Jerob, the acting captain. He asked, "Who are you that you come requesting entrance to Kalaven?"

"My lord, who we are is of little importance. The message we bring, however, is," one of them answered.

"Who is the message for?" asked Jerob.

"For all who inhabit this great city. Would you hear it now?" she asked.

"Tell us," Jerob instructed.

"My lord, there is a great invasion force forming, but two weeks north and east of here. My people and I have been watching them closely for some time now. It is our belief that when they come to invade, they will succeed."

She waited for her words to sink in before continuing. "They have a man and woman among them who are of the people. The man teaches them to fight. They are learning . . ." she stopped again and looked around him. The group of sentries had stiffened and the air felt tense. "Shall I continue?" she asked.

Ketherey came forward to answer her. "I ask that you continue this conversation before the Queen and the First Guardian." His voice sounded very strangely constricted. The air about them crackled with anticipation.

Recognizing anguish in the man who spoke, one of the young outsiders quietly said, "Allow me to ask my mate about this. We thought only to deliver our message and leave." She sounded nervous. Touching her companion's hand, she engaged her in private conversation. The second woman shook her head no several times, each time less adamantly. When they released hands, she said, "She fears you will capture us and not allow us to leave."

"I would have thought of that before I came here," Ketherey answered quietly. The two strangers looked around at the men and women who encircled them. It was obvious they were already captured.

"You are correct. We will accompany you." This time it was the other young woman who answered.

With a nod to them, Ketherey made a quick hand signal to Jerob, who sent the sentries back to their posts. "Come with me," he said to the couple. They stood up gracefully and bowed to Ketherey.

"My lord, I am called Corta and this is my mate Ondeen. Whom have we the pleasure to greet?" Her words seemed to soften Ketherey's mood somewhat, for he removed his mask, revealing his face to them.

"I am Ketherey sul Jemapree," he answered with a small bow.

The other young woman gasped, clearly surprised. "You are my uncle, Ketherey," she whispered.

Now it was his turn to look surprised.

"My mother is Finta sul Jemapree. I am Ondeen sul Finta." She smiled, something that he knew only by the way her eyes crinkled at the edges behind her mask.

Finta sul Jemapree—his and Benyar's older sister—had been one of the many who had left Kalaven to become known as the Lost Feralmon. Still tied to the old ways of living the life of a nomad, Finta had had two mates and refused to live under Zeraya's edict of putting one aside. Their parting had been tearful.

"How I long to gaze upon Finta's face again. Tell me she is well," answered Ketherey quietly.

"She is very well, uncle. However, she will be furious when she finds out what we have done, Corta and I." Ondeen bowed her head.

"That is another thing I would have thought of before coming here. If her temper is still intact, you should know better by now," Ketherey said dryly. "Come, let us bring your news to Zeraya and Benyar."

Hearing the names, Ondeen started. "Zeraya and Benyar are the Queen and the First Guardian? My uncle, Benyar?" she asked.

"Yes, your other uncle," nodded Ketherey. "Shall we go?"

No longer fearful, they nodded in agreement, eager now to follow him into Kalaven. Because Ketherey and Benyar were family, more importantly because he had acknowledged them as family, she and Corta knew they would not only be well cared for, but also be granted permission to leave.

They hurried through the city streets masked, following close behind Ketherey. Upon reaching the palace, Ketherey sent a servant ahead to inform Zeraya and Benyar that he was arriving with visitors who carried an important message.

The royal couple had just themselves returned to the palace from their audience with Honia. They sat in the audience hall listening to the reports of several scouts who had returned earlier this morning. *It will be interesting to hear what they have found,* Ketherey thought to himself as they hurried through the palace. Ushered quietly into the hall, he and the young couple stood off to the side, listening intently as one of the scouts was finishing her report. So far none had seen the army Corta and Ondeen warned of.

Benyar had noticed Ketherey enter with two outsiders who were cloaked and masked. Anxious to find out who they were, he motioned for Ketherey to approach as soon as the scout concluded her report and stepped away. Ketherey went to one knee before Zeraya and Benyar, then bowed his head.

Behind him Ondeen and Corta bowed, but neither bent her knee. They were too busy staring at Zeraya. Belonging to a tribe of outlaw Feralmon, they had no close contact with the current news of Kalaven. Their culture, in fact, considered those in Kalaven to be traitors to tradition. Feralmon were, after all, nomads. When Zeraya had declared they must all live permanently in one place and build a city as well, putting aside the old ways, there had been dissension. Her abolishing multiple mates had driven a wedge between the two groups that nothing could mend.

Only a handful of the Lost Feralmon knew that Zeraya lived again, her Lifestone restored to her. Few knew just how long she had lain in stasis close to death. Ondeen and Corta had long known of Zeraya's injury and stolen Lifestone, but no more. They were very confused at her youthful appearance.

"My Queen, my brother. I bring two messengers before you who have new, disturbing information. I ask that you hear them."

"Come forward and state your message," Zeraya's impatient voice cut the air, and the room changed because of it. Everyone watched in silence. Knowing that these two people before her were from the Lost Feralmon, and expecting to see familiar faces beneath the masks, Zeraya decided to act first and ask questions later. She summoned guards forward with a discreet hand gesture and within seconds they had surrounded the couple.

"My Queen, there is no need for this," offered Ketherey. "If you will allow them to state their names, their identities will assure you they mean no insult or harm."

"I will consider what you advise, Ketherey, after I learn who they are," Zeraya informed him. "Show us your faces and tell us your names."

Slowly complying with her order, Ondeen and Corta pulled back the hoods of their cloaks and unfastened their masks. Both of them wore their hair in warrior braids, but in a much simpler, older style. Their skin was darker than anyone else's in the room, for they had lived under the sun and stars all their lives. Barely twenty years of age, it was obvious they were the children of the Lost Feralmon.

"I am Corta sul Sarda," she said, a bit bewildered.

"I am Ondeen sul Finta," the other woman said, raising her head long enough to shoot a bold glance at Benyar, lowering her eyes when she saw the look in his.

Upon hearing his sister's name, Benyar catapulted from his chair. "You are Finta's child?" There was genuine elation in his voice.

Carefully studying the young woman's face, Zeraya could see her resemblance to Benyar, Ketherey, and even to Ranth; their eyes, mouths and chins were similar in shape and size.

"Be welcome among us, your family," Zeraya offered with a genuine smile as servants brought them the welcome cup. Each gratefully took a cup, bowed before drinking, then drained the contents. Setting the cups back on the tray, Corta and Ondeen exchanged wary glances. They were confused by Zeraya yet too polite to ask how she could look no older then they.

"Now, tell us your business. What have you seen that our scouts did not?" asked Zeraya, her voice startling them.

Ondeen cleared her throat and began. "As you may know, the northern army from the place known as Tonnerling has been wintering on the Thrale River. We learned from our sources that they await reinforcements. Another thing we have learned is that they have two people among them who are of your people."

At the mention of this the hall became deadly silent. Ondeen continued into the silence, "No one sees much of the woman, but it is rumored she possesses great powers. The man teaches the troops our fighting skills,'' reported Ondeen.

''Have you learned their names?'' asked Benyar.

''Yes, they are called Lord Korab and Lady Septia.'' Before her words were an echo, someone gasped loudly, and all the people in the audience hall began talking at once. Ketherey's face turned ashen.

Leaning forward at the edge of her seat, Zeraya's cheeks flamed, and her knuckles bunched as she tightened her grip on the carved wooden arms of her throne. ''Be silent or leave us!'' she shouted at the room. Everyone obeyed instantly, several people leaving the audience hall in a hurry. Once things had quieted, Zeraya urged Ondeen and Corta to continue.

''Tell us how you know this when our scouts have never reported anything of this nature,'' Benyar said.

''Only twice did your scouts travel close enough to see any of these things. Unfortunately, both times we were too late to prevent their deaths, but found their remains after the enemy had finished with them. From the condition of their bodies, they suffered horrible tortures, and it was better that they died,'' Corta replied quietly.

''We have seen them forming a great invasion force and perhaps against our leaders' judgment have decided to warn you who inhabit Kalaven. Since we have family here, we want to help you.''

''And who is your leader?'' asked Zeraya, very curious.

''We have three,'' answered Ondeen. ''Our priestess and her two mates.''

''And, their names would be?'' urged Zeraya.

''Forgive me, but I am bound by oath not to speak any names other than ours to you without their permission.'' Ondeen bowed her head.

''I understand and will press you no farther,'' Zeraya answered. ''We are most grateful for the information you have supplied us with.''

Then she brightened. ''You, of course, are welcome

among us as family. We will have servants escort you to quarters where you can rest and refresh yourselves with food. Later this evening you will join us at the evening meal and tell us more of your strange tale. Now, because of your report, we have much to attend to. We thank you.'' She dismissed them graciously.

When Corta and Ondeen were gone, she called for Ketherey to assemble the generals, captains, and the swiftest of their scouts. If what Corta and Ondeen had told them was true, they must be prepared for the main force to strike within the week.

''But first, Benyar, I would seek advice from Honia and the oracle for the second time today. This is alarming news, and I feel we must consult with her to confirm what we have heard. What do you say?'' He agreed, and they left at once, putting Ketherey in charge until they returned.

Yet when they announced themselves at the Temple, they were told Honia wished not to be disturbed. It was explained that she was engaged in private prayer which was expected to keep her occupied the remainder of the day. There being nothing else they could do, Zeraya and Benyar returned to the palace to continue preparations for the invasion

The chamber was small, square, and sparsely furnished. There was one window; it provided light only, covered as it was with white opaque glass. In the middle of the room, covering most of the stone floor, was a thickly woven rug of many colors in geometric patterns. Several large pillows were strewn around the room. Beneath the window, at the edge of the rug, was a long, low rectangular table piled with jars and containers on one end; a small scrying bowl similar to the one on the altar in the Temple sat on the other end.

Sitting cross-legged at the table, Honia carefully mashed equal parts cactus and herbs in a small stone mortar, after which she took the pestle and ground the ingredients into a paste, chanting as she worked. Satisfied with the consistency, she added water a little at a time from a glass pitcher until she had a thick, green beverage. Setting aside the pestle she put the mortar to her lips and drank the draught in several large gulps, grimacing at the bitter taste.

Honia was preparing herself for a deep communion with the oracle. She had been searching for answers to the many questions that plagued her these days, foremost being why her prize, Septia, would betray all she held sacred. Honia continued to blame herself for Septia's betrayal. After all, she had loved her as her own child. Taking a deep breath, Honia leaned back against the pillows and closed her eyes, thought moving freely through her.

Holding the office of High Priestess of the Feralmon, Honia sul Urla had never married, nor entertained the thought of taking a mate and having a family of her own. She kept herself apart, though there was no dictum that demanded she must. There had been other women before her who held the post, who had taken mates and had children. For reasons only Honia knew, she refrained from the pleasures of love, sex, and family.

Shortly after Septia had been banished into the desert for her crimes, Honia had scried to ask the oracle why Septia had betrayed her people so horribly. Curiously it seemed to refuse to answer her question. Instead, over the scrying bowl a picture of the ancient text she had studied for years took form, a text forbidden to all eyes but hers. Then she saw Septia sitting by the light of one small candle, bent over the book, and by the way the shadows fell across her face, Septia appeared to be much older. Honia had assumed it was a vision from the future, one that she had seen previously when she asked the oracle who her successor would be.

At the time, Honia had accepted that vision as admonishment to study the written word in greater depth. For the first time since she had taken office, the oracle had not given her a direct answer. Not only was it disconcerting, but Honia had been shaken to the roots of her soul. She who had forsaken everything for this post, this sacred trust, was not answered; worse yet, she had been ignored. She fasted and prayed for days. When she put the same question to the oracle, again the answer was a vision of the book with Septia hunkered over it by candlelight. Feeling that she had failed her people, Honia was near to stepping down from her post when Shunlar had appeared with her marvelous child.

A smile crossing her lips, Honia recalled the day Tavis had chosen his name and the profound intelligence of the child. The oracle had amazed them all by taking shape and offering him the rune for his name with the hand of the goddess herself. That moment had been the turning point for Honia. Believing again that she had not been forsaken, it had taken a small child to convince her that her calling was real.

Why, then, hadn't the oracle answered her questions in a more direct manner? Why had it shown her again the picture of Septia reading the ancient text? Might it be trying to point her elsewhere? Several days later, when Honia sought the ancient text for a way to save Ranth's life, she discovered what the oracle had been trying to tell her, for the text was missing.

This was what the oracle had meant all along when it had shown Honia the vision of Septia reading. Blinded by her need to understand, filled with grief for this daughter who had betrayed everyone, Honia had been preoccupied with Septia's other crimes and misinterpreted the oracle's vision. She had never been shown the future at all; she had been shown the answer.

Fueled by her desire for power, Septia had stumbled across secrets that made her dangerous not only to the people, but to herself as well. For, hidden in the written words of that sacred text were spells that, if read by one who did not use the proper protocols, would entrap the person, greed taking precedence over all other emotions. Though she had been specifically warned of this by Honia, Septia was young, and her youth clouded her judgment.

Sighing, Honia remembered that just this morning Zeraya and Benyar had come seeking the answer to the strange disappearance of Ranth and Avek. Upon consulting the oracle, to their amazement, a winged woman had taken form over the scrying bowl. It appeared to be a mate abduction, but was that simple answer the real one? When Honia recalled seeing the woman holding Ranth, she remembered that his back had been facing her and that the words etched onto his skin were glowing through his clothing.

Positive that she alone had been privy to that particular nuance, Honia interpreted that to mean that Ranth had been taken away so a cure could be found for him from Bimily's people. With the text missing, Honia was powerless to save his life. If the truth be told, she was secretly happy and a bit relieved that the matter was out of her hands.

Today, as she had done since Septia had been found out, Honia prayed to be shown the truth. This time, something different was about to happen. The air in her private meditation chamber stirred, and she inhaled the pungent aroma of night-blooming desert cactus, which marked the arrival of the goddess. The water in the scrying bowl began to swirl.

Emptying her mind of all previous thoughts, Honia opened it fully to receive the answer as great waves of emotion began washing over her. Effortlessly, as if she were shrugging a cloak from her shoulders, the feelings of guilt surrounding Septia's betrayal fell away. Instead she was given a feeling of hope for herself and her people.

The hair on her arms rose. A woman appeared before her eyes, dancing in the air above the blue scrying bowl, with a clarity more precise than anything Honia had ever experienced. The High Priestess sat up. The face kept changing so that no matter how hard she tried, Honia could not determine if she was young, old, pretty, or plain. Yet when the woman addressed Honia, she knew beyond a doubt that she spoke to the goddess herself; her voice was unmistakable. As she listened, Honia was told that all of her questions would be answered and she would learn the truth about Septia.

''But be prepared, daughter. Your own demise will

also be made known to you,'' the voice of the oracle foretold.

''My only wish is to know that I have served you and my people faithfully,'' Honia prayed with her head bowed, hands clasped at her forehead.

''That you have, and well,'' answered the voice.

When Honia raised her head the woman was gone, but her presence lingered. Tears trickled down her cheeks as Honia watched the vapors over the bowl begin to shift and reveal a scene from the past to her. She was shown the moment when Septia decided she must have a Lifestone. Her heart nearly failed when she learned the truth of what Septia had planned with Korab; that they would stop at nothing, not even murder, to become holders of Lifestones.

As the past unfolded before her eyes, she watched Septia placing a hold on another young priestess's mind. Honia was made aware of the strength of her touch and all the ways in which Septia hid her talent. Honia flinched, watching the young priestess being compelled to steal the missing text, while Septia was imprisoned, and deliver it to a person whose face Honia could not see. As Honia watched in horror, the realization crept over her that Septia and Korab were still alive!

''Yes, daughter. You have guessed the truth. They yet live,'' hissed the voice in her head.

Fighting the panic rising in her, Honia could only watch as the scene changed and she saw Korab instructing the soldiers of Tonnerling how to fight with the techniques of the Feralmon. She was appalled not so much by the fact that he was alive but that he continued to do what he could to destroy his own people.

The water in the scrying bowl by this time had begun to swirl and spill over the edges. From its depths came yet another dark apparition of Septia, practicing the rituals she had pulled from the stolen text and teaching them to Korab. In that moment Honia learned that Septia had discovered the passage in the text concerning the Dark Lifestones. Praying it was not so, she could only watch as the oracle showed her how Septia prepared herself and Korab to pair with one.

A temporary clouding of the image occurred and when it cleared, there was Septia answering the call of the Dark Lifestone in the Temple, in Kalaven. Instantly Honia knew this was a scene from the future. As Septia stepped into the chamber of Lifestones, her face turned toward Honia and for a startling moment, in the vision, their eyes locked. Completely unnerved, Honia gasped and looked away. When she turned back to the vision it was to see her body being struck by a flash of lightning and falling to the ground. In the background Septia could be seen leaving the Temple, clutching the Dark Lifestone, an escort of the enemy soldiers her bodyguards. When the High Priestess returned her attention to the body lying facedown outside the Chamber of Lifestones, Honia recognized it as her own and became very still.

Mercifully, the scene shifted once more and Honia was shown a great gathering of people, her people, yet somehow they were very different. When one or two faces in the crowd looked familiar she realized that she was looking upon the Lost Feralmon. The group was assembled before a priestess who was flanked by a man and a woman, all three wearing similar ceremonial robes. She, like Honia, was scrying. The priestess in the vision raised her face to peer directly into Honia's eyes. She opened her mouth and said, "I entrust Corta and Ondeen into your care. Treat them well, our children." The priestess nodded to Honia and as she closed her eyes, Honia's eyelids became heavy.

As the scene began to fade, Honia had to force herself to stay awake. Through her blinking eyelids she was shown one final vision: two young women standing before Zeraya and Benyar.

Heartsick by what she had seen of the future, a moan escaped her lips, and her consciousness slipped away. Having spent the entire day communing with the oracle, Honia was on the verge of collapse. The days of fasting and praying prior to this scrying had used up her fragile strength.

The moan did not go unnoticed. The women of the Temple had been keeping close watch on Honia, and when the woman outside the door heard the strange sounds coming from the chamber, she quickly summoned Honia's successor, Calenda sul Honia. Calenda and several others entered the room and very gently picked Honia up and carried her to bed. By that time her body was burning with fever. The women silently, efficiently, began to mix herbs and sent for water and towels for cold compresses to apply to her forehead.

As she tossed and turned, her moaning caused all of the women who cared for their mistress to worry. Never had they seen her in such a state. Her constant thrashing made it almost impossible to get any of the medicines near her mouth. Those who did touch her as they placed compresses on her drew their hands away immediately, her fever was so hot. At first, Calenda was the only one who could get near. When her hand was pushed away from Honia's forehead with great force, she realized her mistress yet communed with the oracle, as if held in its grip. Helpless to do anything but watch, they knelt around Honia and prayed. Finally, around dawn, Honia's fever broke, and she quieted, sleeping peacefully at last.

"Sisters," Calenda addressed everyone in the room, "let us take some rest while we can. Honia will sleep now and so must we. There are others who will watch over her and call us if need be." The women agreed with her. Yawning, they rose stiffly from their chairs or the floor, where they had spent the night in prayer. Calenda placed four novices in charge of Honia and instructed them how to administer the herbs. Somewhat comforted by the knowledge that her mistress was in good hands, Calenda left for her bed.

But the events of the night had troubled Calenda. She fell asleep only to begin dreaming immediately of Septia and Korab. When her hand had been pushed away with such force from Honia's body, Calenda had seen bits and pieces of Honia's vision. Now, strangely, she was being shown in vivid detail just what made Honia suffer so. After several hours she was mercifully released from the dream. Calenda woke and dressed, praying that what she had learned was not true, knowing in her heart that it was. She stopped by the kitchen for some bread and cheese. Thinking Honia might be well enough for food, she made up a tray for her mistress and carried it to her bedchamber.

Honia was awake and dutifully swallowing a great gulp of the herbal elixir, her face twisted in a grimace as she drained the cup. "Ach. Next time may I please have some honey mixed with that?" The young novice who attended her looked horrified and bowed repeatedly to Honia as she took the cup away.

"Child, it's not your fault. Don't look so frightened. I will be feeling much better soon, thanks to your help." Her kind words brought a reluctant smile to the young novice's face.

As Calenda entered with the tray, Honia brightened. "Ah, food. Something to wipe my palate clean after the bitter tea."

"Yes, Mistress. I am happy to hear you feel like eating. That is a good sign," Calenda answered. "Perhaps when you have finished you will tell us what happened to you." She waited patiently as Honia ate small bites of food. It was clear to Calenda that Honia had paid a dear price for the information she received from the oracle. But, being the healers they were, Calenda knew she and her companion priestesses would soon restore their beloved mistress to health.

Only after Honia had eaten something did she realize how weak she was. But her duty called to, more like pulled at, her. Finished with her sparse meal of broth and bread and cheese, Honia commanded Calenda in a voice that was barely a whisper, "Send to the palace for Corta and Ondeen." Puzzled, one young priestess bowed and left to carry out her order.

Twenty-Four

For Bimily the waiting had become intolerable. She had little to occupy her time during the day, and though she was genuinely happy to see her family again, she was very much a stranger to them. Much of the day she was left alone while her parents and her sister went about their lives. Her strength had returned yet she found the idle hours tiring. With little to occupy her mind, she worried.

Four days had gone by and no word had come from the Elders about their decision on the fate of her friends. They remained in the underground chambers where they had first been placed, in the same state of deep sleep. Bimily was still forbidden to go near them.

Bimily was about to begin pacing again when there came a knock at the door. Instantly there, she opened it to see a very handsome young man standing on the step. His hair was a mass of blond curls that glinted in the light and his eyes were the gray-green color of the sea on a stormy day. His perfectly formed mouth smiled and flashed perfectly straight teeth. It took some time for her to remember to speak. His effect on Bimily seemed to please him.

"Good day to you, Bimily. I am Tarlsen. Do you remember me?"

"Tarlsen? You were still a young boy when I left. Please do come in, though I am the only one here. How can I help you?" To herself she muttered, *It's amazing how several hundred years can change a person.*

"I have been sent to summon you. The Elders are ready to speak to you about your friends and request your presence." Now his eyes changed and she read something dark in them. Fearful, Bimily left with him at once for the great hall.

There were few present to witness Bimily's audience, something that made her uneasy. She also didn't care for the way her footsteps echoed as she followed Tarlsen down the center of the hall. At the dais, he bowed low before the three seated Elders. "Bimily is here as you requested," he announced. This time when Tarlsen smiled at her, Bimily couldn't help but feel something very wrong was about to happen.

Bimily had just greeted the Elders when the doors opened noisily at the far end of the hall, pulling everyone's attention away. Bimily turned to see Shunlar following Erroless down the center of the hall. Shunlar smiled with relief when she saw Bimily, then she directed her full attention to the Three Elders who sat waiting in their cushioned chairs.

She bowed with the slightest show of respect. "Please my whims, I am Shunlar, daughter of Marleah and Alglooth. Why have I been placed in the Spell of Dreamless Sleep for so long?" While her words in Old Tongue were proper, Shunlar's icy tone conveyed displeasure.

Leatha answered, "You are not a welcome presence here in Vash Darlon. If you can convince us that you should remain alive, you will be allowed to leave. Your memory of this place will, of course, be erased."

Though Leatha's answer would have normally made her very angry, Shunlar remained calm and simply announced, "Please my whims, but I have been instructed to tell you I demand The Thousand Things."

To say that her words startled the Elders would be an understatement. Everyone in the hall became silent, rigidly watching what was taking place before them. The words were a secret response only one of their kind could have uttered.

Thricia's voice broke the silence as she carefully

asked, "Where did you learn these words?"

"I learned them in a dream. I demand The Thousand Things," Shunlar repeated.

Before another word could be uttered Menadees was up and out of his chair. Poised at the edge of the dais he stared hard at Shunlar until she felt she might faint. It took almost all of her strength to look away and break the connection between them. Once she had, Shunlar was panting and pale and leaned heavily on Bimily for support. Menadees, too, felt the break. He began to make a sign in the air with his hand when suddenly the doors to the hall crashed open behind them.

In the threshold stood Alglooth, his wings extended, his chest heaving, and his hair billowing around his face in such a way that it gave him a fearsome look. From his appearance, it was plain that he had exerted himself near to the point of collapse. He slowly walked the length of the hall, with all eyes on him. By the time he had crossed the room, his wings were folded under his cloak and his height covered with an illusion that made him look shorter and thus more human. Reaching the dais he embraced Shunlar tenderly, whispering something in her ear. When they parted, he turned to the Elders and bowed.

"My name is Alglooth. I am the son of Grazelea and Porthelae. This woman is my daughter, and I am here before you to demand to know why you hold her a prisoner. It seems all she has done is assist one of your own in returning to you. If not for my daughter's help, Bimily might not be alive now." Though he spoke quietly, sparks and smoke spewed from his mouth and nostrils.

Menadees remained standing on the same spot at the edge of the dais. "Your daughter has just mentioned something extraordinary. Tell us of your dream, Shunlar," instructed Menadees, the gesture of his hand and the tone of his voice placing a compulsion to speak over her.

But no one was more surprised than he when his spell failed to work. Alglooth had placed a protective cover around Shunlar, Bimily, and himself the moment he had embraced his daughter. Nothing anyone did could pass that barrier. Knowing fully what Menadees attempted, Alglooth answered when Shunlar did not.

"Shunlar has dreamed the dream of The Thousand Things, which I sent to her. She summoned me after you had placed her in the dreamless sleep. What she carries in her arm can do no one any harm. It may be a source of irritation to some of you, but I assure you, the goodness of her heart has prevailed. The Lifestone of Banant can do no damage where it is.

"As for whether or not she will be allowed to leave here," Alglooth paused for his words to sink in, "there is nothing any of you can do to stop us from leaving whenever we wish to. However, you yet hold three men prisoner, and since we wish no harm to come to them, we will not leave until they are awakened and set free." No one doubted that Alglooth was sincere.

Erroless, who had been sitting off to the side of the hall, watched what had just taken place with great amusement. He approached. "So, you are the son of Grazelea. Welcome to Vash Darlon, nephew." He opened his arms and embraced Alglooth. Startled, Alglooth returned the embrace. In the blink of an eye he and the old man disappeared, leaving Shunlar and Bimily standing together. Just as they were about to protest, they, too, disappeared.

Smelly, sulfurous smoke filled the air and Menadees wrinkled his nose. Leatha was furious. Thricia looked insulted as she heard Menadees's laughter fill the hall.

"What in the name of the ancestors is so funny?" Leatha growled at him.

"Why, the unpredictability of today. I suspect it is their humanness that brings it about. Can you recall this much excitement in eons? What will happen next, do you think, now that they have Erroless with them?" Before anyone could say another word, Menadees also disappeared, his chuckling voice echoing in the hall.

Twenty-Five

ALGLOOTH SEEMED A BIT UNSETTLED. HE WAS just about to ask after Shunlar and Bimily when they blinked into the room. They looked as stunned as he did to be there.

"Well, well. Make yourselves comfortable. I'm sure you have many questions, and I will answer them to the best of my ability." Erroless watched patiently as his three guests looked around the room.

They were in sumptuous surroundings. The room's walls were covered in beautiful tapestries that had scenes of dragons frolicking in the air. Nearly every inch of the floor was covered by carpets so plush their feet felt as though they were sinking when they stepped upon them. The overstuffed leather chairs looked soft and inviting, piled with pillows of brightly embroidered fabric. From tables and ornately carved wooden cupboards spilled forth jewels, golden plates, and goblets, jewel-encrusted swords and daggers, tumbling and scattering across the floor.

"This is my treasure room. Only those I wish to admit can enter. For the time being you are safe and may speak freely."

"Why for the time being? What is going to happen?" asked Alglooth.

"The Elders, I can imagine, are now conferring and attempting to find a way to bring you back. Probably only Menadees suspects where we are. He is the only one of them that thinks clearly in a crisis. But, I digress. The reason I have brought you here is to tell you what we have learned about the words on Ranth's back. Not to mention the fact that I wasn't at all comfortable with how things were being conducted in the hall."

"Can they find a way to bring us back?" asked Shunlar.

"No. Not while I am alive, at least," he answered with a wink.

"Erroless, you called me nephew. Is this true? Are you my uncle?" asked Alglooth.

"Yes, it is true. Your mother, Grazelea, was my sister. We of Vash Darlon were dragons before we were shape-changers. In fact, you have many other family members here in Vash Darlon. Some will be pleased to discover who you are, while others will not. We are a very closeted people, and it is my hope that you will not think too harshly of us. To some you are an abomination because of the circumstances of your conception. I don't agree, but I am only one person." Erroless looked apologetic. Alglooth, on the other hand, had a look of amazement on his face.

"Now to the business at hand. Bimily, I will leave this up to you because Alglooth and Shunlar trust you. It is time to open your mind to them so they may learn the secret of the Lifestones."

"But I thought only our people could open that memory," Bimily answered him.

"Think about what you have just said, my dear," he gently told her. "They are of our blood. Though it may be thinner in Shunlar, it is there nevertheless."

Bimily looked bewildered, but she did as Erroless asked. Asking Shunlar and Alglooth to sit on either side of her, she placed her hands over theirs. "As Erroless said, I have a deeply embedded memory of our people that you must now be shown. Coming from any other source, this would most probably sound too fantastic to believe. Once I open my memories to you, it is Erroless's belief that you will find these recollections are enclosed in your minds as well." Then she closed her eyes and accepted their presence into her thoughts.

The strength of her mind was dizzying to Shunlar. In a flash she and Alglooth were transported to a verdant countryside that was inhabited by great dragons of every color and hue who were engaged in flying, playing, eating, hunting, and even sleeping. Never had she thought there could be so many. *Which one are you?* Shunlar asked.

Why, can't you tell? I am the pretty one with the copper-colored scales and beard, Bimily answered, amusement in her voice. Even now she teased.

Then her voice changed, becoming more sober. *Have you ever wondered why it is humans have chosen to build great cities where they have?* Without waiting for a reply, Bimily continued. *It is because all of the great cities are built over the sites of the burial caves of our ancestors and great magic resides in these caves. Humans are unconsciously drawn to these places. And the secret of that magic is this: The heart of each dragon becomes a Lifestone when she or he dies.*

How do you know this? asked Shunlar.

My people were once dragons. When the human population began to grow, someone got the notion to spread the rumor that dragons were evil beings. They were hunted and killed. Collectively my people decided to leave behind the dragon's shape forever. Once it was done, it was forbidden for any of us to take on that shape at the cost of being stripped of our powers.

When a dragon died, a fire consumed the body and only the bones and the heart remained. The heart would then be buried with others in secret caves known only to the dragons. The hearts eventually came to be called Lifestones by humans and certain humans who were deemed to be "pure of heart" were called to bond with a Lifestone; the essence of a dragon. The pure of heart were individuals who were recognized for their potential to use their hearts and minds together for the good of their people.

The Lifestones had been buried for centuries in secret places, Kalaven Desert being one of several secret caves. There are other caves where there are more Lifestones, but only my people know their locations. You will soon remember, because I am unlocking the memory, that there is a secret cave in Stiga, one in Tonnerling buried under tons of lava rock, and one between Vensunor and the Valley of Great Trees.

As stunned as they were to learn this great secret, Alglooth and Shunlar knew Bimily was telling them the truth. As she spoke, the words had the effect of unlocking a treasure chest, causing something inside their memories to surface. An overwhelming feeling surged through them, a knowledge of who they were combined with new depths of power.

What happens to a Lifestone when the person who has bonded with it dies? asked Alglooth.

When the holder of a stone dies, unless it is passed on at the holder's death, the stone loses its power and becomes merely a brilliant gem. All of my people will become Lifestones when they die, and so will I.

Slowly Bimily moved her hands apart from theirs, gently closing off the mind-touch.

"Thank you, Bimily and Erroless, for this information. Now I begin to understand the actions of your people, I should say, our people, more than ever before. But tell me, do they suspect that we possess the shared memories?" asked Alglooth.

"I don't know what they suspect. Frankly, I wasn't sure at all if you had it in you, nephew. I am relieved to know you do." Erroless smiled.

"Erroless, could I have come to harm if they had not had the deep memory of our ancestors?" asked Bimily with a wary tone.

"Probably not, but we'll never know now, will we? And, no harm has been done. Now I will tell you what we have learned about Ranth." Their attention was fully focused on Erroless as he spoke. Shunlar clenched her fists as she listened. Soon tears filled her eyes, but she refused to blink them away; she just kept a blank look on her face as they ran down her cheeks.

"As you know, *azkrey gaht* means 'helpless captive,'

in a tongue that is older than most of our people can remember. They are very powerful words, for not only do they take away one's will, making that person vulnerable to manipulation by another, as if that weren't enough, *azkrey gaht* is a spell to draw death to the one so marked. It is only thanks to his Lifestone that Ranth has remained alive, I assure you.

"What we have concluded is that there are four alternatives for him to take; three of them not pleasant. To begin with, only the one who placed the words on Ranth can change them. Since whoever did this is likely one who wishes Ranth dead, I believe it very unlikely he or she would be easily persuaded to change the words.

"Another choice would be to have the words removed. Painful indeed because it involves peeling away layers of skin. Nasty business," Erroless muttered.

"The most painful and worst alternative as far as I'm concerned is that he must die by another hand and then be brought back to life with the help of his Lifestone. I wouldn't choose that course, no.

"Then there is the choice of becoming another. That is to say, he must change his name. To do that, he must take another name in the same place, in the same way he did when he first was named. I don't suppose any of you know how or where that happened?"

"I do," replied Shunlar. "He drew his name from the Cauldron of the Great Mother in the Temple of Vensunor, where he was raised."

"Ah, then he is not truly of the Feralmon, is he? I see now how appropriate Ranth is for his name," chuckled Erroless. In Old Tongue, Ranth meant "changeling."

Erroless was beginning to seem older by the minute. The strain of removing three people from one location to another as he had done was showing. His voice sounded thready, and he was becoming more stooped. Bimily noticed it first.

"Are you quite all right?" she asked suddenly. "My eyes aren't playing tricks on me, are they?"

"Depends on what you're seeing." Apparently his wit retained its edge. "When I tire these days, I begin to appear as old as I really am. Yes, positively ancient," he mumbled. "You're going to have to leave here soon. If I am going to be able to argue intelligibly to have your three friends released soon, I must get some rest. Come here. Gather round and I'll teach you how to translocate," his arms opened, motioning for them to come closer.

Surrounded by Alglooth, Shunlar, and Bimily, Erroless explained to them through mind-touch how to translocate themselves. *Tsk, tsk. Bimily, you should have learned this long ago. You would have if you hadn't been so stubborn and left so early.* Shunlar and Alglooth felt Bimily blush at the way Erroless admonished her.

It's really quite simple, just not easy. He chuckled at the joke he made.

With a chime-like quality to his voice, Erroless began the instruction on how to translocate. They all heard someone say, *Oh*, or, *Of course, how simple* when they saw how it was done, but none of them were sure who said the words.

Do you understand the technique? Erroless asked. *Yes,* they all answered. *Well and good, then. We shall see each other shortly. For now, I must sleep and rebuild my strength. Until later, my friends.* Then as an afterthought he added, *Just be sure you have a clear picture of where it is you want to go. Otherwise, you could end up anywhere at all.* They all heard him chuckle one last time before Erroless translocated them to the underground chamber where Ranth lay.

Twenty-Six

ONCE THEIR IDENTITY HAD BEEN CONFIRMED, Septia and Korab were treated well, much to their great relief. An entire month had passed since they had been captured in the desert by the small band of Tonnerling scouts. In that time they learned as much as they could about the men from the north and their customs. Women, it seemed, were treated as objects of desire and value and little else. Septia could sense a feeling of underlying distrust for her whenever she had the occasional encounter with any of the men. Sometimes she caught a lustful leer from a passing soldier, which was immediately dealt with by Korab. Never was she alone with any man except the two body servants, and they treated her with respect bordering on fear.

The first three weeks, Septia's time was occupied by applying salves to her burned skin, drinking gallons of water, and sleeping to recuperate from the ravages of the desert. Septia needed more time before she would consider herself fully recovered. One reason was that she had transferred a very large measure of her life's essence to Korab to ensure that he had had the strength to carry her to safety. It had worked, in part.

Septia had also given birth just four months prior. Always one who succeeded at whatever endeavor she undertook, being torn from her child had made her weaker in spirit than she ever suspected it could. On several mornings Septia found she must force herself to find the will to live. Since being separated from Iola, Septia felt at times as if she carried a phantom child with her. She found herself easily startled and cowering at the oddest moments, prepared to hide or take a blow with her back or arms rather than have anything happen to the child who was no longer in her arms. This made her anxious, for it was utterly unlike her usual behavior.

The only thing that gave her a sense of purpose each day was the ancient text that she had now read twice from cover to cover. Though her torn spirit begged to be left alone to mourn Iola's loss, the text gave her the desire to begin again each day. Once she began reading the script, Septia's sense of purpose would return, and, with a vengeance, she would begin mapping out what must be done to achieve her goals. First and foremost was the goal to prepare herself to be called by a Dark Lifestone, whose existence she and Korab had stumbled across in the text. The second was to be reunited with Iola.

Unlike his mate, Korab greatly improved in strength within one week, and he had immediately begun to meet with General Bergoin and his officers to discuss strategy. He learned that the battles they fought had been a test of the newly trained Tonnerling soldiers, most of whom had never before participated in a real battle.

Korab had gotten no information from his people about the fighting. He and Septia had both been imprisoned for their crimes when the war began, and because he was the person who had instigated the war, everyone shunned him. When they were taken to the desert to die, the enemy was in retreat, something that his people knew and counted on. They preferred he and Septia die from exposure, expecting he might not be killed if the enemy were to capture them. They didn't know how right they were.

No one realized how devious or powerful Septia's influence was. If not for her control over one of the young priestesses who attended her daily, they would have died as they were intended. But her control held and in secret meetings with hirelings, gold was exchanged, messages were passed, arrangements were made for the water and supplies to be hidden, without questions.

Even though initially the Tonnerlingans had outnumbered the Feralmon, they were no match when it came to actual fighting, and many died because their combat skills were so poor. Korab intended to fix that, but only because he wanted to win. When he learned how badly trained these men were, it disgusted him. He knew Septia could fight most of them blindfolded and win, with only half of her strength regained.

The Tonnerlingans were larger in stature than the Feralmon, but coming from a northern climate on the edge of the sea, they were also unaccustomed to living in the heat of the desert. It gave the Feralmon a very welcome advantage and perhaps the only one, given they were outnumbered three to one.

Kalaven had proven to be much more difficult to invade than the Tonnerlingans had imagined. Since so little was known about the Feralmon, the first wave of the fighting force was astonished when they discovered that not only was there a great city but also that Kalaven was well defended. The entrance to the city was a natural fortress in the rocks that proved impenetrable.

Green troops all, the Tonnerlingans were forced to stop their attempted invasion after half of their force was left wounded or dead. With so many men lost or unable to fight, morale dropped so low that many chose to flee rather than face death or maiming. The remaining force opted to bury their dead and tend their wounded as far from the desert as they could get. Thus the long wait for reinforcements began.

Further, there was little or no game to speak of in the desert, nothing that northern men considered food anyway. The giant, poisonous lizard and the small, elusive, stringy antelope that the Feralmon ate were next to impossible to track if a person did not know how, and the men of Tonnerling were not and had never been hunters.

With winter setting in and supplies running low, the commander of the army decided to set up a permanent base camp close to the Thrale River, where the men could find food and tasks they were familiar with. With great nets and traps woven and put into place, the men began to feel confident once more, something their leaders had counted on. It was this waiting remnant of an army that Korab and Septia found themselves living among as they healed.

It was early morning and the air in the tent had become close and oppressive. Septia and Korab sat facing each other, drenched in sweat from focusing on a pattern of breathing while chanting, an exertion that seemed near impossible. Since dawn they had been working at the task of perfecting a mind technique from the pages of the ancient text that Septia had managed to have smuggled from the Temple. Once they had mastered it, the text assured, this chant would strengthen their minds, enabling them to handle the powerful, Dark Lifestones. Korab called a halt to their exercise first.

''Enough,'' he gasped. ''I have had enough of this for one day. What I desire now is you.'' He gave her a genuine smile, which easily persuaded Septia to agree with his wishes. One of the unexpected side effects of these exercises was a heightened sexual appetite. Now that her strength had returned she could genuinely enjoy it. With his appetite properly cared for, and a mind control subtly placed, Korab was proving to be quite an amenable man.

''Lord Korab,'' the servant outside the tent called at the flap.

Korab ignored the man's voice. He was too busy consuming Septia.

They were interrupted by Gustov Maren calling out, louder this time, ''Excuse me, Lord Korab. Captain Veelim has brought two prisoners who say they are your people. Will you see them?''

Cursing under his breath, Korab hurriedly pulled on his breeches and shirt. Septia had a very amused look on her face as she dressed. Though Korab would never admit it, he was excited by the possibility that it could be his oath-brothers, Tadim sul Kleea and Natha sul Ankar, and some of his followers from Kalaven who had finally arrived. The fact that none had found him yet, when they had all vowed to do so, chipped away at his ego daily. Both fully clothed, they appeared at the tent flap and stepped out into the morning light.

Kneeling before them were a man and a woman who were bound and gagged. The burly soldier who knelt between them was pressing their foreheads into the dirt. From the looks of them, they had been treated badly by the band of scouts who had captured them. Their clothing, or what was left of it, was torn and bloody in places. Their hair had been cut off bluntly at the nape of their necks and what remained clung to their heads, matted and crusted with blood and dirt. The large soldier grabbed both by their hair and pulled them up to standing positions in their bare, bleeding feet. Korab recognized them, though their faces were bruised and filthy.

"Cut them loose. They are mine, as they said." Korab watched as two guards removed the gags from the prisoners then unsheathed daggers and began to cut at the ropes binding their arms. The man who had removed the woman's gag gave her a sinister leer, which Korab observed.

"I would advise against causing the woman harm," Korab warned, perhaps too late. "She can retaliate in the most unusual ways."

The words were barely out of Korab's mouth when the guard's expression began to change. He choked and struggled for his breath. As everyone watched he fell over, clutching his throat, his face turning blue. The guards who were cutting the ropes stopped abruptly and backed away several steps, their eyes growing wide.

"Don't hurt him too much," admonished Korab, though his voice didn't sound serious. "We need every man possible to take Kalaven." But the woman seemed not to be listening. Her attention was on the man who lay at her feet, no longer breathing.

"Trust me, that one won't be missed." Then she remembered herself before Korab and bent low before him. "My lord Korab, I claim my right to kill him for what I suffered at his hands. Blood for blood."

"I don't give you permission to kill him. Revive him. Now!" Korab shouted. Her eyes slits of fury, the woman trembled, obviously in turmoil, fighting hard to obey the order. With the muscles of her jaw working, she kicked the man several times as hard as she could before spitting on him. Finally he twitched and coughed, sucking in air in great gulps.

By that time the soldiers were about to panic. Korab gestured impatiently for them to continue cutting the ropes from the captives' arms, something they did as fast as they could. Though neither the man nor woman made a sound when the ropes fell away, he knew all too well from their expressions how much pain they were experiencing.

"Take them to the healer's tent and see that they are treated well, by my order. Feed and bathe them, and find them proper clothing. When they are rested, bring them to me." He watched as the two captives were carefully led away. The soldiers guarding them maintained a distance from them and their comrade, who had been dead and brought back to life. Korab could hear several of them muttering under their breath about wizards and magic.

This is good, Korab thought to himself. *They now have another reason to fear me. It should make them all the more willing to do as I command.*

Septia hadn't uttered a sound as she watched. Once they were back in the privacy of their tent, she asked, "Who are they, Korab?"

"They are assassins, weapons that I sent to find and kill Ranth's woman and her child."

Septia regarded Korab closely before saying, "You never mentioned anything about assassins to me. How long ago was this done?"

"Do you remember the morning you came to me, upset because you discovered that Ranth's woman had given birth?" She nodded. "I wanted to protect you, make you feel secure knowing that our child would have no rival." Septia came to Korab, put her arms around his neck, and kissed him, a tear trickling down her cheek at the mention of their daughter, Iola.

"Since they are both here, I must assume they have not found her." He sounded angry yet he was gentle with Septia as he removed her arms from around his neck. He began to pace.

"Why must you assume they have not found her?"

"The man is alive. That woman's orders were to follow him to make sure he killed the one called Shunlar and her child. When the prey was dead, her orders were to kill him. Since they have turned up here, together, I must question them to find out why my orders have not been carried out."

Septia didn't like the look in Korab's eyes and knew there was only one way to quiet him. The servants who had poured the bath water waited nearby to attend to them. Septia ordered them out. She helped Korab undress and urged him to step into the deep wooden tub. When he was settled, she disrobed and got in. Soon the water began spilling rhythmically over the edges.

Late that evening the two assassins were brought to Korab and Septia's tent and quietly ushered inside. They went to their knees before Korab and pressed their foreheads to the ground, something that was not easy for them to do in their battered conditions. Dressed in clean, although ill-fitting clothing, both of them had their faces covered in makeshift masks, as a sign of recognition that their lord was not pleased with them. They remained kneeling before the seated Korab for a long time while he methodically raked them with his eyes. Finally he gave permission for them to stand.

"Rise and greet the Lady Septia, my consort," Korab ordered in a quiet, steely voice. "State your names."

"Orem, my lord Korab. Lady Septia." His hoarse voice conveyed the pain he endured from the simple acts of standing and bowing. He was sweating and reeked of fear.

"Deeka sul Bareth, my lord Korab. Lady Septia."

Her whispered greeting sounded pinched from the effort of rising to her feet and bowing.

Septia acknowledged their presence with a nod. She reclined on pillows behind Korab's chair, slightly off to his left side, so that she had a clear view of the two assassins. From there she felt certain she could observe everything and remain a benign presence.

"Show us your faces," Korab ordered.

Keeping their eyes lowered, Deeka and Orem slowly unwound the cloth that covered their faces.

The air around the man who called himself Orem moved with a rippling quality that Septia recognized immediately as some sort of spell, positive that the woman had placed it on him, something he seemed not to notice. She wondered if Orem was extremely dense or just stupid, but concluded he must have some bit of intelligence to have remained alive at his age.

Deeka, the female assassin, also had placed a strong cover over herself, so strong that Septia could not be sure that she really looked at the face of the woman standing before her. Orem seemed to be afraid or perhaps it was exhaustion that made him tremble so, while Deeka's stillness was magnetic.

Korab, too, could see that Deeka maintained a hold over Orem. He remembered very well his first and only encounter with Deeka. Though they had merely exchanged words, she had filled him with such strong lust that he had nearly spilled his seed where he sat. Recalling that, Korab had placed a strong protective cover securely over himself and Septia before Deeka entered their tent so she could not affect either of them during this audience.

Korab's controlled voice, while low, was thick with displeasure. "Explain to me how you came to be captured by these men."

"My lord Korab, we rested, thinking we were safe. While we slept, we were surrounded," Orem answered, keeping his eyes on the ground. "We underestimated their stealth and tracking skill."

''And how many days were you their unwilling guests?''

''My lord, I cannot be sure. A hood was kept over my head, and I did not see the light of day. It may have been five days. It may have been longer.''

''Kept a hood over your head you say. Then you saw nothing of what Deeka suffered at their hands, though I can guess by the way she tried to strangle the guard.'' Korab glanced at Deeka, before he continued.

''From the looks of you, you were treated badly. Why is it that they cut your hair?'' Korab asked with a hint of curiosity.

''My lord, they meant to frighten us. They said something about mourning for myself. They were laughing.'' Orem's voice remained low, his eyes trained on Korab's feet, a small tic pulling at the corner of his right eye.

''Sounds like they intended to kill you, or at least make you believe they would.'' Then Korab's head jerked up. ''What language did they speak?''

An awkward silence filled the air. Finally Orem answered. ''They spoke in their tongue and in ours. I can speak theirs, but I did my best not to let them know it.'' Korab gave him a hard look before turning his attention on Deeka.

''What happened to you?'' He asked her in that same cold, uncomforting tone.

''My lord Korab, while they interrogated Orem, they treated me as if I was not capable of anything clever or intelligent. I was not questioned, but used as an animal would not be.'' Her voice was clipped, the hate rising with each word. Deeka stared at Korab while she spoke. ''One night I overheard one of them speak your name. Reading his thoughts, I found out you were here, and I begged him to bring us to you. Finally he grew tired of me and brought us here. He should be dead now,'' she stated matter-of-factly.

''Why did it take so long for you to bend him to your will?'' Korab asked, extremely interested, knowing what she was capable of.

''My lord, when we were captured I was knocked

unconscious. It took me several days even to realize what had happened to me."

Korab stared at the bruises on Deeka's face for a long time before turning away from her. He asked Orem in the same controlled voice. "The job you were hired to do. Tell me it was accomplished."

"My lord, it was not," Orem answered shakily. Terrified, he quivered and his acrid smell became more unpleasant.

"Tell me you have a good reason," Korab shot back, clearly angry.

"I . . . I . . . cannot. All I can s-s-say is that she proved stronger than we anticipated." Orem stuttered, the nervous tic becoming more pronounced.

"You say *we*. How is it that the two of you traveled together, you and Deeka? Obviously for your pleasure. You took her into your confidence as well as your bed, didn't you?" Korab unmercifully accused Orem, who quailed under his grilling. Deeka merely stood calmly, staring at Korab through half-closed eyes.

"Yes, Lord Korab," Orem answered miserably, his whole head twitching this time.

"Together you could not kill one soft woman," Korab taunted.

"She did not have the child with her when we found her. We decided to capture her and question her until she would tell us where the child was. Forgive me, but if we had killed her, the child would have remained alive, and we would have had no way to find him," Orem explained.

"Indeed, and just what means did you use? Surely a woman such as she would have answered to force, or were you afraid to use force? Did you threaten her with pain and death?" Korab demanded.

"My lord, she was drugged, bound, beaten, and given no food or comfort for three days, and still she would not answer." This time it was Deeka's steady voice that explained. "We discovered who she was in the mercenary camp outside the gates of Vensunor. Not a camp follower, as one might have expected, but a warrior who is well trained in the use of sword and dagger."

"A warrior you say?" Korab mused.

"Yes, and her companion is Avek sul Zara." Deeka allowed the name to roll languidly off her tongue.

Korab's head came up slowly, and his expression changed. "Avek has partnered with Ranth's woman?" He turned to Septia with a strange look of contempt.

"My lord, though I have failed you the first time, I know where the woman and her child have gone," offered Orem. "We were on her trail and would have finished it had it not been for our capture. I ask only that you set me free and allow me to complete this task for you. I swear I will not fail you." Finished, Orem slowly got to his knees, difficult and painful for him as it was. He bent fully over, touching his forehead to the ground. Deeka remained standing.

"Where is she?" Korab demanded, turning his full attention back to Orem.

"She traveled to Kalaven with the child," replied Deeka.

"Into our very hands she goes. With Ranth's son," Korab murmured. But Deeka had heard him, and as understanding crossed her face, she frowned and lowered her eyes.

"No, you will not go free," Septia suddenly announced as she rose from the floor and placed herself between Korab and the two assassins. "You had your chance. Now you will die for failing," she promised, her eyes blazing horribly.

Korab seemed to propel himself from the chair. He called loudly, "Gustov Maren." The tent flap opened and the man appeared. "Have these two removed from our sight. Return them to their tent and see that they are closely guarded."

Guards appeared. Deeka went willingly, since none of the men dared to touch her. Orem, however, had to be practically dragged out, spent from his interview.

When they were alone again Korab turned on Septia. He grabbed her by the shoulders, picked her up, and shook her violently. "You will never usurp my authority again, ever!'' he shouted as he threw her down onto the pillows.

''You would have had them killed eventually,'' she answered. Somehow Septia managed to look just as in control of the situation lying amidst the pillows as she had standing, defying Korab to his face.

''Yes, but in my own good time. I will order their deaths myself, in my own time.''

''I want the pleasure of killing Shunlar, and her child, before Ranth's eyes. He must suffer the way I have. I want him to know the pain of having his child taken from him, as I have. But I want him to watch it die.'' Septia's eyes nearly glowed with hatred.

Korab regarded her for several minutes before leaving the tent.

Twenty-Seven

Korab seethed with the newfound knowledge that Shunlar and Tavis were alive. Mercurial at the best of times, his temper was positively out of control. Septia had not only angered him by overstepping his authority in front of the two assassins, she had positively frightened him besides. The look in her eyes caused him to question her sanity. *Does she have the strength to continue?* he wondered. The way Septia behaved of late had him watching her closely and sleeping with a dagger close by, especially during their lovemaking.

Walking around the encampment, with no particular destination in mind, Korab heard the familiar tromp of Gustov Maren's boots behind him. In a small way he was comforted; something at least had the feel of familiarity about it. The last month had been the most difficult in his life, and now this. *Orem, the scum, the worm,* Korab muttered under his breath. *He will suffer,* he vowed. *He failed me. I can't have failure, not now.*

Though Korab received the most deferential treatment from the men in this camp, he was aware of their real feelings about him. Being the strong telepath that he was, Korab could hear their private thoughts, information he kept to himself. Unlike his people, Tonnerlingans were not skilled in the art of telepathy. If any of them knew he constantly read their minds in any encounter and in all of the meetings he attended, he would lose his advantage. The strain of holding his tongue, of being civil and not saying what he really wanted to say to these men pushed him to his limits.

He kept walking, still muttering to himself, until he realized he was standing before the tent wherein Orem and Deeka were held. A strange calm washed over him, and his smile made Gustov Maren almost stop breathing. Korab gestured to his constant shadow.

Gustov Maren nodded understanding of the task Korab put to him. He bowed and hurried off to find the soldiers who had captured the two assassins, particularly the man Deeka had nearly killed when they were brought in.

Gustov Maren was learning just how much he hated the life of a soldier. At one time he had entertained the thought of becoming a monk, living a life of meditation and chastity. Trying to live it had been another thing altogether. His family was large, and he was not the eldest son, so he worked for his father and eldest brother at various menial jobs in the family business after returning from the monastery. Expendable as the fifth son in line of inheritance, he had been sent away to fight in the war by parents who wanted to maintain their family's good reputation.

But he had learned one very interesting bit of information while studying with the monks, and that was that there were people who could read your thoughts or control you by touching your mind without your permission or knowledge. The old monks taught the old ways, and one of the lessons was how to protect your mind from being touched or manipulated by another.

He did that now as he ran in search of the men Korab had sent him to summon. For weeks Gustov Maren had suspected that Korab and Septia were strong telepaths. Today he decided to take this opportunity to test his theory. When he entered Deeka and Orem's tent with the four men, he let himself become frightened to the point of feeling physically ill. He trembled and let his thoughts run rampant. He imagined what was going to happen next, and he prayed he would not be required to attend to any of the goings-on inside the tent. He did not have a strong stomach when it came to torture. Hitting a man in a fight, getting a few blows in with a weapon or fist was one thing. When the blood started running and bones cracked, his stomach turned. As if on cue, Korab looked his way, read his mind and kicked him out, telling him to allow no one to pass.

Now he was certain, but, truthfully, he was not comforted by the knowledge, as frightened as he was. The one thing Gustov Maren suspected was that he also had a very effective tool. For hadn't he just gotten himself put out of the tent, as he wanted? Could he learn to do more, even to the point of manipulating the way Korab treated him? The thought frightened him, and he gave up thinking about it. Instead he concentrated on the chant that would put a protection around his mind, praying that Korab would not have occasion to try to probe his thoughts and find him out. Until then, Gustov Maren sat guard on the other side of the tent flap, thankful that he could only hear the muffled sounds of what took place inside.

The sight of Korab bursting unexpectedly into the small tent where he and Deeka were held prisoner told Orem that his life was over. Though he had lived most of it doing to others what was about to happen to him, Orem was in no way prepared to die in the same fashion. He thought of begging for mercy but knew it would serve no purpose, and perhaps only prolong his pain.

Korab wanted to punish someone, had wanted to for so long he couldn't remember a day when he hadn't. The look in his eyes told Orem there were no words that could save him, and so he surrendered to it. Something in the quiet way he did that made Deeka turn toward him, but only for a moment. He saw the look of self-preservation in her eyes and turned away from her first.

To her he mumbled, "May you fare better than I." After which Orem stood slowly and waited for Korab to give the order to the four soldiers who filed in, all ill at ease. Utterly silent though they were, the men began to sweat, and soon their nervous stink permeated the air. Wrinkling his nose in disgust, Korab snarled out his orders.

To Deeka he turned first. "You are to sit and watch. His fate will be yours, but because of the way you both failed me, I have no desire to let either of you die quickly."

To the soldiers he warned, "Don't touch his face."

The soldiers shifted on their feet, guessing their part in what was to unfold. One of them grinned an uncomfortable half smile. Two others slowly wrapped leather thongs around their knuckles. Without speaking Korab touched their minds and took control of their limbs. As a unit they surrounded Orem and began pummeling him until he fell. When he was down they continued, using their feet as well as their fists.

Not one of the soldiers was fully aware of his actions. Before their eyes Orem's face took on the physical likeness of Korab's enemies, and all the men were seized by a great hatred and a vengeance for people who were unknown to them. One by one they saw him as Benyar, Ranth, Zeraya, Honia, and countless others who had offended Korab over the years in some way. Standing off to the side, Korab watched the men carry out his work, his hands balled into fists, clenching and unclenching, his breathing becoming faster.

The darkness of the tent was suddenly changed as a shaft of light spilled in. Korab turned his head slowly, moving his eyes at the last instant to see who intruded. Holding the flap open, Gustov Maren was on one knee with his head bowed and turned away as Septia bent to enter the tent's small opening. Korab scowled at her, then turned back to the men who were carrying out his orders.

She came in, took a place near Deeka, and watched with a forbidding expression. After only a few minutes, she had seen enough. She left, Korab ignoring her exit. In her spot near the opening sat Deeka, her eyes closed, a small bead of sweat on her upper lip the only sign that she was at all concerned by what was happening to Orem.

Sooner than he would have liked, Korab recognized that Orem was near death. Satisfied only by the fact that he had been able to make the man suffer, he watched as Orem took a last liquid-sounding breath and expired with a shudder. Then he called the men away with a sharp command to step back. Standing over Orem, Korab kicked him hard once and when he didn't breathe or move, he backed off. The four soldiers were trembling from the shock of what they had done. They were spattered in blood, and one of them swallowed hard so as not to embarrass himself in front of the savage Feralmon lord.

"Go now. We are finished for tonight. If you wish, you may have her as a reward," Korab pointed at Deeka. When none of the men came forward, he sent them away with a dark guffaw of laughter.

"Gustov Maren," he called loudly. When Maren appeared before him, Korab sent him off ordering, "Bring the Lady Septia to me. Ask her to bring the book." As an afterthought he said, "Take this woman from my sight and do whatever you want with her. When you're finished, kill her. But beware of her. She can make you do things you'd never have a mind to do."

Gustov Maren nodded slowly and waited for Deeka to precede him from the tent. The woman moved soundlessly and it made him quiver. He followed her for several paces, then called for her to stop.

"Look, I don't want to see you harmed or killed, the way your friend was. Do you understand me?" he asked. Sickened by what he saw of the remains of Orem, his face was nearly green.

Deeka looked him over slowly and reached toward him with a mind-touch. It was broad daylight and they stood in the midst of the soldiers camp, the bustle of daily life going on around them. She knew this was her only chance to escape. Her touch glanced off him like a pebble striking a smooth marble surface. Amazement registered on her face.

"You can do that, too?" Gustov Maren whispered at her, rubbing his scalp, looking at her as if she were a demon.

She came closer, and he grabbed her arm. As his fingers closed around her wrist he looked her in the eye, and whispered, "I will help you escape, but you must help me, protect me." She nodded.

"My life will be forfeit if Lord Korab knows I let you escape. Teach me how to make and hold a firm memory in my head of me killing you in a very believable way and I will get you a horse and supplies."

Why would you do this for me? she asked, and he heard her voice in his head.

Going pale, he swallowed and answered her in much the same way. *I could not help your friend, and I doubt I will be able to help myself if Lord Korab or Lady Septia suspects what I have done. I must learn to keep them out of my mind in exchange for which I will arrange your escape. Will you help me?* She studied him for several seconds before nodding. Together they continued on to his tent. In front of several men they embraced, making it clearly look like they had one purpose in mind.

He looked around at their audience and grinned. "See that she is not disturbed or touched. I will return shortly for my reward." He patted Deeka on the behind as she ducked into the tent. The men sitting around shook their heads and laughed.

"Aye, that we'll do. What should we do with your body parts when they come flying out through the flap?" Rude laughter followed, but all the men were too afraid of Deeka to try to get near her, and Gustov Maren used that to his advantage. On his way to Septia's tent he began thinking of holding the woman in his arms, finding it near to impossible to think of anything else. Deeka had planted a memory already, and Gustov Maren found it increasingly difficult to walk.

He delivered his message to Septia, as Korab had ordered. When she looked him over after he had finished speaking, her icy glare made him shiver.

"Truthfully, I would rather have Linq and Dennik accompany me to Lord Korab's side. It seems you are preoccupied by something else. Enjoy the moment, for it is all you will have with her." Septia hissed the words and dismissed him.

By the time Gustov Maren returned to his tent he was sweating. Inside, Deeka had made herself comfortable on his pallet. She smiled at him in an amused way, which made his knees go weak.

"Come sit beside me and I will teach you several things. One of which will be how to safeguard yourself from unwanted mind controls. In exchange you will find for me a very sturdy horse, weapons, and supplies." Her voice had a strong compulsive quality.

"Lady, I have already agreed to set you free. I vow to keep that promise, on my family honor. In exchange all I ask from you is what I have already asked, nothing more. No harm will come to you while you are under my protection." Gustov Maren's voice had gotten softer and he found himself sitting next to her on the pallet, a strong desire to touch her rising in him. The air felt soft and fuzzy and he lay down, closed his eyes, and was instantly asleep. A dream overtook him with the subtlety of an avalanche; of Deeka standing beside him, pouring a pitcher of arcane knowledge into the top of his head, which had been cut open like a melon.

As soon as Deeka saw that he was asleep, she placed one hand on his chest, the other on his forehead and began planting the memories in his mind, memories that Gustov Maren would forever wonder at, never knowing if they were real or imagined. But she also held to her bargain and taught him how to place a cover over his mind that would prevent anyone from placing a Spell of Compulsion on him. Anyone who tried would experience an illusion of a woman's voice whispering in their ears, lasting for mere seconds, yet extraordinarily strong. Afterward they would be left with a desire so strong they would likely bed anyone or anything. She laughed at her great joke.

* * *

Let him have his fun, Septia thought to herself as she hurried to Korab. *He'll most likely be dead by next week anyway.* The influx of new troops, the long-awaited reinforcements, had been arriving on great rafts all week. The invasion was scheduled to take place very soon, the exact details of which Septia was not privy to, but she knew it was soon because of the way the camp bustled, preparing gear and packing supplies.

Carrying the heavy text herself because she permitted no one else to touch it, Septia hurried to Korab's side. Behind her trailed the two body servants, Linq and Dennik, keeping a good four paces back. When the soldiers saw her pass by, they rose and bowed to her. None would think of barring her way or stopping her for any reason. They were all too afraid of this "sorceress of the desert" as they called her behind her back. Many times of late when a particularly vile thought had passed through a soldier's mind, Septia no longer controlled herself. She retaliated instantly by sending the man's muscles or bowel into spasms.

Soon she had crossed the camp and was at the tent where Orem's broken body lay. *What could he have in mind, calling me here with the text?* she wondered to herself. Steeling herself for the sight she knew awaited, she entered the tent, relieved to see that Korab, or someone, had covered the body with a blanket. He sat upon a small stool, bent over, his forehead resting on his clenched, entwined knuckles. Hiding her thoughts securely, she wished he had also done something about the smell.

"My lord, I am here with the text as you requested," she said, keeping her demeanor soft. She wished none of Korab's wrath to come her way. With graceful finesse she reached toward him with the merest tendril of a calming spell to quiet his seething temper. It didn't work.

"I want you to find a spell in that great book for me, Septia. I require something that will draw the woman Shunlar to his body and hold her there, stuck like a fly to a glue pot, should she escape or leave Kalaven. Orem failed me in life; perhaps he can yet fulfill the contract in death." Korab turned to her, his eyes glazed and cruel. "Can you find such a thing in that text?"

She nodded. "I will try, but . . ."

"Don't try. DO IT!" he screamed at her.

Septia backed away from him. "Korab, I cannot guarantee there is such a spell. So far, I don't recall finding one, and I have read it cover to cover."

"Now it's Korab. A moment ago it was 'my lord.' " In one swift motion he was beside her and he grabbed her arm, squeezing it hard. The book he pulled from her arms with his other hand and dropped it on the floor. His hand free, he tore her dress from her shoulders. Trembling, Septia raised her face to him as he kissed her, letting his appetite take its course.

Much later that evening, long after the last fires had been banked low, and all but a few sentries had gone to their beds, Gustov Maren peeked out from his tent. Behind him came Deeka, dressed in some of his old clothes, a pack slung over her shoulder. They walked straightaway to the makeshift rope corral, where Gustov Maren explained to the sentry who Deeka was, making up a story that she was a special courier. With help from Deeka, the lame story worked and the sentry yawned and waved them by.

Choosing her mount, she decided upon a small animal, with sturdy legs and a barrel chest; a rather scruffy-looking horse that was probably used as a pack animal. This one, she knew, was strong and would carry her far without ever being missed. Her own horse found her while she was in the middle of the herd, but she decided it was best to leave the handsome gelding behind as it would make Gustov Maren's story about her death more believable. Scratching her horse between his ears, she patted it for a last time and, sighing, put the halter on the sturdy little mare she had picked.

Quickly saddling the mare, she secured the blanket and pack of food to the saddle with leather ties. Turning to Gustov Maren, she saluted smartly as he had taught her. Then she pulled her dagger from its sheath and handed it to him, hilt first.

"Trade daggers with me, man from sea. Give this to Korab as further proof that I am dead."

He did as she asked and she touched his arm gently in way of thanks. "You will not remember tonight, nor will the man who stands guard here. You saved my life, and I am in your debt. Should we meet again, I will do the same for you, if the need arises."

Gustov Maren watched her mount and ride away then, his memory already clouding over. He returned to his tent and slept, but his dreams were horrible and bloody. When he woke, he believed he had killed Deeka and he was not able to keep food down for the entire day. His duty was, and continued to be, to stand guard outside the tent of Korab and Septia. Thoroughly distraught over the deed he believed he had performed, he was at his place when Korab stepped from the tent after breakfast. Knowing Korab would likely question him as to Deeka's whereabouts made Gustov Maren jumpy.

But when Korab saw him and the condition he was in, he merely read his thoughts and knew why he suffered. For the remainder of the day, whenever Korab encountered him, he cast a disgusted look his way; not because Gustov Maren had killed, but because the act made him ill. He supposed he owed this soldier thanks, not that the man deserved any in Korab's estimation, yet he couldn't bring himself to say anything to him. At least he didn't have to concern himself with what to do about the woman. As far as he knew, she was dead, buried, and Korab cast her from his thoughts.

But Deeka sul Bareth the assassin had escaped. She was not lying in a shallow pit with her throat cut. No, she was very much alive. Since she could not take her revenge on Korab immediately, she decided to return to Kalaven and wait. In the interim, before the army attacked the city, she would find Shunlar and her son and watch them. Maybe she would use them as bait when Korab showed up. She rode on, the pain making it difficult to think of anything clever, recuperating as she was from the brutal treatment she had suffered at the hands of the scouts who had captured her and Orem.

Even stiff and sore as she was, Deeka rode through the night, putting as much distance as she could between herself and the army, pushing the little mare to her limit. She knew this part of the country well, and it would take a very crafty individual to catch her now. Having Orem with her had slowed her down, distracted her; she always traveled best when alone. She would miss the comfort of him, she knew, but men like Orem were easy to come by.

Four days later she approached the entrance to Kalaven. There were other ways to enter Kalaven besides passing through the sentries, secret ways that the likes of Deeka knew. In the city at last she began making discreet inquiries, only to learn that Shunlar was gone and had taken Avek and Ranth in what appeared to be mate abduction. The idea that Shunlar had taken both men endeared her to Deeka. She decided then that she would not kill Shunlar, merely use her as bait. The child had been left at the palace in the safekeeping of his grandparents, Zeraya and Benyar.

Thinking time remained for her to plan, Deeka decided to spend a few days recuperating in her home at the edge of the city. Having no way to know that she had arrived a mere three days before Kalaven was to be invaded, Deeka barely managed to escape when the soldiers entered and the fighting broke out. Shunlar had, yet again, gotten away from her, and Deeka, once more, found herself running for her life.

Twenty-Eight

THE MARCHING SO FAR HAD BEEN WORSE THAN Septia could have ever imagined, unaccustomed as she was to riding. She and Korab had been given the geldings that Orem and Deeka had ridden. The animals were sleek, tall, desert-bred Kalaven horses who responded to their new riders well.

Every detail, to prepare the army for stealth, down to the last man's sword buckle, had been carefully orchestrated by Korab. He instructed the men how to sew masks to protect their faces from the blowing sand and sun. Their gear was packed so that no squeak of leather nor clink of metal against metal would make a sound and give them away. The same went for their clothing, weapons, and tack, though there were few riding horses. Only the general and his captains were mounted; the remaining animals carried supplies. Using the saddles and bridles of Orem's and Deeka's horses as examples of Feralmon design, the men made the necessary changes.

As the only one among them who knew how best to survive in the desert, Korab had insisted they travel at night once they passed beyond the forest and the protection of the trees. About noon the fourth day they reached the edge of the trees, where a vast expanse of grassy plain stretched out before them. Beyond that, far in the distance, there was no sign of green or trees, just some scrub bushes that quickly thinned out and became the parched, golden color of desert.

The heat of the afternoon sun quickly refreshed the memories of the general and the troops who had begun this campaign the year before. They remembered all too well how they had limped away from the desert, defeated. Convinced that Korab was right, they stopped and made camp, resting under what available shade they could find until sunset.

Breaking camp at dusk, they marched until they had crossed the plain and entered deep desert. Unaccustomed as they were to marching through sand, every man had to push to make it until sunrise when at last, exhausted, they dropped off to sleep as soon as they had constructed their makeshift tents. The pack horses loaded down with waterskins were relieved of their burdens, which were passed around sparingly. It would be another two days before they came to the first oasis, and they could not be sure if there would be water there as it was the beginning of the dry season.

The closer they came to Kalaven, the more the terrain changed, becoming less desert-like, though it remained dry and exceedingly hot. As the ground went from sand to hard-packed clay and rocks, marching became an even more miserable experience for man and beast. When at last they came to the final oasis, they were happy to find water in abundance. There they rested for an entire day. Scouts went out and returned every hour on the hour to report that there appeared to be no activity in the desert around the city.

That night, when Septia and Korab retired to their tent, they went over the details of their plan one last time. They had lived for more than a month within an encampment of men who knew nothing of telepathy nor the concept of closing their minds off so that others could not read their thoughts. They realized this was a problem of massive proportions, for how could they approach Kalaven—where everyone was a telepath—with this many chattering minds and not be heard?

Having no desire to give their secret away to the Tonnerlingans, Septia came up with the idea of creating a fog so dense that it would hide the men and the noise of their minds as well. The men would be none the wiser that the spell was twofold in nature.

At the appointed hour, the well-rested army formed ranks and began the final part of its march toward Kalaven. Septia and Korab rode at the front, with a small contingent of handpicked warriors marching silently on either side of them. The army kept pace behind them, all camouflaged by the wall of fog that slowly advanced before them.

Recognizing that they had reached the entryway to the city and would soon encounter the sentries, Korab gave the signal to halt. He helped Septia dismount and stood aside as she raised her hands and spoke aloud to the wall of billowing gray fog. At her words, it stopped. Assembling their handful of men around them, they stepped into the mist, hiding men in strategic places among the rocks. With the last soldier in place, Septia and Korab continued on alone.

As they walked in the fog, Korab took hold of Septia's hand. "We are here, at last. Soon all will be as we planned it Septia." He stopped and grabbed hold of her shoulders. The mist fell in cool, thick droplets upon their faces and they kissed fiercely one last time before continuing on. The mists parted dramatically as they stepped from the fog together.

The first sentries they encountered were taken off guard, just as they had hoped. Bowing low, Korab and Septia straightened and came closer until one of the sentries recognized who they were. He immediately turned his back on them, and the others who were situated in the surrounding rock followed suit, exactly as Korab counted on them doing.

Squeezing her hand was his signal. Septia spoke the words of a spell, creating a wind that blew the fog away. Then she concentrated on the sentries in the surrounding rock. Slowly a glowing light formed over each sentry. Able to see their targets, the Tonnerling soldiers hidden close by loosed their arrows, and the sentries were all killed. With the main entrance to Kalaven open, the waiting army began the invasion.

It was the middle of the night when Tonnerling troops overran the city. Stealth was their ally at first and many were murdered in their beds, but soon the cry of battle had the inhabitants of Kalaven awake and fighting.

Septia had gathered the select group of warriors to her once the sentries were down, leaving Korab with the troops as planned. Weaving a spell around them for secrecy, they hurried in eerie silence through the streets to the Temple at a fast pace. Practicing the secret techniques from the forbidden text daily had finally paid off. For days Septia had been hearing the urgent call of a particularly strong Lifestone.

The column of men entered the Temple at a run with drawn swords, Septia in their midst. At that hour very few torches were lit. In the dark, in closer proximity to the Lifestone that called to her, Septia was able to see currents of the spell she had placed around her and her guards, churning in a circular motion. They kept pace with each other, their booted feet clumping noisy echoes off the walls. Instructing her guards to line up on both sides of the doorway to the Chamber, Septia prepared to enter.

The voice banged against her skull and her breath caught. Pain, real pain—the likes of which she never knew was possible to endure—encompassed her. Her entire being was drawn to a faceted, vaguely heart-shaped, smoky crystal with a line of black through its middle that stood apart from the others. Septia reached for it. A current arced from the stone to her hand and it flew through the air into her open palm.

For several seconds she was surrounded by pain and fire, and she was blinded. Blinking hard, Septia finally regained her eyesight, but it was as though she looked through a clouded glass. When she exited the Chamber and was once more surrounded by the waiting soldiers, more than one of them trembled. A current of light that made their eyes hurt would intermittently arc around the Dark Lifestone in Septia's hand.

The loud voice of Honia sul Urla demanded that they stop. Standing before them with her hand held high to bar their exit, Honia was accompanied by four young priestesses. The tight formation around Septia parted, allowing her to pass from their midst. Raising her hand and pointing the Dark Lifestone, Septia unleashed a bolt of lightning at Honia who screamed and fell to the ground. One by one, Septia pointed at the young priestesses, who cried out in pain and fell near Honia.

Her mission accomplished, Septia left the Temple. By that time the city was ablaze; the fighting had broken out everywhere. The clan pavilions were burning, as was nearly every building. The air was punctuated with the battle cry of Feralmon warriors and the streets were beginning to run with blood. But Septia would not be deterred by the battle raging around her. She hurried toward her final goal—the palace and her daughter, Iola—her accompanying guard running to keep pace with her.

Suspecting that Iola was in the same room that had been her nursery, she headed directly there. Septia had but one thought and that was to find and take back her child. Pity the guards who stood in her way, for she merely raised her hand and pointed the Dark Lifestone at them, blasting them with a bolt of lightning-like energy. Wanting to waste no time with fighting, she had her soldiers force the door, then Septia killed the small band of warriors that had been left to guard her child. Two nurses were left huddling around Iola's cradle when Septia lowered her weapon. She decided not to kill them; instead she took control of their minds and they instantly stood and bowed to her, their faces void of expression.

Frightened by the strange sounds, the infant, Iola, was screaming. Nearly overcome, Septia took Iola from her cradle and began to weep, from the sheer exhilaration of being reunited with her. Holding her daughter again, Septia felt her milk begin to run and she put her to her breast. It was then that she heard the muffled sound of a small child crying. Around her the Tonnerling soldiers had backed away, politely averting their eyes from Septia as she nursed.

She shouted, "Find the source of the crying!" It made several of the men jump as they scrambled to search the room. In a corner far to the back of the room they found Tavis, his face buried in the bosom of a dead woman.

"Bring them to me," Septia ordered.

One man lifted the boy and another brought the fallen warrior, placing her at Septia's feet. She looked down at the face of Fanon, peaceful in death, and a shiver ran through her. Deciding not to tell Korab how his mother had died, Septia turned to the small boy who was no longer crying, but watching her intently.

"And who are you?" she asked, knowing by his looks that he could only be Shunlar and Ranth's son. When he wouldn't answer her, Septia turned to one of the nurses. "Tell me this child's name," she demanded.

The young woman answered in a flat voice, "Tavis sul Shunlar." Septia's wicked smile made more than one of the soldiers nervous.

The Tonnerling troops had been warned that women, not just men fought, and fought well. But when Kalaven was breached and the first armed women were encountered standing shoulder to shoulder with the men, many of the soldiers who still found it difficult to believe were killed by their female opponents when they hesitated or brought their weapons down, only to find swords in their bellies seconds later. Seeing that soon convinced the others that they must fight, no matter who wielded the sword.

Korab had taught the green troops well. His tactic to put the lesser able-bodied fighting men in the front, saving the strongest fighters for the final strike made sense, for as the battle raged on for hours, the Feralmon, who were the better fighters, began to tire. When the last wave of the ablest fighters surged through the streets, the Feralmon warriors who had remained behind to protect the backs of the few who escaped knew they would die.

The Tonnerling army razed Kalaven, taking no male or female adult prisoners as Korab had ordered. The death toll was staggering, but Benyar and Zeraya escaped, among others. Ketherey also managed to escape, but his wife, Fanon, was dead. Their daughters, Tilenna and Cachou were captured, but because they were Korab's sisters, were protected and strict orders were given that they were not to be touched; Gustov Maren was put in charge of seeing to that, knowing his life would be forfeit if anything happened to them. They would be taken to Tonnerling and given to someone as wives, as would all the girls who were taken prisoner. Only the younger boys were taken alive, at Korab's instruction.

Korab's mood was foul when he learned his aunt and uncle, Zeraya and Benyar, had escaped him. When told that Septia had captured Tavis, he seemed to brighten. His mother's death affected him strangely, however, and he spoke not a word to Septia, just went directly to bed. He and Septia spent that night quartered in the palace sleeping in the same room with Iola, Tavis, and the two nurses. Septia would not allow her child to be taken from her sight.

The general and his captains also had taken rooms in the sumptuous royal household. Rising early the next morning to the sound of the soldiers looting the palace did nothing to improve Korab's mood. Septia, the children, and the two nurses were gone. Gustov Maren wasn't standing at his place just outside the door when he emerged. Remembering where the man was, Korab left in search of Septia and breakfast.

With Septia's assistance the Tonnerlingans took possession of the Lifestones the next day. She had learned how they could be moved without harming those who dared disturb them. Once the removal was complete, the army, having cremated their dead, headed back to Tonnerling with the Lifestones, their prisoners, and their prizes of war. It would take them the better part of a month to reach Tonnerling, traveling as they were with children. Though most of them would be treated fairly well, the boys were destined for lives as slaves. The girls would end up not too much differently, as wives to the soldiers who had captured them, with no rights or say in the matter.

Twenty-Nine

It was dark and damp. "No one move," Alglooth said quietly. Blowing a stream of concentrated fire across the room, he saw that there were two torches set into brackets on the wall. He lit both. Able to see again, Shunlar gasped. Before her on a bed in the middle of the small chamber, lay Ranth, still held within the Spell of Dreamless Sleep. Alglooth stepped closer to Ranth, examining but not touching him.

As she circled the bed, Shunlar could tell Ranth had remained in the same position he had been in since the Spell of Dreamless Sleep had been placed on him. It made her angry to see him like this, as clearly as the words on his back promised: a helpless captive. It was as if the words that had been etched into his skin were coming to fruition.

"Why were your people able to bind him with this spell? Why didn't his Lifestone protect him?" Shunlar asked Bimily.

"Because of who my people are, a Lifestone is like a spirit to them. It can be spoken to, dealt with, if you will."

"Bimily, can you do nothing to unbind him? Perhaps you can speak to the Lifestone and reason with it. Tell it Ranth is in danger here," Shunlar suggested.

"That would be like trying to convince a fish it might drown."

"Well," interjected Alglooth cheerfully, "it seems you have only one recourse, and that is to ask your father what he can do."

"What? Do you mean you know how to break the spell? I assumed that only the person who placed the spell would be able to remove it. You're telling me you can do this?" Shunlar sounded frantic, and smoke erupted from her nose.

"Calm yourself, daughter. You're beginning to change. I would not recommend doing that here. As to your question, yes, I can and will sunder the spell," Alglooth answered.

"You who are bound by the Spell of Dreamless Sleep, awaken when I speak your name three times. Ranth sul Zeraya." Alglooth's voice was strong and commanding. Twice more he repeated Ranth's name, his hands moving in the air over Ranth's body, weaving a distinct pattern in rapid succession each time he did so.

The sound of a familiar voice calling his name woke Ranth. Finally, he was able to shake off the sleep, and his eyes fluttered open. Somehow he had the feeling that he hadn't wakened for a long time. The air smelled of damp and his own unwashed body. His mouth and throat were dry, and his tongue felt swollen from disuse. All of his joints were stiff, and he wondered where he was.

Feeling a little frightened, he reached for the pouch around his neck. The Lifestone began to glow, a golden light seeping through the leather that became so bright the three people around him were able to see the bones of his hand beneath his skin.

"Shunlar? Is that you? Where am I?" he asked in a hoarse voice.

"I am here," she answered him. "Bimily, too, and Alglooth has joined us." While she watched, the golden glow of light gradually outlined his entire body.

"You have been a captive of my people in Vash Darlon," answered Bimily. "We are here to set you free, though once we've done that we'll still have to escape," Bimily reminded them as well as herself.

"Can't we just fly from here? Each of us could carry

one of the men,'' Shunlar suggested, excited by the thought.

''First we must awaken them. Deadweight is so much heavier. Alglooth certainly is capable of carrying a sleeping man, but I'm not sure I am. Not enough time has passed yet for me to have regained my full strength. Avek will not be easy to carry even awake, with his bulk. Then, we must pass the wards that surround my people's valley. Which reminds me, how did you manage to pass them, Alglooth?''

''The wards were very weak, and I flew through them easily. Your people have grown lax and complacent. Nothing lasts forever; spells need to be constantly checked and strengthened. But, I suspect that since I was able to enter Vash Darlon undetected, the wards will not be so easily passed on the way out. I'm certain someone has checked them by now.

''But what you said about not enough time puzzles me, Bimily. I would think that eight weeks would be sufficient time to regain your strength, wouldn't it?'' he asked.

''What are you talking about? It's early spring. Not more than four days have passed since I was healed and restored of my powers,'' she answered.

Now it was Alglooth's turn to look shocked. Shaking his head, he answered, ''It is full summer. Three months have come and gone since Shunlar left the Valley of Great Trees with her son. We assumed she and the boy were yet in Kalaven with Ranth. When did you leave Kalaven and arrive here?''

''It was the month of the first rains, though we saw little of them, being so far south and in the desert. When we arrived here, we were instantly trapped and put into these underground chambers. I have not seen the light of day since. Only Bimily has.'' Shunlar eyed her friend suspiciously.

''I have only seen Vash Darlon, and it appears to be spring here. Is it a lie, Alglooth? Have my people kept me trapped under illusion also?''

"You have been here much longer than you think," he answered.

Shunlar became pale. "No," she whispered, covering her face with her hands. "Tavis will think I have abandoned him. I told him we would return soon. Two months is like a lifetime to a small child. We must leave here immediately." No one disagreed with her.

"Ranth, can you stand or walk?" asked Shunlar. He had been lying on the bed listening to their conversation, taking everything in. Shunlar helped him sit upright.

Answering for him, Bimily said, "Because of his Lifestone, Ranth should have no problem walking. It's the condition of Loff and Avek that worries me now that I know how much time has passed."

As if to answer her, Ranth's Lifestone began to pulsate in bursts of light. His eyes glazed over and he cocked his head to one side. The pulsing light stopped, he straightened his head, blinked, and, looking worried, said, "We have to revive them, now." His voice sounded frightened.

"Are their lives in danger?" asked Alglooth.

"My Lifestone has warned that if they remain in this state much longer they will never awaken. Some damage may have already been done."

Shunlar's eyes filled with tears, and when she exhaled, smoke curled from her nose. "If my brother and Avek suffer at all from their treatment at these people's hands, someone will die." Everyone believed she meant it.

"Daughter, we have no time to waste. Let us revive Loff and Avek. Then we'll return to the only safe place I can imagine, Erroless's chamber. He will assist us in leaving here. I am sure of it." Alglooth asked, "Which one of you can translocate us to Loff and Avek?"

"I can," answered Bimily. She concentrated and the four of them were instantly in the room where Loff lay sleeping. Ranth was startled by suddenly being in another room, but it seemed to pick up his mood. Before they moved on to the chamber where Avek lay, as Alglooth was sundering the spell placed on Loff, Bimily and Shunlar instructed Ranth how to perform the translocation technique.

What Ranth's Lifestone had told him was true. Loff and Avek looked emaciated, and it was impossible for them to walk unassisted. Both of the men had to be supported so that they could simply stand. They were told about the translocating just seconds before it happened, so they would have no time to panic.

When all six of them suddenly appeared in Erroless's familiar surroundings, he was not alone. Leatha, Menadees, and Thricia had joined him and they were not pleased to see the three captives revived and standing, though unsteadily, before them.

"You have overstepped the limit of our patience this time, Bimily!" Leatha shouted. "Now you *will* have your powers taken from you." Bimily's face turned completely white.

As Leatha advanced on Bimily from across the room, Alglooth quickly set Avek in a chair and stepped between the two women. "Threats are unnecessary. I am the one you should be addressing. Or do you assume I am helpless?"

Leatha was shocked. "But . . . but . . . How could you do this?"

"Tsk, tsk. Leatha, he is Grazelea's son. All of her powers seemed to have transferred to him, especially her memories. He holds the secrets, as does his daughter." Erroless waited for the suspected reaction from the Three Elders as they began to comprehend his words.

"Now it is time to let them continue safely on their way. Their world, after all, is at war, and people they care for may be in grave danger, Shunlar and Ranth's child among them. You must remember, they are my family. I will do everything in my power to see that they leave here safely." The calm way he eyed the Three Elders told them he meant what he said.

"Erroless, Loff and Avek can't travel in their condition. Look at them. They're undernourished from being kept in the dreamless sleep for so long. Why didn't you tell me that we have been here for two months?'' Bimily asked, aghast.

"So, you have discovered that also?'' The old man shook his head. "You must forgive us for what has been done to these men. I only came to their aid once I had found out who Shunlar was. Because of her, they are still alive. Others among us wanted to let them waste away and die in their sleep. It would have been totally painless. Now that they are revived, you can see what has happened.''

"I demand The Thousand Things!'' Shunlar spewed ash and fire across the room as she shouted the ritual words.

By those words they were bound to return everything that had been taken from her, restored to its original condition. Her brother, Loff, Ranth, and Avek were all suffering from being in the dreamless sleep for so long. In the dream of The Thousand Things, items of great worth had been returned to Shunlar when she uttered those words, but each piece had been damaged in some way. Shunlar knew now that those items were metaphors for the three men standing with her. The Three Elders knew also. They weren't happy about it either, trapped as they were.

Erroless winked at her, grinning broadly. Leatha, Menadees, and Thricia, however, were not smiling.

"Which of you will reply to her?'' Erroless shouted into the quiet. "She must be answered, and her request fulfilled. These three men must be restored to health, as the words of the ritual demand.''

"Please my whims, you will all be restored and returned,'' answered Thricia quietly. She and Menadees and finally Leatha bowed. Slowly each of them approached one of the men. They opened their arms, encircling but not touching Loff, Avek, and Ranth. Bowing their heads to them, they all disappeared.

Shunlar screamed, a stream of fire following the sound into the empty space. Alglooth was at her side, his arms around her, trying to console her. She was near to hysteria and beginning to change into her half-dragon, half-human self. She leaned heavily against her father, sobbing, as her hair turned white and her wings beat the air frantically.

"Erroless, tell me this is not another foul trick of those three!" Bimily shouted.

The old man looked exhausted again. He stumbled to a chair and sat down in it with a sigh. "Believe me when I say your three companions will return soon. The Three Elders are bound by custom and will not do harm, I swear it. They have merely taken each one to be healed and restored to the state he was in when first you arrived in Vash Darlon. The only thing that will not remain is their memory of their time here and the location. As soon as you leave here they will cease to remember all that happened to them. This I cannot change." He looked apologetic.

Shunlar nodded acceptance of the terms, there being nothing else she could do.

"When next we see Loff, Ranth, and Avek we must be ready to leave immediately. I suggest we find something to eat, then rest so we can think clearly. Erroless, can you provide us with food and a place to rest?" Bimily asked.

"There is a vacant cottage that I will transport you to. Food will be provided and beds, for I am sure you will welcome sleep. When the healing work is complete, all three of the men will be returned to you there, no sooner." Erroless bowed to them, and they bade him a farewell. "Go now. Eat and rest. I will be there when the time comes to see you safely on your journey."

With those words they were translocated to a spacious cottage where, true to his promise, a sumptuous table of food awaited. Surprised at just how hungry they were, they took places at table and ate a very large meal. Through a doorway that was off to one side of the room, they found a corridor with bedrooms for each of them. Bidding his daughter and Bimily a good sleep, Alglooth placed a ward around the house that would waken him the instant anyone stepped across it. Then he laid his head down for a long, well-deserved rest.

It was late morning when Alglooth was awakened by someone disturbing the wards and entering the cottage. Leaping from his bed he called out to Shunlar and Bimily, waking them as he hurried into the main room, leaving a trail of smoke behind him in the corridor. Bursting into the room from the corridor, they discovered Ranth standing in the center of the room looking more robust than he had in a long time. The smile he gave Shunlar made her blush, something she wished she hadn't done when she saw the way her father raised an eyebrow.

Before anyone could utter a word Ranth crossed the room, grabbed Shunlar in a tight embrace, and kissed her. Then he let her go abruptly.

"If you don't mind, I am famished," he announced. He barely nodded to Bimily and Alglooth. The table was again filled with food, and Ranth began piling a plate with meat, cheeses, and bread. Unable to resist the aroma of the food, Bimily and Alglooth joined him at table. Only Shunlar held back, still stunned by the way Ranth had greeted her.

As she was about to sit beside her father, Loff and Avek suddenly appeared with Erroless between them. Both young men appeared to be restored to the peak of health and physical strength. Loff smiled when he saw Shunlar, and he gave her a brief sisterly hug before he was beguiled away by the table of food. "I'm starving," he announced as he bade everyone a good morning, spearing a peach with his dagger.

Strong arms went around Shunlar's waist from behind. She had hardly finished blushing from Ranth's kiss and here was Avek, nuzzling her neck, whispering in her ear. Her cheeks went red again when she saw that Alglooth watched intently. His eyes went from Ranth to Avek and back again. Then he gave Shunlar a look that she could not read, smiled, and went back to his breakfast.

Soon she was the only one standing, and Bimily called out to her, "I suggest you sit and eat now, for with these three at the table soon only the plates will be left, and even that's questionable the way they're packing it in.''

''Erroless, can you explain why they're so ravenous?'' Bimily thought to ask.

''It is due to the healing process. And, don't forget, they have not had solid food for some time.''

''Will it be permanent, this stuffing themselves like horses?'' Shunlar asked, laughing.

''Sister, pass me that plate of smoked meat,'' interrupted Loff as he chewed furiously on a leg of fowl. None of them seemed to notice how fast or how much they were consuming.

The plate was passed to Loff, but not before Ranth and Avek took several slices for themselves. Loff finished what was left as Shunlar, Bimily, and Alglooth sat back and watched.

Before Erroless could answer, the food on the table was gone. Avek, Loff, and Ranth leaned back in their chairs, patting their stomachs. Loff belched loudly and was rewarded by a comradely slap on the back from Ranth.

''It appears that their appetites will be greater for a time, but they will return to normal, I assure you,'' he answered, winking at Shunlar. She looked nervously from Ranth to Avek who were both grinning at her in a strange, lopsided way. It was then that she realized Loff was intently staring at Bimily, and not in a brotherly fashion.

''Great,'' she mumbled under her breath.

''Seriously, how long will these effects last?'' Alglooth wanted to know.

''Once you pass from Vash Darlon they will return to their normal behavior. I would suggest, however, that you make ready to leave soon. Time passes differently here. In the span of what appears to be one day, several have passed since the men were taken away to be restored to their former fitness.'' Exchanging nervous glances all around, they rose from the table.

''Are we ready to leave now?'' asked Shunlar. Nods and words of agreement came from everyone.

Looking from Avek to Ranth, Shunlar said, "I need both of you now to help me find Tavis and rescue him if need be. In two months' time the war must have reached Kalaven. Are you both prepared to leave and do whatever it takes to help me find Tavis?"

"I am," answered Avek with a positive nod.

"Ready," said Ranth.

"Good. Last night we decided that Loff and Bimily will go to the Valley of Great Trees to let our family know we are alive and well. Bimily has agreed to teach Cloonth, and whoever else is capable of learning it, the technique of translocating. They will then take the children to Stiga and begin settling in there so that when we find Tavis, we can join them. Alglooth will be coming with us."

Erroless had been watching Avek closely when Shunlar had spoken. The young man seemed to take her announcement about Stiga in a strange way. It was then that Erroless recognized the look in Avek's eyes as love, recognizing the question on Avek's mind as clearly as if he had spoken. It was: *What of me? Will I be welcomed in Stiga?*

Without thinking, Erroless answered him. "Yes, Avek, you will also live a long, prosperous life in Stiga." Avek bowed his head and blinked away tears as Shunlar placed her hand on his shoulder.

"Since Alglooth has no visual memory to guide him to Kalaven," Shunlar continued, "we must link minds to travel there. Ranth, because your visual memory of the palace is probably the most accurate, it makes sense for you to guide us. Do you agree?" she asked. Ranth did.

Bidding Erroless farewell was not without regret or a touch of sadness. Alglooth promised to return with Cloonth and the children for a visit, if it would be permitted. Erroless assured him he would see to it that they would be welcomed with open arms.

Outside the cottage their horses waited for them and they were given enough supplies for many days' travel. Only Alglooth remained afoot, having no need of a horse. Before mounting up they bade a final farewell to Bimily and Loff.

Erroless had assured Bimily she had the strength as well as the power to transport herself, Loff, and their horses safely to the Valley of Great Trees. Of course, Loff must be the one to select the exact location since he knew the Valley so well. Without another word they raised their joined hands in a good-bye and winked out of sight. In a spark of blue light the outline of their bodies danced upon the air for mere seconds after they were gone, the sure signature of Bimily.

"Now it is our turn," announced Ranth quietly. "We will arrive at the entrance to the palace stables. Do you recall the spot I mean, Avek?" Avek nodded as they joined hands.

"Shunlar, Alglooth, it looks like this," said Ranth as he passed the image on to them. Together they spoke the words that would translocate them.

Having translocated several times, Shunlar had begun to notice that there were subtle differences each time and that more details appeared during the transfer time also. Perhaps it was because she was so anxious about finding Tavis that she let her mind notice someone calling out her name. Suddenly, as if a great hand grabbed her by the scruff of her neck, she was pulled off in another direction, and because they were linked together by physical and mental touch, Alglooth, Avek, and Ranth were pulled along, too.

Sand blew in all directions at once as they landed with a jolt in the middle of a sandstorm. The horses immediately began to whicker and stamp their feet in fear. Avek's beast even tried to buck him off his back. The only one not having difficulty was Alglooth, and that was because he had no mount. Once they had settled the animals down, they tried to figure out where they were.

Shunlar felt herself being strongly drawn to something on the ground. Dismounting she struggled toward it in the blowing gale to have a closer look, the men following close behind. What she saw nearly made her vomit. It was the remains of a man.

Tied spread-eagled between four posts, the emaciated body was torn and broken like none she had ever seen. Beside her Avek, Ranth, and Alglooth looked over the remains as the wind died down. The sand stopped blowing long enough for them to see clearly the face of the corpse. It was the only part of him that hadn't been touched, in fact it looked as if his face had been dipped in wax and preserved.

A strange compulsion to have a closer look made Shunlar step nearer. Alglooth quickly grabbed her by the elbow. Pulling her back, he warned, "Don't get any closer. Can't you see the wards that were placed over him?" Shunlar shook her head to clear it. She hadn't seen anything.

Behind them Ranth had gone to his knees and was retching in the sand. When Avek offered his help, Ranth waved him away.

"Orem," Shunlar whispered, suddenly recognizing the face. Giving Avek a sideways glance, she saw him nod and turn away from the corpse with a grimace.

"Daughter, you knew this man?" asked Alglooth.

"Yes. He and a woman named Deeka were traveling with Avek when we first met. It looks as though he met up with someone who disliked him more than I did," she answered coldly. "By the moons, I'd like to know who set this trap, for it surely is one," she concluded.

"I fear someone who has a great deal more power than I suspected set it. Only one other person comes to mind who could have possibly learned you traveled in this part of the world, and that is Deeka," said Avek. "Now I am beginning to believe it's true that she and Orem were the ones who captured you in Vensunor."

"Father, can anything be done to break the wards?" asked Shunlar.

"Probably, but it would take time we don't have. Now that you know this trap is here, you must do whatever it takes to avoid it. Time and the elements are already dissolving the spell, something the maker did not foresee. If not for that, we all would have been trapped. Be assured that we will find the person who placed this here. Since there is nothing we can do for the dead man, let us go to Kalaven as we planned.

"Tavis may not be there; we must prepare ourselves for that possibility. If, by chance, we encounter the person who set this trap, perhaps they will reveal themselves to us by their behavior. I, for one, am most curious." Though he remained calm on the outside, Alglooth was seething, evidenced by the smoke that poured from his nose and mouth. He clearly had had enough and now he desired one thing: revenge. Someone had threatened his child. He would see to it that they never threatened her again. A low rumble reverberated in his chest.

The storm began blasting them with sand, making it impossible to see. "Shall we try it again, then?" Shunlar screamed into the wind. They got as close as the horses would allow and grasped hands all around.

Not wishing any of his companions to know how severe his pain was, Ranth did his best to hide the physical sensation of it behind a wall. He winced as the pain in the small of his back grabbed again. The moment they had landed he knew that the spell had been placed by Korab, not Deeka, as Avek thought. But the pain prevented him from speaking.

Thirty

THIS TIME THE FOUR OF THEM LANDED IN THE courtyard of the palace near the stables, the exact location Ranth had intended for them. The horses were nervous but before they could react, Ranth reached out to their minds and they quieted down immediately.

The smell of smoke hung in the air. Around them the walls of the stables had been reduced to broken clods of brick and stone. Kalaven had been razed; the city was empty. Clan pavilions were no longer standing; what remained of the large tents were piles of burned hides and scorched earth. Even the elaborate palace that had been his home for nearly two years was a smashed ruin.

There were no bodies anywhere, yet it was evident that many had been killed. Desperate to find some sign that Tavis yet lived, Shunlar began a frantic search for his heat trace. Storms had come and gone in the weeks since the city had been destroyed, making it impossible for Shunlar to identify distinct heat traces; they had all become degraded by time and weather. When she found the faint trail that remained, it appeared to end abruptly under the rubble of a collapsed, burned-out building. No heat trace of Tavis could be found anywhere else. Seeing that, Shunlar bellowed, her anger and frustration transforming her until she had become half-human and half-dragon. Only Alglooth could come near to comfort her. Together they paced and spoke in hushed voices.

From several paces away, as Ranth watched her being consoled by her father, pain lanced through his back, making his knees suddenly weak, and he lost his balance, falling to his knees. His will to live drained from him, like a jug of wine being emptied onto the sand, and he succumbed to the pull. *Useless. Weakling. Failure. Might as well die.* The accusatory voice in his head was Korab's, and it cut him to his core. His body began to shudder in a convulsive way and before anyone could stop him, he unsheathed his dagger and sliced a deep cut across his wrist. The last thing he remembered was Shunlar screaming, "No!"

But he didn't die. When Ranth woke much later he found himself in his bedroll, safely sheltered in the ruined Temple. His wrist was bandaged and his Lifestone securely tied to his wrist to encourage the wound to heal. Hearing someone stir beside him, he turned his head and saw Shunlar sitting cross-legged.

She regarded him with a blank expression. "We are taking you to Vensunor, where you are going to choose another name. In Vash Darlon, Erroless told us that to do so would stop the markings on your back from killing you. If we must leave you there, we will, for nothing is going to stop me from finding Tavis," she stated flatly. Then he watched her stand, nod curtly to him to emphasize her point, turn, and walk away.

Avek replaced her at his side to offer support, but more than that, to ensure Ranth wouldn't harm himself again.

"Why did you attempt to take your life?" Avek asked with genuine concern.

"My brother, since we found the body in the desert, the pain has begun. I can't explain why, just that a voice ordered me to do what I did." Trembling, his voice constricted, Ranth explained his actions to Avek, sweat pouring from his body. "The voice was so strong that I couldn't ignore it. The pain grows by the minute. Just let me die." By the way he sucked in a fast breath and shuddered, Avek knew Ranth was succumbing to the curse Korab had carved into his flesh.

"Brother, you and I are bound by an oath. I will not and cannot let you die, if it is possible to save your life. We will do it together, you and I. Shunlar and Alglooth have raised a good point. Later tonight, when you have rested, we leave for Vensunor. Think no more of dying but of living. Soon this will be over, and we will find your son. Think of him and find the will to live, somehow, I beg you." Avek bowed his head when he finished speaking.

"I have not the strength to do it," Ranth answered.

"Then I will gladly lend you some of mine," said Avek.

Ranth considered what Avek offered for a long minute. Finally he nodded in acceptance, unable to speak, his throat tight with emotion. Very gently Avek placed his hand on Ranth's shoulder, directing his energies toward Ranth. As if sipping water from a cool well, Ranth accepted Avek's offer of strength. He relaxed immediately, Avek's calm slowly lulling him to a peaceful sleep, free of pain for the moment.

That night Alglooth stood first watch while the others slept in the ruins of Kalaven's Temple. All day he had had the gnawing sense that something was not quite as it seemed, and it continued to grow. Earlier in the day, he and Avek had explored what was left of the city while Shunlar kept watch over Ranth. Of the buildings, only the Temple remained, and that was because it had been carved from the bedrock of the mountain. The outside and inside had been heavily damaged, the tapestries and the wooden altar completely destroyed by fire, but the warren of rooms remained. The worst discovery, however, was that the Chamber of Lifestones had been desecrated, emptied of the revered Lifestones.

When Alglooth asked Shunlar to look upon the site, there remained plenty of evidence of who had taken the stones left behind in the heat traces, but she could only identify those of Honia and several of her priestesses; the others were unknown to her. Sadly, Honia and the women had died there, no doubt attempting to stop whoever had plundered the Lifestones.

Yet the feeling that there were other factions at work could not be shaken as Alglooth sat watch over their camp in the ruins. He heard a noise; the scuff of leather upon stone. Able to see in the dark, he quickly turned his full attention to the spot from which the sound emanated. Then he saw them. In the dark several cloaked figures were sneaking up on them from the depths of the Temple. Knowing they could not see him, Alglooth waited until they surrounded him and his three sleeping companions. When they were in place, Alglooth leaped into the air, breathing a stream of fire that lit up the darkness and caused those who had sneaked up on them to freeze in their tracks.

Instantly awake, Shunlar and Avek, their weapons in hand, rolled from their blankets, taking up a defensive position on either side of Ranth, who remained in his bedroll, too weak of will to defend himself. The six who surrounded the camp remained frozen in place and as Alglooth's flame faded, the terrified expressions on their faces seemed to hang in the air like masks.

Seeing herself and her companions surrounded, Shunlar became angry, and she let her anger change her appearance. She grew taller, her wings unfurled, and she coughed a stream of flame across the six feet of space between herself and the closest attacker. Then a strange thing happened. The attackers all went to their knees and pressed their foreheads to the ground. Alglooth came forward with a torch in his hand, slowly circling the group who were groveling in the dirt.

"Get up," he shouted. Carefully, they sat up but remained on their haunches, refusing to look at him. By the torchlight he recognized them as Feralmon.

Avek came forward and began questioning them. In that way they learned what had happened to Kalaven. When he asked them about survivors, they told him that Jerob sul Ansilla and Zara sul Karnavt, his parents, were not among them. Benyar sul Jemapree and Zeraya sul Karnavt had been wounded, but they were both alive and recovering.

"What of a child named Tavis?" asked Shunlar, stepping up beside Avek. Her anger quieted, she looked like her normal self again. He put his arm around her as Ranth watched from his bedroll.

"There are no children left from Kalaven. If he was under the age of ten, he has been captured and taken away with all the other children. I am sorry." The man who answered bowed his head.

"You say that the army marched from here nearly four weeks ago?" Alglooth asked.

"Yes. They were led by two who had been banished and whose names are not to be spoken." This time the voice that answered was female.

That got Ranth's attention. "Septia and Korab?" he blurted out.

"Yes," came her quiet answer.

"I suspected that at least my cousin yet lived. Did they return here for their child?"

"Apparently so, and the Lifestones, which they have taken. They also took the young females, but only the youngest males who were not yet considered men. Anything else of value that couldn't be carried away was destroyed."

"Tell me, are we to believe you are friends when you come like thieves in the night? Who sent you?" Ranth's voice rose in anger.

"We were about to ask the same question of you. Who sent you here to the ruins of Kalaven? Though you two look like you are of the people, who are your friends?" This time another person spoke.

"I have lived here all my life," answered Avek. "If you will, I am Avek sul Zara, though she was my foster-mother. Jerob, whom I asked about, was my father. And yes, our two friends are very trustworthy. This is my cousin, oath-brother, and the son of Zeraya and Benyar." Avek got very quiet then, wondering about the fate of his two sisters, Menity and Falare, and his young brother, Jessop.

"We offer our sympathy for your loss. I am Corta sul Sarda." She bowed.

"And I am her mate, Ondeen sul Finta. My mother

is sister to Benyar and Ketherey." She addressed Ranth.

"It appears that we are family. I am Ranth sul Zeraya. Tell me, are my parents' wounds serious?" Ranth asked, curiosity barely covering the anger in his voice.

"Cousin, Zeraya took a blade thrust in her shoulder from the back, but she will be fine. Benyar suffered mostly cuts that are already healing. It is our uncle, Ketherey, who has suffered the most. His mate, Fanon sul Eliya, is dead, his daughters have been captured by the enemy, and he has lost an eye and his left arm," answered Ondeen quietly.

As the grim news sank in, Ranth recovered from the shock first, fortified as he was by Avek's strength. He unwound the leather thong that bound his Lifestone to his wrist. Slipping the thong over his head, he concealed the stone under his tunic. Pulling on his boots, he rose slowly and strapped on his sword and coiled his bedroll, stopping only to give a weary smile to Shunlar.

"Let us go to my parents now. To wait further would be foolish. I, for one, cannot sleep, knowing our son is in the hands of the enemy." He bent back to his task, and they followed his lead. Within minutes everyone's gear was packed and secured onto the horses' backs.

They followed the six Feralmon back the way they had come, through the Temple. Passing the empty Chamber of Lifestones, Ranth noticed that each of them bowed. One of them lit a torch, and they continued down a long corridor that began to smell of damp. They reached a dead end, where the entrance to a tunnel was concealed behind a large stone. One of the Feralmon whispered a few words in Old Tongue and the stone moved away, revealing a tunnel large enough to allow the horses to pass. Leading their horses, they walked single file down a steep path for what seemed like a very long time, until at last they stepped into a vast cavern. Around them stood carved columns, pillars, and the remains of stone buildings long ago abandoned.

"What is this place?" Avek asked Corta as they crossed what was once a grand courtyard garden with fountains and stone sculptures.

"We don't know who built it nor who might have lived here," Corta answered. "All we know is that there once was a flourishing society here. Over the years we have explored most of the buildings. We even found the remains of a library, but the letters are not known to us. Our High Priestess has tried, unsuccessfully, for years to decipher their meanings. She continues to this day. Perhaps your friend Alglooth could look upon some of the tablets. Of course, I would need to ask permission first."

"Of course. But first we must speak to Zeraya and Benyar. Once we know your location, we leave for Vensunor. Ranth's life has been endangered by Korab, and there he must change his name so that the curse laid upon him can be lifted." Avek spoke quietly and explained how Korab had marked Ranth. Corta looked pale by the time he had finished. She took in the information, then excused herself and caught up to Ondeen, the two of them whispering intently to each other.

Passing the ruins in the mountain, they emerged some hours later on a windswept bluff overlooking another valley. Below them they saw the fires of their destination. It took several hours of climbing downhill to reach the camp of the Lost Feralmon, where they were granted entrance and taken immediately to Zeraya and Benyar. By that time it was dawn.

Zeraya and Benyar were both elated to see them alive. Zeraya was introduced to Alglooth and immediately afterward begged forgiveness from Shunlar for allowing Tavis to be captured. Shunlar had no doubt that Zeraya had suffered. She looked worn and tight around the mouth, but what surprised Shunlar most was that she carried a child. Zeraya had lost a fair amount of blood, having been stabbed in the back. Benyar told them how he had slung her over his shoulder and fought off the soldiers who tried to kill them. Both had narrowly escaped. If it had not been for Ketherey, they would be dead.

After their stories had been told, they were shown to a tent where they rested for most of the day. As night descended Alglooth and Shunlar left together, ostensibly to take a walk around the camp. Returning as the evening meal was being served, they were beckoned over to the fire and food. Avek and Ranth watched in anticipation as they approached.

"We must leave here as soon as possible," announced Avek, when Shunlar and Alglooth were settled.

"Agreed. I have decided to fly from here tonight on a search for the Tonnerling army," said Alglooth. "You three will go to Vensunor traveling by the new means learned from Erroless, as you no doubt have already guessed. After we have eaten, let us say thank you and farewell to our hosts." Ranth and Avek were relieved to learn they were all in agreement.

Saying farewell was as difficult as Ranth thought it would be. His mother wanted him to stay, but to his surprise, his father stood up for Ranth's right to leave and find Tavis.

"My son, as I did many years ago, leave now on this quest. I hope your journey takes you only a matter of months, not years as it did me. At least you know who has Tavis and where they mean to take him. You also have a mate whose abilities far surpass anything we have ever known. May the goddess smile upon you and bring you to your son very soon." Benyar and Zeraya embraced their son and the others, sending them on their way.

Before they could mount, however, Corta and Ondeen rode up, their scant gear packed and loaded upon the backs of two sleek desert horses.

"Oh no. We travel without you," protested Shunlar.

"But you might need a hand. Besides, we are anxious to see this place called Stiga that Avek told us about last night," answered Ondeen. "We have already been given the blessing of the High Priestess. See, here she comes now."

Behind them strode a tall, dark woman, accompanied by a couple equally as tall and elegantly dressed. All three wore their hair pulled back in a warrior braid, their complexions dark, their slanted eyes piercing. Coming to a halt before Shunlar, they bowed. Behind them most of the encampment had followed, and they were slowly surrounded by the entire group. Many of the people held torches or lamps high upon poles, and the area became bright, a sea of faces regarding Shunlar and her companions. Even Ketherey was there, leaning heavily upon a woman who resembled him greatly, his sister Finta.

"Alglooth, we greet you," the High Priestess, Esla sul Veeta, spoke into the night, her voice one used to giving speeches as well as commands. "We who are the spiritual leaders of this small band beseech you to take these two of our children with you. Let them travel under your protection, and they will prove worthy warriors. After all, it has been foretold that they will be instrumental in saving the child Tavis sul Shunlar," Esla added with a glint in her eye.

All he could do was agree. Alglooth bowed to her, accepting Corta and Ondeen into his care with that gesture. "We leave now, and though I have agreed to their coming, I travel separately. When I have found the army, I intend to follow it so that we may rescue my grandson, Tavis. Regrettably I cannot take Corta and Ondeen with me at this time, but they will be safe within the walls of Vensunor, under my daughter's care."

"This is known to us. We agree and accept the terms." Esla and the couple with her bowed to Alglooth and the others before turning and retracing their steps. The friends and family of Ondeen and Corta said their farewells in quiet, and gradually the crowd dispersed. When they were alone, they rode a short way away from the camp and bade a farewell to Alglooth. He unfurled his wings and was gone in two strokes.

When they explained to Corta and Ondeen just how they would travel to Vensunor, it was with wide eyes that the two women clasped each other's hands, then grabbed hold of the offered hand beside them. Minutes later, when they landed in Vensunor, just inside the Temple gates, their eyes were wider still.

Thirty-One

THE SUDDEN ARRIVAL OF LOFF AND BIMILY IN the Valley of Great Trees startled everyone but Gwernz. Shortly after Loff finished explaining to Marleah how they managed to blink into existence in front of her house, Gwernz arrived at the door, with a very pregnant Klarissa beside him. Loff recognized immediately that Klarissa no longer limped and when he could comment on it, she explained that Gwernz, with help from the Great Trees, had made the bones of her leg knit properly.

Bimily asked to be taken to Cloonth so that she could be told Alglooth and Shunlar were fine. Together they left for the cabin that Cloonth, Alglooth, and the six children called home, telling as much of their story as they could while they walked.

Though the children were just over one year old, they had developed fast. All of them could speak Old Tongue, as well as the language of the Valley. The two boys, the only ones with wings at the moment, greeted them at the door. Taller than most children their age, they would all be six feet and more when they were grown. Their hair was white-blond, and each one's eyes were a different shade of amber.

''Klash, Hew, who is there?'' called Cloonth from the back of the room as she hurried to the door.

She was so excited to see Bimily and Loff and anxious for news of Alglooth and Shunlar that she nearly forgot to introduce Bimily to the children. When Cloonth had collected her wits, she began, starting with the firstborn, Emberlootha, or Ember for short. Next was Vailcooth, or Vail, then Torqueoth, or Torque, followed by the fourth girl, Furlenth, or Furl. The boy's formal names were Klashonth and Hewgoth.

"Alglooth has asked that you and the children leave immediately for Stiga. It seems that Shunlar and Ranth have it in their minds to settle there," she said a bit mysteriously. She had no wish to disturb the children with any unpleasant news.

"And what of Avek?" asked Cloonth and Marleah together.

"It will be interesting to see what develops," murmured Bimily.

"Tell me that my grandson is safe and that he has chosen a name. Ranth did acknowledge him as his child, didn't he?" asked Marleah.

"His name, chosen according to Feralmon custom is Tavis sul Shunlar. And yes, Ranth is very proud of his son." When Bimily looked at the children nervously, Cloonth shooed them away to the outside to play.

"Now, what is there that you haven't told us, my friend?" asked Cloonth, a very worried tone to her voice. Marleah gnawed at her bottom lip, her brow furrowed. With a sigh Bimily began the tale of all that had happened to her, how Ranth and Benyar had saved her life, how they came to be captured by her people, and finally where Ranth, Shunlar, Avek, and Alglooth had gone.

When she finished Marleah decided then and there to join them, and they immediately began making preparations to leave for Stiga with the children, as Alglooth had requested.

Gwernz, but more especially Klarissa, was anxious to hear any news of Tonnerling, but they could give them none. Spending the two months in Vash Darlon as they had, they knew nothing about what had taken place in the world. The army of Tonnerling, they suspected, had by this time carried out their plan to invade Kalaven.

Klarissa looked pale after hearing that news.

Later that night, after the children were asleep, Bimily told Cloonth, ''Since seeing my people again, I have learned a new and most valuable skill. In fact, I am going to teach it to you, but not the children just yet. They are too young, and it could prove dangerous for them to learn how to translocate at such a tender age.'' Cloonth agreed, for as far as she was concerned, they already knew more than enough to get them into trouble as it was.

''My children learn new skills every day; in fact, they absorb information like parched earth. If it would not be too inconvenient, I would prefer we travel by this method when they are all asleep; otherwise, they will learn how to simply by participating.''

Astounded to hear that, Bimily didn't question Cloonth. ''Very well,'' she agreed. ''If we can be packed up and ready to leave by this time tomorrow, I see no reason why we can't travel when they are asleep. To be sure they're not aware of how we move them from the Valley to Stiga, I suggest we place a ward over their minds to shut out anything they might hear while they sleep.'' Cloonth agreed.

Everything went smoothly, as planned. With all of their belongings and the children, plus Loff and Marleah, they arrived in Stiga by translocation the next night. Cloonth had shown them the mental image of the house she and Alglooth lived in as their destination. Shortly after arriving they realized they were not the only people in Stiga, for the smell of fire was in the air—and not just fire, food as well. Making sure the children were settled, it was decided that Bimily would be the one to find out who these people were, because of her shape-changing ability.

Though she had not taken another shape since being healed by her people, Bimily knew she had no choice. Truthfully she was frightened. Having nearly died because she couldn't change back into her human form, the last thing she wanted to be was a bird. Unfortunately, a bird was just the animal she needed to best spy on their new neighbors.

As she had done so often in the past, Bimily concentrated on the animal form. A blue light shimmered and sparkled around her as she took on the shape of an owl, a nocturnal hunter. Shrinking in size, Bimily hopped across the floor, spread her wings, and flew from the doorway. Several of the houses she glided past silently had been cleaned up and restored so that they looked inhabited. The sensitive ears of the owl heard the sounds of breathing, both animal and human, and her nose inhaled the smell of food in the air.

Circling higher she banked off toward the plain, where she could see in the distance a small herd of cattle and a larger flock of sheep and goats. There were two fires winking at her, likely the herders keeping watch over their animals. Swooping close enough to recognize the faces as Tonnerlingans, she panicked, flying back to Stiga at breakneck speed with the information.

Her first impulse was to run; these were the people who had captured her, after all. Slowly, Marleah and Loff calmed Bimily down. Once she was able to think straight again, they came up with a plan. Marleah and Cloonth would hide with the children. In the morning Bimily and Loff would venture out into the city square, where they would meet with some of the people. If anything were to go wrong, Loff reminded her, they could always just wink out of harm's way.

The next morning she and Loff casually strode into the square, where a crew of builders were setting up to begin a day of restoring another of the great stone houses. The women were outnumbered by the men, about four to one, and one of them, Bimily noticed immediately, was a lovely, young blonde, dressed in the same breeches and tunic as the men. The other women were dressed in simple brown, ankle-length nun's robes, as were some of the men.

The appearance of Bimily and Loff casually striding into their midst stopped conversation. Soon they found themselves surrounded by a crowd of about one hundred people, mostly men, who addressed them in several languages. Finally, one of them spoke the tongue of Vensunor. The crowd began to part to allow a couple who were dressed in the brown tunics of a monk and a nun to come forward. Between them they supported a positively ancient man who, upon seeing Bimily and Loff, greeted them with a great toothless grin. He straightened, one hand clasping the pouch that was beneath his brown, woolen robes, the other clutching his staff. His hair and beard were thin tufts of white that seemed to move of their own accord.

"Sir, you honor us this morning with your presence," one of the men in the crowd announced. Everyone bowed to the old man.

"Be welcome among us," his old voice rang out. Bimily and Loff bowed to him but didn't speak.

"Excuse my poor manners. I am Da Winfreyd. This is Brother Boringar and Sister Nomia, my successors. We have recently arrived in this, your city, and hope to restore it to its former grandeur, with your permission, of course." He bowed to Bimily, leaning heavily on his staff.

"Da Winfreyd," Bimily bowed to him. "I am Bimily and this is my friend, Loff, from the Valley of Great Trees. But I am curious as to why you would call this my city."

Da Winfreyd squinted hard at her and seemed to be conversing with his Lifestone. "Ah," he said after a moment, "it seems I have mistaken you for another." He shook his head in an odd way, but Bimily didn't press him further.

"We also are newly arrived here and, frankly, we are very surprised to see so many others, and so hard at work. Tell me, are you from Tonnerling?" she asked, straight to the point as always.

A murmur went through the crowd, and Da Winfreyd raised his hand for quiet. "We are indeed. It is our wish to live here in peace, beginning a new way of life where all are treated well, taught the true meaning of a spiritual life, and given the freedom to come and go as they please, as all who once inhabited Stiga did in the past."

Ariaste and Dolan, who were standing off to the side came forward, smiled graciously at Bimily and Loff, and bowed. Addressing Loff, Dolan asked, "If you are from the Valley of Great Trees, perhaps you know my sister Klarissa? She married Gwernz last year and left Tonnerling to live in the Valley with his people. I am Dolan Vinnyiusson, and this is my wife, Ariaste." They bowed together once more.

Loff and Bimily exchanged a smile. This was unexpected yet very welcome information. Loff answered, "Yes, I know Klarissa, and she and Gwernz are very happy; in fact, they will have a child at the beginning of next year. Gwernz is my uncle, you see, and if you met him, you also met my sister, Shunlar," he added, raising his brow.

"Indeed, we were well met, having sheltered them both under my roof for the winter," Dolan added. He didn't miss the glance Ariaste gave him.

"So, it would seem we are family, Dolan of Tonnerling. But, how is it that you are here and not fighting in the war against Kalaven?" Another murmur passed through the crowd.

"We have much to discuss about that, friend Loff," Da Winfreyd interrupted. "But, I prefer we do it sitting down, for my old legs won't hold me up as long as they once did. If you will come with us, we will tell you everything we know of the war and what has happened since a remarkable discovery was made in Tonnerling. I believe it will interest you both." Da Winfreyd had a conspiratorial look about him.

The crowd parted once more to allow them to pass, the workers staying behind to continue with the rebuilding of Stiga. Dolan and Ariaste joined Bimily and Loff asking many questions as Da Winfreyd led the way, Boringar and Nomia on either side of him. Before the comfort of a warm fire they sipped tea and learned that the war with Kalaven had been declared over before the invasion had taken place.

"The war was instigated in the first place," Da Winfreyd told them, "because a certain faction from the Feralmon came to Tonnerling one day offering Lifestones. Since everyone had assumed there were no more to be found in the world, the knowledge that Kalaven had a cave filled with stones was astounding."

Da Winfreyd told them that the discovery of a cave of Lifestones in Tonnerling a year later had changed everything. "Because we now had a source of our own, there remained no reason to seek Lifestones elsewhere. It took some doing, but I was able to convince the city fathers that a war seemed futile," he continued.

Sadly, he and the others had no way to know that Kalaven had been destroyed and that the army was already returning their way with the stolen Lifestones, stolen children, and, worst of all, Korab and Septia.

"The majority of the men you have seen in Stiga are soldiers who formed an escort for myself and my people. Upon reaching Stiga, the army they had anticipated meeting and stopping had already rafted down the Thrale. In an attempt to recall the troops, a small band of soldiers was sent riding as fast as possible after the main army, with their new orders to stand down. We pray they have been successful.

"These few weeks here, the soldiers who remained behind have decided their lot in life would be much improved if they were to remain in Stiga rather than return to Tonnerling. Here they will be free men, after all. The society they abandon adheres to a strict social structure that can only be climbed by arranging a fortuitous marriage within a small circle of families. Being the lesser sons of merchant families, they had been given the order to ride from Tonnerling as fodder for the war, something they were well aware of. The grand houses they are restoring are available for any one of them to claim as their own, something most have already done," Da Winfreyd explained.

"The other men who labor by their side are men of the cloth who accompanied me and Brother Boringar, numbering twenty. Helping alongside them are the same number of women from the abbey, whose valuable skills include the planting and growing of herbs and vegetables. While the men toil building and repairing the structures, the women are doing their part hauling fertile earth to the terraced plots, and setting gardens into place where the land has long lain untilled and choked with weeds,'' he concluded.

Bimily recognized at once that Da Winfreyd was asking for her approval and permission for them to stay. ''I for one am most pleased to see all the building and restoration taking place. Yet the persons you should speak with are the real inhabitants, Cloonth and her mate Alglooth. Trust me when I say they will welcome you,'' she added when she saw the worried looks on their faces.

''Loff and I will leave you now so we may bring Cloonth and her children here. It will relieve her greatly to know that her family will be safe. I must caution you, though, she does not look entirely as you do, nor do her children. Their blood is mixed with that of the dragon,'' Bimily concluded.

She waited for one of them to speak, knowing her words had a great impact. Da Winfreyd was shaking his head and conversing with his Lifestone. Shortly, Ariaste and Dolan put their hands to their chests and did the same.

First to speak, Dolan quietly said in Old Tongue, ''Please my whims but give Cloonth the message that she and her family will be doing us great honor. I, my wife Ariaste, and those who followed Da Winfreyd here from Tonnerling vow that she will be protected from harm. My Lifestone has told me this.''

Very much relieved at hearing his message, Bimily and Loff thanked Dolan. With a mischievous grin, Bimily grabbed Loff's hand, and said, ''I will return shortly,'' then they winked out of sight, a sprinkling of blue sparks floating upon the air.

Returning within the hour with Cloonth, the children, and Marleah, Bimily took great pleasure in introducing them to their newfound friends. Knowing they were safe came as a great relief to Cloonth. It would not be necessary to hide, and the work of settling into their house could begin.

Even with so much work to do, all of them were anxious for word from Alglooth. Bimily was again elected, after only two days, to begin a search for him. She believed, as did the others, that he was unharmed, had found the army and was following it. She was correct. Slipping easily into the shape of a large hawk, she flew from Stiga in the early morning hours of the third day to begin her search. She found Alglooth near the end of the day flying high above the army, which looked to be marching straight for Stiga.

"Why didn't you come to Stiga to let us know you had found Tavis?" Bimily asked as the army seemed to be inching forward through the forest far below.

"I couldn't leave if it meant taking my eyes off my grandson or his captors. I had to be certain Tavis remained with them and was unharmed. I fear that the two Feralmon who lead this army possess powers that are beyond their abilities to control.

"There is also a band of warriors, possibly from Kalaven, who follow the army. They are small in number and I believe their intent is to recapture the children. They made one raid and took three children. Since then they have remained hidden, and it is my belief that it is only because there are wards placed around the children that no further attempt has been made to infiltrate the camp," he answered. "They may have sent for reinforcements, for I noticed that two had returned in the direction of the desert. But, if and when they do, I must be there to offer my help, for I will not place Tavis's life at risk."

"My friend, you may not like the news I bear, but Stiga is inhabited by a group of around one hundred Tonnerlingans. They have met Cloonth and the children and anticipate meeting you as well." Bimily held her breath, knowing Alglooth's propensity to remain hidden. His reaction was to accept her words in silence as he glided on a wind current, keeping his eyes on the troops that snaked their way slowly across the heavily forested countryside. They continued to circle overhead, looking much like two large birds of prey to any below who noticed. When the first riders left the trees, Alglooth came intensely alert, and when at last he spied Tavis, he pointed him out to Bimily.

Leading the army on horseback marched the general, several of his captains, with Korab and Septia riding close behind. Directly behind them rode two young women, but their hands were tied to the saddles and their horses were connected by a rope each to a man who rode alongside them. Bimily recognized them as Tilenna and Cachou, Korab's sisters. Slumped in their saddles, heads hanging low, their body language shrieked their shame to any who cared to notice.

Behind them came Tavis. Kept apart from the other children and closely guarded, Tavis rode in a horse-drawn cart that was more cage than cart. Surrounding him rode six armed men who never left the side of the cage for a second. Some of the time Tavis sat looking up at Alglooth, but he never pointed nor drew anyone's attention to him. At other times Tavis slept or wept, Alglooth could not be sure which, but the young boy appeared to rub his eyes often.

The youngest children had been piled into larger versions of the cage Tavis rode in, five of them moving along steadily behind his cart. The older children, their hands bound before them, were connected by a rope around their necks, tied together in groups of ten that strung back for yards. Close to two hundred children marched along in this way, keeping pace with the soldiers, who urged them on with a shout or a switch, and it wrenched Bimily's and Alglooth's hearts every time they saw one stumble and fall. The soldiers that guarded the children would merely pick the fallen one up, and set him or her back on their feet in an effort to keep the line moving.

Around Korab, Septia, and the children a strange line was faintly visible that made the air within it wobble. It was a ward of protection. Alglooth explained to Bimily as they glided along on a current, that when it had been noticed that three children were gone, the troops guarding the children were doubled and the wards set in place. Since that time no more attempts had been made by the Feralmon.

When Alglooth found the army, they had been following the river north for water as well as a source of food. Though they had taken the small herd of cattle from Kalaven, these men were accustomed to and preferred a diet of fish. Having taken the horses of the Feralmon, about half the army now rode. All the wounded who could ride had been given horses, and the others who could not were carried along in carts. At the rate they traveled, they should reach Stiga within the week. None seemed to be concerned for the children they pushed to their limit to keep up, who grew thinner each day.

Thirty-Two

It was close to impossible for Delcia and Morgentur to be taken unawares; they had been expecting Ranth's arrival for days. The Cauldron had informed them that he was closer to death than even they were willing to disclose. A novice had been posted in the courtyard near the stable, and as soon as Ranth, Shunlar, Avek, Corta, and Ondeen had translocated there, Delcia and Morgentur had been notified, and Ranth was given over into their care.

He was taken directly to the Chamber of the Cauldron of the Great Mother, and would not be leaving that esteemed presence for days; neither would Avek. His oathbrother continued to grow weaker by the hour, and Avek refused to leave Ranth's side.

Ranth walked most of the way to the Chamber, but as he approached the doors, he faltered. Beside him, Shunlar took hold of him with her right arm. She felt a slight burning in her forearm where the sliver of Banant's Lifestone had become part of her bone, but ignored it. Ranth looked at her sharply, but said nothing. His curiosity squelched by the markings on his back as they grew stronger, Ranth was not even aware that his Lifestone was trying desperately to make contact with him.

Just inside the open doors stood Delcia and Morgentur. Though they tried to hide their concern for Ranth, whom they had taken in as their own so many years ago, they failed. He looked terrible. The loss of blood he had suffered from his attempted suicide combined with the power of the nefarious symbols etched on his back were taking their toll. He had dark circles under his eyes, which were dull and listless. His generally robust physique was thinner, and his muscles looked flaccid, as if a poison were pulling every bit of his strength from his body.

They quietly ushered Ranth, Shunlar, and Avek into the room. Avek had never been in the Chamber, and the might of it took his breath away. Before him spread a seamless, red-marble floor, the center of which contained a large fissure, from which a vapor was rising. Suspended over the fissure on three thick golden chains hung the Cauldron of the Great Mother, fashioned of green, opaque glass. Runes of light appeared and then vanished from the sides as the vapor rose and seemed to caress the sides of the Cauldron. Overwhelmed, Avek went to his knees and hid his face.

"Come, my son. Look upon this gift of the Mother. She awaits," spoke Delcia and Morgentur in unison. He raised his head, stood, removed his sandals, and shakily made his way across the floor.

Shunlar and Ranth stood in the same spots they had nearly two years previously, when the Cauldron had had a message for them. Thinking of that day, Shunlar looked at Delcia, and asked, "Do you have the means to make Ranth whole again?"

"The Great Mother of us all does," was their answer together. When Avek stood with them, on the other side of Ranth, Delcia and Morgentur spoke the ritual words of welcoming. The Cauldron responded by sighing, as if it were a living object.

The vapors rose and wrapped around the waists of the five people who were assembled, beginning with Ranth. Next it curled around Shunlar and Avek, winding its way about Delcia and Morgentur. Then Ranth's Lifestone began to glow brightly, and soon he was encapsulated by light. He swooned, and Shunlar and Avek lowered him to the floor gently. Stepping back they all watched as the glow increased. Soon his clothing became ash and fell away so that the scarification on his chest and arms was visible. Delcia and Morgentur had never seen such scars, but they maintained their serene countenances even as their eyes looked on in disbelief.

Shunlar and Avek sat next to Ranth, cross-legged, and the two leaders of Vensunor's Temple followed their example. For hours Ranth lay quietly as the light continued to burn away all of the markings on his body. He became too hot to touch. His night-black hair, too, was reduced to ash and as they saw it fall away, new growth appeared and began growing at a slow rate, as white as the ashes covering him.

Shunlar, becoming restless, stood and began to pace in the Chamber. Delcia approached her. "My child, this will take much time. I see no reason for all of us to sit this long vigil. Perhaps it would be best if you left and rested for a while. We shall all take our turns watching over him. Let us leave the men alone with Ranth for now. Later, when they need rest, we will take their places." Shunlar nodded her understanding, and they left the Cauldron's Chamber.

However, after they had been under the Temple's roof for an entire day, Shunlar could not take the waiting. In that time she and Delcia had taken two turns sitting by Ranth's side. He continued to change slowly before their eyes. Soon he would have a full head of hair, eyebrows, and beard of white. Avek stayed with Ranth, leaving only to relieve himself, choosing to take his meals and sleep in the Chamber when Shunlar and Delcia sat over Ranth. Nothing could persuade him to leave his oath-brother's side.

Knowing that Ranth was well cared for, Shunlar decided to venture into Vensunor for a few hours when her next break came. Though she wanted for little while under the care of the Temple, there were some things the Temple did not provide, and one of those was *taloz*. Shunlar needed to be away from worry for just a few hours so that she could think clearly, even if it meant getting drunk first. She longed for the familiar sights and smells of a tavern, and that was where she was headed, that is, after she dumped Corta and Ondeen. They insisted on going with her, for they were as bored as she was.

Choosing not to tell Avek, they left in the late afternoon with several others from the Temple who were going to market for the evening meal. Corta and Ondeen were quickly mesmerized by the sights of the market around them and since she felt they were safe, she left them with the women and their baskets of food, or thought she did. As soon as Shunlar turned the corner, they noticed she was gone and followed.

Vensunor was the overcrowded city she remembered it to be. There were several blocks of market she must pass before she had her bearings and started down the lane that would take her to her favorite tavern, the Dragon's Breath Inn. Ahead of her she saw a heat trace that stopped her in her tracks when she recognized whose it was.

Deeka.

She who had captured Shunlar the last time she was in Vensunor. She who Shunlar suspected had set a trap for her in the desert with Orem's body. Deeka was here in Vensunor.

I knew our paths would cross again, just not so soon. After I kill her I'll really enjoy a drink, she said to herself. Following Deeka's heat trace for several more blocks, Shunlar came to the tavern with the inn above it where Deeka was obviously living. Now all she had to do was wait.

Tucked into a doorway Shunlar began to watch the passersby. She'd only been hiding a few minutes when Corta and Ondeen slipped past. *So, they have followed me. Let them watch then,* she thought. *Maybe they'll learn something.*

An hour went by, and Corta and Ondeen passed her several times. It was obvious from the looks on their faces that they couldn't believe that Shunlar had given them the slip. Another hour, and they passed twice more, but the second time they were being followed.

It was Deeka. Dressed in the clothing of a mercenary

from Vensunor, not her Feralmon leathers and cloak, Deeka slowly sauntered after the two younger women, who remained oblivious to the danger behind them.

Once Deeka had passed her hiding place, Shunlar stepped into the street. She loosed a dagger, which struck a wagon two feet in front of Deeka with a satisfying thunk.

Recognizing the dragon-shaped hilt of Shunlar's dagger, Deeka crouched and whirled around in time to see Shunlar dodge to the left. Deeka threw a blade that grazed Shunlar's cheek, close to her eye.

Shunlar's second throw came fast, but Deeka managed to turn aside swiftly so that the blade glanced off her shoulder and clattered to the stones.

People passing by in the street who realized what was happening immediately turned and ran in the other direction.

Corta and Ondeen, hearing the sound of metal flying through the air had turned around just in time to see Deeka avoid the second dagger. Drawing their weapons they took a position at the assassin's back, leaving her no avenue for escape. She felt them, for she glanced over her shoulder once, then quickly turned her full attention back on Shunlar, who now had her sword drawn.

"This time I am armed and able to fight back," challenged Shunlar. "Did you think I'd forget? I found your little message left with Orem," she spat at her.

For a moment a curious expression crossed Deeka's face, one which she covered just as fast. "I don't know what you can mean. The last time I saw Orem, Korab was busy killing him. About that time I left his esteemed presence." She jumped at Shunlar, jabbing her weapon at her with a series of quick, snake-like strikes. On the offensive, Shunlar brought her sword up fast to the right, then the left, covering the front of her belly, a dagger in her left hand, as Deeka tried to gut her with an upward thrust.

Soon they were both panting and sweating. Deeka had a determined scowl on her face, but, try as she might, she could not get within Shunlar's defenses. When all else had failed, Deeka hit her with a burst of mind-probe energy.

Shunlar staggered back and winced, shaking her head to clear it. "You spawn of a dung beetle," Shunlar cried. "Now we finish this!" Angry at last, she let herself change, the bloodlust so great she didn't care who saw. It took Deeka by surprise, and she stumbled, nearly dropping her sword. Righting herself, she attacked with a fury Shunlar had seldom seen.

Truly fighting for her life, Deeka spent herself trying every possible strike she knew to maim or kill, but in the end she was no match for Shunlar in her half-dragon form.

As Deeka raised her sword above her for a two-handed strike, Shunlar saw the opening and went down on one knee, thrusting upward into Deeka's heart with her right hand. Her left hand reached up, not so much to block Deeka's downward blow, as to prevent the sword and woman from falling on her.

"You came after me and mine. I couldn't possibly let you live," Shunlar said, smoke curling from her lips.

"No," Deeka exhaled as the sword slipped from her limp fingers, dead before she fell.

"By the moons," Shunlar murmured to herself. Only then did she notice she was bleeding from a cut on her right cheek, where Deeka's dagger had narrowly missed her eye. Feeling another sting on her left thigh, she saw that her leather breeches were split and covered with blood. Panting as Corta and Ondeen joined her, she pulled her sword from Deeka's chest, wiped it on the corpse's cloak and sheathed it with a final gesture.

"What do people do with bodies in this city?" asked Ondeen seriously.

"Someone will come with a cart before too long," Shunlar answered, before turning and walking away. The crowd of people that had gathered on both ends of the street parted for Shunlar and her companions to pass.

Much later, after splitting a bottle of *taloz* with her two young friends, Shunlar returned with them to the Temple, injured but profoundly satisfied that Deeka was dead. Avek raised his eyebrows when he saw her, but her steely look prevented him from asking how she had managed to get such a slice on her cheek. When he saw her leg, he looked at her and pointed at it.

"I have sent Deeka on her way," was all she would say as she took Avek's place beside Ranth, wincing as she sat down.

Though his features remained the same, Ranth had changed in the hours since she had last seen him. His muscle tone had improved, filling out his chest again, his arms and legs. His skin was smooth once more, and he now had a full head of hair and a beard of white curls that cascaded around his head in loose ringlets. His skin tone retained the brown cast of his people. He stirred when he heard Shunlar's voice and his eyes, when he opened them, were no longer black. He looked at the world through eyes the color of amber, much like those of Alglooth and Cloonth.

Blinking several times at the four people who surrounded him, Ranth wasn't sure everything was quite right from the surprised expressions he saw. "What is it?" he asked, his voice deeply resonant. "What has happened now?"

"You are the same and different," answered Shunlar. "How do you feel and what do you remember?"

"Little, other than I felt very warm for a long time. Now I grow cold." Picking his head up, he looked down at himself and saw that aside from the fact that his clan markings seemed to have been erased, he was naked save for a thick covering of ashes. Even the leather pouch that held his Lifestone had been burned away, the heart-shaped amber Lifestone lying on his breast. "Yet I feel wonderful."

He grinned, took the Lifestone in his hand, and jumped to his feet in a fluid motion, leaving everyone else sitting on the floor, ashes floating in the air around them. Ranth began to leap into the air and turn somersaults around the room, stopping when he stood before the Cauldron. He bowed his head and waited as Delcia and Morgentur came to stand on either side of him.

"Now it is time for you to choose another name," Morgentur told him. He and Delcia spoke the words of welcome. Several minutes went by as they waited for the Cauldron to respond to their greeting. Nothing happened. Finally, gradually, a small puff of vapor squeezed out from the fissure. Another came and soon great puffs were billowing up and curling around the Cauldron. Encouraged by Delcia and Morgentur, Ranth put his hand into it.

Holding a fistful of tablets, he gave them to Morgentur and reached again. The second fistful he gave to Delcia. Without looking at them, they said the ritual of closing, and the vapor abruptly vanished.

On the table off to the side, they placed the runes, and as their eyes appraised each one they began to laugh. "It would seem our Mother has chastised us. Look here," Morgentur pointed.

All the runes were the same. Each one was the rune for Ranth.

"I don't understand," said Shunlar, puzzled.

"It would seem his name is fitting as it stands. Ranth means 'Changeling,' in Old Tongue, after all," answered Delcia and Morgentur together.

Ranth laughed aloud, his voice echoing off the walls of the Chamber of the Cauldron. "Now I am ready to confront Korab and take back our son, Tavis."

"Brother, don't you think you'll be needing at least a cloak?" asked Avek, with a wry smile.

It was then that Ranth remembered his clothing was gone, burned away by the powers of the Cauldron and his Lifestone working in consort.

"Then perhaps you can find me something suitable to wear before we leave?" He smiled back at Avek. Not to be outdone, Avek handed him a set of Feralmon traveling leathers and a hooded cloak.

When Ranth had finished dressing, Delcia and Morgentur spoke. "We have had a message awaiting you and Shunlar for some time now. When you were last with us, the runes you and Shunlar picked before you left on your separate journeys were somewhat puzzling in meaning. Now more than a year later we know the Cauldron foretold of the physical transformations and the severing of vows both of you would undergo before standing here again.

"We believe that you are destined to return to Stiga and settle there, so that once again it will be a thriving city where knowledge is prized above all else, shared equally between female and male.

"The mountain calls to you and others of like kind. There, where you will step above the world, a great treasure awaits you in Stiga.

"But we caution you, the path is difficult and marked with death—whose, we do not know for certain. We urge you to have great care, for much of the future of Stiga belongs to you." Delcia and Morgentur bowed to Ranth, Shunlar, and Avek when they had finished speaking.

Hearing Delcia and Morgentur speak the words, "step above the world," sparked Shunlar's memory. Suddenly she saw herself sitting in the women's pavilion beside Zeraya. She recalled how the sand had been blown away by a mysterious breeze and they had seen black letters appear. Zeraya had translated them: *Wrought in pain, severed by death, bound by oath. Step above the world to live once more.* Shunlar was more certain than ever that the deaths would not be hers or Ranth's.

Confident that they would be safe, Shunlar told them of the events of that evening in Kalaven, after which they thanked Delcia and Morgentur and left the Cauldron's presence to prepare to depart for Stiga immediately.

Thirty-Three

As it happened, when Shunlar, Ranth, Avek, Corta, and Ondeen translocated to Stiga, the Tonnerling army was already there, camped on the plain. Marleah and Cloonth were taken off guard when the five of them winked into existence suddenly in the small courtyard behind the house. Ranth's appearance was the most unexpected, for he looked more like Alglooth than ever before, though he had a beard. They were greeted by the six children, who remembered their older sister and Avek. It took them no time at all to warm up to Ranth, his hair coloring and eyes being so like theirs and their parents.

Yet it was difficult for Shunlar to see her young half-sisters and -brothers and not pine for her son, Tavis. Cloonth excused herself and went off seeking Alglooth. They returned with Loff, Dolan, and Ariaste. After introductions were made, Alglooth told them all that had transpired in the days since they had parted.

"Alglooth, do you tell me that my son is here with the army?" asked Ranth.

"Yes he is. I have left Bimily with Tavis so that I could come and make my report to you. Tavis seems to be fine, except for the fact that he is guarded day and night. Until now I have not taken my eyes from him. The army just arrived last night, and I have yet to find a way to get inside the ward Septia has placed over Tavis and the rest of the children."

"And what of the other children?" asked Avek suddenly. "My sisters and young brother are among the captives, and I mean to take them back. None of the children who were taken in Kalaven will leave this place unless it is over my corpse. I mean to free them all." Avek was adamant. Until now, not one word of this had he spoken to Shunlar or Ranth.

"Today our spiritual leader, Da Winfreyd, will be riding out to the plain to meet with the general. We are planning to negotiate on the children's behalf. None of us want to see them sold into a life of slavery," Dolan answered.

At his side, Ariaste nodded her agreement. "If you would like, we will arrange for you to ride with the party when the time comes. Da Winfreyd sent us to tell you that he would greatly enjoy meeting you. If you come with us, we will take you to him now." Ariaste bowed to them all.

True to her word, Da Winfreyd was waiting for them. He rose when he saw Shunlar and bowed to her. "Now I know that I was not dreaming when we first met. If you recall, I saw your transformation," he said to her. "It is indeed an honor to meet you again, and I will do everything in my power to save your child." She thanked him with tears in her eyes.

"In one hour's time we will ride out to meet with General Bergoin, his captains, and the Feralmon couple, I believe their names are Septia and Korab." Turning to Ranth and Avek, he asked, "If I may inquire, since you are dressed in the garb of your people, would you consider hiding that clothing under, say, a monk's robe?"

"To what advantage?" they both asked.

"Perhaps surprise might be called for now. If they can be caught off guard, it may be to our advantage when negotiating for the children."

In agreement, robes were brought for Shunlar, Ranth, and Avek, which they donned over their clothing. Shortly afterward, the small party, numbering about twenty, assembled, and they rode from the city down onto the plain.

Boringar rode on one side of Da Winfreyd and Dolan on his other. Behind them rode three soldiers, after which came Avek, Shunlar, and Ranth. Alglooth, Marleah, and Loff were next, and behind them rode Corta and Ondeen. Riding three abreast, the small troop headed down toward the meeting place. Because Stiga was built into the mountain, the road they traveled on as they left the city proper was well above the plain, and they were able to see the entire army stretched out before them.

As shelter from the sun, a long canvas had been stretched between a series of poles. Before it General Bergoin, six of his captains, and Septia and Korab sat ahorse, already waiting for them. The rest of the troops were assembled behind them in orderly ranks. Well off to the side, surrounded by guards, were the wagons where Tavis and the younger children were imprisoned. The older children were lying on the ground, exhausted by their ordeal.

Seeing them made Shunlar's heart beat faster. She cast a look at Avek, and it made her heart ache to see the way he searched for his family. She knew he was calling out to them, when suddenly, as if they were of one mind, all the children stood up. Along the lines of them, three hands went up, then down just as fast. He had found them and given all the children hope. Now it was just a matter of time. Avek looked at her with a satisfied expression. He nodded, then directed his eyes straight ahead.

When they reached the shelter, everyone dismounted and took their places beneath its shade. The army was under the impression that Da Winfreyd had come to bless the troops and lead them home. Imagine how amazed they were to find out he had come to settle Stiga.

"As your spiritual advisor I ask that you set the children free at once. Turn them over to our care and leave them behind. Our people have had a long tradition of abhorring slavery. How is it that you can do this now, after all this time?" he asked, shaming the men who were assembled before him.

Septia immediately saw him as a threat. "Old man," she called out to him disrespectfully, "take your words elsewhere. We have given these men the spoils of war, as promised. You can't stop us; nor do your words have import any longer." She reached toward him holding the Dark Lifestone in her hand and blasted a hole in his chest before the horrified eyes of everyone.

Watching him fall, the army went into chaos, except for General Bergoin and his captains who remained stone-faced and did nothing in retaliation. Korab ordered the general to quiet his men, which he did immediately. It became clear to those who could see his face that Bergoin was not aware of what he was doing, controlled as he was by Korab. The soldiers outside the shelter began to back away, many of them drawing swords as they did. Not to be outdone or taken advantage of, Korab turned on them and ordered them all to stand down in a voice that made them wither.

Ranth took that moment to make himself known to Korab. He pulled off the brown monk's robe, and, when he did, Avek and Shunlar followed his lead. At first, Korab and Septia only recognized Avek. Ranth, after all, now had white hair that fell loose, to the middle of his back, and a white beard. His eyes were no longer a piercing black, but a golden shade of amber.

"You should be dead by now," Korab sneered at Ranth when he recognized him at last.

"I want my son back. You have the Lifestones. You have your child, and if you let mine go, I am willing to spare your life," Ranth said in an even voice.

"No!" screamed Shunlar. "For what he did to you and for stealing our son, he deserves to die. I'll kill him if you aren't prepared to," she threatened.

"Well, it seems we have a difference of opinion as to your fate. Shall we compromise? I am willing to fight you for Tavis," Ranth offered, his golden eyes flashing.

"Fight you? Why should I? All I have to do is call these men forward and you're a dead man. I intend to raise the boy and teach him how to serve me. He will always have a home and a place to sleep, at my feet, where he belongs,'' Korab taunted.

The soldiers were beginning to mill about behind his back, distracting Korab. ''General!'' Korab screamed. ''Quiet those idiots. Now!'' The general again did as he was ordered.

''See what power it is that I possess. Soon you will learn to obey me, too,'' he said to Ranth.

But before Korab could issue another order, Ranth reached toward him with such a forceful grip of mind control that it slammed into his head and nearly knocked him over. Septia saw Korab falter and reached to steady him. It was a mistake. By touching him she was caught in the forced rapport, and the unexpected intrusion of it came like a blow to her head. Septia fell as did Korab from the sheer strength of it. Both of them lay on the ground, writhing in pain.

As Shunlar looked on, Ranth gasped. Having never performed a forced rapport on anyone, he had a feeling of being unclean. When Septia became included, Ranth almost lost the contact. He had to choose one, and he chose Korab, pressing himself deeper in Korab's direction. On this plane it appeared he was chasing Korab through long, dark, tunnels. Finally Ranth managed to catch up to Korab and grabbing his shoulder, he spun him around. *Yield to me,* Ranth demanded.

Never, Korab yelled back defiantly.

Suddenly Ranth was pushed away as the contact was broken.

Clutching the pouch containing the Dark Lifestone, Septia was on her feet again, and she brandished the Dark Lifestone before her like the weapon it was, pointing it at Shunlar. A strong beam of light poured from it. Instinctively, Shunlar raised her right arm to shield her face. The beam of light touched the exact spot where the tainted sliver of Banant's Lifestone had become part of her bone, as if caught. Her eyes wide, Shunlar watched as her arm began to glow. Holding her arm like a shield, she used her full strength to force the beam back at Septia.

Anger churned inside Shunlar and soon she grew taller, her hair turned white and she unfurled her span of wings. She screamed a stream of fire at Septia, who became enveloped by the flame but, protected by the Dark Lifestone, remained untouched.

"Don't come any closer," Septia warned. She reached for Korab and shook him by the shoulder. *Take hold of your Lifestone and draw strength from it,* she ordered him mind-to-mind. Korab shook his head and gasped but did as she ordered. Once he had taken hold of his Lifestone, he regained some of his color and sat up. Then, very slowly Korab got to his feet.

"Now you will die," he promised Ranth menacingly.

He rushed at Ranth with his sword swinging in great arcs around his head. Ranth parried each thrust calmly, letting Korab's anger push him on. No one interfered as the two men, similar in weight and size, fought hard and fast.

Korab leaped at Ranth, kicking out with his foot at his head, which Ranth easily ducked. Another leap, but this time when Korab landed he swept out with his foot and Ranth went down.

As Korab gleefully came in to strike, Ranth warned, "Too late, cousin. You were given fair warning, and I even tried to save your life. Now you will die." With those words, Ranth threw his dagger straight to Korab's heart.

Septia screamed and fell to her knees on the ground beside him, losing her hold on the Dark Lifestone. The pouch swung in the air. Korab's life drained from him as she cradled him to her bosom. She became stone-still, then let his body slide to the ground. Her head bowed over him for several minutes. When she raised it the look in her eyes held murder.

She again took hold of the pouch around her neck and as her arm came up, before she could unleash the power on anyone, Shunlar let fly a dagger. It found its mark in the side of Septia's neck, and she fell, clutching her throat. Several seconds passed, and no one moved. Then together both Septia's Dark Lifestone and the one Korab was wearing popped loudly, smoke rising from the pouches hanging from their necks.

The army suddenly began to move again. General Bergoin swooned and would have fallen had it not been for the fact that he was sitting down. "What in the name of the holy stone is happening? Where are we. Why are these people dead? Captain! Someone explain this." He was clearly confused and demanding to know what had happened.

Brother Boringar came to their aid. He explained everything in a tight voice as he held his mentor and friend, Da Winfreyd, dead in his arms.

Upon hearing Brother Boringar tell him that the order had been given to stop the war and release the prisoners, General Bergoin easily agreed to release the children. He ordered for them to be fed and escorted to safety within the walls of Stiga.

Avek had taken full advantage of the confusion and was already in the midst of the children when the order to free them was called down. He had found his two sisters and brother, Menity, Falare, and Jessop sul Zara. When Septia died, the wards she had placed over the children vanished, making it possible for Avek to approach and begin cutting them free. The three of them were in a tight embrace when Shunlar spied them.

Then she saw a sight that did make her heart leap. Tavis on her hip, Bimily strode toward her, followed by Corta and Ondeen. Bimily had stayed with Tavis, in the shape of a mouse, watching over him and keeping him entertained. Corta had slipped past the guard and freed Tavis as Ondeen distracted them.

"Ah, my friend. It would appear that your family has again expanded," Bimily pointed out. Shunlar could only nod as she spied Iola being carried by Tilenna, as she, Cachou, and the two nurses ran to Ranth. Close behind them came a soldier who, upon meeting Ranth, bowed low. Gustov Maren, as Shunlar would soon learn, had become quite smitten with Tilenna.

"Aye, it would appear that it has." Shunlar smiled. Gathering her family around her, Shunlar gave Tavis reluctantly over to Marleah's arms before long.

Avek had himself been surrounded by hundreds of children, and he laughed and talked to them, reassuring them that all would be fine now. They had been rescued.

Nearby Ranth cradled Iola, who clung to him, as he did his best to console Tilenna and Cachou.

Bimily and Loff were standing with their arms around one another, and Shunlar just shook her head when she saw the way Bimily blushed when Loff kissed her.

The sun was nearly setting when they returned to Stiga, bringing Da Winfreyd's body back in a cart, some three hundred children following after in silence. Their training started in early childhood, after all, and they knew the way to show proper respect.

Shunlar rode, carrying Tavis. On her left side was Ranth, with Iola clinging to his neck. On her right rode Avek, with young Jessop behind him. Menity and Falare shared one horse and Tilenna and Cachou shared another mount beside them. Gustov Maren walked quietly beside them, his identity hidden beneath a monk's brown robe someone had discarded when the fighting had broken out.

The army having supplied them with blankets and food, the older children took over the care of the younger ones, as they often had done in their clan pavilions. Given their freedom, they proved to be more self-sufficient than ever and had grouped into their respective clans once again. Corta and Ondeen became invaluable over the next days: The children looked up to them when they discovered the two women were of the Lost Feralmon.

Within the week most of the Tonnerling troops marched out with General Bergoin leading them home. Those who chose to stay behind in Stiga were welcomed. Men who had wives waiting in Tonnerling sent letters, urging them to join them in their new life. Many who did stay were young soldiers who had tired of war and become smitten with some of the older Feralmon girls during the march.

Their biggest problem was finding enough food for

all the extra mouths. Avek was happy to organize hunting parties, though not many of the Tonnerlingans were able hunters. The Thrale River became a source of food then. Within the week, life took on a semblance of normalcy, if men and children outnumbering women fifteen to one could be called normal.

The small band of eight Feralmon who had been following the army returned to their people with the news that the children were waiting in Stiga. Two weeks later, on a bright sunny afternoon Alglooth announced that there was a huge band of close to four hundred Feralmon approaching, led by Zeraya and Benyar. They were the survivors from Kalaven who came for their children. Too used to living in a city, they had no desire to rejoin their Lost Feralmon tribe in the desert life of nomads. Zeraya was quite happily pregnant and found she was eager to live an ordinary life and set aside the duties of a queen. She and Benyar looked content for the first time since Ranth had seen them together.

Many children were reunited with their parents, but many were not. Soon, however, there were no orphans. Each child whose parents had been killed was adopted either by the Feralmon or Tonnerlingans. Since the army had returned, scores of women had begun appearing regularly each day, to the great delight of the single men and the waiting husbands. With the arrival of so many people, Stiga became a teeming city overnight.

Thirty-Four

THE DEATH OF DA WINFREYD BEHIND THEM, Boringar and Nomia took their places as the spiritual leaders of Stiga. Both of them were well educated, respected, and suited to the job, as Da Winfreyd knew they would be. Left in charge as they were, it was to Boringar and Nomia that General Bergoin went for advice as to what to do about the Lifestones.

When the time had come for Septia and Korab's tent to be dismantled and their belongings packed, the soldiers who had the duty found they could not come near the four large chests. All but forgotten, the Lifestones of Kalaven seemed to have a life of their own and kept everyone away. It was clear they would not be leaving with the army for Tonnerling.

Equally puzzled by what to do with them, Boringar and Nomia called upon Alglooth and Cloonth for advice. They went to see for themselves, taking Bimily and Shunlar along. The four of them knew there was another cave of Lifestones somewhere beneath Stiga, and when they encountered the Kalaven Lifestones, deep memories from their dragon ancestry surfaced, showing them the location. Able to hear the voices, a chorus instructed them it was their wish to be reunited with the remains of their friends far beneath Stiga.

Alglooth turned to Boringar and Nomia. "Since you were designated as the spiritual leaders of Stiga, it is time you learned some of the secrets. Come with us, and we will show you where these wish to be placed." They encircled the four chests and grasped hands all around. The Lifestones began to glow, and the chests rattled. All of them saw in their mind's eye the cave beneath the Temple, and within seconds they translocated themselves, Boringar, Nomia, and the chests there.

As soon as the feet of those who had entered the chamber touched the soil, the luminaries in the walls began to glow brightly. Stepping apart they watched as the chests popped open, spilling the Lifestones onto the chamber's floor. Uncovered, the Lifestones began to glow, matching the hundreds of luminaries on the cavern wall. A feeling of great elation and joy flooded them as colors danced before their eyes, music filled their ears, and whispers could be felt, heard, and smelled, touching all of their senses at once. When quiet finally settled around them, the feeling they were left with was one of returning home.

Blinking and looking around, they discovered that they were not the only ones in the cavern. They had been so entranced by the Lifestones that they hadn't noticed the arrival of Ariaste, Dolan, Loff, Marleah, Ranth, Avek, and the children, all of whom had been called there by the Lifestones. And behind them came others.

Completely at ease, Shunlar noticed that Ranth and Avek, who stood on either side of her, had each placed an arm around her, an embrace that she returned.

When the lights slowly began to dim, they became aware of the sound of small voices singing. Looking for the source they saw Iola, Tavis, and the six offspring of Cloonth and Alglooth sitting among the Lifestones from Kalaven, playing with them.

"The Lifestones you see before you are all that remains of dragons once they die. Because their love of life was so great, it was difficult for them to pass completely from it," said Alglooth.

"When they can, they call to a human to bond with. In this way they live again, but this time as companions and advisors to humans.

"Lifestones are the hearts of dragons, you see. Only the pure of heart are called and chosen. The purest of hearts being those of children," he concluded.

Tavis looked up. In his tiny hands he held a faceted, amber, heart-shaped stone pulsing with light. Tavis grinned as he listened to the voice of the dragon's heart.